To D[illegible]

Dad & Mom

Dec 2017

The Rescue

BRIAN ROBBINS

WestBow Press books may be ordered through booksellers or by contacting:

WestBow Press
A Division of Thomas Nelson & Zondervan
1663 Liberty Drive
Bloomington, IN 47403
www.westbowpress.com
1 (866) 928-1240

ISBN: 978-1-5127-6171-9 (sc)
ISBN: 978-1-5127-6172-6 (hc)
ISBN: 978-1-5127-6170-2 (e)

Library of Congress Control Number: 2016917771

Print information available on the last page.

WestBow Press rev. date: 12/19/2016

This book is gratefully dedicated to my wife Carey, my mother Vianna, Martha Watts, and others who have believed in me. Thank you for being encouragers in the truest sense of the word.

Contents

Darkness in motion

Sarah knew she shouldn't be there.

She just couldn't help herself. It was her one weakness, her one guilty pleasure. She wasn't even sure how she had ended up back at this place. Lately, though, it seemed to be happening a lot. At the end of the day, sitting alone in her room, she would begin to wrestle with the familiar feeling that if she walked downstairs and tried to be part of the family, her isolation would only increase. It was in those moments, when the only other option was to face head-on the emptiness of her life, that she would find herself mindlessly putting on her shoes and jacket and rushing down the stairs and past the entrance to the living room.

"I'm going out," she would mumble as she pulled the hood over her black hair, feeling at once the guilt of knowing she could be a better daughter and the anger that it was up to her, the child, to make things right. No one would respond. And so she would go out, into the night, where her feet led her without fail to this place, a dark spot in the darkness of the city, a place where she felt something that, while it wasn't hope, was better than despair.

And now she was here again. She knew it was wrong. But it felt, to her, less wrong than the alternative. Darkness in motion somehow seemed better than a darkness where nothing happened at all. Here at least there was a semblance of life, in a world that seemed to be more and more a place of death. Here at least people smiled and enjoyed themselves, enjoyed being alive. Something inside of her sensed that it should, it must, be possible to enjoy life without using others, without giving yourself away so cheaply. But she had to admit that she didn't know what that would look like. As far as she knew, she was the only one who even thought there was anything wrong with this place. And she was so, so lonely. So she came, more and more often, when her hunger and frustration outweighed her guilt. She was tired of the guilt. Why should she be held back when everyone else seemed so free to give themselves to the experience? But she couldn't. Somehow, she knew that it would be a betrayal of herself, of who she really was, although she couldn't explain where she got the idea that there was anything more to her than what people saw. Certainly not from her family. And not from the world around her. It came from within. And that was the problem. It seemed that no one else she knew was engaged in the same internal battle that was tearing her apart. Everyone else was so simple, so shallow. So happy. At times she hated caring, hated the nagging voice within that told her people could be better, that even she could be better. It felt like a curse.

Sarah realized with anger that time was passing, that her thoughts were keeping her from enjoying what she had come to see. She shoved them aside and turned her attention outward, comforting herself with the same simple words that she used every time she gave herself permission to come here: *It's not like I'm actually dancing. I just like to watch.*

A fellow observer

There were others watching, of course. In the shadows around the edges of the room, other people talked, rested, and enjoyed the spectacle. Sarah told herself that she was different from them. She really did enjoy the dancing for its own sake. She thought it was amazing and beautiful what people could do with their bodies, up to a certain point ... and then she did her best to filter out everything else that went on here. She told herself that if there were a place where there was only dancing, where dancing was pure, she would go there instead. She smiled as she imagined such a beautiful, uncomplicated place. Then a deep discouragement returned as a voice in her head said, "Yes, Sarah, but you would be the only one there."

She looked around the room. What drew these people here? How many of them came because, like her, they had somewhere else they didn't want to be? Her eyes rested on a man standing across the room near a doorway. Like everyone else, he was dressed in dark clothes. He had the standard black leather trench coat, which all the men she knew seemed to wear when the sun went down like a uniform, like a suit of armor. But there was something different about him, and it took her a moment to put her finger on what it was. He had no visible tattoos on his face, neck, or hands, which was rare, but not unheard of. His haircut was short and plain, which was a little unfashionable, but that wasn't it either.

Then she realized that he wasn't moving. Music pulsed throughout the large room, filling the empty spaces so completely that you could almost touch it. Everyone else, including Sarah herself, was caught up in its rhythm to one degree or another, whether they were dancing or not. They bounced and twitched and swayed subconsciously as they talked, drank, and laughed together. But this man wasn't talking to anyone, and if he heard the music at all, it seemed to have no effect on him. It was strange, and interesting. What was he doing? Was he looking for someone? He seemed intent, focused, as if the music and dancing were mere distractions he chose to overlook in his pursuit of some other, greater purpose. Was he a Soldier? She wondered what an undercover Soldier would be doing in a place like this. Their presence in the city had been greatly reduced since all drugs had been legalized. There were very few crimes that were serious enough to merit the attention of the Army anymore. Still, for a moment, the fleeting thought that some kind of arrest was about to take place, and that she could be caught up in it, filled Sarah with horror. It would provide her father and brothers more than enough ammunition to remind her, yet again, that she was no better than anyone else. She felt another flash of frustration with herself. Why did she have to be so different? An arrest, even a wrongful arrest, would be a badge of honor to the other girls she knew. But Sarah would hate it. She would hate the attention, hate the fact that now people would assume that she was just like them. It would bother her, and no one else would care, and that would bother her even more.

Suddenly Sarah realized that she had stared too long, and now the man was looking back at her. Now she had another reason to be frustrated with herself. She had gotten sloppy. Avoiding eye contact was one of her rules, part of the set of skills she had developed to keep from being noticed in places like this. She used to go to another club that was closer to her house, but one night a man there had tried to follow her home, so she had switched to this one, a remodeled warehouse called The Grind. Since then, she had worked hard at blending in, and took pride in the fact that she could slip in and out without attracting any unwanted attention. But now the stranger was looking right at her with those eyes that pierced through the music and the shadows.

And now he was walking toward her.

Sarah lowered her eyes and pretended to be watching the dancers, but it was too late. They had seen each other, and there was no sense in pretending they hadn't. Surprisingly, as he approached, the man broke into a smile. And not just any smile. It was a smile that didn't fit in this place. His smile was full of … she couldn't say what. Goodwill? Sarah laughed at herself for using, even knowing, such a word. The people at work were right that she read too many old books. Still, the word fit. The look on this man's face expressed what she imagined a good father might feel toward his daughter. Sarah's own father rarely smiled except when there was an especially dirty comedian on the Wall late at night. But she preferred her father's indifference to the kind of attention she got from most of the men of the city. There was something predatory about the men at work and on the streets, and if they smiled at you, you could be sure they had their own selfish reasons for doing so. This was different. Even so, she told herself to keep her guard up.

"Hi," said the man, "I'm Justin."

"I'm Sarah," she said, "Wow, your name is almost as old-fashioned as mine." What was she doing? She had intended to get out of this as quickly as possible, and now she was starting a conversation with this stranger, and insulting him at the same time. Why did she say that?

"You don't like your name?"

"No, I do, actually, it's just that it's really old, and most people think it's funny. I'm named after my great-grandmother. I guess she was this amazing lady. But sometimes I wish I could be more like everybody else." What? What was happening? Why couldn't she keep herself from talking? She hoped he wouldn't take this last statement to mean any more than that she wanted a more modern name, but she knew that it came from a much deeper place. It seemed that her loneliness was working against her. The chance to connect with another human being was overruling all of her instincts to protect herself. And there was something about him that was different from the types of guys she was used to protecting herself from.

"Well, why would you want to be like everybody else? Maybe you're right and they're wrong."

He said this casually, innocently, and it was impossible to tell what he was thinking. Was he just making conversation? Did he know this was one of the nicest things anyone had ever said to her, possibly the one statement that would tempt her to completely let her guard down and trust him? In any case, it was too much too quickly for Sarah. She attempted a lighthearted laugh and said, "Yeah, maybe," and turned to watch the dancing. Obviously the conversation wasn't over, but she had no idea where to take it from here.

Justin graciously changed the subject. "Do you dance?"

"Me? No. No, I just watch." She said this while keeping her eyes forward, but realized that this was rude, so she turned and asked: "How about you?"

He gave a chuckle that was impossible to decipher. "Not like this."

A moment of silence passed, and then something in Sarah wanted to get out of this situation as quickly as possible.

"Listen," she said awkwardly, "I have to go home to … sleep. It's been a long day. It was nice to meet you, Justin." She turned to go.

He smiled his strange, friendly smile again. "It was nice to meet you too, Sarah."

As she turned to walk away he reached out and put his hand on her shoulder. For a split second she was very uncomfortable, but he released her as soon as she turned around.

"Sarah, I know this will sound strange, but I might as well tell you now. You'll be seeing me again."

"What?" Now she was scared. "Look, you're not my type, okay? Please leave me alone."

Now his smile was becoming annoying. Was he amused by this? "Sarah, it's not what you think. Please don't take this the wrong way. You're a beautiful young girl, but you're not my type either. I just wanted you to know that you'll be seeing me around, and when you do it's nothing to worry about."

"Are you going to follow me? If you follow me, I'll call the Army."

Justin took a step backwards and raised his hands in a gesture of surrender. "This is not going the way I wanted," he said. "I won't follow you, so don't worry. But I can't change the fact that we will see each other again, and when we do, just remember, I'm one of the good guys."

"I didn't know there were any good guys," Sarah mumbled as she scanned the room for the nearest exit.

"We're around. But these days, we're spread pretty thin."

Sarah was already moving. "Look, just leave me alone," she said loudly over her shoulder. "And don't follow me!" And with that she pushed her way through the crowd toward the door. Several people turned and stared at her as she left, but no one made a move to get between her and the man she was obviously frightened of. *It figures*, she thought as she emerged from the noise and heat into a gentle nighttime rain. *People don't care.* When she had taken a few steps away from the light of the club, the darkness of the night in this part of Portland swallowed her, and even the false protection offered by the crowd of strangers at the club was gone. *Alone again.* Suddenly panic welled up inside her. Before she knew it, she was running uncontrollably, like a child afraid of the dark. The slap of her feet on the wet pavement echoed off of the buildings on either side of the street, the sound coming back to her and increasing her fear that the man had followed her. But she resisted the urge to look back. She was too good a runner for that. Back in school her favorite coach had been Mr. Henderson, the English teacher who had always been patient with her and sensitive to the way she was treated by her teammates. She could hear his voice in her head now, telling her to pay attention to her form. *Run tall. Drive with your arms. Stay loose.* The slapping stopped and now she was flying. A moment passed and then she knew it didn't matter whether anyone was following her or not. She was uncatchable. It was her one gift, a skill that had earned her respect from people, when everything else about her seemed to distance her from the rest of the world.

She didn't stop for several blocks, slowing to a walk as she came within reach of the lights of the MAX station that would take her out to the suburbs. Finally, she looked behind her into the shadows. No one was there. Soon the train arrived. The ride home was the same as always, the bleak fluorescent lights revealing the bleak faces of people who didn't really want to be there. They stared at the floor or disappeared into alternative worlds on the screens of their phones. Some were finishing a long day at a job they didn't especially like, some were on their way to start the night shift, and many had nowhere to go and were simply staying out of the rain. The silence on the MAX wasn't awkward; it was the way everyone wanted it. The only awkwardness on the trains came when some naïve person tried to start a conversation with a stranger. Sarah was used to the silence now, and found it comfortable, although when she had first started riding the MAX after graduating from high school she had been shocked by the sad reality that the adult world was such an unfriendly place. But she hadn't caused any awkward scenes by trying to talk to anybody. She wasn't the kind of person who started conversations.

3

Home sweet home

Sarah was a Sleeper. She hadn't been lying to Justin, although looking back she was sure he had been insulted at the pathetic reason she gave for excusing herself. Most people she knew got by on two to three hours of sleep a night. But shortly after her twelfth birthday, Sarah had an allergic reaction to her first dose of Ampheine. Doctors had then tried several other sleep-replacement drugs, but none worked. This meant that while all the rich kids at school were enjoying the new-found freedom of staying up most of the night playing video games and watching the Wall, and all the poorer kids were taking night jobs to help support their families, Sarah continued to need eight hours of sleep every night, which was considered childish and lazy.

It was a great disappointment to her family. Having little money, her parents had been counting on the additional income she would bring in at some simple job, stocking shelves in a megastore or something like that, once she reached the appropriate age. When they divorced two years later Sarah had blamed herself, although more recently she had begun to see her parents' all-consuming selfishness for what it really was, to the point that, on good days, she pitied them. On other days she was still angry and hurt. Her mothers' self-centeredness took the form of an outright rejection of her husband and children in order to "make a fresh start." For her father it was more subtle. It was the way he chose not to try, the way he filled his life with various forms of passive entertainment and offered nothing of himself to anyone. Her two brothers, who were older and no longer lived at home, didn't seem to mind. They had their own lives now, jobs and girlfriends and electronic distractions, and they had learned their parents' lesson well: except for the rare occasions when it somehow benefitted them, they took little interest in others. The only attention they paid to Sarah was when they had an opportunity to mock her for one of the many ways in which she was different. Fortunately, now that they were out of the house, this happened less and less often.

Of course, this situation was no different from most other families. None of Sarah's classmates in school had lived with both of their parents. She didn't know about the people at work, but she assumed it was the same. It was normal. But again, the problem came from the fact that it seemed to bother her more. Something inside her would not be satisfied with broken or empty relationships. Something insisted that things could be better. This was why it broke her heart to sit in the living room with her dad and stepmom, watching the Wall, longing for some sort of connection with someone, and knowing that she would only be misunderstood if she pursued it. She had tried, actually, a few times with her stepmom. Her father had married a woman who was nice enough. Her name was Jalen. They fought less than her parents had because she didn't demand as much. Sarah thought she seemed grateful just to have found someone who would take her in and keep her from being alone. A fair amount of her attention seemed to go toward new clothes, silly trinkets, money, and being liked by those who didn't really know her. Although Sarah didn't especially respect her, she was still kinder than most people, and even defended Sarah when her brothers said something especially mean. From time to time they would have a pleasant conversation that would give Sarah enough hope that she would probe a little deeper. She would ask a question designed to reveal if Jalen, too, might wonder in quiet moments about the meaning of life, if she ever looked at the way people lived and felt like there was something wrong with the world. Then, to Sarah's disappointment, her stepmother would reveal her discomfort by changing the subject to a sale that she was looking forward to at a certain store that weekend, inviting Sarah to come along if she would like. Sarah would accept, grateful for the kind gesture, and more convinced than ever that she was all alone in the world.

When she came through the door that night, her father gave her his typical greeting, a mindless insult that didn't require him to take his eyes, or his thoughts, off of the shows he was watching on the Wall.

"Going to bed?"

"Yeah, Dad," she said as she made her way up the stairs.

"Yeah, well, I guess you'd better."

Selfish. Lazy. Different. She was used to these little jabs, and they didn't cut as deeply as they used to.

Sarah didn't especially like the Wall. Having an entire wall of the living room devoted to a giant screen that could display multiple shows and websites at the same time was now common even in homes where the income was as modest as her father's—and in most homes, as in hers, it was on all the time. Every once in a while, she enjoyed watching a show about dancing or animals, or a love story if the nudity wasn't too bad. But the huge screen and its bright colors gave her a headache if she watched for too long, although no one else seemed to have that problem. In school, much of her homework had been done on the Wall, but now that she worked, she could avoid it most of the time. And the things her dad watched in the evening were mindless, degrading, and made her ashamed of him. Secretly, she was glad she was a Sleeper. She would much rather not see or do anything than endure hours of the Wall with her dad. His love for it bordered on addiction. Once when Sarah was younger, her brother Julian had received a dart set for his birthday, and he had set it up on the wall of his bedroom that happened to be the back side of the Wall. A few days later, being a typical boy, he had thrown a dart at full strength and missed the board entirely. The tip of the dart had gone through the sheetrock and pierced a key wire that had put the Wall out of commission for several days. Her dad had been furious. He stomped and growled around the house until even Sarah was glad when the repairman came to replace the wire. It was then she realized that, while she had very little interest in it herself, the Wall played an important part in her life, because it kept her from having to deal with her father.

Sarah was especially grateful to be a Sleeper on this night. She welcomed the chance to put her head on the pillow, close her eyes, and not think about anything for a while. She had to be at work early the next morning, so she got ready for bed as quickly as she could.

As she lay down, she thought about Justin. *You'll be seeing me again? I'm one of the good guys?* What did it mean? Most likely, he had some kind of mental illness, and either she would never see him again, or he was just a stalker of a different type, and she would have to find a new place to go in the evenings. The thought made her tired. Why couldn't anything be easy? Why did she have to work so hard to protect this one small thing in her life, a momentary escape she could only partially enjoy because of the guilt? Why was there no one who cared, no one who protected her? Weariness and sadness filled her heart, and she could not explain the inner strength that helped her tell herself that it was worth hanging on, worth getting up tomorrow and going to work. Something good must be coming. Then she remembered something that had brought her some comfort lately: last week's discovery. She slipped her fingers under the pillow to assure herself it was still there. It was silly, but just touching it did make her feel a little better. It was a little piece of evidence that she was connected to something good, and she chose to dwell on that thought, to give hope a foothold inside her as she surrendered to her body's need for sleep.

You'll be seeing me again

Sarah worked in a café in the heart of the city called The Cup and Saucer. As a child, she had always said she wanted to work in a bookstore, without being able to explain why, which had provided her father and brothers with yet another opportunity to mock her. But by the time she was out of school and looking for work, bookstores were nearly non-existent. The strange attraction she felt toward books, real books made of paper that you could hold in your hand, and the fact that they were harder and harder to find, had increased her feelings of loneliness as she grew older.

She was grateful, though, for her job as a waitress. It was much better than her first job had been, working as a cashier at a huge electronics store. She was still forced to interact with strangers more than she would prefer, but she worked with reasonably friendly people, in a small environment that was less stressful for her timid personality. And she had Torin, another waitress who was outgoing, energetic, and immediately likeable, and yet seemed to understand and respect Sarah's shyness. She found ways to protect Sarah from angry customers and from Dak, the night manager who was loud, flirtatious, and had a temper. It was partly because of him that Sarah worked the early shift as often as she could. Torin was a gift, and Sarah didn't like to think about how she would handle this job, or any job, without her.

This morning, Torin greeted her with a friendly smile as she entered the café.

"Morning, girl. How was your day off?"

"Fine. I slept in." Sarah did not have to feel badly about being a Sleeper with Torin.

"Good for you. Do anything fun?" Torin was always trying to get Sarah to have more fun, and this morning she was glad to have something to report, to prove she was not that different from everyone else.

"Met a crazy guy at The Grind. He said he was 'one of the good guys,' whatever that means, and that we'd be seeing each other again. Acted like he already knew me. It was weird."

"Good looking?" Torin asked. She was also constantly pushing Sarah toward men, telling her she was beautiful and that she needed to "get out there." Judging from Torin's own life, Sarah was pretty sure she didn't want to be "out there." And the question about Justin made her uncomfortable for some reason. It seemed inappropriate, though she didn't know why. But she played along.

"Um, yeah, I mean, handsome. Sort of old. And super clean-cut. Like, old-fashioned."

"Hmm ... might be just your type!" Torin raised her eyebrows and gave Sarah a lighthearted smile.

Sarah rolled her eyes and ended the conversation by turning her attention to some customers who had just walked through the door. She settled into the routine of work, and the day passed quickly. She covered part of someone else's shift that afternoon, came home exhausted in the evening, made a simple dinner for herself, and retreated to her room. She was in no mood to visit the Grind anytime soon, and besides, her dad and Jalen were out somewhere, which gave her the perfect opportunity to spend more time with her new discovery, which she preferred to do alone with her door locked.

Later that night as Sarah prepared for bed, she was suddenly aware of the distressing feeling that her life was becoming smaller.

In school, despite the anxiety of being surrounded by the variety of people who were different from her—hopeless kids, self-confident kids, kids who could just blend in—she had at least had a small social circle, and plenty of distractions. Homework and running had made it a busy, somewhat enjoyable time. But without that ready-made community, she found that she had less and less to occupy her mind, and less and less to look forward to.

In fact, if she was totally honest, the only real bright spots in her life right now were Torin's friendliness and the object under her pillow. How did that happen? Is this what life would be like from now on? What would make it better? There was The Grind, of course, but that wasn't a true bright spot. It was a dirty bright spot, like the circle of the sun shining through the cloudy skies that were so often overhead. This analysis of her life filled Sarah with a mixture of sadness and anger. Of course, she couldn't identify exactly who she was angry with, although that was becoming a little clearer lately. She had trouble getting to sleep that night.

In the morning, Sarah passed the work hours mindlessly, and the vague anger filling her mind made her even quieter than usual. She comforted herself with the thought that after work she could visit her favorite spot in downtown Portland. She prided herself on being a public transportation expert, and could make her way around the city easily. It had become her habit to take time to explore the area around the café, in wider and wider circles, taking a different combination of buses and MAX trains to get home each time. One day she had discovered a little place called Westside Park, a strip of grass with some picnic tables just one block wide and two blocks long, tucked away between skyscrapers. There was a little sandwich shop nearby where she would get lunch and a coffee. For some reason it was strangely satisfying to be served by the staff there after a long day of waitressing, and the novelty of spending her own earnings on her own lunch had not worn off yet. It was fun to feel like an adult, a capable, self-reliant city girl. Or at least to give that impression to the strangers who walked by, distracted by their own lives.

On this day, Sarah was glad to see that her favorite bench was unoccupied. She settled down with her lunch, folding up her jacket to sit on because the bench was wet. At least it wasn't raining at the moment. Sarah had lived with rain, with wet benches and wet shoes and wet pant legs, for her whole life, and she rarely noticed it. But the sunshine today was especially welcome. After the dreariness of the past few days, it felt like she was being smiled upon. She took a bite of her sandwich, a drink of coffee, and allowed herself to relax, entertaining herself by imagining where the various people on the street were headed, what their lives were like. She watched a young couple for a while, talking and flirting and making plans together, and then noticed the bright orange flyer on the lamppost next to them. When they moved on, she strolled over and took it down.

It was for a concert of one of her favorite local artists, a young woman named Gayia who played guitar and sang at trendy coffee shops in the evenings. She was tall and slender like Sarah, with long dark hair like her, and in fact looked so much like her that they could have been sisters. But Gayia's facial features were striking and beautiful, and she accentuated them with just the right amount of make-up, whereas Sarah not only believed that she was plain, but actually preferred it that way; she was uncomfortable drawing even positive attention to herself. Gayia sang with such power and confidence and beauty that Sarah always left her concerts filled with a mixture of admiration and envy. Why couldn't she be more like that? Sometimes the feeling was so strong that she almost wished she hadn't gone. Still, the music was beautiful, and it was something to do that got her out of the house. The concert was that night at a coffee shop called Brew. Maybe she would go. She returned to her bench, picked up her sandwich, and continued to scan the park for interesting people to watch.

And there was Justin. Sarah caught her breath. Was he following her after all? He was standing on the opposite sidewalk on the street that ran along the edge of the park, a good distance away, talking to a tall, muscular young man with curly dark hair. He was wearing a shorter black leather coat this time, but otherwise looked much the same. Again she was struck by how clean-cut he looked. His friend, wearing jeans and a pale green t-shirt, had the same semi-military look and demeanor that he did. For now, he didn't seem to know she was there. But it was a strange coincidence. There were four million people in Portland. What were the odds he would be there in Westside Park, *her* park, at the same time she happened to be there? What was he doing? Who was he? She was torn between wanting to watch him and not wanting to be seen. She pulled the hood of her jacket over her head and bent lower over her lunch, but glanced his direction as frequently as she dared.

He seemed intent on his conversation with the young man. They were nodding in agreement, and Justin was patting him on the shoulder. Then the two of them looked, briefly but unmistakably, in her direction. What? Oh no! She shrunk even lower on her bench. When she looked up again a moment later, Justin was walking down the street away from her, which was a relief. But the other man was once again looking toward her. Or was he? Now it seemed he might be looking past her, off over her left shoulder. His gaze was intense enough that she found herself unable to keep from turning around and looking behind her. It was a typical scene, people strolling through the grass or bustling along the sidewalks. But on the far corner of the street on the other side of the park, there was a group of four men, all in black, covered with tattoos, piercings, and with various shades of blue hair. Burnouts, people called them. Young men who had embraced the legality and availability of drugs to the fullest. They had formed a common identity around their drug use and were often seen in small gangs like this. Black leather and blue hair were their trademarks. Sarah stiffened a bit, then told herself to relax. Part of becoming an independent city girl meant learning to act comfortable around people who made her afraid inside. She knew it was wrong to be judgmental, but she also knew that the city was full of bad people doing bad things. She was careful to avoid groups like this one when she saw them on her evening outings.

Seeing a gang of burnouts at Westside Park, in broad daylight, was strange. They were like night creatures, rarely seen in the daytime. And Sarah was already rattled because of seeing Justin. This made it hard to tell if she was imagining things when it seemed that they, too, were looking at her. Not all at once, but when she glanced briefly at them she felt sure she had seen at least two of them look her way. On the next glance, one was whispering in another's ear while a third was stepping off the sidewalk to cross the street toward her. What was happening? She looked back toward Justin's friend. He, too, was moving in her direction, the intense, focused look still on his face. Sarah was frozen. A moment of sheer, inexplicable panic passed, in which she was tempted to run, to scream, though she knew it would be an overreaction to the situation. This faded, however, when it became clear in a few steps that the tall man was definitely not looking at her, but beyond her. His long strides quickly took him past about 20 feet away from her bench, and it almost seemed that the space between them, and the fact that he walked around people on the far side, was meant to reassure her that she need not fear him. He shot an incredibly brief, expressionless look in her direction. Had he actually looked at her, or was he just another man on the street with somewhere to go? In any case, he didn't slow down as he passed. He was all business, and his business was not with her.

She watched him as he made his way to the other side of the grass. The men had all crossed the street by now, and were standing, looking a little unsure of themselves, at the edge of the grass where it met the sidewalk. Justin's friend approached them directly. There was a striking contrast between them which increased as he drew nearer. He seemed even taller, big and strong and confident. They were shifty, with pride and secrecy in their eyes. It reminded Sarah of lions and hyenas from the nature shows on the Wall. Whatever was happening here, it was doubtful that this was a meeting of friends. What would someone like him have to do with people like them?

When he reached them, a conversation started, but they were too far away, and the city was too loud, for Sarah to hear what was being said. She could only see the strong back of the young man, and the guilty, angry way the others responded when he addressed them. He pointed down the street, lecturing them like a teacher or a parent. Then he gestured behind him without turning around—toward her? The men glanced toward the bench, then he caught their attention again with some final word to which their only response was a look of sullen hatred. Then he stood there. They stood as well, glaring at him for a moment, before reluctantly, with menacing looks toward him and, Sarah thought, toward herself, turning and crossing back to where they had been standing before. Then they made their way down the street in the direction he had pointed. They took their time, with frequent looks back in his direction, knocking down a trashcan and then yelling and laughing back and forth to each other loudly enough to intimidate everyone within earshot. But the noise faded as they continued down the street, seemingly in obedience to whatever Justin's friend had said to them.

The young man stood still, watching them until they were gone. Then he turned and looked back in Sarah's direction, but again seemed to look past her, taking a survey of the park, the surrounding streets, the corner where he had stood with Justin. Then, apparently satisfied with what he saw, he crossed the street with those long strides and quickly disappeared from sight.

A place to sleep

For the next several minutes, Sarah sat on the bench and wrestled within herself. Part of her was certain that something significant had just happened, something that involved her, even centered around her. She had the same feeling she had struggled with throughout school, especially in track, when she was the focus of far more attention than she was comfortable with. She wanted to hide, to disappear. Her simple, humble world had been threatened, and it made her angry that she couldn't just have peace, that she couldn't just blend in and be left alone. Without any good reason, she found herself focusing her anger on Justin. It was his fault. If he hadn't singled her out in some way she didn't yet understand, everything would be fine. She knew on some level that this was unfair, but it made her feel better to blame him.

Another part of her was arguing that nothing had happened at all. A man she had met once had randomly appeared and had a short conversation with someone she didn't know. He did not approach her or make her uncomfortable in any way. His friend had then had some sort of confrontation with a gang of burnouts who might have had any number of questionable reasons for hanging around Westside Park in the middle of the day. None of it had anything to do with her. This was the most logical interpretation of what she had seen. If she was going to live and work in the city, she needed to get over these childish fears and start walking around with the same shielded, confident attitude the people around her projected.

The internal battle continued on the train ride home. It was her goal, someday, to move into the heart of the city. She hadn't talked with her dad and Jalen about it yet, but the time seemed to be coming. She loved the idea of having her own little apartment where she didn't have to apologize for being herself, of walking to work and being too busy and too poor to visit home much. She had been looking for some other part-time job she could do in the evenings. When she found it, she planned to move out. The idea was frightening, but also exciting. It was because of this goal that she finally made the decision to listen to the logical part of herself and ignore, as best she could, the events in the park. She would come back to the concert tonight. She would not give in to silly fears.

No one was home in the middle of the afternoon. Sarah showered, and lay down on her bed. It was about two hours before she would leave for the concert. She reached under the pillow and retrieved her discovery. She laid it on the bedspread in front of her and stroked the cover for a moment, delighting in the simple pleasure of the soft leather and then the feeling of her fingers gently turning the thin pages. How could anyone not love books, especially old books? She paged through the book slowly, absently, without a specific purpose, until she came to a page where a familiar hand had scribbled a short note in the margin. She began to read and was soon engrossed in the words. She resettled herself on her side and gave her full attention to the task and the joy of reading, soon forgetting the events at lunch, her work, her family, and everything else.

"Sarah?" Jalen's voice was calling from downstairs. She had fallen asleep. She blinked, yawned, and went through the usual feelings of confusion and embarrassment that confronted her when she woke from an unplanned nap. Her dad would certainly give her a hard time if he knew she had been sleeping in the daytime.

Quickly, she closed the book and stuffed it under the pillow, then stood and straightened her clothes and hair. Then she looked at the clock, a digital display that was built into the window of her bedroom. 6:20! She had planned to leave for the concert at 6:00 to get a good seat at The Brew. Angry with herself, and with her father too for no specific reason, she freshened up in front of the mirror and then opened the door to make her way downstairs for a quick dinner on her way out of the house. Jalen was at the top of the stairs.

"Oh, good, you are here. We were wondering. We thought you might be ... asleep," she said timidly.

"Nope. Getting ready to go out." Sarah really did like Jalen, and in some ways felt sorry for her, but she also found it easy to dismiss her.

"Oh." Jalen was disappointed. "We brought dinner, and were hoping you'd sit down with us."

"At the table? Like, sit down, sit down?"

"Well, no, your father has a show he wants to watch."

"Uh-huh. No thanks. I'm on my way to a concert."

Again, Jalen expressed her disappointment through a simple "Oh." She was not above manipulating people to get what she wanted.

"Hey, Sleepyhead, come sit and eat with us!" Her dad yelled over the noise of the Wall from the living room.

"Sorry, Dad, I'm going out." Sarah was irritated but trying to get out the door with minimal conflict. She had already revised her plan and would find something to eat when she got downtown.

"Well, yeah, you worked a whole 6 hours today, plus a nap. Time to go have some fun, huh?"

"Shut up, Dad." Sarah said, mostly to herself, but also not caring if she was heard. Lately she was developing a hard edge to her generally quiet personality, and was quicker to lash out because of the vague, growing feeling that the whole world was turning against her. She brushed past Jalen and made her way down the stairs.

"Don't you tell me to shut up!" He turned his head from the Wall but did not stand. Sarah did not slow down as she passed the doorway into the living room. She had a hand on the doorknob. "Hey!" Her dad yelled. He turned toward the Wall and said "Mute!" It went instantly silent, which made his voice seem that much louder. "If you're going to live in my house, you're going to treat me with respect, and you're going to spend time with your family!"

"Watching stupid garbage on the Wall is not family time, Dad!" Now Sarah was losing control, speaking with a boldness fueled by anger and pain. This had been a long time coming. She stepped back into the doorway where she could look him in the eye. "We haven't been a family since Grandma Sophia died!" Her grandmother had always been the one to organize big family get-togethers. Sarah had enjoyed spending entire Saturdays in the kitchen with her making homemade tortillas. "If you want to be a family, how about pretending you care what's going on with me? How about coming to see me at work? Do you even know what my life is like right now?" Tears came to her eyes, surprising her and cutting short her outburst. Now she just wanted out, because she knew her father was as ill-equipped to deal with her tears as with her sleeping needs. She realized in that moment that she no longer counted on him, on her home, for anything except a free bed. She turned and fumbled for the door, slamming it behind her, not wanting to hear his reaction.

One of the good guys

Sarah was glad for the short walk to the MAX station; it gave her time to collect herself before anyone would see her. She cried a few angry tears while she marched along the sidewalk, focusing her frustrations by developing an accelerated plan to move out of the house. It was satisfying to think about declaring her independence from her family completely and dramatically. They might be shocked, even a little sad. Sarah's conscience would not allow her to enjoy this thought without some guilt. She knew it was wrong to delight in someone else's pain, and she had read something recently about the right way to handle anger. But in moments like this it was easy to tell herself that she didn't need to worry so much about being a nice person. No one else did.

Her mood changed, though, once she was settled on the train. The truth was that her anger was a surface emotion. Deep down, what she really felt was sadness. There was a pain caused by her father's emotional absence that moving out would not immediately cure. What if the life she was imagining for herself in the city turned out to be a lonely one? Sarah enjoyed solitude more than most people, but she also appreciated relationships more than most. She longed for a deeper connection with others, to be a part of some kind of family or community where people loved and accepted each other, full of easy and joyful relationships like the one she had with Torin. She didn't have that at home, but what if she didn't find it in the city either? She leaned her head against the cold window of the train and allowed herself a few minutes of despair. But it didn't last. Hope returned, seemingly from outside herself, and she was grateful. She would keep going. Something good was coming. Somehow, she knew it was. It had to be. She turned her thoughts to finding something to eat between the MAX station and The Brew.

The concert was a pleasant distraction. Once she was settled into a seat near the back of the room, warming her hands on the coffee and pretzel she had bought along the way, Sarah lost herself in the music and again marveled at Gayia's talent. *Musicians are amazing*, she thought. She remembered all the attention she got when she was winning races in school, and the feeling that she really didn't deserve it because it came so easily to her. She was just doing what came naturally. Was it the same for people like this?

It didn't bother Sarah at all to be attending the concert alone. Despite being shy, she was not without some self-confidence. The nameless hope she had felt on the train ride was still with her, and in this moment being out alone at night in the big city felt like independence, not friendlessness. After a while, though, a new feeling came over her, completely unexpected and confusing. She was struck by a line in a song that had always been one of her favorites. "Love doesn't last, no love can't last, but it's beautiful while it's in your hands." *That's not true,* thought Sarah. *That can't be true. There must be such a thing as real love you can count on, or what's the point? It's not real love at all if it's temporary.* It shocked her to find herself disagreeing with this person she had admired so much. Gayia sang the line with such conviction, such power in her beautiful voice, that before tonight Sarah had always found herself moved by the song. Now she found herself listening with a newfound skepticism. In the songs that followed, she found time and again that behind the talent, behind the voice and the guitar and the cleverness of the lyrics, there was emptiness. The words were mostly about failed relationships, or about finding pleasure in the moment in the face of an uncertain future. After a while they all started to sound the same.

Sarah was not the type of person to draw attention to herself by leaving early, so out of politeness she stayed the length of the concert. But as soon as it was over, while the crowd was standing and clapping, she snuck out the door and into the chill of the night. Walking to the MAX station, she was completely absorbed in her thoughts, her feet guided by memory as she tried to process what had just happened. She was intrigued by the new door that had been opened in her mind. Was it possible that she had a better understanding of life and love than this woman who put her thoughts to beautiful music and sang them to crowds of sophisticated city people? It was exciting and strange. At the same time, it was as if one more piece of her world was unraveling. One more simple pleasure she could no longer enjoy. Why couldn't she just have an easy, happy life? Why wouldn't her mind let her have the shallow peace others seemed to have? Resentment grew within her and waged war against the excitement. It was all so confusing and made her want to blame someone, to demand answers. Who would help her make sense of the invisible battle she was fighting? What was going on? How could hope be growing within her when it felt like so many things were being stripped away?

Sarah pulled her gray hooded sweater tightly around herself as she walked along, not making eye contact with the few people she saw: couples walking briskly, homeless people peering up hopefully from doorways. She turned a corner, still thinking about the concert and the questions that seemed to be consuming her life lately. This was the last stretch; at the far end of this street she saw the lights of the MAX station. But between her and the station, silhouetted against the pale light, were four or five figures, swaggering and talking loudly. They were a long way off, perhaps 200 yards, but their voices carried easily in the relative silence of the city at night. The darkness and fog, which had the effect of subduing others, seemed to put them at ease and increase their confidence. They were in their natural element. This was their time. They passed under a streetlight as they made their way toward her, and Sarah caught a glimpse of bright blue hair.

She froze for a moment. What should she do? Would they simply let her walk by? Should she turn around, run? She didn't see anyone else on the street. Probably there would be a few people at the MAX station, and there under the lights in a public place she would be safer than on the streets. Behind her was only darkness. Were they looking for her, or just there by chance? Had they even seen her yet? Fear, a feeling that she was all too familiar with lately, again welled up within her. Suddenly Sarah felt that her dreams of being an independent city girl were foolish after all. She was too young and fragile and naïve. She would repent of all her rebellious thoughts and be the best daughter she could be if someone would magically appear and whisk her home right now. She would even apologize to her dad. *Someone help me*, she thought, knowing that it was pointless, that it was up to her to get out of this mess she had created in her own foolishness and pride.

Then there was a hand on her shoulder. Sarah screamed involuntarily but it was stifled by another large, strong hand over her mouth, which was removed quickly as soon as her scream was ended, as if to assure her that she wasn't being attacked. She looked up into the face of the tall, strong man from the park that day. Justin's friend. Where had he come from? He placed a finger over his lips and whispered "Quickly," and half guided her, half pushed her with the hand on her shoulder toward the nearest building. Bewildered, Sarah obediently stumbled out of the lamplight and then turned to face him, her back to the cold concrete wall. The man stood over her, dressed all in black, and placed his hands on the wall on either side of her head. His large black coat nearly enveloped her. She was frightened, but only a little.

"What are you doing? Who are you?" Sarah whispered fiercely.

"Not now. Close your eyes."

"What?" Was he going to kiss her? She knew it was a silly

thought, but if anyone could see them at this moment, they did look like a couple in an embrace.

He repeated himself, and the tone of his voice was like a patient father who needs his child to hurry. "Close your eyes so they can't see you. The lights reflect off of them," he said.

Oh. She blushed internally at the silliness of her thoughts at a time like this. She shut her eyes. It was an act of faith, but Sarah found it easy to trust the stranger. Despite the questions spinning in her mind, she had surprising peace in this moment as she waited for further instructions. The answers would come. She did, though, take a peek out from under his arm to see the gang drawing quite near.

"Close them," he reprimanded her. She obeyed. She heard the men walking by. They were talking loudly, cursing and jostling each other as they had on the street earlier that day. She remembered thinking then that they intentionally made people uncomfortable with their unpredictability and irreverence. They seemed angry at the whole world, and they made you feel that at any moment they might lash out at you simply because you weren't one of them. Sarah was grateful for the protection of this stranger, although as they passed by she began to tell herself that it had been silly to think she was their target. Everyone was their enemy. She just happened to be in their path. Then one of them spoke above the chatter coming from the others, silencing them all:

"Hey, where'd she go?"

Involuntarily, Sarah's eyes opened wide in fear. The tall man's face was right in front of her, as if to prevent her from doing anything foolish. "Wait," he said quietly but forcefully.

The men began arguing. "She was right here!" one of them said.

"No, she was further up the street. Probably saw us and took off. Come on!"

"No, man, she was right here! Look around!"

They spread out and began to search, poking their heads in

doorways and down a nearby alley. Sarah's heart was racing. She and the stranger were just standing there against the wall. They would be spotted at any moment. Her protector had frightened these men off (if they were the same ones) earlier in the day. Why didn't he turn and face them? She felt panic rising within her and looked at him pleadingly, desperate to speak, to do something, although she didn't know what.

"Wait," he said again. He was completely calm. Did he have a plan? What was it?

The men were making their way further down the street, and now they were calling out in mocking voices: "Where'd you go, little girl? Don't be afraid!" and then bursting into laughter. They were moving more quickly as they became convinced that she was ahead of them and would need to be chased down. One, however, was slow to follow them. After checking out a doorway on the other side of the street, he wandered back to the streetlight where she had been standing when her protector had grabbed her. He stood directly underneath the light and turned slowly in a complete circle, peering into the shadows all around. Then the sound of his footsteps came straight toward them. He was hidden from Sarah's sight behind the tall man's coat, but in fear she closed her eyes again, tightly this time. Her fists clenched in fear and she held her breath. He stopped and stood just a few feet away. Surely he was looking right at them. How could he not see them? Several long, silent seconds passed.

"Hurry up, man, let's go! We're going to lose her!" his friends yelled. He lingered a moment, then trotted down the street to catch up to them. Sarah allowed herself to breathe again. She raised her head to face her protector. Just as she opened her mouth to unleash a flood of questions, he put his hands on her shoulders and spoke:

"Now, Sarah. Run."

It took a moment for her brain to register the fact that he had used her name. "Wait, you know me? Who are you? What is going on?" she had a hard time keeping her voice low.

"Now is not the time. You don't want to miss the train. Run, and don't look back."

"How do you ... what is going on?" This time her voice wavered. She was close to tears.

"Sarah, you have to trust me. Your questions will be answered. You have to go now." There was a slight edge of impatience in his voice.

She looked down the street into the darkness where her stalkers had vanished. "What about them?"

An unexpected smile flashed across his face. "Don't worry about them," he said. "Go home." And he lifted his hands from her shoulders and turned to walk down the street into the darkness, in the direction the burnouts had taken.

When he turned a corner, Sarah realized she was still standing and not running. Suddenly she felt alone again, and the darkness seemed like a force that wanted to swallow her up. She turned away from it, toward the distant light of the MAX station, but it was no comfort to have the darkness at her back. She could feel its presence behind her. She started to run, weakly at first. The last few minutes had left her drained. Then she saw that a train, her train, was pulling into the station. The trains did not wait long. Here was a challenge she could face. She gave herself wholly to the immediate task of running, and found some joy in it. She had about 20 seconds to get on that train before the doors shut. She covered the distance easily and slipped between the doors and into a seat, out of breath and relieved that she hadn't had to stand at the station where there was nowhere to hide. It crossed her mind that her protector had an impressive knowledge of the MAX schedule.

7 Loosening the roots

The ride home was long enough for the exhilaration of the run to fade away, and the feeling of being completely exhausted returned as Sarah contemplated the events of her day. First there was the incident at Westside Park. Justin, his friend, the burnouts: it seemed clear now that whatever happened there had been about her. Why? She was nobody! Why all this attention? Who were these people, and what did they want with her? Then there was the fight with her dad, the disillusionment of the concert, and finally the appearance of Justin's friend on the street at just the moment she was in danger. *At just the moment I asked for help.* Sarah's hand came to her mouth at this realization. She sat up and looked around the train, almost as if there should be someone else who could appreciate the importance of this coincidence. But of course there was no one. She was alone. These things were happening in her own private world, and no one else cared. This thought reminded her again of her parents. She hoped they would be asleep when she got home. The last thing she needed was to have to deal with them anymore after a day like today. She was reaching her limit, and would have no trouble putting aside the many questions the day had raised for the sake of a good night's sleep. The questions would be there in the morning. She could already feel the warm softness of her bed.

But when she exited the train and turned the corner onto her street, she saw that the lights were on in the windows of her house. Her pace on the sidewalk slowed. *Ugh*. Maybe they were engrossed in something on the Wall and she could just slip past without a long conversation. She had to work in the morning, which was a good excuse to go straight to her room. But when she opened the door and stepped inside, something happened that told her the night was about to get even more tiring: The familiar light and background noise coming from the living room ceased. Her dad had turned off the Wall.

"Dad?" Sarah stuck her head around the corner and looked into the dark living room. He was coming out.

"Um, come here, Sarita. We have to talk." He was clearly uncomfortable. He had called her "Sarita," a sort of Spanglish nickname, when she was little, and this seemed like an attempt to remind her of better times. *Back when we had a relationship,* she thought. Difficult conversations—conversations of any kind, really—were not her father's strength. He walked past without really looking at her and made his way toward the kitchen, where the lights were on. She followed him and saw Jalen sitting at the kitchen table, her hands fidgeting nervously.

"What's up?" Sarah asked as lightheartedly as she could. This was strange. The fight as she had left the house had not been the first, and the way they usually dealt with situations like that was simply to not deal with them. Were they actually going to follow up and face this conflict head-on? Maybe they would ask her to move out, and then she wouldn't have to bring it up! She was nervous, but optimistic. "What's going on?"

"Sarah, we have to talk about this." Jalen looked at her with a weak smile, and then back down at the kitchen table, where Sarah saw for the first time that her book was lying on the tablecloth. Its leather cover was closed, its gold lettering reflecting the bright lights above the table: HOLY BIBLE.

Sarah's face flushed red. Her emotions changed quickly to embarrassment, then anger. "Hey, that's mine!" She yelled, and reached to reclaim her precious discovery. But her dad's hand came down quickly on the book and held it in place.

"Sarah, wait. You need to hear what we have to say."

"Yeah, what? That you're sorry you went into my room and looked through my stuff?" Sarah shot an accusing look at Jalen, who quickly looked away.

"Sarah, you live in our house. And we're concerned about you. We have a right to check up on you."

"Concerned? About what? I'm not a kid, dad, and you can't just come in my room! That," she pointed at the book, "was under my pillow. You couldn't have found it if you weren't searching through my things!"

"Exactly, Sarah. It was under your pillow. You've been hiding it from us. Is there anything else you're hiding? You want us to give you privacy, but we can only do that if we can trust you." While her dad wasn't much for mature conversations, arguments were another matter. He said this in a tone of superiority, sounding very much like a concerned, reasonable parent dealing with an irrational child. It was infuriating. But he had succeeded in turning the tables and putting her on the defensive. Her face flushed again at the truth of his accusation. She had been hiding the book. She was flustered and didn't know what to say next.

"Fine. Say what you want to say." She took a seat at the table, folded her arms, and stared straight ahead.

"Sarah, this is serious. I know you live in a world of your own, but I watch the news on the Wall so I can be aware of what's going on in the world."

A thousand sarcastic comments flashed through Sarah's mind, but she held her tongue.

"Having a Bible can get you into real trouble. This," he held up the book. The very act of his touching it made Jalen squirm with discomfort. "This is a dangerous book. It promotes violence and hatred. When I was a kid, I had friends who got kicked out of school for having a Bible. People used to go to jail for giving them away on the streets. Society is better off without it. I didn't even know you could find one anymore. Where did you get this?"

"But it's not illegal, right?" Sarah was proud of herself for knowing a little more about the world than her dad gave her credit for. "It's not against the law to have a Bible, dad."

Her dad sighed. "No, Sarah, at this time, in the state of Oregon, it is not illegal to possess a Bible in the privacy of your own home. But it is illegal," he quickly continued, "it is illegal to display one in public. It is illegal to supply one to a child. And it's only a matter of time before they're outlawed altogether. But more importantly, Sarah, why on earth would you want one? We're worried about you, Sarah! Now answer the question: where did you get this?"

"I got it when we were cleaning out Grandma Sophia's house. It belonged to Great-Grandma Sarah." She had been saving this one up. Surely this would change things. Her grandma had died about 6 months ago, and in the weeks that followed she and her dad and brothers had spent weekends cleaning out her run-down old house so it could be sold. One day, up in the attic, in a box labeled "Mom's Things," she had come across the Bible. Something about the gold lettering and the fact that she had never seen one before made it seem mysterious, intriguing, like she had found a hidden treasure. When she opened it, she found that her great-grandmother's handwritten notes filled the margins of nearly every page. Sarah had always been curious about this woman whose old-fashioned name had been passed on to her, and the chance to learn more about her was too good to pass up. She had slipped the Bible into her purse without telling anyone and taken it home. Now, she hoped that knowing it belonged to his grandmother might soften her dad a bit. She wasn't some gullible young girl being drawn into a strange cult; she was just curious about her heritage. But he didn't soften. He rolled his eyes and exchanged weary glances with Jalen.

"I see." For the first time, he opened the book. Jalen scooted back in her chair as if something dangerous might leak out of it.

He scanned a few pages, focusing on the hand-written notes. "Have you read it?"

Now Sarah was in a tight spot. She had begun by reading the notes in the margins, driven by curiosity about her great-grandmother. She was grateful that the writing was in English; her Spanish was not that good, and she knew from family stories that if the book had belonged to her great-grandfather he would have written in the language of his heart. Great-Grandma Sarah, though, had attended school in the U.S. from a young age, and was, like Sarah herself, more comfortable with English. The first time she opened the book, Sarah had rejoiced at the chance to get to know her namesake. But the notes were most often some sort of commentary about the text, and they had naturally led her to the point that, more and more, she found herself reading the book itself. She continued to tell herself that her interest was simply in her family history. But lately, it was more than that. She found herself looking forward to quiet evenings of reading the old book. It was comforting, and interesting. But how much of this could she safely share with her dad?

"Just Great-Grandma's notes," she said. "I just wanted to get to know her better." She delivered the partial lie along with the most innocent look she could muster, directly into her dad's eyes. She didn't feel good about it, but she didn't trust him enough to share the truth either. This seemed the best way to alleviate his concern and maybe still walk out of the room with the book.

He returned her gaze. She was not a good liar, and he had known her for her entire life. He was silent for a moment.

"Hmmm. Okay. Well, she was my grandmother. Maybe I should get to know her better too. I'm disappointed you hid this from me, Sarah. It belongs to me more than it does to you. I have to tell you, you're going to have some work to do to regain our trust. You might want to do some thinking about that before you fall asleep tonight." He picked up the Bible and walked out of the room.

◆

Sarah heard it slap down on the coffee table, heard him sigh as he settled into his usual spot on the couch and clicked on the Wall.

"Well. Are you hungry?" Jalen asked coldly. The argument and the presence of the dangerous book in the house had all been too much for her. She was clearly angry with Sarah for introducing this tension into her life, but willing to put her anger aside for the sake of making peace.

Sarah looked at her incredulously but did not answer. She rose and walked numbly up the stairs and into her room, where she shut the door, flipped off the light, and lay down on her side. She stared blankly into the darkness for a moment, but soon the tears came, softly at first, then great sobs as one disappointment piled on another in her mind. She knew Jalen could probably hear her, and she knew she would do nothing. She paused to set her alarm for work the next morning, then continued to cry for a while in the darkness, and eventually fell into an exhausted sleep.

8 Questions

When the alarm went off, Sarah rose and went about her morning routine in silence. Her dad had left early for work, and Jalen was nowhere to be seen. She found herself on the train to work without really knowing how she had gotten there. It was raining hard, a good day to keep your hood on and ignore the rest of the world. The events of the previous day were still so overwhelming to her that just thinking about them was too tiring. She told herself that all she wanted was a normal day at work, and then quiet time in her room reading a book, any book. She would think about the future tomorrow.

Torin was friendly and upbeat as usual, but she sensed that Sarah was in no mood for conversation, and was sensitive and gracious enough to leave her to her thoughts. The morning passed quickly, and the second her shift was over Sarah said her goodbyes with a false smile, pulled her gray sweater on, and began the march through the rain to the MAX station.

Her long strides took her past Java Stop, a popular coffee shop on one of the busiest streets in downtown Portland. The rain was getting heavier, and the shop had an awning that offered some protection, so she stopped and shifted her purse to the inside of her jacket so her things wouldn't get too wet. As she was adjusting her hood, she happened to look through the glass into the warm, inviting shop. Sitting alone at a table right next to the window, just inches away from her, was Justin. He offered her a friendly, innocent smile, and gestured to the empty seat across from him.

Sarah was again filled with a vague, unjustifiable anger at this stranger she knew only by name. Her life seemed to have been unraveling ever since the night they met at The Grind, and somehow she blamed him. Seeing him there was another intrusion into her simple world. She wanted to be left alone, by her parents, Justin and his friend, the burnouts, everyone. Still, there was no doubt she was going inside. She wanted answers.

She shook the rain off her jacket as she sat down and spoke before she had time to think about what she wanted to say. "What are you doing here?" she asked bluntly, with a note of accusation in her voice.

Justin seemed not to notice her tone. He looked around the room with a cheerful, innocent smile. "I like this place. Do you ever come here?"

"Why don't you tell me? I'm starting to think you know everywhere I go."

His smile broadened, but he didn't respond to the remark. "So," he said with sincere friendliness, "how have you been since I saw you that night? Have you been back to The Grind lately?" He seemed intent on pretending he had no knowledge of what had happened to her in the days since they had met. But he had to know. She glared at him.

"No, no dancing for me. I've been doing a lot of running lately."

"Running? Good for you. That's a good hobby. Keeps you healthy. And you never know when it will come in handy."

Was he talking about last night? Did he know? He seemed to be enjoying this little game, but Sarah was not. She struggled for words for a moment, then unleashed her thoughts:

"Look, I don't know who you are. But I know you know what is going on in my life. Everything has been a mess since I met you. And you were there yesterday, in the park, with your friend, who scared off the burnouts. And then he was there, last night, when they were looking for me, and I don't know why they might be after me, or where he came from, but you know, and you have to tell me, because it isn't fair that my life is falling apart and no one cares and I don't know what's going on, but you do! So please tell me!" She was at a point near tears by the end of this outburst, and felt once again how tired she was, not physically, but in her heart and mind.

Justin studied her patiently for a moment before answering. He seemed to be calculating how much information he should share. There was also genuine pity and concern in the way he looked at her, as if she were a fragile child who wasn't completely capable of understanding the forces at work in the larger adult world. But when he did speak, the playful smile crept back into his face, and he gave another infuriating answer which had the strange effect of assuring Sarah that her life was not as awful as it felt at the moment.

"So, let me get this straight. You suspect that I am somehow involved in … protecting you. And this makes you … angry. Am I getting that right?"

"Well," she stumbled, "I'm angry because I don't know why I need to be protected, and why the world won't just leave me alone. And because you won't tell me the truth."

Again he stared at her for a moment. Then he seemed to reach a decision.

"Okay, Sarah. My friend, the one you met last night, is named Thaddeus. He is watching over you."

"Why?"

"Because I told him to."

"And who are you?" She was getting louder. A few heads in the busy shop turned toward them, so she lowered her voice and continued. "And who are they? And why me?"

"As I told you before, Sarah, I'm one of the good guys. They," he looked out the window down the street in the general direction of Westside Park, "are the bad guys. And you have become a person of interest, to us and to them." He leaned closer to her, and all the playfulness was gone from his voice. "I am going to do everything I can to keep you safe, Sarah. But you will have to trust me. Before it is all over, you are going to have to do a lot of trusting. The answers will come. But sometimes trust is just as important as answers."

It was maddening. Now he was finally talking, but his words simply raised more questions.

"Okay," she said, not really understanding his last statement, "but can I at least have a few answers? Why am I a 'person of interest'? And what do you mean, 'before it's all over'? And—" she struggled for words, and finally said, exasperated, "why should I trust you? How do I know you're the good guys?"

"I think you know we are, Sarah. I'm not worried about that. I think we've proven we're on your side. And something inside you tells you to trust me."

"How do you know what's going on inside of me?" His statement felt like an invasion of privacy, all the more invasive because it was true. For all her loneliness, there was a side of Sarah that enjoyed being a private, complicated person, and it was insulting for a stranger to presume to know her inner thoughts.

"It's my job to know, Sarah. Don't take it personally. It's a good thing to be known. You're not as alone as you think you are."

For some reason, she took great offense at this. "You don't know me," she said as she backed away and stood to put on her jacket. She was flooded with the thoughts and feelings she had experienced when she first met Justin. For a moment, fear gained the upper hand in the battle inside her. Words like *stalker* and *crazy* filled her mind.

Justin raised his hands in surrender, the same way he had that night in The Grind. He also scooted back in his chair, as if to assure her he was no threat. He spoke slowly and calmly, but his words continued to press the issue.

"I do know you, Sarah. I know things are getting worse at home with your dad and stepmom. I know you have a hard time enjoying the things you used to. I know you haven't been going to

The Grind because you don't really want to. You are changing, and that's not who you are anymore."

This was too much. "I don't know what you're talking about. Look," she said as she pulled her arms through the sleeves of her jacket, "thank you for the offer of protection, but I'll be fine. Please leave me alone." She spoke as calmly as she could, but she was moving quickly, driven by fear and confusion. She had to get out of this conversation as soon as possible, get out and get away from this stranger who knew far too much about her life and her heart. She turned her back on him and moved toward the door.

Justin did not pursue her. He simply called after her, raising his voice slightly to be heard above the crowd, "I know about the book."

Sarah froze. She turned and stormed back toward him. Now all heads in the shop were turned toward her, but she didn't care. She slammed her hands on the table and leaned toward him, her voice low but intense. "How do you know about that? What, do you have cameras? Is that all you are, some kind of psycho stalker?" She wanted her words to hurt him, to scare him off. She was also thinking about the conversation with her father, and a little afraid that she could be in some sort of trouble. Did Justin work for the Army after all? She hadn't broken any laws. But she did have a vague, guilty feeling about the book, like she was doing something that was wrong, even if it wasn't illegal. Is that what all this was about?

"No, Sarah. There are no cameras. I don't need cameras. And I really am someone who is for you, not against you. I'm sorry I've scared you. I'll tell you what. Let me just give you something to think about, and then I'll leave it up to you if we meet again. I'll be here tomorrow at this same time, and you can decide if you want to have another conversation or not. If you don't come, I promise I'll leave you alone, as much as I would hate to do that. Fair enough?"

"Sure," Sarah replied with a fair amount of skepticism in her voice.

"Okay, Sarah, here it is: All these things that have been happening to you, your interests changing, the tension at home, the confusion about the future, the fear ..." At this Sarah looked away sullenly, like an embarrassed child, but he continued: "All these things, as painful as they are, are a natural part of the process of disconnection."

"Disconnection?"

"Yes. When you're going to transplant a young tree, first you have to loosen the roots. Your roots are being loosened, Sarah, because you need to be transplanted. You don't belong here ... and you know it."

Sarah was grateful there was no pressure to respond. His words made perfect sense, and at the same time were completely overwhelming. "Anything else, or can I go?" she asked blankly.

"Yes, there is one thing. A hope you have, Sarah, a dream that you're going to have to let die."

"What's that?"

"The world is not going to leave you alone, Sarah. I'm sorry. It just doesn't work like that." He paused. "I'll be here tomorrow."

Sarah turned and walked out into the rain.

9 What is real?

"*You don't belong here.*"

Justin's words rang in Sarah's head as she leaned against the cold glass of the train window on the ride home. She stared out at the apartment buildings, the strip malls, the people dressed in black walking the wet sidewalks. She had never felt like she belonged. At school, at home, at work—she had always been different. Certainly, there were moments of joy in her life: reading, running, joking with friends like Torin. In school, she had been a fairly good student. She enjoyed accomplishing a task, doing something well and receiving credit for it. She didn't even mind her job. But there was something deeper. Even when things were going well, she was never comfortable. She could enjoy herself at times, but she couldn't relax and enjoy the world around her. For all her confusion and anger, she found herself admitting that Justin's words were some of the truest she had ever heard. They resonated within her at a deep level, touching a part of her that it seemed had only recently begun to come awake. She realized that she felt the same way when she read her great-grandmother's book. It was an inexplicable certainty, the conviction that *this is right* which was so strong that she knew to question it was to be untrue to herself, to be untrue to truth itself.

She remembered that Justin had done this before. On the night they met, he had said something in casual conversation that had penetrated her very soul:

"Why would you want to be like everybody else? Maybe you're right and they're wrong."

It had been as if this statement was designed, even then, to assure her that she was known and accepted, to inspire trust. The kindness and accuracy of his words had scared her then, too. It was true that today he had angered her, and frightened her, with his knowledge of her thoughts, and the details of her life, with the presumptuous way he assumed he knew her heart. But the truth was, he was right. *"Something inside you tells you to trust me."* She wanted to trust him. Her world was a lonely one, and at the moment, riding the MAX through the gray city, the prospect of being understood, of knowing that someone else accepted her, saw the world as she did, was such a hopeful one that it outweighed all her fears. *"You don't belong here."* Was there a place where she could be herself, where she would feel at home?

Sarah found herself hoping that when she got to the house that night, her parents would do something that would be the final straw, something that would make her so angry that it would be easy to leave and never come back. She began to envision it in her mind: she would walk through the door, her father would pick on her sleep habits, or bring up the book again, and start an argument in which she would finally unleash all her anger and disappointment toward him, wounding him so deeply that then there would be no going back. She would see it as a confirmation, as the closing of a door that would leave her no choice but to trust the mysterious stranger who offered her protection and a new life.

But it didn't happen. Her father wasn't home from work yet, and Jalen was so pathetically pleasant that Sarah couldn't bring herself to pick a fight with her. Her conscience got the better of her and she actually helped her stepmother make dinner, and when her father got home he thanked them both and settled himself down on the couch as if there had never been any tension between them. Jalen made a sympathetic comment about how stressful his job was.

"He works so hard for us," she said, which made Sarah feel like an ungrateful child who was nowhere near ready to face the world on her own. She went to her room confused, angry that she didn't have Great-Grandma Sarah's book to read, but very aware that the one who took it away was providing her with a soft, warm bed. She tried to distract herself by reading another favorite book, but she soon found that she was mindlessly scanning the pages without reading them, her thoughts elsewhere. Justin would be waiting at Java Stop tomorrow. Was she going to trust him? What was she going to do?

She was still unsure in the morning when she left for work. When she walked through the door of the Cup and Saucer Torin greeted her pleasantly, and Sarah was grateful for the opportunity for some normal, lighthearted conversation. They joked about an obnoxious customer from the day before, and Torin told her about her latest relationship problems with her boyfriend, who had moved back into her apartment over the weekend. Then she said, as if she had just remembered something,

"Hey, did you get plugged?"

Getting "plugged" was the latest trend in communication technology. It involved surgical implants in your throat and one ear, which were connected wirelessly to your phone. It was a new enough process that it was still fairly expensive, and although it was becoming more and more common to see people walking down the street talking into the air in conversation with someone on the other side of the city, it would have been a little surprising for a waitress to be plugged. Torin knew that Sarah was usually suspicious of new things, so the question was a strange one.

"No," Sarah laughed. "Who would I call? You?" She could make fun of herself with Torin. "Can you imagine?" She pretended to touch a button on her waist. "Torin, can I get another pot of coffee over here?" She laughed again at her own joke, forgetting for half a moment the burdens she had carried into the room that morning.

But Torin wasn't laughing. She had a strange, confused look on her face.

"What? What is it?"

"You're not plugged?"

"No? Why would you think that?"

Torin shrugged. "Well, I saw you in Java Stop yesterday, and it looked like you were in the middle of this really intense conversation. Anyway, I didn't see your phone, and I was like, 'Wow, good for her. Standing up for herself *and* with the latest tech!'"

Sarah was slow to realize what this meant. Confused, she said, "I was … talking with Justin."

"Ooh, who's Justin?"

"Remember that guy I told you about from The Grind last week?"

"Mr. Old Fashioned? Good for you! You didn't tell me anything happened with that! So, what, you're already fighting?"

"No, it's not like that. We're not together. I'm still not sure I trust him." Sarah still felt like she was trying to catch up in the conversation, like something was off.

"Well, you're going to scare him off revealing your angry side this soon, Honey. Trust me; I've learned the hard way that conversations like that always go better face to face. Next time make him drop what he's doing and come meet you. Good for you for going after it, though!" And she stepped lightheartedly back to the kitchen to pick up an order that was ready.

Sarah was paralyzed. Her mind swirled. Torin didn't see Justin? He wasn't there? She stumbled to the little restroom in the back that was just for staff, and locked the door. Slowly she sunk to the floor and put her head in her hands. Justin wasn't real? She thought back. She had never seen him interact with anyone else, except for Thaddeus. Was he a figment of her imagination too? But he had been so close, even touched her that night on the street. She remembered the night at The Grind. No one had cared when she ran away from Justin. Did no one see him? In the park … The burnouts had seen Thaddeus, spoken with him. That, at least, was one point in favor of the idea that these men actually existed. Either that, or the burnouts had been imaginary too. What about yesterday at the Java Stop? Justin didn't have a drink. He said he liked the place, but he just sat alone at a table without anything on it. She tried to imagine what that scene would look like to the others in the shop if he weren't real: her talking, shouting, slamming the table, walking back and forth. Definitely more like a crazy person than someone who was plugged. Her face flushed red.

In many ways, some sort of mental problem would be the simplest explanation for her life lately. Depression, fear, confusion, anger, believing she was being pursued ... maybe she was losing it. It wouldn't surprise her family if that were true. And of course, everything Justin knew about her would be explained away if he existed only in her mind. Maybe it was as simple as a pill she could take that would finally make her like everyone else. This was a comforting thought, although it also felt a little like giving up. Then tears came to her eyes as the unfairness of it all overwhelmed her. What was going on? She felt less sure of herself than ever. It came to her mind that in a couple of hours, she would finish her shift, and she would have to decide whether to go back to Java Stop. If she went, unsure that he was real, would he still be there? If she was imagining him, and she didn't go, would he keep his promise to leave her alone? She smiled through her tears at the ridiculousness of the situation. Being crazy might turn out to be a great source of entertainment.

"Sarah, you okay?" Torin's voice asked through the door.

"Fine," she said as she stood and wiped her eyes, thinking that it was a good thing she didn't wear much makeup. She looked in the mirror to clean up, and then looked deeper, staring herself in the face. "I'm not crazy," she said, hoping it was true. She quickly washed her hands and rejoined Torin just in time as two groups entered the café. The rest of the morning was busy and passed quickly. Somewhere in the bustle she determined that she would go and see if Justin was there. Of course she would. Answers were more important than ever.

The plain truth

All the long walk through the city to Java Stop, Sarah prepared herself mentally for what was about to take place. She walked quickly as she formed questions and wrestled with the various possibilities. She was angry at Justin, whether he existed or not. It was only as she walked through the door and heard the tinkle of the bell above her head that she considered the fact that there would be witnesses to this confrontation. The place was once again alive with the buzz of a dozen conversations. The prospect of appearing crazy—again—forced her to calm herself a bit. Justin was there, at the same table, with the same infuriating smile on his face. He stood graciously as she approached and gestured to the empty chair.

"You came," he said, obviously pleased.

Sarah ignored his greeting. "So, you're not real?" She asked in a low accusing whisper.

His eyes widened and he appeared confused. "I'm very real," he stated simply.

"But Torin didn't see you."

"No she didn't. A great deal of reality is unseen by most people. No offense to your friend, but she is hardly the determiner of what is real."

Sarah was completely thrown off. With this short comment

he had rendered useless every argument she had been prepared to make.

"Wait. What?" she stumbled. "You are real, but she can't see you? I mean, real outside of my mind? You're not just something I made up because I'm crazy?"

He laughed cheerfully. "Hardly."

"Well … what does that mean? And don't give me that 'trust' stuff again. I need real answers this time or I—" she realized she had nothing to threaten him with, "—or I'm just done."

"Fair enough," he said. "I can see we're not going to make much progress until we settle this question for you. So let's start with this: in about 20 seconds, a group of men in black with blue hair, the ones from the other night, will be walking down the sidewalk across the street. And they will be visible to everyone in this shop. You can ask any of them," he gestured around the room.

Sarah looked out the window. Sure enough, in a few moments the group appeared, coming around the corner from a side street in their usual loud, obtrusive way. She looked back at Justin, and he nodded toward a woman at a nearby table. Doubtfully, Sarah leaned over and addressed her as casually as she could.

"Excuse me, but do you see that group of guys across the street?" She was already preparing to explain away her question if the answer came back negative.

"Yeah. Burnouts," the woman said disgustedly. "Coming out in the daylight now. I wish the Army would do something. Don't worry, honey, they're all noise. You're safe in the daytime." And she returned to whatever she was reading on her phone.

Sarah resettled in her chair. Justin gestured with his hands as if to say "You see?"

"Okay," she said, relieved that it appeared her mind wasn't failing her, but still deeply confused. "It's a little impressive that you knew that would happen," she admitted. "So why can't anyone see you? Who are you?" She hesitated. "What are you?"

"People can see me. You can see me. And there are others," he nodded toward the burnouts as they disappeared down the street.

"Them?" she asked doubtfully. "Why them?"

"For exactly the opposite of the reason that you can. Don't worry, Sarah, answers will come. Now, if it's okay, I'd like to talk about the original reason for our meeting today."

"No, wait. Who are they?"

"They are men who have given themselves over to certain influences, at a great cost," he said with a sudden sadness in his voice. "They are the enemy, because they have aligned themselves with the Enemy."

Sarah was getting used to answers that only raised more questions. "Why are they here? I mean, in the clean part of the city, in the middle of the day?"

"Because you're here."

Sarah fought back a wave of fear, and her voice broke as she asked her next question: "Then why are they leaving?"

"Because I'm here."

Sarah was silent.

Justin once again made an effort to lighten the mood of the conversation. "So, if we have settled the question of whether I exist or not," this seemed to amuse him, "can we return to the reason for our meeting?"

Sarah was overwhelmed. "Which was what, exactly, again?" she asked apologetically as she slumped in her chair.

"Yesterday," Justin replied with great patience in his voice, "I told you that you don't belong here, and that you are being uprooted, prepared for a dramatic change. We both know that something in your heart tells you this is true. You know it has something to do with your great-grandmother's book, and with the way you have struggled to find peace for as long as you can remember."

Sarah squirmed, but his words were not as hard to take as they had been the day before. Still, she was withholding judgment until she knew more.

"Go on," she said.

"Well, this is the part of the conversation where, I'll be honest, I'm a little nervous about scaring you off. But we're running out of time," he glanced out the window, "and you need to know, because soon you'll be asked to make a decision."

He paused, took a deep breath, and looked directly into her eyes.

"Yes?" she was growing impatient.

"Sarah, look out that window. You see all those people, all those big buildings? Everyone so busy, so caught up in their lives, all the things they want and need and plan to do?"

It was impossible to tell where this was going, and Sarah was getting frustrated. She glanced out the window. "Yeah, sure."

"Sarah, thirty days from now, these streets will be filled with people screaming and crying. Missiles will strike these buildings, and soldiers will march through the city. Everything about daily life in this place will change forever. It will be a time of fear and great pain, and—" his voice broke off as his eyes filled with tears, but he regained his composure quickly and seemed to force himself to focus back on Sarah, "and I am here to get you out. I am here to rescue you."

11 A lot to take in

Sarah was silent. Under other circumstances, she might have laughed. She knew that if she were telling the story of this conversation to Torin, they would both be cracking up at this point. But something about Justin's voice, his sadness, and everything that had led up to this moment, caused her to think that maybe, just maybe, this was the truth after all. If he had been a crazy stalker, he would have revealed that he loved her or something awkward like that. Part of her felt that this was right, this was the answer she had been looking for. But only a part of her. It was hard not to be skeptical about a statement as wild as the one Justin had just made. She needed to know more.

"In thirty days? How could you possibly know something like that?"

Justin's familiar smile returned. "I have it on very good authority."

"What does that mean? What, are you some sort of scout for the army that's coming?"

"No. If I were, why would I care about rescuing you? No, I am not a part of any human government. I am a servant of God, Sarah."

Sarah's face turned red as her thoughts flashed to her great-grandma's book. She glanced around the room nervously and slunk down in her chair before she remembered that no one else could see or hear Justin. She replied in a frightened whisper:

"A servant of ...?" she glanced upward, unable to bring herself to say the word. Apart from history teachers in school, she wasn't sure she had ever heard anyone use that word unless they were cursing. She lived in culture that prided itself on having been cleansed of all traces of God. That was a word for ignorant fanatics of past generations and backward parts of the world. And then recently she had read it in the book, and it had been like discovering a treasure she didn't know she was looking for. It had caused her to stuff the Bible under her pillow and peek out the bedroom door to make sure her parents weren't nearby. Now Justin was saying ... she realized what this meant, if it were true.

"So you ...?"

"Yes. I understand it's a lot to take in."

The word neither of them had used presented itself to her mind, leaping off a remembered page as if it were highlighted in gold: *angel*. People in her world did use that word, but in silly ways that had never created in her imagination anything like the man sitting across the table from her, who exuded such confidence and quiet strength. She sat staring at him, shrinking back in her chair with a fear that was very different from what she felt toward the burnouts. She felt unworthy, dirty and small. Then a fresh thought entered her mind, unexpected, as if suggested by some other voice outside of herself. She looked back out the window and became angry.

"Well, why would ..." she lowered her voice, "why would *He* do that? Kill all these innocent people? Why all that pain and destruction? It doesn't seem right."

"It is right. They are not innocent, Sarah. You know that."

"But it made you sad to talk about it."

"It is sad. It is heartbreaking. But it must be. And it's important that you don't get distracted." He leaned forward and placed his hand on the table in front of her, like a parent trying to get a child's attention. Sarah's hand was also on the table, and she withdrew it. "What you need to decide is whether you will come with me and leave this place. There will always be questions, but they will be answered along the way."

Half of Sarah heard and understood what he was saying. The other half was preoccupied with a fresh thought, a new realization of the significance of his words.

"What about my family? What about Torin?"

Justin looked her in the eyes and shook his head slowly.

Sarah's hand came to her mouth and her eyes filled with tears. "I don't believe you. It can't be. He wouldn't ... No. No." She stood quickly, bumping the chair and table, and made an awkward exit from Java Stop for the second day in a row.

Denial

Sarah was an intelligent girl, and she was very much aware of the contradiction in the thoughts that filled her mind on the ride home. It made no sense at all for a person to say that she didn't believe in God and at the same time to be angry with Him. But she was angry, and it felt like the best way to express her anger was to refuse to believe. That last word she had spoken to Justin, "No," filled her heart and mind for the rest of the evening, like a wall she had erected to prevent any further thought or discussion about the matter. When she got home she headed straight for the kitchen and prepared for herself a huge plate of junk food, then plopped herself down in front of the Wall. She found a show about fashion, which she watched mindlessly for an hour until Jalen came home. Then the two of them watched it together for another hour, laughing and talking and thoroughly enjoying themselves. Then her dad came home, Jalen prepared dinner, and they all sat on the couch and watched an action movie her dad had been wanting to see. It was the most enjoyable evening any of them had had in months. No one dared spoil it by bringing up any of the tension of the past week. Her parents were obviously pleased, and by the end of the evening even Sarah herself was genuinely relaxed. This was what she needed. Just life, normal life. To stop worrying about the future. *Ha*, she said silently to the Force she did not believe in.

When her alarm woke her in the morning, an unbidden thought flashed through Sarah's mind as she raised herself from her pillow: *29 days*. She pictured missiles striking skyscrapers, smoke and dust and injured people running and screaming. She closed her eyes again and sank back down, and was instantly weary. She could not avoid it. Justin's words would not leave her alone. Somehow she knew this would happen every morning. *No*, she said to the imaginary Justin in her mind. *It can't be. No.* And the wall was erected again. She reminded herself that this was her last day of work for a few days, and she resolved to enjoy herself, to do some things she wanted to do. She would spend the day in the city. She loved the city. She was relieved to look out the window and see that it wasn't raining. She would get lunch from a street vendor, and maybe do some shopping. It would be a good day.

After work she took a bus to a park in another part of town, with picnic tables and a playground where children laughed and played. It was a beautiful spring day, a little cold but nice enough in the sunshine. She ate her lunch, a hot chicken sandwich from a roadside cart that warmed her inside and made her smile, then went across the street to some shops where she strolled lazily and found a new sweater she liked. A large library was nearby, and eventually she found herself inside, drawn by her love of old books, real books, the kind printed on paper. One of the reasons she loved living in Portland was that there were still libraries. In many cities they had disappeared, being completely unnecessary, as everything that had ever been written could be found on the internet. But here there were still some people like her, who loved the feel and the smell of a room full of books. She browsed a familiar section of classic old fiction and picked out *The Swiss Family Robinson*. Lately she had been re-reading some of her favorite books from childhood, and she loved this story, the romance and adventure of living off the land in an exotic place. She was a city girl, and everything about the book was completely foreign to anything she had personally experienced—including the happy family. She wondered today if that was the real reason she liked it. She took the book to a far corner of the library, settled down in a soft chair, and immersed herself in a fantasy world.

After a while, she stood and stretched, went to the restroom, and returned to her chair. Settling back into her seat, she glanced absently at the tall bookshelves that filled this part of the library. Directly in front of her, down low on a shelf of large, uninteresting-looking books, one title caught her eye because of one word: "religious." She turned her head sideways and looked closer. *The Religious History of the United States of America*. She was intrigued, and began to get up from her seat. Then she remembered. *No*, she thought, and sat back down. She would not open that door. She told herself she didn't care about religious history. She was enjoying a well-deserved day of relaxation. She opened her book and tried to return to the fantasy world. But her thoughts would not leave the book on the shelf. She kept glancing at it, and every time she did it made her angrier. It seemed clear to her that it was the book she should be reading. That it was somehow important. But she didn't want to. She wanted to escape, to deny. She wanted to be left alone. But Justin had said that wasn't an option. *Justin*! Somehow he had found his way back into her thoughts. *No*, she said to Justin, and to the God she refused to acknowledge. She forced herself back into her book, and read for another hour or so, determined to enjoy it and only half doing so. But she pressed on, mostly to spite the book that called out to her from its place on the shelf. Finally she finished a chapter, stood up, and strode purposefully past the shelves and out to the main entrance. She checked out her book and quickly made her way out of the building and down the steps to the sidewalk, thinking about dinner and intentionally not thinking about the Religious History of the United States of America.

It was nearly dark out. Sarah had been in the library longer than she realized. She had often been teased by her dad and brothers for getting lost in books, but today her time was her own, and it made her smile to realize that she had the freedom to waste an afternoon doing what she loved. She told herself that when she moved into the city, she would do this all the time. *But there will be no city. Not like this. Everything will change forever in 29 days,* said a voice in her head. *No,* she replied to it, and distracted herself by looking for a place to eat. She found another street vendor and quickly ate a hot dog while standing next to the booth to take advantage of the warmth and the light. Suddenly she wanted to be home as quickly as she could. She told herself that she wasn't scared, just tired, but the truth was that she did not feel safe, and once again, somehow, it seemed that it was Justin's fault. God's fault. Yes, Justin had protected her from the burnouts, but now the truth was out: He worked for the real bad guy. The Destroyer. Before the two of them came along, she had enjoyed nights in the city. Now her dreams were being taken away, for reasons that had nothing to do with her. It wasn't fair. *Leave me alone,* she said to both of them.

From this part of the city, the quickest way home was the new underground portion of the MAX system, which Sarah had only ridden a couple of times, since the section between her home and work wasn't finished yet. But from here she could ride it to a bus station, and then catch a bus the rest of the way home. Riding the subway felt like the perfect end to a long day of work and play in the city. She descended a set of steps to an underground station, studied a schedule on a screen that told her which train to wait for, flashed her payment card at an automatic gate, and stepped onto the platform to wait.

This particular station was strangely empty. The noise of the city at night echoed down the concrete stairwell into the empty space where Sarah waited, but it seemed muffled and distant. A few people stood at a safe distance from one another, lost in private worlds on their phones, until the noise of the coming train brought them partially back to reality, enough that they could step through the open doors and find a place to stand or sit, hardly looking up as they did so. Sarah's train was the next one, which would arrive in about 15 minutes. When they all passed through the doors and the train sped away in a rush of wind and noise down the tunnel, she realized with a chill that she was all alone.

She felt foolish. Why had she come through the gate this early? It crossed her mind to go back, to rush upstairs into the activity of the sidewalk, catch a bus to an above-ground MAX station, but that seemed silly. She was as safe here as she would be in those places. There was no way to completely avoid this kind of situation. It was part of life in the city. Probably everything would be fine. She retreated to a far wall she could lean against and look down the tunnel into the darkness, wishing the train to arrive. After a few moments she looked at her phone and sighed. Exactly two minutes had passed since the last train left. She tried to distract herself by planning her day off tomorrow. She would sleep in, watch the Wall, browse the internet for apartments in the city when her parents weren't around. It would be another good day. She deserved that.

There was a noise in the stairwell. Loud voices. She looked up and saw black shoes, black pants. Lots of metal and tattoos. Ugly laughter. And finally, blue hair. There were five, six, seven of them. Eight, nine. The last two positioned themselves at the base of the stairs. Why? Then she knew. To keep others out. They were claiming this stop as their own. She was frozen against the wall. They hadn't looked at her yet, but she didn't kid herself they were there for any other reason. The group made its way to the automatic gate, and one flashed a payment card. Two of them quickly stepped into the gap of the open gate, planted their boots and leaned into the swinging arm, forcing it open while all the rest pushed through. They released the gate and it swung shut with a clang.

Once on the platform, the group scanned the area and quickly spotted Sarah cowering against the wall. She let out an involuntary whimper as they spread out and made their way toward her, each with his own ugly, menacing smile. This was the closest she had ever been to men like this, although she had seen them many times in the city, and of course several times lately. They were a mixed group of tall and short young men, with varying skin color, but had several things in common. Of course there was the blue hair. Up close, it was easy to see that some were naturally blonde and others had dark hair, but each had cut his hair short, dyed it a bright blue, and spiked it straight up into the air. They all wore black, which was not uncommon in the city, but with them there was no variation. Not just their leather coats, but pants, shoes, shirts, socks, gloves—everything was black, the only exception being the metal spikes embedded in their jackets, gloves, and belts. They were heavily tattooed, which was not all that unique, and some had various piercings.

But what she noticed for the first time on this night was their eyes. There was a wildness, an unpredictability, a strangeness in their eyes that was far and away the most frightening thing about them. Just looking at them, you had the vague sense that something in their minds was not right. Something, possibly, beyond the chemicals in their blood. Nearly all drugs had been legal in Oregon for most of Sarah's life. As long as you weren't driving a car, the Army didn't care what you put in your body, and it was common to see people on the street who were obviously under the influence of something. Burnouts were known to be high on at least one substance at all times; it was something they prided themselves on. But looking at their eyes as they approached her, Sarah had the distinct sense that it was something more than drugs that that made these men dangerous. An old-fashioned word flashed across her mind: *evil.*

A shorter, skinny one stepped to the front of the group as they approached. Sarah was trembling with fear, well beyond the point of trying to pretend she wasn't terrified. She had no intention of saying a word to these men, and would not have been able to get words out even if she wanted to.

"Well, here we are at last," said the man, looking her in the eye for a moment and then glancing wildly around the platform. "You're a hard one to catch up with. Fast. You're a runner, huh? And where's your friend? Could use him right now, huh? Pretty special to have a friend like that." He looked her in the eyes again, this time with surprising clarity. "You must be pretty important."

The group had continued to move closer as he spoke. They were very close now, surrounding her in a half-circle against the wall. It was everything Sarah could do not to sink to the ground and cry. She said nothing, and tried not to make eye contact.

The man reached out and grabbed her chin and gently but firmly turned her face to meet his gaze. His fingers were cold. He leaned closer to her and spoke with false concern: "I know you think we're the bad guys, but you've got it all wrong. Your friend lied to you. You deserve to know the truth. We're here to make you an offer."

Sarah could not help the doubtful look on her face. He chuckled and continued, "I know, we come on strong, but it's true. You see, Sarah—yeah, we know your name—you've been missing out. We've experienced things you've never dreamed of. Our minds have been opened. We know you're tired of your family, tired of the routine." He paused to look her up and down in a way that flooded her mind with fresh fears. "And you could be so great with us. You have no idea. So we want to give you a chance. If you come with us, let us show you some things, I promise, no one will hurt you."

As he said "show you some things," the man had reached into a pocket and extended toward her a handful of various pills. Sarah shrank back from them. It was an invitation to cease to be herself, to open herself up to whatever had made these men what they were, and she was repulsed by it. She still found herself unable to speak.

The man took a step back. "Oh, poor thing. We've frightened her." He looked around at his companions and chuckled. "She's speechless. Can't come up with the words, honey? Let me guess: you want to say something like 'What if I refuse?'"

Sarah stared at him.

"Well, I can answer that. Unfortunately, Sarah, we are in a little bit of a rush. This is sort of a one-time only offer. You need to come with us now, or," he shook his head with mock sadness, "well, it would just break my heart."

At these words he pulled back one side of his trenchcoat to reveal a long metal blade.

One thing the Army was serious about enforcing was the ban on all firearms. For many years now, gun manufacturing had been illegal for anyone but a few military contractors. The penalty for possession of even a small handgun was so severe, and the efforts of the Army to eradicate them from the black market so thorough, that owning a gun had become even more unheard of than owning a Bible. And so people like these men, for whom violence was a necessary part of life, had turned to blades. Blades were easier and cheaper to make than guns, and far less of a loss if they had to be disposed of in a hurry. Men like this usually carried one or two small knives, as well as a larger, sword-like blade, cheap and homemade but effective, on the inside of their coat. Skill with these weapons was a source of great pride for them. It was also a key feature of many of the movies Sarah's dad watched late at night on the Wall, but this was the first time she had seen one up close in real life.

The look on the wild young man's face as he revealed his weapon made it clear to Sarah that he would enjoy using it as much as anything else he might do to her. She had always imagined, watching movies in the comfort of her living room, that she would be brave in a moment like this, say bold, clever things and stand up to her attackers with an inner courage that would surprise them and give her the split second she would need to sprint away to safety. But this wasn't like the movies at all. She was filled with nothing but fear, and there was nowhere to run. With a pathetic cry, she hid her face, cowered against the wall and shrunk to the ground as he removed the blade from his belt.

Nothing happened. He didn't strike her, and didn't say anything. With her hands still shielding her head, she looked up to see that a figure was standing between them. His back was to her, facing the burnouts, but she knew. It was Justin.

13 Time to go

The men stepped back at the appearance of Sarah's defender, but their leader quickly recovered himself, and spoke with just as much hatred and pride as ever.

"Good. I'm glad you're here. We can deal with you too. We're stronger than before. Stronger all the time. Our days of running from you are over."

Justin was utterly calm. "You are not as strong as you imagine. I give you one warning: I have been given authority over your lives. I will spare you tonight if you turn and leave now." He reached into the folds of his trenchcoat and drew out a blade of his own, clean and gleaming even in the dim fluorescent light.

Sarah's fear lessened only slightly. Her mind was spinning with the impossibility of Justin's sudden appearance. His presence was a comfort, but he was one against seven. A vague thought passed through her mind that somehow the evil within these men made them stronger, that Justin would be bound by certain rules they would ignore if it came to a fight. He was too good, too pure, too naïve, she thought, to be of any help against such men, who cared nothing for right and wrong.

But the burnouts didn't seem to think so. They shrank back noticeably when he revealed his weapon. Except for the leader. He yelled at them without breaking eye contact with Justin.

"All right! He wants a fight! Let's give it to him! Let's do it!" His eyes were wilder than ever, and his face contorted as his voice rose to a scream. "It's time! We're ready! Come on!"

The others drew strength from his confidence. They drew their own blades and stepped nearer, their own faces filling once again with such a hatred that Sarah's mind was instantly flooded with an overpowering desire to leave. Not just to get away from this dangerous situation, but from the world as a whole. She wanted to get as far away as possible from anywhere that such ugliness could exist. *Everything is so wrong,* she thought. *Who can live in such a place?*

Meanwhile the leader was still screaming. "Come on, hero! Make a move!"

Justin spoke quietly, and although his back was to Sarah she thought she detected a note of pity in his voice. "Please don't do this."

Then the leader struck. He swung quickly with a false blow that was meant to draw Justin's blade away from his body, then brought his blade down from above with tremendous force, just like Sarah had seen the men do in the movies. But Justin defended it easily, and then went into action. The two men on either side of the leader then struck at the same time, but he handled them both as if he had known what they would do before they did it. He was amazingly fast. No matter what they did, even when another joined in, his blade was always just where it needed to be. Sarah watched in awe.

Then she screamed. As Justin defended himself from the four attackers, and even began to press them back away from the wall, the three others moved away from him, off to the side toward the train tracks, and then rushed toward her. "Justin! Justin!" She scrambled to her feet and stumbled in the only direction she could, back toward the corner of the platform, where she would be trapped once again.

Justin spared only the briefest of glances in her direction, assessed the situation, and then turned his back once again. Sarah was angry and confused. "JUSTIN!" she screamed again as the man nearest her lifted his blade.

And then Thaddeus was there. Sarah blinked in surprise, and as quickly as she did the sword in his hand had knocked the man's blade to the ground and was plunged deep into his chest. Sarah gasped in shock and confusion. Had he actually killed the man? When he withdrew the blade there was no blood, no wound, but her attacker slumped to the ground and did not move. She looked over and saw that two of the men who had been fighting Justin were lying still on the cold concrete. As she watched, he disarmed another and brought his blade across the man's belly without slowing down on his way to defend against a stroke from the other one. In a flash he forced the man's hands up over his head, spun, and delivered another killing stroke. They both fell to the ground and were still.

The platform was quiet. She turned again and saw that Thaddeus had finished his attackers as well. There was a scrambling sound back by the stairwell on the other side of the gate, where the two other members of the gang were sprinting up the stairs. Thaddeus gave Justin a questioning look, but Justin shook his head. He turned to Sarah, who realized that she was crying, and didn't know when she had started.

"Are you okay?" Justin asked.

Sarah was a mess, but she nodded through her tears. Physically, she was fine.

"I'm sorry you had to see that. I understand you're upset, but we have to leave now. The next train will be here in a moment, and things will become much more difficult for us if you become a murder suspect."

"Are they really dead?" she asked.

"Yes. Finally. They gave their lives over to death a long time ago. Sarah, I'm sorry, but this is not the time for questions. We need to leave now." He held out his hand to lift her to her feet.

Sarah became calm. "Okay," she said, taking his hand. "Okay, I'll go."

"Good. Let's get you home."

"No, I mean I'll go. I'll go with you. I'm ready to leave."

Justin smiled and nodded. "Okay. Good. We can work out the details tomorrow. Go home and get some sleep. You have the day off tomorrow, so sleep in, and then go out for lunch somewhere close to your home. I'll find you. Thaddeus will watch over your house tonight. You'll be safe."

They heard the whoosh of the train coming in the distance. Sarah wondered why the platform was still completely empty. They rushed through the gate and up the stairs, and found themselves in a sea of people suddenly coming down. In a moment the train would arrive, and the bodies would be discovered. She pulled her hood over her head and made her way down the crowded sidewalk toward the nearest bus stop, escorted by her invisible guardians.

Exit strategy

28 *days.* Sarah woke late to the sound of Jalen vacuuming downstairs. She lay in bed for a long time, feeling heavy and tired, as though she had run a race the night before. For several minutes her thoughts took her back and forth to the two sides of the question that lay before her.

True, she had told Justin she would leave with him. The attack by the burnouts, and his appearance and defense of her, left no doubt that he was on her side, and that she had somehow become important to both sides of a battle she didn't fully understand. But Justin worked for the God who was planning to strike the earth with fire and pain, and who apparently had no problem with His servants taking lives in street fights. Her thoughts went to Jalen, the simple woman vacuuming her carpet downstairs. True, she was shallow and weak and had made some mistakes in her life, but did she deserve the destruction that was coming? Sarah suddenly felt more pity for her step-mother than she had ever had before. She could barely handle it when the power went out; what would she do in a war?

But something within Sarah knew that these arguments were hollow, even though she didn't yet have satisfying answers to her questions. The truth was that she knew, she *knew*, that leaving with Justin was right. She knew that what she had seen in those young men's eyes the night before was just an extreme version of what she had felt every day of her entire life from the world all around her. She knew that the intangible, indescribable feeling—no, it was more than a feeling—the awareness that came over her when she was reading her great-grandmother's book was the truest, most trustworthy thing she had ever known. She knew that her resistance, the denial she had lived in for the last day or so, was foolishness. She had to leave. She had to trust. *Fine,* she thought. *The sooner the better, then. I'll meet with Justin, we'll make our plans, and leave as soon as possible. I won't even say goodbye.*

She got ready and went downstairs. Jalen was cleaning the kitchen.

"You hungry, dear? I could make you something," she offered.

"No, thank you, Jalen. I'm meeting someone for lunch." Sarah found that she had a hard time looking Jalen in the eye. Suddenly her plans to run away felt like a betrayal. How could she leave everyone to face what was coming without warning them?

"Oh, that friend from work? What's her name? Torin?"

"Yeah, Torin. I mean yeah, that's her name, but that's not who I'm meeting. It's, um, it's a guy," Sarah mumbled.

"Oh, really?" Jalen was obviously excited but trying not to overreact. For quite a while now it had been clear that Sarah's lack of interest in guys was a great concern to her. One more reason to think something was not quite right with her step-daughter. The truth was, Sarah was as interested in meeting a guy as any girl her age, but had very little hope that she would be able to find someone who was a match, someone who really understood her. She knew about Jalen's concern and had gotten good at ignoring it. But she picked up on her misunderstanding and made the split-second decision to take advantage of it. She had not meant to suggest that this was a romantic interest, but Jalen's assumption made her realize that this would be one logical reason she might suddenly disappear. This would be the lie she would use to explain what she was about to do.

"Um, yeah, a guy. I'm meeting a guy for lunch." She faked an excited smile.

"Someone from work?"

"No, just someone I met at a club. We've seen each other a few times now, and so far it's going really well."

"Well, that's exciting!" Jalen gave her a big hug and then shooed her out of the room. "What time are you meeting him? Don't waste time with me, for goodness sake."

"Oh, no, I'm okay. I should get going though. Thanks, Jalen."

"Have a great time!" Jalen called after her as she made her way down the hall to the door. Then she added as an afterthought: "Oh! What's his name?"

"Justin," Sarah said. "His name is Justin." And she hurried outside, shutting the door behind her.

Of course, Sarah didn't feel great about lying. But she told herself she was doing it out of kindness. Jalen had obviously been pleased at the possibility of a romance in her life, and the things that were coming her way in the near future would be so hard to understand that a little deception like this hardly seemed important one way or the other. Besides, Justin hadn't given her any instructions about how to handle her family; she was doing the best she could on her own.

She walked a few blocks through the residential neighborhood of her parents' house and around a corner to a strip mall that contained a small liquor store, a place to get cash advances on paychecks, a convenience store, and a deli. Sarah was uncomfortable as she opened the door of the deli; she didn't especially like the people who worked there, or the food for that matter, but it was the only place to eat within walking distance, and she had no desire to take public transportation at the moment. It was a little early for lunch, and all the tables were empty. A man washing dishes in the back of the kitchen seemed to be the only one there, and he hardly looked up when she entered. She stood at the glass counter awkwardly for a minute until he finished his task, and even then he only gave her about half his attention. She ordered a simple sandwich, which he made mindlessly, then added some chips to the plate and ran her cash card without ever making eye contact. Sarah smiled at the thought that this was the perfect place to have a conversation with an invisible stranger. Her clothes could have been on fire and this man wouldn't have noticed.

When she turned to choose a table, Justin was sitting in a booth in the back corner of the room. Sarah joined him with the hint of a smile on her face.

"It must be fun to be able to do that."

"Do what?

"Appear and disappear. Travel all over the place. Can you move … instantaneously? Can you just be anywhere, anytime you want?

"No, it doesn't exactly work like that." He didn't seem anxious to do any further explaining. Sarah found his mysteriousness a constant source of frustration. Was it just that he was such a soldier that he was used to only communicating what was absolutely necessary? Or did he enjoy keeping her in the dark?

"Well, how does it work? I mean … okay, let's start with this: Are you … physical? Like, are you, you know, really even here?" Sarah had been wondering this for a while now. Both Justin and Thaddeus had touched her at times—lifting her to her feet, shielding her from danger, things like that. They had also had what was clearly a physical interaction with the burnouts last night. And those men could see them, too. But to the rest of the world they were invisible, and they could appear out of nowhere, as they had at the MAX station. She was sure that Justin had not come into the deli through the door. She felt that if she were going to travel to who-knows-where with him (another question she had), she had the right to know what kind of being she was dealing with.

"That's a good question, Sarah. I think the best answer is that I am real, and I am limited. There is only One who can be everywhere at once, and I'm not Him. I exist in a particular time and place, like you. I'm not exactly physical in the way you mean it, but I am capable of being physically present when it's important to do so."

"Okay. But appearing out of nowhere, right when I need you, knowing what I'm doing and where I'll be ..."

Justin smiled. "I said I was limited. But I'm not as limited as you. And I have an excellent Source of information."

"So why can I see you? And feel you?"

"Well, think of it this way. You're bilingual, right? English and Spanish?"

"Well, not really. I know some."

Okay, well I'm guessing you know enough to know that words don't always have an exact translation, but even when they don't you can usually get the point across. "Espero" means "I hope," but it also means "I wait," and neither translation is perfect, but either one is close enough that the other person gets the general idea."

"Okay. So?"

"So, what you see here in front of you," he gestured to himself, "is an imperfect translation. You might say this is not the real me, but it's me translated into your physical world. I am a spiritual being, and this is what I look like when I'm translated into the physical."

Sarah nodded, feeling that she was actually close to understanding this one. But there were more questions. "Then why don't other people see you?"

Justin smiled again. "I guess you could say they don't speak my language."

"And I do?"

"You're learning. Now, can we get down to business?"

"Okay. I'll have more questions later, though," she warned him.

"That's fine. We'll have plenty of time to chat once we get on our way."

"Great. When do we leave?" Sarah was trying to commit herself fully to what she knew was the right course of action, and not to think about all the reasons—Jalen, Torin, death and destruction—to question what was happening.

"In a week." Justin said matter-of-factly.

"A week! What? No … I'm ready! Why not now? Today, tomorrow?" Sarah was scrambling. She couldn't imagine looking everyone in the eye for another week, knowing what they were facing and that she was leaving them forever. "I said I would go; let's go! We only have 28 days, right?"

"The trains move quickly. We don't need that long. And we will need money for the trip. You have a paycheck coming next Monday, a week from today. It will be enough to get us where we're going."

"Which is where, by the way?" Sarah's tone was accusatory once again. "Where are we going? And why on earth would He," she pointed upward and lowered her voice, "why would He make me go through a week of living a lie? And can't—" now she was whispering "—can't God come up with some cash some other way? Does He really need my paycheck? This is ridiculous." Sarah knew she was throwing a fit like a little girl, but she felt justified in doing so. She was taking a great step of faith, and making great sacrifices, but this was asking too much.

Justin stared at her for a moment before answering. She had seen this fatherly, disappointed look before, and it only served to reinforce her feeling that he was being unfair. But she found it hard to return his gaze. When he spoke, he continued to look directly into her face, despite the fact that she was avoiding eye contact. He spoke slowly and carefully.

"Sarah, I told you that I am not unlimited. That includes my patience. I am not as limited as you, for which you should be grateful. I'm going to try to ignore your attitude right now and answer your questions as best I can. But let me say that I hope we don't have to have too many more experiences like last night before you'll begin to trust."

Sarah stared at the table.

"We are going south, beyond the borders of this land. And

yes, He is unlimited. At any time, He can do anything He wants. He could provide any amount of money, in any way He chose. In this case, He is choosing to provide through your paycheck on Monday. He could also simply cause you to disappear and reappear at our destination. But He is not doing that. And anytime He does something, or does not do something, it is because that is what is best. Always. This next week is important. I don't know why, but I trust. If you do not trust, the alternative is to stay here."

"No," Sarah mumbled without looking up. She had questions, but his lecture had deflated her. "No, I understand. I'll go. I'm sorry."

Justin was silent for a moment. When he spoke, his voice had softened a little. "It's okay, Sarah. I know this is hard. You're being stretched, which is a good thing—it's how we grow. But it's never easy."

Sarah looked closely at him. She was still feeling the sting of his rebuke, but she couldn't resist following up on this comment. "We? How 'we' grow? So you … you're not perfect?"

Justin laughed out loud. "Hardly! I have much to learn."

"So does that mean you get things wrong sometimes? I mean, do you ever do the wrong thing?"

"I think the word you're looking for is 'sin.' And no, I don't do wrong in that sense. I live in complete obedience. But I don't know everything, and I have many areas in which I can grow."

"Like what? I don't get it. If you don't …" she lowered her voice because she realized she was about to use another outdated, unpopular word, "if you don't *sin*, then how can there be room for improvement? You already trust Him completely, so what kinds of things stretch you?"

Suddenly Justin was the one avoiding eye contact. He seemed to be caught off guard by her question. He hesitated before saying, "You probably wouldn't understand."

"No, come on, I want to know! What's hard for an angel?" The playfulness had returned to Sarah's voice.

Justin sat up straight and pushed back from the table, as if preparing to leave, although there were clearly more details they still needed to discuss. He was visibly uncomfortable. "As I said, Sarah, we will have plenty of time to talk on our journey. It's important that we don't overwhelm you. Perhaps we could meet again tomorrow to outline the rest of our plans."

Sarah kept pressing. "Oh, don't you worry about me. I'm not the one feeling overwhelmed at the moment. What is it? Why won't you answer me?"

He didn't speak. Sarah crossed her arms and looked at him questioningly for a moment, and then her eyes widened. She raised a finger and pointed at him, then slowly turned it around and pointed to herself. "It's me!" She said. "It's this! It's dealing with me!" She pretended to be deeply offended. "So, you never sin and you can fight evil and travel at the speed of light, or something, but you find it hard to put up with a sweet little girl like me?"

Justin's face flushed red with embarrassment. "It's not … it's not you. Don't take it personally, Sarah. I just haven't done this in a while. I'd forgotten what it's like to work one-on-one. Apparently, my Lord wants me to grow in patience. But that would be the case working with any human. Again, I'm sorry. I would have preferred if this had not come up."

Sarah laughed. "Justin, I'm not offended. I know I'm a pain. But now I have another question: Are you saying that God gave me a guardian angel who's out of practice? You're rusty? Haven't had to put up with humans in a while? What have you been doing, resting on a cloud for a few thousand years, and now people are more than you can handle? " Now she was thoroughly enjoying this opportunity to pick on him.

Justin's tone now became serious, and at the same time humble. "Sarah, I am not your guardian. I mean—I will be on this journey, but that's not where I've been serving. We all start out as guardians. I served well in my position and was given greater responsibility. I have been a … supervisor, you might say, for a long time now. I oversee a number of guardians—for example Thaddeus, who is assigned to you."

"Thaddeus is my guardian?" Sarah was humbled, and a little embarrassed. For some reason this information touched her heart at a deep level. It made her feel known, loved, and personally cared for. People talked about "guardian angels" all the time, but always as a joke, and she had been half joking in her comment to Justin. But the fact that this great, strong being had been personally assigned to her was like someone putting their finger directly on the place in her heart where she had always felt that she was no one special. On another level, she was also hoping that Justin could not read her thoughts—that Thaddeus was cuter, and that she imagined she might prefer his company to Justin's on a long journey.

"He is a faithful servant. He has watched over you for your entire life. It's an important assignment, and he has served well."

"Then why isn't he here now? Why am I going with you, and not him?" She didn't mean for it to come out that way, but Justin gave no indication that he was insulted.

"His assignment is nearly complete. I am relieving him because getting you out is a high priority, and it will bring about the end of my responsibilities here as well." Sarah gave him a look that made it clear his answer had not been helpful, so he continued. "Think of it this way: If the owner of this deli knew that the mayor of Portland was coming in for lunch today, no matter how much he trusts his employees, he would probably make the sandwich himself."

Sarah nodded slowly. "I see. You're not going to tell me why I'm so important, are you?"

Justin smiled. "Not today."

"Will you tell me how long it's been since you 'worked one-on-one'?"

"Four hundred years."

The conversation had taken on such a familiar tone that this detail served as a shocking reminder to Sarah that she was not talking to a peer. She swallowed and asked, "And how many 'guardians' did you 'supervise'?"

"Around nine hundred million."

"Oh." She paused. "Not exactly resting on a cloud."

"Not exactly." He smiled. "*Now* can we get down to business?"

"Yes."

"Thank you. As I said, we will leave next Monday. You'll go to work in the morning, and your paycheck will be automatically deposited into your account as soon as your shift is over. You'll take a backpack to work with you that day, with a few changes of clothes, including a hat, gloves, and a warm jacket. You will go straight from work to the bank and take out all the money in your account in cash. Then you'll go straight to the main train station downtown and get a ticket for southern California. I'll meet you on the train."

"Why the warm clothes if we're going to southern California?"

"Because you never know."

"Okay. And why cash?"

"So your purchases will be harder to trace. We will probably be followed. That's also why you are not to bring your phone."

"Okay. Anything else?"

"No. Just try to live your life as normally as possible for the next week. After the defeat last night, you will probably be left alone for a while, but Thaddeus will be watching over you all the time, although you may not see him."

"Where will you be?"

"I have other business to attend to between now and then. And that reminds me: in the next few days you'll start to hear things—on the news, from people at work—about events in the world. War, accidents, crime, that kind of thing. Under no circumstances are you to indicate that you have any knowledge about what's coming. You will make yourself suspicious to the Army and it will become much harder to leave quietly."

"But does that mean I can't warn my family and friends? I mean, I've been thinking: if I'm worth saving, aren't they? Shouldn't I at least be trying to convince people to come with me? Shouldn't they get a chance to trust too, or to change their ways, or something?"

"You have the right heart, Sarah. And normally, the answer would be yes. In this case, you will have to take my word that we are beyond that now. It's too late for those kinds of opportunities."

This was hard to accept. "Can't I at least try?"

"If you can do so without revealing anything about your plans or what is coming. But take my word for it, Sarah, that time is past."

Sarah was thoughtful for a minute. "That also means I can't say goodbye."

"That's correct. I'm sorry, Sarah."

She sat quietly for a moment. Then she had a new thought: "Can I take the Bible back?"

"What?"

"My dad took my great-grandma's Bible away from me. It's not like he's reading it, and I don't want to steal, but … I miss it."

Justin's answer was decisive, and he seemed pleased at her request. "Take it," he said.

"And that's not stealing?

"No. It was intended for you."

"But I mean, technically it belongs to my dad."

Justin smiled. "Technically, it belongs to the Author. Take it. You'll need it this week. Read every chance you get, but keep it safe. And bring it with you on Monday."

"Anything else?"

"Just this: try not to talk about the future at all—about what's coming, or about anything else. I know you want to prepare your loved ones, Sarah. But our Lord never wants us to live a lie."

Sarah blushed. "Got it."

"Okay. See you Monday." Justin stood and made his way toward the door, and Sarah followed. There was no sign of the man who had made her sandwich. Justin stood aside while Sarah opened the door and they both walked through. Outside in the bright sunlight, Sarah shielded her eyes for a moment and then turned backward to ask Justin a question that had just occurred to her. But he wasn't there.

Every opportunity

Sarah walked home in a bit of a daze. The feeling reminded her of walking out of a movie theater in the middle of the afternoon, when the whole world feels wrong for a few minutes because you expected the darkness of nighttime, and the shock makes it hard to appreciate the sunshine. She was inexplicably cold the whole way home, as if the warmth of the day were not meant for her. She began making plans for a nap.

Walking up the sidewalk, she was glad to get home; it would be a relief to be indoors. The outside world felt like too much to handle right now. As she reached the door of the house, though, she heard the noise of Jalen bustling in the kitchen, and she felt herself stiffen. She realized that her home was not actually a refuge from the world at all, but just a place where the challenges of this world presented themselves in another form. She would find no real rest here, not anymore. She envisioned the next seven days of living, working, waiting, and carrying a secret burden. As this moment, she felt completely unequal to the task. And so she did something, not realizing at the moment that it was the very first time: she prayed. She closed her eyes and said in her heart, *"Oh, please help me through this week."*

That was it. It was a simple, monumental moment. Up until this point all of her thinking about God had been just that: thinking, not interacting. A subtle shift had occurred in her spirit; she had replaced *Him* with *You*. It was different from that night on the street, when she had cried out for *someone* to help. This time she knew exactly Who she was addressing—it was still a cry for help, but it was a personal one. And the answer was immediate. She turned the doorknob and crossed the threshold of the house with a strength and confidence not her own, and passed the rest of the afternoon in productivity and peace, completely forgetting about her nap.

Jalen was loading the dishwasher when she walked in. She turned and gave her a warm smile. "So," she said, "tell me about lunch!"

"Oh, that. Yeah, I'm not sure he's the one." Sarah knew she had to backtrack out of her earlier story, but wasn't quite sure how.

"Oh, why not?" There was disappointment in Jalen's voice. Sarah suddenly realized that there was a selfish side to Jalen's interest in her love life. She wanted her to find happiness, but she was also nudging her toward independence. Sarah pictured Jalen and her dad talking in bed at night, wondering when they would have the place to themselves and would no longer have the burden of responsibility for her. She could imagine her dad being skeptical that any guy would want a shy, bookish Sleeper, and Jalen meekly pointing out her good qualities, hoping for the best. Did either of them really love her? Amazingly, she realized that she doubted so, but that the thought did not hurt her deeply. She did not expect love from them, and she did not need it.

"I think we're just too different. He's a nice guy, but we don't have a whole lot in common." Sarah smiled inwardly as she realized that Justin was right: she didn't have to lie.

"Well, are you sure you're giving it a chance? What kinds of differences are we talking about?"

"Well, for one thing he's a lot older than I realized, and I'm just not comfortable with that."

"Oh. Well, I'm sorry, honey. You know I just want you to be happy."

"Thank you, Jalen. I do know that. I'm grateful for you ..." Sarah left the rest unsaid, but they both knew it: she was grateful for Jalen because she served as a cushion between Sarah and her father. She made life in this broken home tolerable. Sarah found herself filled with love and pity for this woman, and she decided to take a risk and reach out to her as best she could. "Can I ask you a question?"

"Sure, honey, anything."

"Do you believe in God?"

Sarah flinched at the insensitivity of her own words. She had not intended to be so direct. She had meant to introduce the topic gently, asking if Jalen believed in an afterlife, or what she believed about spirituality, or something like that. People didn't talk about God. The existence of God was an offensive, backward idea to most people, and if it wasn't they were unlikely to admit it. She kicked herself inside for introducing such an important topic in such a clumsy way.

"Oh." Jalen was clearly disappointed. She had felt she was making headway in connecting with her stepdaughter, and now Sarah had again revealed herself to be different, odd. "Well, honey, no, I think most people realize, with all Science has shown us, that there isn't a God." She sounded like the parent of a Kindergartner.

Sarah decided to press on. "Well, okay, but you must believe that there's more than just ... stuff, you know?" Sarah grabbed her own arm as an example. "I mean, there's more than just matter, right? Do you believe in life after death, I don't know, souls, anything spiritual at all?" Again, she struggled to find the words. She had pictured a heartfelt, personal conversation, and now if felt that she had moved from being offensive to being insulting. Jalen probably felt like Sarah was calling her an animal. *Great.*

"Well, honey," Jalen seemed to stiffen a bit, "yes. I have my private beliefs about spiritual things. I consider myself to be a spiritual person, although I certainly don't buy into any old-fashioned ideas about heaven and hell and all that. I've made a few mistakes in my life, but I've been a good person, and I believe my spirit will endure when I ... pass on. But why do you ask? Are you feeling all right?"

"Yes, fine. I've just been thinking a lot about that kind of thing lately. Doesn't everybody?" Sarah tried to sound as young and innocent as possible.

"I guess sometimes. But honey, you're young and beautiful; you should be worried about work, love, family—you know, real life. Don't trouble yourself about things no one can know for sure. You have a sweet spirit and whatever happens after death isn't something you need to be afraid of. But young men your age aren't looking for someone who sits around thinking about death. Worry about that when you're old, baby. It's a long way off."

Sarah's head filled with possible responses. She wanted to tell Jalen that death was not far off at all, that spiritual things were just as real as jobs and family, that she had believed a hundred lies the world had told her, that it was crazy to acknowledge the existence of a soul without asking where it came from, that the fact that an idea was old didn't mean it was any less true, and so much more. Some of these thoughts were even new to Sarah herself, but in this moment they were clear, obvious. At the same time, however, she was aware of a sort of resistance, something that made her stop short of actually saying any of these things. It was more than Justin's warning; it came from within. Somehow, she knew that it would be pointless. Jalen's heart was not open, and words would not open it. So she just smiled a hollow smile and politely changed the subject.

"Yeah. Thanks, Jalen. Hey, I don't have to work today, and I need a new jacket. Want to come with me into the city?

Jalen was clearly pleased with this request. For some reason, Sarah knew that she would be perfectly safe in the city if she wasn't alone. The dark forces that were pursuing her wouldn't reveal themselves to Jalen; it was important to them to keep people like her ignorant of such things. They took the MAX downtown to a trendy outdoors store and Jalen bought Sarah a jacket, hat, gloves, and a couple of long-sleeve shirts, insisting that she pay and never once asking why Sarah needed such things in the middle of spring with summer on the way. They were shopping and she was dressing up her stepdaughter to make her attractive to some young man who would see past her oddness and make her happy and get her out of the house, and that was enough for Jalen.

After shopping they got dinner at an outdoor café, then caught the train home to find Sarah's father already on the couch watching the Wall. He complained about having to warm up his own dinner, but Jalen calmed him down and Sarah left them to watch the news. As she made her way up the stairs, she heard Jalen say, "Oh, my!" She turned and went back into the living room, where the Wall was filled with images of chaos, of Soldiers from the Army and people screaming and crying. There had been a deadly explosion in the shopping district where she and Jalen had spent the afternoon. It was unclear if it were an accident or some sort of attack. 18 people were dead and many more wounded. "We were just there!" Jalen had her hand over her mouth and was near tears.

"Yeah, there was another one in San Francisco," said her dad. "And some terrible traffic accidents back east. I don't know. Sometimes it seems like the whole world is going to hell." He said this with a mixture of anger and superiority in his voice, as if to say that if he were running things, the world would not be such a mess. Sarah recognized this attitude at once—she had felt the same way herself several times recently. Seeing it in her father made her want to distance herself from such thinking as much as possible. She also saw with clarity something she had never put words to before: her father was angry with God. She smiled a bit at the contradiction, again knowing it from firsthand experience. *You can't have it both ways, Dad,* she said to herself with a bit of an internal smile, *you can't hate Him if He's not real.*

Sarah slipped up the stairs and then, instead of going down the hall, she stood for a moment at the door to her parent's room.

She had intended to wait until they were both gone, but knew that once they were both seated in front of the Wall for the evening they were not likely to move for many hours. They were, effectively, absent. She went in, and was even so bold as to turn on the light. She bypassed the bed, knowing that her dad had no interest in keeping what she was looking for near to himself. She was the only one who had that desire. So she turned to the closet, and realized that she was not anticipating a difficult search, partly because of her father's laziness, and partly because she expected guidance. She was right. The book was under a pile of clothes he never wore on the upper shelf above the clothing rack. She took it down, turned off the lights, went quickly to her room, and shut the door.

She flopped down on her bed and read for an hour straight, delighting in the words as never before. Something about having been denied the opportunity for a few days filled her heart with deep gratitude for this book. She was now focused much more on the actual printed words than on the notes scribbled in the margins by her great-grandmother. Much of what she read made no sense to her, but this did not discourage her. She skipped over confusing parts with a confidence that one day she would understand them, and found that before long she always came to something that seemed to be just for her, something that filled her with wonder that such a book could exist, and that so many people could be missing out on it.

When she heard Jalen stirring in the kitchen below, Sarah reluctantly put the book in the bottom of an old school backpack, then stuffed her new clothing purchases on top of it and put the bag in the back corner of her closet. She got ready for bed and lay awake for a long time, deep in thought. She felt as if her world were changing from black-and-white to color. There was so much more to life, good and bad, than she had realized. Her parents' heartbreaking rejection of God, and the incredibly real and devastating consequences they would soon experience, felt at certain moments like a weight that would crush her. The fact that this story was multiplied a million times over just in her own city was more than she could fathom. But at the same time, there was something else happening inside, something positive. There were new horizons opening within her soul as she read the book, talked with Justin, and began to see the world more for what it really was. There was an unexplained and undefined hope of what was in store for her that sometimes filled her heart to the point of bursting. These things could only be described as *life*; she felt that another word was needed to describe what she had known before, what Jalen and her father and all the people around her settled for every day. Whatever that was, it was less than life. *This* was life. She felt in this moment that she could not pretend otherwise, or turn her back on it, ever again, no matter how painful things might get in the days to come.

Sarah had already made up her mind that she would make no attempt to have a spiritual conversation with her father. First of all, she and her father didn't have conversations about anything. There was no foundation upon which to stand. Second, she was certain that the door was closed. Justin was right. That time had passed. He was not open, and he was not her responsibility. But as she drifted off to sleep, Sarah told herself that there was someone she was not willing to give up on so easily. Torin had treated her so well, and was in many ways a good person. Surely there must be hope for her. Tomorrow, at work, she would do her best to offer life to her friend.

16 The ticking clock

But the next day, Tuesday, was Torin's day off. Sarah had forgotten this, and when she got to work and realized it, she was thrown off for her entire shift. She had awakened with a sense of urgency (*27 days until the end of the world*), and the train to work had seemed especially slow. And now there was nothing to do but take orders and pour coffee. For some reason, she had an internal sense that it would be wrong to slack off at work, despite the fact that very soon it wouldn't matter at all. So she tried her best to stay on top of things and serve her customers well, but she was restless and distracted all day long, thinking about the fact that she was leaving town forever in 6 days and now she wouldn't get to talk to Torin today. She had stayed awake a long time the night before thinking about what she would say, and hadn't come up with anything she felt very good about, but she was still determined to try. She could try to call Torin, but didn't have any real excuse to do so. Torin was a work friend; they were too different to spend time together socially. She would have to wait until tomorrow. She finished her shift, rode the MAX home, and sat around the house for the afternoon and evening, reading, watching the Wall, and trying to distract herself. That night she found herself unable to concentrate while reading the Bible, and eventually gave up without ever reaching the point where it felt like it had done her any good. She was careful to tuck it back into her backpack before she went to sleep.

The next morning she was surprisingly sleepy when her alarm went off, and lay there for a few moments not really thinking about anything. Then came the familiar involuntary countdown: *26 days*. Then her thoughts went to Torin, and the awkward conversation she had no idea how to initiate. Then to the fact that she was leaving with Justin in just 5 days. She had been putting off packing her things because she would be taking so little with her, but now she suddenly felt unprepared. What if she forgot something important? What if she couldn't remain calm and casual talking with her friend? How many people were going to die? Was all of this really happening? The questions and anxieties grew until within a few minutes she felt genuinely unable to get out of bed, paralyzed by panic. She rolled over so her back was to the bedroom door, which seemed to represent the outside world she didn't want to deal with, and pulled the covers over her head. *What am I going to do?* she asked, partly to herself, partly as a desperate prayer.

She had expected no answer, but after a moment a new thought came to her: *you need to read the book*. She felt under the pillow, and it wasn't there. She lifted the covers and looked over at the closet. It seemed a long way off. Maybe she didn't need to read. She would be fine. Once she was up, she would rather just stay up and get ready. She didn't want to be late for work. It would be one thing if the book were right there, under the pillow, but to get up, dig it out of the backpack, get back in bed and read felt like so many unnecessary steps. But no, she needed it. *Read every chance you get*, Justin had said.

She forced herself up, and once it was in her hands she didn't even return to bed. She sat on the floor against the wall next to the closet door and opened the gold-lined pages delicately, reverently, to roughly the middle of the old volume. On this particular page her great-grandmother's notes filled nearly every open space. Her eyes were drawn to Psalm 46, and she read slowly, "God is our refuge and strength, an ever-present help in trouble. Therefore we will not fear, though the earth give way ..." Her eyes filled with tears. She read on, not understanding all of it, but when she read "Be still, and know that I am God," it was as if He were sitting on the floor next to her. She cried openly for a moment, but a smile was on her face. Her great-grandmother's handwriting in the margin next to this verse said "All will be well."

"Okay, Great-Grandma Sarah," she said aloud, and slowly put the book away. She rose with confidence and went to take a shower. The peace that followed stayed with her through an awkward breakfast with Jalen, throughout which it was somehow clear to her that she didn't need to worry about her step-mom on this day. She knew where her focus needed to be, and she could entrust everything else to Someone who was perfectly capable of handling it. She was polite but preoccupied as Jalen made shallow chit-chat over cereal, and didn't trouble herself with deeper questions about the fate of this poor, weak woman. The peace remained through the bleak train ride into the gray city, the bus ride, and the short rainy walk to work, and then seemed to rise within her to push back against the fluttering of her nerves when Torin walked through the door. She felt strong. She knew that she was, in some way, supported. This conversation would go just as it needed to. Even when the morning rush kept them from interacting for the first couple hours of her shift, she didn't worry. The time would come.

And then it did. Things slowed down, and finally the last two breakfast customers paid their checks and left. Torin took the first opportunity when things slowed down to approach Sarah, and said in her usual friendly way, "So how ya been? Haven't seen you in a few days. Everything smoothed over with Mr. Mysterious?"

Sarah gulped and dove in, nervous but excited. "Actually, I've been great. He, um, didn't turn out to be what I thought he was, but things have been really good in, uh, in other ways."

"Oh, yeah, someone else? It's not like you to move so fast, Sarah! I knew you had it in you, though. It's time those guys realized what they've been missing." Torin had a bit of a one-track mind.

"No, not a guy. Just, well, I've been learning a lot, and, realizing a lot, and, I don't know, it's just been good." As confident as she had been, Sarah was struggling to take the conversation where it needed to go. She was depending on her friend asking the right questions, which felt risky, but she didn't know what else to do. She knew that for Torin, personal growth was not nearly as interesting as the dating scene. Thankfully, though, she took the bait.

"Learning about what?"

This was her chance. It wasn't perfect, because Torin was now wiping tables as Sarah put silverware away, and soon they would probably be interrupted by customers. But she knew it was the best opportunity she would get. So she took it.

"Well, about me, and about, you know, spiritual things."

"Okay, well, that's good, you know. Good for you. That's important. They say you have to know who you are before you find your match."

Torin had responded without looking up from the table she was wiping. Clearly, she still thought this was a conversation about guys, or at least would prefer that it was. But Sarah could not let the moment pass. It was too important. Driven by the strength she had drawn from her morning reading, and also by a brief image that flashed through her imagination of the street outside the cafe filled with screaming people, she pressed on:

"Do you ever think about that kind of stuff? I mean, you know, the big questions? The meaning of life, life after death, that kind of thing?" She prepared herself for a rejection similar to what she had received from Jalen. But Torin surprised her. She stopped wiping a table, stood, and looked across the room.

"Actually, yeah. I read a book once about that kind of thing that helped me a lot. It was great."

Sarah was stunned. She would not have guessed in a million years that Torin took the time to read anything but fashion articles on her phone. But she was excited about where this was headed. "Really? What did it say?"

"Oh, it was so good." Torin was all the way across the room now, working on another table. She seemed to be completely comfortable having this conversation in this environment, with the cooks in the kitchen very likely listening in and early lunch customers bound to come through the door at any moment. "It was all about how everything is spiritual, if you are open to it. It talked a lot about how you breathe in and out, and that's spiritual, you know. Like, our work is spiritual—okay, so I don't totally get that one, maybe not here so much—" she laughed, " but you know, play is spiritual, friendship is spiritual, sex is spiritual, eating is spiritual, everything. Life is spiritual, so, you know, just live! And if you focus on living, truly living, before death, then life after death, if there is such a thing, will just be more of the same."

As Torin spoke, Sarah saw clearly that her friend had discovered a way of seeing the world that allowed her to continue living exactly as she had been, and at the same time to congratulate herself on being a deep thinker and a spiritual person. She never needed to give another moment's thought to life's biggest questions; in fact, she could live exactly the same as someone who never asked such questions. It was a system of beliefs that contained some truth, and yet required no change. It cost Torin nothing; it left her right where she was and told her she was exactly where she needed to be. It was hard for Sarah not to compare this to her own developing beliefs, which very soon would cost her everything she had known. Was Torin getting the better deal? No, not if Justin was right. She couldn't give up. She felt that her position had weakened, but she had not yet given her friend every opportunity to hear the truth she needed.

In the few seconds it took for these thoughts to make their way through her mind, the room was silent. Torin, who, as far as she knew, was still having a lighthearted conversation, looked up from a table to find Sarah standing still, staring at her.

"What?"

Sarah was silent, just looking at her, reading the situation and waiting for guidance.

"Sarah, what? What is it?"

Sarah decided against trying to argue with what Torin had just shared. She didn't feel smart enough, and didn't want to go on the attack. Instead, in what felt like a great leap of courage, she decided to simply tell as much truth as she could without violating the rules Justin had laid down.

"I've been reading the Bible."

"What?" Torin immediately took a few steps closer and lowered her voice. She glanced at the kitchen and asked again, "what?"

"I found my great-grandmother's Bible, and I've been reading it … and I really like it."

Torin was clearly concerned now, and possibly a little offended. "Sarah, that's not funny. Tell me you're joking. You know that's illegal, right? It's a book about violence and hatred and oppression, not real spirituality."

"But that's not true. First of all, it's not illegal to own one and read it in the privacy of your own home, and … it's not like that at all. Well, not totally, I mean—it's not what you think. You should read it. You might really like it."

Now Torin stepped back. She took another glance at the kitchen and spoke quietly but firmly. "Okay, well that was illegal."

"What?"

"Sarah, you just tried to convince me to read the *Bible,*" she spoke this last word as a harsh whisper. "You can't do that, honey. I don't know what to make of this. I mean, I always thought of you as a loving person. Please tell me you won't read that book anymore. Let me send you the one I read. It might really help you. Seriously, Sarah, don't go all wacko on me." She attempted a smile to lighten the mood, but it was unconvincing.

Sarah discovered, to her own surprise, that her loyalty to her newfound convictions was greater than her loyalty to Torin. This was becoming an argument, and while she cared about Torin, she also didn't want to lose. It felt like something too important was at stake. She responded with a firmness of her own: "Okay, how is that any different? You want me to read your book, just like I want you to read mine. So what's wrong with that?"

Now there was fire in Torin's eyes. "You honestly think that's the same thing? How dare you? I'm trying to help you, not acting like ... some religious nut!" Her voice was raised and she was clearly angry. It crossed Sarah's mind that perhaps she was getting a glimpse of one reason for her friend's recurring relationship troubles. In the short term, a little display of temper probably helped her get her way with the men she dated, but then what? She kept her smile to herself, realizing this was hardly the time to bring that up. But what was it time for? She didn't know where to go from here. She hated to give up. There were only 5 days left. But she was out of ideas.

"Okay. Sorry. I'll drop it. I'm sorry. I see what you're saying," (but she didn't). "I didn't mean to argue with you." She offered a sad, apologetic smile.

"Okay." Torin was used to arguments ending this way, and was always quick to seek harmony after they did. "So, you'll let me send you that book?" She put her hand on Sarah's arm in a caring, motherly way, as if it were clear to both of them now that she was the reasonable, mature one.

Sarah paused. "No," she said. "Sorry, but I probably wouldn't read it."

"Oh." Torin withdrew her hand. She studied Sarah for a moment, then turned her back and found something to busy herself with. Sarah didn't know what to do. Then another thought occurred to her. It was probably pointless, but she couldn't keep from speaking it. She cared about Torin. And maybe even more than that, she wanted to leave with no regrets.

"It's just that ..." Torin turned around as she spoke, but her look was sullen. Sarah tried anyway. "I mean, if everything is spiritual, where did that come from, you know? What makes it spiritual? What's the source?" She hoped she was being clear.

Torin gave an exasperated shrug. "No one knows, Sarah. You just go with it." She said this in a frustrated tone, as if she were explaining something that everyone knew to someone who was not very intelligent. She turned her back again and walked away.

The awkward silence between them lasted for a few minutes, and then customers started to come through the door again. They worked together without making eye contact for the rest of the shift. Apparently, the kitchen staff hadn't heard anything, which was good. As the day progressed, Sarah felt, at various times, waves of sadness, anger, and frustration with herself. Had she used the wrong words? Had she messed it up? Why was Torin so stubborn?

When work was over, though, it was the sadness that stayed with her on the long walk through the city back to the MAX station. She could have taken the bus, but the rain had stopped, and she felt that if she stopped moving for too long she would be unable to stop the tears from coming. The truth was, she knew she hadn't messed up. The conversation had gone poorly, but it wasn't a failure. It had revealed exactly what she needed to know. And she wasn't angry with Torin. She loved her, possibly more than she had before, because her heart was growing, and with it her capacity to love. No, she was just sad. She saw what was, and what had to be, and it was heartbreaking. She had no questions at the moment, felt no desire to pour out anger in a childish outburst. The walk was a small comfort, and somehow she was able to keep her heart numb for the length of the ride home, and even down the street to her house and up the stairs to the privacy of her room. No one was home. When she collapsed on the floor and began to sob, she caught a glimpse of the digital time display in the corner of her window, which seemed to her now like a sort of countdown. The seconds ticked by until she turned her head away, hiding for a moment from the unavoidable fact that in less than five days, she was leaving everything she knew for something uncertain, and no one she cared about was going with her.

Last details

When her tears had dried, Sarah lay on her bed, aware that she still had an hour or so before anyone else got home. She felt like she should do something productive, but didn't know what. There was very little to do now but wait out the next few days, which was a prospect that seemed at the same time incredibly boring and terrifying. It felt like being tied to a bomb with a really long fuse. An exhausting battle was taking place in her heart between anxiety and trust, loneliness and peace, anger and hope. She was in danger of succumbing to the same paralysis that had had a temporary victory over her that morning, and when she realized this she quickly got up, went to the closet, and found her backpack. When the Bible fell at her feet, she remembered again that she was supposed to be reading all the time, but she didn't feel like sitting still right now. She would pack. Packing was something productive, and she had been meaning to do it for a couple of days now, so it would feel good to get it done. She took out the new clothes she and Jalen had bought, cut off the tags and re-folded them, then got other clothes out of the dresser and added them to the pile. She put some toiletries in little bags, then found a logical place for everything in the pack, with a space for her Bible at the top.

Was that it? Sarah looked around the room for anything she would absolutely need. Was there something she would miss, or just couldn't stand to leave behind? She was surprised to realize that the answer was no. She picked up a school yearbook and flipped through a few pages, smiling at the pictures but not feeling any deep sense of loss at leaving the book, or the experiences it represented, behind. There were family pictures in cute little frames on her dresser; she told herself they were impractical, mentally avoiding the fact that they could be taken out of the frames if she had really wanted to bring them along. The truth was, she didn't. There were her books, and she realized that even a few months ago there were some she would have had trouble parting with. Not anymore. She scanned the titles, then glanced at the Bible sitting on top of the backpack. It was all she needed. How had that happened?

Sarah sat down next to the pack on the floor, more thoughtful than sad, and spoke aloud to the empty room: "I'm the perfect one to do this." She smiled at the thought of how hard it would be for Jalen or her father to leave town on short notice. They would need a moving truck and a week to pack. She, on the other hand, was barely connected to this place at all. It was like Justin had said: her roots were loosened. They had become even looser after the conversations with Jalen and Torin. She could leave now. It crossed her mind that if she did take pictures or books from her room, it would be that much more obvious that she had run away. The more normal her room looked, the further away she could get before they understood what had happened.

This thought brought with it a great wave of doubt. Was she actually going to do this? It seemed in this moment to be an incredibly ungrateful, spiteful thing to do. She pictured Jalen's face when they discovered she had left without saying goodbye. They would not understand. It would be deeply hurtful. But before Sarah was overwhelmed by guilt, a new thought came, a bit of truth that helped her push back against the doubt. The truth was this: the relationship with her family was already hurtful. Things were not good in her household, just like they were not good in the world. The status quo was not worth preserving, despite the fact that it was, at times, comfortable. If there was something better on the other side of the pain her actions would bring, it was worth seeking. Leaving would not be the cause of the pain, it would simply bring it into the light. And if Justin was telling the truth … she decided not to think any more about that for now; she simply didn't have the energy.

Sarah was packed for her trip, prepared to leave her home forever, and exactly 15 minutes had passed. She picked up her Bible and lay back down in bed. She read until her parents came home, ate a quick dinner, then went back to her room and read some more until bedtime.

Out the door

25 days. On Thursday, Sarah arrived at work to discover that Torin had called in sick. She worked a double shift and came home exhausted, both from the work and from doing her best to avoid Dak all afternoon. After dinner, she attempted to read her Bible, but finally put it away after falling asleep twice. She pictured herself sleeping through her alarm and Jalen discovering the book when she came in to wake her, so she was careful to put it away in the backpack before she got under the covers.

24 days. On Friday, Torin was at work, and was pleasant but distant. The Cup and Saucer was busy and Sarah didn't feel up to the challenge of pursuing a conversation. She went home after her morning shift and read non-stop until bed. Her dad and Jalen were home briefly at the end of the work day, and then went out somewhere for dinner. They yelled their greetings up the stairs on their way out the door, and Sarah mumbled a reply without opening her door or looking up from her reading. The longer she read, the more it felt like the words on the page were more real than the world around her, and things like becoming hungry or having to get up to go to the bathroom were an annoyance, an unwelcome intrusion into the alternate world she inhabited as she read. Eventually, she became tired, and the clock told her she should have been asleep an hour ago. Again, she put the book in the backpack, and the backpack in the closet, before she crawled into bed and fell quickly to sleep.

23 days. Sarah was grateful she had to work on Saturday. With her father home all day, the last thing she wanted to do was sit around the house. And Torin had the day off, so there would be no awkwardness at the diner. At lunch break, her boss offered her another double shift, saying that she didn't have to if she didn't want to, but she took it in a heartbeat. Dak was off that day. It was a chance to stay out of the house, and to make a little extra money, which she would need for her trip, which was now only two days away. *Two days!* Her stomach knotted at the thought. It felt like time was moving faster now, and she laughed to herself when she remembered how eager she had been to leave the day she met Justin at the deli. What if he had asked her to leave right away, without looking back? Would she have found a reason to back out? She felt she was stronger now, more able to follow through on their plan, even though it had only been a matter of days. What had been an impulse, an emotion, was now a decision of the will. Somehow she knew that, despite whatever fear she felt, she would be ready when the time came.

22 days. The next morning, however, was different. From the moment she opened her eyes, it seemed that fear had the upper hand. She was leaving tomorrow. *Tomorrow! Really?* Was the world really coming to an end? Was she really leaving town for an unknown destination with an angel? It was too crazy to think about. She forced herself out of bed and downstairs as quickly as possible. On this day, being distracted, even at the cost of spending time with her father, was better than being alone with her thoughts.

Her father was watching the Sunday morning news on the Wall.

"Morning, stranger," he said without looking in her direction. "What brings you out of your room?"

She decided to ignore the insult. Politeness was the best route to take. The goal for today was to avoid conflict, make as few waves as possible, and get to bed without her parents suspecting that anything was out of the ordinary.

"Morning, dad. I'm off today. Can I watch with you?"

He seemed pleased, and even smiled a bit. For him, watching the Wall was what normal people did, and when his daughter showed interest in it, he felt better, both about her future and his own use of time. "Sure, but no girl stuff, okay? I'm watching the news."

"That's fine." The truth was, she was interested in the news. She was about to enter the wide world outside the city, with a total stranger, who claimed that world was coming to an end. She had never traveled outside of the Portland area except once to Seattle for a track meet, and the hassle of all the paperwork that had been necessary to cross into Washington had made her coach swear they would never do it again. Her dad had told her about his days as a boy, when people traveled freely across state lines, before the Army had introduced strict travel regulations. Like many people, he had been against the restrictions when they were introduced, although it had to be admitted that terrorist attacks had been greatly reduced. Now, forty years later, people had adjusted to the new reality, and complaints were few.

The first news story to come on after Sarah sat down had to do with an increased number of bombings like the one in the shopping center a few days ago. There had been several across the country in recent weeks, to the point that the Army suspected some sort of coordination between them. While burnouts were the usual suspects, they had never before been known to work together across state lines, and the motive for doing so was unclear. Authorities were still investigating.

The next story was about a deadly airplane crash in Houston, followed by a report on the passage of a law mandating abortions for state-certified prostitutes in New York. Then another airplane crash, this time in Los Angeles, and a deadly apartment fire in Las Vegas. The possible outbreak of a serious illness in the Chicago area. After a while, it seemed like an endless stream of death and pain was pouring out of the Wall. Sarah glanced at her father, who was mindlessly taking it all in and snacking on some mixed nuts out of a bowl.

"How can you stand this?" she asked as she gestured toward the screen. She had intended to keep the peace, and flinched internally as soon as the words had left her mouth.

Thankfully, he didn't take offense. "What? It's the news, Sarah. It's how I know what's going on in the world."

"But it's so sad. So many bad things."

He shrugged. "It's the real world. You can't blame them for reporting what's really happening, can you?" He was still looking at the screen, and Sarah had the fleeting thought that he was as engrossed in what he was watching as she had been in her book a couple of nights ago. Was he even aware, at that moment, that he was talking to her and not Jalen? He put a few more nuts in his mouth, which didn't keep him from continuing to talk: "That is weird about all the plane crashes, though, huh? Somebody's not doing their job."

Sarah stared at him for a moment, wondering if he would even notice if she didn't respond. Finally she shook her head and said, "I'm getting some breakfast. I'll be back in a while."

Her father grunted in response and shifted his legs so she could pass without taking his eyes off the Wall. She made her way to the kitchen, poured a bowl of cereal, and sat at the table. It was a relief to be away from the light and noise of the huge screen. Still, she had nothing else to do this day, and had no desire to be alone with her thoughts. She briefly considered going out, heading into the city for a sort of good-bye visit to all her favorite places. But it didn't feel right. She knew she had been protected to and from work this week, but a pleasure trip felt like pressing her luck, and she suspected she wouldn't be able to enjoy a trip like that anyway.

The city had changed for her. She thought about Westside Park, Java Stop, concerts, dance clubs. She smiled at the thought of The Grind, remembering that Justin had told her she had no desire to go there anymore before she had even realized it herself. Those days seemed a world away now, and there was no going back. She would enter the city just one more time.

But there was still the problem of what to do with the rest of the day. She could only sit at the kitchen table for so long. In school, she had always been nervous the day before a big track meet, and the best solution was usually to stay busy. If it was a school day, this was easy. If it was a weekend, then she would eat, rest, watch the Wall, and try not to think about it. She decided this was the best way to approach today. It crossed her mind that perhaps she should stay in her room all day and read, but she didn't feel up to it. She needed not to think today. She also felt that, somehow, she owed it to her parents to be present today. So like it or not, it was the Wall with her dad, for as long as she could stand it.

Back in the living room, her dad was sending a message on his phone with one eye on an action movie.

"Who you messaging?"

"Your brother."

"Which one?"

"Alyx. You talk with him lately?"

"No, Dad, we don't talk." Sarah and her brothers hadn't been close even when they lived in the house. Julian had left home when she was in middle school, and since Alyx had moved out two years ago, she rarely saw either one of them. She knew it was hurtful to her dad that they didn't come around more, and she knew the reason they didn't: he made no more effort to be close to them, to understand them, than he did with her. He expected much but gave little. Aside from a sense of obligation around the holidays, they felt little connection to home.

"We talked about getting together for a barbecue this afternoon, but Julian had to work," he said. "Maybe next weekend."

Sarah felt a twinge of guilt, both about her plans and about the fact that she hadn't even considered saying goodbye to her brothers, much less attempting a spiritual conversation with either of them. They were strangers, who happened to share her name. "Maybe next weekend," she said.

The rest of the day passed slowly. After her dad's action movie, they had lunch, and Jalen came home from shopping. Then it was more of the Wall until dinner, after which she excused herself to go up to her room. Once there, she dug out the Bible, and read for a bit, but soon thoughts of the next day filled her mind and reading became pointless. She double-checked her pack, put it back in the closet, and got ready for bed. She lay in the darkness for a long time, thinking of her father, Jalen, and her brothers, of Torin and the life she had pictured for herself in her imaginary apartment in the city. She mentally revisited all her conversations and interactions with Justin and Thaddeus, everything that had brought her to this point. It was really happening. Tomorrow she was leaving. *Help me,* she prayed. *This is all so crazy. Please, I hope this is the right thing. Please help me to do what's right.* It was a long time before she fell asleep.

21 days. When her alarm went off, Sarah's eyes popped open and she immediately sat up, forcing herself into the bathroom before she could begin thinking, much like she had done on track meet days back in school. She showered, dressed, and took the backpack from her closet, checking it one last time to make sure everything was in place. She peeked out of her room, and when no one was there she went quickly down the stairs to the front door, hiding her pack behind the coat rack. She went to the kitchen, made some toast, and ate it hurriedly. She desperately wanted to get out of the house before Jalen woke. She ate her last few bites standing up, and just as she picked up her pack and opened the front door, she thought she heard someone stirring upstairs. Without looking back, she stepped out into the light of the morning and shut the door behind her. Just as she was about to allow herself a sentimental thought about never seeing this house again, she saw a tall figure standing at the end of the walkway. It was Thaddeus.

It was all she could do to keep from shouting his name. The feeling of relief that passed over her was like a warm shower after a cold day. She was not alone. And she was doing the right thing. Her steps were light as she made her way to where he stood.

"Good morning, Sarah. Big day today." He smiled warmly.

"Yeah," she said, rejoicing in the unfamiliar feeling of being understood. It was as comforting as being protected.

"I'll be with you until you meet with Justin," he said. "It will be important for you to remember that, whatever happens."

"Sure," she said, wishing he hadn't felt the need to remind her of reality so quickly. "Why, what's going to happen?"

"I'm not sure. But don't worry," he said, gesturing down the sidewalk toward the MAX station. "Come on, we should get going."

They walked in silence to the station. The sun was rising on a clear sky, and the spring air was still cold enough to make her grateful when the train came and they stepped on board. Sarah was too excited to sit down, so she stood holding an upright metal pole and began mentally preparing herself for one last shift at the Cup and Saucer. Had she done the right thing in not giving any notice that she was leaving? What would Torin think? How long would it be before people realized she was gone?

She was engrossed in these thoughts when the train stopped at the next station. Several people got on, typical commuters in work clothes clutching coffee mugs. Then three men in black, with tattoos and bright blue hair, stepped through the door closest to Sarah and Thaddeus. Sarah froze and clutched her guardian's arm, grateful to find that she could feel it, although she wondered what this looked like to the people around them. One of the men stepped past them and stood behind her, one crossed the aisle and sat down in the seat facing her, and one walked right up and stood face to face with her, glancing briefly at Thaddeus. He was taller than the men they had faced the week before, and all three of them were larger, more muscular, than typical burnouts. Their eyes seemed clearer, sharper than she expected—they didn't seem to be under the influence of any drugs at all. They reminded Sarah of Soldiers. The tall one looked Sarah up and down, glanced at her pack, then looked her directly in the eye and spoke:

"Good morning, Sarah. Big day today."

Last shift

Sarah was ice-cold with fear.

"What do you want?" she tried to look the man in the eyes and to sound strong, even angry, but her voice trembled. Her mind was a blur. Why didn't Thaddeus do anything? What kind of a protector was he, allowing the men to get so close to her?

The man leaned in and spoke in a low whisper, so that none of the other passengers could hear: "We want to kill you, Sarah Martinez."

Sarah was surprised to find that this threat did not increase her level of panic. On the contrary, it made her realize something, and she grew calm. She looked around. Everyone else on the train had backed away and refused to make eye contact with her. The appearance of these men on a morning commuter train in the suburbs was a shock to them. Some of their faces were white with fear, others red with shame, knowing that they should come to the aid of this defenseless young girl (they could not see Thaddeus, of course), but that they would not. She looked from them to Thaddeus, who stood like a rock on her right side, and whose left arm she was still clinging to. He regarded the men with a stern look, but gave no indication of being alarmed. She looked back at the man standing before her.

"But you can't," she said. Then she raised her voice and spoke with genuine confidence: "You can't kill me, can you?"

The man looked her in the eye for a moment, then turned his attention to Thaddeus. He looked her protector up and down, sizing him up but carefully avoiding eye contact. Then he turned back to Sarah and said with a menacing smile, "Not yet." He moved across the aisle and sat next to his companion. The other man, the one standing behind them, also sat down. Sarah turned and looked pleadingly at Thaddeus, not caring, at this point, how crazy she might look to the other passengers. He put his hands on her shoulders and spoke firmly:

"Sarah, nothing has changed. This is not a surprise. You stick to the plan, okay? Go to work. Follow Justin's instructions. I am with you. Do everything you would normally do, and don't act like anything is out of the ordinary. 'All will be well,' remember?" He smiled, and she did too, remembering her great-grandma's note, and not even questioning how Thaddeus knew about it. She turned her gaze forward, down the tracks, and allowed the MAX to carry her one last time toward the city and the day that awaited her. For the moment, she was not afraid.

When she stepped off the train, she felt the burnouts following her, but she looked straight ahead and marched all the way to work without looking back. It was chilly, but she chose not to take the bus. If these men were going to follow her around all day long, they could start by walking ten blocks in the cold morning air. When she entered the cafe, she turned and could see that they had taken up a position at a bus stop on the other side of the street. They stood without talking, just glaring in her direction. Then, after receiving directions from the tall one, one of the others left and made his way up the block and around the corner. Sarah knew he would be in the alley behind the building, guarding the back entrance. This was fine, she told herself. She didn't care. Thaddeus was with her and she had work to do. Thaddeus took a seat at a small table in the corner, one that was seldom used because it barely sat two people. She smiled at him and set her backpack in the chair opposite him, then turned to make her way toward the kitchen. Torin was just coming out.

"Hey, Babe," she said cheerfully, "Haven't seen you in a while!" She made her way across the room and flipped on the neon "Open" sign that hung in the front window.

"Yeah. Our schedules haven't really worked out. I've missed you!" It was true. She had missed her friend, and had been hoping for the chance to make things right before she left. But something told her that if she brought up the debate from the other day, it would be impossible to repair the friendship. So she decided (as she suspected Torin had) to let it go.

"I've missed you too." Torin gave her a warm smile. "So how have you been? Anything new going on? What's with the backpack?"

Sarah was grateful for this last question, which allowed her to sidestep the other two. "Oh, just some things I'll need later. Didn't want to forget them in the back room."

"Okay. No one sits there anyway."

Torin was about to say something else when the bell over the front door tinkled. The first customer of the day. Time to act professional. The girls turned to see the tall burnout standing in the doorway. He smiled at the knowledge that his presence made the room, as it did all rooms, instantly uncomfortable. Torin stepped protectively in front of Sarah.

"Can I help you?" She said in a voice that was less than friendly.

The man shrugged innocently. "Just here for some breakfast."

Sarah was angry, but refused to be intimidated. To Torin's surprise, she looked the man directly in the eyes and said "Sit anywhere."

He scanned the room and gestured toward the table with the backpack, knowing that he and Sarah could see Thaddeus sitting silently in the corner, but Torin could not.

"Anywhere, huh? Can I sit at that table?"

"Go ahead," Sarah said evenly.

He shrugged again. "No, I think I'm good with the counter."

He crossed the room and seated himself on a barstool. Sarah turned to make her way behind the counter, but Torin grabbed her elbow. She gave her a look that said *What are you doing?* and pointed to a sign on the back wall that read "We reserve the right to refuse service to anyone." Sarah suspected that her fiery friend had always wanted to refuse service to someone, but knew that making a big scene would only satisfy this man all the more. She was feeling strong; all would be well. She shook her head and said quietly, "It's fine."

Behind the counter, Sarah served her stalker coffee and stood silently while he looked at a menu. When Torin stepped back into the kitchen, he lowered the menu and asked in a low voice,

"What's your game? What are you doing here?"

"I don't know what you mean. Just doing my job." Sarah was proud of herself for staying so composed, and tried not to notice the size of his tattoo-covered arms as they rested on the counter.

"You know exactly what I mean. We both know what today is. What's the point in stalling?"

"Look, I have other things to do," Sarah said, grateful that at that moment two more customers had come through the door. "You're the one who's stalling. Now what can I get you?"

The man shook his head and chuckled. "I'll just have a bowl of oatmeal. But I should warn you, I'm a slow eater. And keep the coffee coming."

Sarah didn't answer. She passed his order on to the cook and made her way to where the other customers had taken their seats. For the next hour, the man sat at the counter and watched her work, occasionally glancing at the corner where Thaddeus sat. Finally, he stood up and stretched, and Torin hurried over to run his cash card, then stood behind the counter with her arms folded and watched him leave while Sarah took an order from another customer. When he was gone and they found themselves side-by-side wiping down a table, she whispered to Sarah:

"What was that about?"

"Oh, that guy? Weird, huh? I've never seen one of them come into a place like this before. Hey, did you see that old guy from last week walk by the window a few minutes ago? I think he thinks you're cute." Sarah was trying her hardest to change the subject, but Torin wasn't ready to let it go.

"He acted like he knew you. And look, now he's just standing over at the bus stop with another one of them. They give me the creeps. If he's not gone in a few minutes I'm calling the Army."

"Oh, who knows what those guys are thinking? I'm sure they'll get bored in a few minutes and take off." The café was now busy enough that she could leave at this point without it seeming like she was avoiding the conversation. She attended to another set of customers, then more after that, and was genuinely wrapped up in her work until after the lunch rush subsided. All the while Thaddeus sat at his table, needing nothing and completely content to simply keep watch. Suddenly, Sarah realized that she had only a half an hour left on her shift. She glanced across the street and saw that the men were still there. She set about cleaning up tables. Fifteen minutes. Ten. Now she realized it was not walking out and facing the men in black she was afraid of, it was saying goodbye to her friend. This moment had snuck up on her, and she was unprepared. Torin interrupted her thoughts.

"All right, they're still there. I'm calling."

"Don't do that." Sarah realized that this was an inexplicable request. Why would she protect these men? Even she didn't know. But she knew that today had to be as uneventful as possible, right up until she stepped on the train. And she knew what Torin didn't know, which was that the best possible protection she could have was already sitting in the corner of the diner.

"What? Why not? Is everything okay?"

Sarah checked her watch. Less than five minutes now. She looked around the diner, which was nearly quiet. Without explanation, she took Torin by the arm and walked into the back hallway.

"Sarah, what are you doing? What is going on?"

"Listen to me, Torin, I want you to know something." She took a deep breath. "I want you to know that I am going to be fine."

"But, those guys—"

"Don't worry about those guys. Listen, this is important. I'm really sorry about the other day. I hated arguing with you. I wish ... I wish I could make you understand."

"Oh. Well, it's okay. I was kind of mean. I'm sorry too. Sarah, is something going on?"

Sarah hesitated. She looked into her friend's eyes for a moment, then plunged ahead: "I won't be at work tomorrow. I want to ask you a favor: can you pretend like you don't know anything?"

"Well, until you said that, I didn't know anything."

"I know. But I'm telling you because I want you to know I'm okay. Don't worry about me. Just ... don't say anything, and don't worry. I'm going to be okay. Can you please trust me?"

"Okay," Torin said slowly, trying to be supportive. "But you are scaring me a little bit. Is there anything I can do?"

"Just, think about what I said. The other day—"

Torin cut her off, shaking her head. "Sarah, don't ..."

"Just think about it. Please." Sarah gave Torin a hug, which caught her off guard, but when Sarah squeezed even harder she responded and squeezed back. Sarah released her and looked her in the eye, then said, "I have to go."

Sarah turned to the automatic time clock and punched in her code, signaling the end of her shift. She knew that once the code was entered, her pay for the past two weeks would be automatically calculated by the computer and immediately deposited into her bank account. She stepped past Torin, who was still watching her with bewilderment, and crossed the room to her backpack. She put in on her shoulders, being careful to pretend that Thaddeus was not there as he rose from where he had sat motionless for the past 6 hours and followed her to the door. In the doorway, she turned and looked around the room, then back at Torin. "Bye," she said, and stepped quickly outside into the busyness of the city before the oncoming flood of sadness could overtake her.

When Sarah and Thaddeus turned down the sidewalk to begin

the walk toward the bank, the two burnouts at the bus stop started walking too, keeping pace with them without crossing to their side of the street. When they came to an intersection and had to wait at the crosswalk, the one who had been waiting in the alley came up and stood behind them, offering a mocking smile but saying nothing. She glanced at Thaddeus, who gave her a look that said *All will be well. Stick to the plan.* At the next intersection, two more appeared and fell in behind them as well. They had the same strong, soldierly look as the other three.

"How are they doing this?" Sarah whispered to Thaddeus.

"They're plugged," he said calmly.

It was true. Sarah glanced across the street and saw the tall one, the leader of the group, touching a finger to his ear and speaking into the air. A moment later, as they continued to make their way toward the bank, another burnout, also touching his ear, stood on the sidewalk half a block ahead of them. His eyes scanned until he had spotted his leader, and Sarah and Thaddeus, then he turned and started walking ahead of them in the direction they were going. They were being hemmed in. Sarah began to panic.

"Repeat Justin's instructions to me," Thaddeus said.

"What?"

"Justin. What did he tell you to do?"

"Oh. Um, go to the bank, take out all my money in cash, go to the train station, get a ticket for Southern California, and he'll be on the train.

"Okay. So we do that."

"What about them?"

"Don't worry about them. They don't want a scene any more than you do. They're waiting to catch you alone."

"So, I just stay with crowds and I'll be okay?"

"Stay with the crowds and stay with us. Without a guardian, they might be bold enough to attack you in public. If enough time goes by and they don't get the opportunity they want, they'll get desperate. They could probably get away with it. People are scared of them, and they could disperse before the Army showed up."

"Thaddeus, why do they want to kill me? Why do they care if I leave?" Sarah knew she was asking Thaddeus a question Justin had been unwilling to answer, and she felt like a child playing one parent against another. But it all seemed so unfair at the moment that she felt she deserved some answers. Thaddeus surprised her with his reply:

"I actually don't know, Sarah. That's not my department. I just keep you safe."

"Not your department? Wait, you don't know what this is all about?" His blind obedience was baffling. This was her guardian angel! Shouldn't he know the plan for her life? "You haven't tried to find out? Aren't you curious?"

"No, Sarah, I trust. I will know what I need to, when I need to. I've seen enough to know it will be a great story when it's all over." He smiled, but Sarah did not.

"Does Justin know?"

"Yes."

"Do you do whatever he tells you?"

"Yes."

"And that doesn't bother you?"

Thaddeus laughed. "Where I come from, Sarah, no one abuses power. They use it to bless. They serve. They love. Only someone from this world would ask a question like that. Here we are."

The bank was ahead of them on the other side of the street. When they stopped at the crosswalk, the burnout ahead of them kept on walking as if he had nothing to do with them. Those behind them turned a corner and went up a street in the opposite direction. Sarah saw that the two on the other side of the street had disappeared. Then she saw the two uniformed Soldiers standing at the door of the bank, each with a huge machine gun in his hands and a pistol at his side. Of course. Burnouts hated the Army, and the Army didn't trust them and didn't need much excuse to arrest them. They could determine what the charges were after the fact, and they would often be right. The burnouts would never challenge them directly, especially in the daylight.

Sarah entered the bank. "Remember," Thaddeus whispered to her, "everything is normal."

Sarah nodded and approached an open teller. She dug a card from her purse and presented it to the smiling, professional-looking woman.

"I'd like to get some cash, please," she said with a nervous smile.

"Certainly. You know, you can use an ATM for that," the woman said, gesturing to the back wall of the room.

"Yes, I know, but I have a limit on that."

"Of course. How much will you be taking out?"

"Um, can you tell me how much I have in there?"

"Certainly. Just run your card." Sarah slid her card through a scanner and then pressed her thumb onto the small glass plate that was attached to it. The woman turned a screen toward her so she could read the little green numbers for herself. Not quite ten thousand dollars. It wasn't very much. But Justin had said it would be enough.

"Okay. I'd like all of it."

"Oh, I see. So will you be closing your account with us today?"

Sarah was unprepared for this question. If she closed the account, it would look more suspicious, like she never planned to return.

"Um, no. Can I take all the money out and just leave the account open, you know, like for the future?"

"I'm sorry, you would have to leave a minimum of five hundred dollars in the account for the account to remain active."

What should she do? Justin hadn't told her. She couldn't consult Thaddeus with all the other bank customers around. She would just have to make a decision. Would she need that money? She decided that it was more important not to appear desperate.

"Okay then, I'll just take nine thousand and leave the rest." She hoped this was the right decision.

"Very well, then. And you said cash? Are you sure you wouldn't like me to put that on a cash card for you? It would be much easier to carry, and safer if it's stolen."

Another decision. The woman was right. But Justin had said cards would be too easy to trace.

"No, thank you. Cash is fine." Sarah smiled politely and tried to seem relaxed.

The woman looked at her questioningly, but said "Very well" and punched a series of commands into her computer. She counted the cash out onto the counter and then slid it all into an envelope, which bulged and proved difficult to close, as if to prove the woman's point that this was not a good plan.

"Um, could I have a couple of extra envelopes?"

The woman took them from a drawer, smiled stiffly, and then said "Will there be anything else?"

"No. Thank you so much," Sarah said meekly and quickly turned and tried to walk calmly to a counter at the back of the room. There she divided the money equally into three envelopes, put one in the inside pocket of her jacket, one at the bottom of her backpack, and one in a hidden compartment near the top. When she finished, she turned and looked around the room. No one appeared to care about the plain girl with the backpack and her measly nine thousand dollars. Grateful, she shouldered the pack and walked out the door with Thaddeus by her side.

"Well, I guess now it's the station?" She tried to appear relaxed.

"I think you should get some food first."

"Really? Is that okay? I mean, is it safe? Is there time?"

"Yes. Don't worry, Sarah, Justin knows what he's doing. There's time. Get some food."

This was a relief. She was hungry, and still wrestling with anxiety about the actual moment of stepping onto the train that would take her away forever. They were close to one of her favorite hot dog stands. On the short walk from the bank, the burnouts began appearing again, but their presence now reminded Sarah of wolves pacing behind a fence at the zoo. They couldn't touch her; at least not now. It felt good to stop and get a hot dog and fries, even to sit down on a bench to eat her food as if she had all the time in the world, while they stood around, leaning against light poles, forced to operate on her schedule. She ate with gratitude and watched the bustle of the city around her.

She had people-watched on this street countless times before, but it was different this time, as if she had already left town and was back for a visit, seeing the city as someone who was now an outsider. The feeling was the same as the night she had packed her bag: a surprising lack of sadness, an unexpected peace. A few short weeks ago, her dreams had revolved around finding her place in this city, on these streets. Now she felt a sort of pity for the people around her, whose worlds were so small. Whatever was in store for her, it was bigger than this. She finished the delicious hot dog before it had even finished steaming, licked the salt from the fries off her fingers, stood and threw her napkins in a nearby trashcan, then turned and smiled at Thaddeus.

"Okay." She took a deep breath and adjusted the pack on her back.

"Okay," he said with a smile, and gestured down the street in the direction of the train station. "Lead the way, Sarah."

Boarding

There was only one station in Portland where the big, fast trains, called "zip-trains," left for other parts of the state and beyond. When the Army had closed the state borders, it had also eliminated all non-military air travel within the country. International flights departed from New York, Houston, and Los Angeles almost every day, but travel abroad was discouraged and visas were extremely difficult to get. The zip-trains were fast enough to cross even the larger western states in little more than an hour; a trip from one coast to the other took around 12 hours or so, taking into account the regular stops at state lines for paperwork and security checkpoints.

The walk to the central station was not far, but even in the few short blocks the entourage of burnouts accompanying Sarah and Thaddeus doubled in size. They appeared from side streets as if on cue, nodding at each other, touching their ears and whispering into the air, so that by the time the station was in sight people on the sidewalks were whispering to each other, lowering their eyes and stepping aside to let the men pass. There were four on the other side of the street now, three behind them, and three in front, who seemed to have no doubt where they were headed. When they arrived at the big arched doorway into the station, these men stepped aside and waited. As Sarah approached, one of them opened the door and gestured for her to enter like a butler in an old-fashioned movie. The others laughed at his boldness and sneered at Sarah as she stepped past them into the station.

There was an obvious hush in the large, bustling, open foyer of the station when they entered. Burnouts used the MAX fairly often, but generally weren't seen in the smaller towns, and could never get clearance to cross state lines, so they had no use for the zip-trains. Several people gasped at the sight of ten of them, in broad daylight, pouring through the doorway into the station and following the quiet young woman up to the ticket counter. Sarah was still doing her best to ignore them, but had been hoping they would turn back at the door as they had at the bank. There were Soldiers at security checkpoints just beyond the ticket counter; surely they would stop there? They seemed to have no intention of this, though, and her anxiety grew as she sensed, without turning around, that they were taking their places in the line behind her.

When her turn came, Sarah approached the counter and realized she had been thinking more about her stalkers than about what she would say at this moment.

"Where you headed, Sweetie?" asked a kind-looking older man sitting at a computer screen behind a protective glass window.

"What? Oh, um, I ..." she looked at Thaddeus, who, to her surprise, spoke.

"San Diego." He was not talking to the man, but to her. It took a moment for her to remember that others couldn't hear him, either.

"San Diego," she said quickly.

"You sure about that?" he asked with a smile.

"Yes. San Diego. Sorry," she gave him a warm smile, "I'm just a little distracted."

He looked past her to the crowd of big, dark, imposing figures lining up behind her. "I don't blame you," he said under his breath, and then, as he began typing on his keyboard: "Good, California. Make my day a little easier."

"Why's that?"

"You haven't heard? Problems on the trains today, lots of them.

A couple of accidents in the Midwest, and some kind of explosion on the New-York to Florida. California's one of the few places I can send you. Lots of frustrated folks today," he gestured to the room behind her, "and I don't blame them. Seems like the whole system's falling apart ..." Then he stopped himself. "Sorry. I'm sure the California train will be fine. It'll be one thousand and thirty-one dollars, with taxes and fees. That is, if I haven't talked you out of it."

"Not at all. It'll be fine." Sarah dug in her purse for the money, smiling to assure the nice old man that he hadn't lost a customer. She counted out the amount and passed it to him, along with her ID card. But something about his comment reminded her of what her dad had said about the plane crashes on the news, and she had a vague feeling it was somehow related to everything that had been happening in her own life lately. "Out of curiosity, though, what do you mean about the system falling apart?"

"Well," the man leaned a little closer to the hole in his window and said in a low voice, "I mean, one of those accidents was a collision. Head-on, at full speed. That has never happened, not in the forty years I've worked for the trains. That means someone was *really* not doing their job. Makes you wonder ..." he shook his head, then sat up straight again, looked around, and resumed a more professional tone: "Have you traveled out of state before?"

"Not by myself, no."

"Okay, Sweetie. Here's how it works: When you get on the train, you need to fill out this form, explaining the reason for your travel, et cetera," He passed a form to her through a narrow slot at the base of the window. "At the California border, the train will stop and you'll need to go through another security checkpoint. You'll need to have your ID and your travel form, and you may be asked some questions. Shouldn't be a problem for someone like you ..." he again eyed the men behind her, shaking his head. "Then you just have to find a directory in the station for the train headed to San Diego and scan this card to board—that's your ticket onto both trains." He passed her a card through slot. Make sense?"

"Yes, thank you."

"Okay, have a good trip, Sweetie. Next!"

Walking away from the counter, Sarah couldn't help but look back to see how the man would handle his next customers, the first of which was her original stalker, the tall one from the morning train who had eaten at the Cup and Saucer. She couldn't hear the interaction, but she did see items being pushed back and forth through the slot in the window, and then the man turned and began walking toward her with a smug smile on his face.

Sarah quickly turned away, and found that she was approaching a stern-faced Soldier with a machine gun slung on his back and a pistol in a holster on his belt. It was the closest Sarah had ever been to a gun, and it immediately made her feel that she had something to hide. His blank, humorless face gave her the irrational feeling that he would find out some dark secret of hers, refuse to let her through, and embarrass her before the crowd of strangers and burnouts. This was silly, of course. She had nothing to hide. He asked for her ticket and ID, which he scanned and then returned to her. He gestured toward an x-ray machine, where she stood while another Soldier inspected her image in a screen while her backpack passed through a separate scanner. After a moment she was directed toward a third Soldier, who looked her up and down and asked, "Destination?"

"Um, San Diego."

"Purpose for your visit?"

She looked at Thaddeus, her invisible companion, who smiled a mischievous smile and said "Recreation."

She had no time to process the fact that it seemed an angel had just told her to lie. "Um, recreation."

"Okay. And what's in the bag?"

The question confused her, because the previous Soldier had just seen a scan of her backpack. Then a wave of anxiety washed her face white, which she tried to hide by turning and looking at the bag as if she were struggling to remember its exact contents. Her

Bible! She did have something to hide. Did they know? Would they take it? Had she broken a law? The thought of it being taken away was a greater fear at this moment than anything the men in black behind her could do. But she tried to appear cool.

"Um, clothes, toiletries ... something to read."

She knew it was strange, but hoped it would just seem quirky. Paper books were uncommon, but not unheard of. But the Soldier was just asking routine questions. He had already begun to eye the men who were being processed behind her. "Very well. Trains are straight ahead." He pointed down a wide hallway lined with screens displaying the day's various train schedules.

As she hurried down the hallway, he heard the same Soldier's skeptical voice addressing her stalker: "Destination?"

"Medford."

She glanced at Thaddeus, striding beside her and easily keeping up with her panicked pace. "Medford?"

"Smart." Thaddeus acknowledged. "They know they won't get clearance into California, but they can stay with us to the border." Decades ago, when terrorism had been at its peak, the increased security measures had required that some state borders be moved closer to major cities, so that travel could be more closely regulated. Medford was the last city on the Oregon side of the border, with Ashland immediately on the other side in California.

"But how does that help them?"

Thaddeus shrugged, but did not seem concerned. "I don't know. Don't worry, Sarah." He looked over his shoulder. "You had a little scare back there, didn't you?"

She nodded. "I thought they were going to take the Bible and arrest me or something."

He shook his head. "You have to stop worrying, Sarah. You're safe. While you're with us, nothing is going to happen to you unless we allow it. The Army is not in charge of your life, and neither are the burnouts."

They were nearing the end of the hallway, which opened onto

the loading area. They heard the whoosh of a train leaving the station and felt a breeze push past their faces. Sarah thought about this last statement for a moment as she looked back to see if anyone was following them. The hallway was empty.

"So they're not strong enough to, like, overpower you? I mean, you can't be killed, right? What if there were a lot of them?"

"We can't be killed ..." He hesitated and became thoughtful for a moment, as if lost in a memory, then quickly came back to her and gave a reassuring smile. "Don't worry, Sarah. I don't foresee it being a problem."

"He said he was going to kill me."

"No, he said that he wanted to. Sarah, I'm telling you, don't worry. Now let's find your train."

They emerged into the daylight and the fresh spring air, which seemed to reinforce what Thaddeus had said. Things would be fine. Sarah's pursuers were creatures of darkness, and this was not their domain. There was still no sign of them coming through the hallway. Probably, she told herself, they had not gotten past the security checkpoint. She scanned the huge monitor that hung from a beam of the rain shelter that covered the loading area. Her train was straight ahead about a hundred yards, and was just beginning to board. Once they learned this, it was obvious that the old man had been right: much of the area was empty, and several trains sat motionless under unlit message boards. The California train was the only one leaving the station, the only one with a line of people waiting to board. They walked quickly, and when they reached the train a woman took her ticket and ran it through a handheld scanner. Sarah looked back down the walkway and saw no sign of anyone else coming.

They located their seats and Thaddeus moved to take the window, leaving Sarah to sit in the middle, with an empty seat on the aisle next to her.

"Can I have the window?" she asked, more out of shyness than any desire to see the countryside. She hated the thought of being stuck next to someone talkative for the long ride ahead.

"No, I think this is better," Thaddeus said. As he did so, there was a noise ahead of them, and Sarah looked down the aisle to see one, two, three men with blue hair entering the train, examining their tickets and looking up and down the rows to find empty seats. She quickly sat down and ducked behind the seat in front of her, then peeked between the headrests to seek where they were seated. Two more came aboard. Then another. She hid herself again.

"What is happening?" she whispered to Thaddeus. "How on earth did they get through security?"

"They were prepared. ID cards, money, no weapons or even baggage. The Army hates them, but they would have to have a reason to deny them access to public transportation." He seemed amused by the situation, as if all of this effort was impressive but useless. He looked her in the eye, and said slowly, "Sarah: don't worry."

She sighed. Then there was a shadow, and a man all in black sat himself in the empty seat next to her. She felt she would explode. Taking a huge breath, she forced down the fear that was rising within her, and turned to face him, trying to think of something clever and brave to say.

But it was Justin.

Answers

"Where have you been?" Seeing Justin was a great relief, but Sarah couldn't keep herself from venting the fear and anger that had risen up within her before she recognized him.

"It's good to see you too, Sarah." He had a particularly obnoxious habit of ignoring her rudeness in a way that made her feel guilty about it. "I've been taking care of a few things. I'm here now, though."

"I see. You have big, important things to do. Never mind that half the city has been stalking me all day."

Justin studied her with a fatherly look for a moment, then answered: "Actually, Sarah, as of this moment I have nothing more important to do. You will have my undivided attention from here on out. There are, believe it or not, a few other things going on in the world, but I have taken care of my other responsibilities, and I'm all yours now. I hope Thaddeus' service to you has not been too unsatisfactory."

Sarah sank in her chair and looked at Thaddeus, then Justin, then down at her lap. "He's been great. I'm sorry."

"It's fine, Sarah. It's been a stressful day, and it's not over. But you can relax now. You should fill out your travel form, and then you can read or something. We'll be on the train for about an hour. And you should know," he said, anticipating her next question, "that you're under no obligation to converse with us. Angels don't get bored, we don't need to be entertained, and our feelings are not hurt when we're ignored."

"And you're patient," Sarah added.

"Yes, we are."

Anxiety and embarrassment passed, and when they did Sarah was able to feel gratitude. She looked around the train and saw that the burnouts were scattered throughout the cabin, having boarded late and being forced to take whatever seats were left empty. All of them were at least 3 rows away in either direction. She realized that it was no small thing that the two seats on either side of her were empty. The feeling she had experienced when she stepped out the door that morning and first saw Thaddeus returned. It was good to be protected.

The train began to move. As it pulled away from the loading area and past some concrete barriers, Sarah had a clear view of the city. They passed between skyscrapers, crossed the Willamette River that divided the downtown area from the rest of the city, and then the buildings got smaller. They picked up speed, and there was barely time to reminisce about her former dreams of independent adulthood here before they were out in the suburbs, then on an elevated track running parallel to the highway going south. She sighed, closed her eyes momentarily, and turned away from the window. She had done it. Again, she was not overwhelmed by emotion, but was aware that this was a significant moment. The truth was, she had been in the process of releasing her family, the life she knew, even her future, for some time now. Her roots had been loosened. But there was a finality that came with the changing landscape around her filled her with a certain sadness. *But not regret,* she told herself. *This is right. This is right. Isn't it?*

"I'm proud of you," said Justin.

"What?" Sarah was caught off guard by this statement.

"You've taken a big step of faith. From my position, it's easy to see that it's the right thing, but I know you're giving up a lot and stepping out into the unknown. I'm sure that's scary."

"Well, yeah. Although I don't know how much I'm actually giving up. It's not like my life was that great."

Justin smiled. "Well, the path to a better life always involves a step of faith. And you are giving up the feeling of security, which is a major obstacle for some people. You're doing the right thing, Sarah, and I'm glad."

"Did you know what decision I would make?"

"Hmmm. I'm sorry, that's not something I can really talk about."

"Why not?"

Justin hesitated. "Well, in most cases, I would say no, I don't know about the decisions people are going to make. I don't have access to that kind of information, nor do I need it. In this particular case, however ..."

"What? He's told you everything I'm going to do?"

"No, not at all. But I was given some information about the future, some of which I was authorized to share with you, the end result of which is that you are sitting on this train."

"Which you knew would happen?"

"I was fairly certain."

"Because you had inside information?"

"Yes."

"Because I'm special."

"Yes."

"Why?"

Justin looked at her thoughtfully. He was clearly undecided as to whether it was a good idea to answer this question.

"So we're back to this," Sarah said. "I have to say, this whole thing would be a lot easier if I could have a few more answers. I mean, all these guys are after me for no reason, and I have to leave my family and my job and my life because the end of the world is coming, which makes no sense, because if it's the end of the world I don't see how it matters where I am, and all you keep telling me is that I have to trust, but what am I trusting in? I don't know anything. I'm just blind in this whole thing."

"Who." Justin said.

"What?"

"Not what. Who. Who are you trusting in?"

Sarah hated being reprimanded like this, but she knew it was the perfect thing for him to say. She paused long enough to really consider the answer to the question.

"Someone I barely know."

Justin nodded. "That's fair. Okay, Sarah. I'll give you answers."

"Really?" Sarah noticed that even Thaddeus, who had been silent and motionless through the conversation thus far, perked up at this.

"Really. But you have to promise to listen better this time."

"What does that mean? I listen."

"You do? You just said the end of the world was coming. Tell me, when did I ever say that? If you're operating on that assumption, no wonder you're confused."

For a single second, Sarah wrestled with an internal panic that was equal to any fear she had felt in the previous two weeks. Had she been deceived? Had she been lured away from home by a simple lie, tricked into leaving her life behind for who knows what evil purpose? Were these two beings she had been trusting the true agents of darkness? What did he mean?

"But, you did say ..." she stumbled, "what about the missiles and soldiers and all that?"

"All of that is happening, in twenty-one days, just as I told you. But it will not be the end of the world. Think about it, Sarah: if a human army is having a victory, whether it's the good guys or the bad guys, it's not the end, not for them. The end of the world will be far worse than what I told you about."

She had to admit that this made sense. The moment of doubt and panic passed, and she relaxed a bit. "Oh. Okay, so it's just

Portland, then? Or the northwest or something? And we'll be fine in California?"

"No, it's bigger than that. Sarah, what do you think I've been doing for the past week?"

Sarah shrugged.

Justin leaned forward and lowered his voice, which caused Sarah to lean in as well. He spoke humbly.

"Sarah, I am the supervising angel for all the guardians in what you know as the United States of America, and I have been for the entire history of this nation. For the past week, I have been withdrawing and dismissing my men. We're pulling out, Sarah. It's over. In 21 days this country will no longer exist, and what remains will be chaos and war and global power struggles that will mean terrible times for the people who survive the initial attack. Trust me, you do not want to be here." As he spoke this last sentence, Justin's voice filled with the same grief Sarah had heard that day in Java Stop.

Sarah had never imagined that she would feel sympathy for an angel, but in this moment her heart filled with compassion. Did this mean Justin had failed to do his job well? No, of course not. Still, even if he did not feel responsibility for what was coming, he would at least have a certain love for this land he had cared for all these years. But something in her heart felt that it would be awkward, maybe even inappropriate, to offer him comfort. She felt that Justin would probably want her to change the subject, so she did:

"So what does all that mean for me?"

"Well, it means that right now, you are sitting in the safest place in the entire country," he said with a smile.

Sarah thought about all the bombings, the plane crashes, the train wrecks of the past several days. *Somebody's not doing their job.* The implications of the withdrawal of protection Justin had just described overwhelmed her. She felt the weight of worldwide events pressing down on her, and suddenly felt very privileged and undeserving. Except of answers. She deserved those.

"No, I mean what does it mean that I'm being escorted by the last two angels in the country while everyone else is suffering and unprotected?"

Justin looked her in the eyes. "It means, Sarah, that you are the last one."

Sarah gulped. "The last what?"

"The last believer."

Surely this could not be true. "What?"

"The last believer, Sarah. You are the last person in your country to place your faith in God."

Sarah sat stunned and silent. It explained everything. She went through a sort of mental checklist of the experiences, thoughts, and questions of the past two weeks. This was the answer, and she knew it. Something inside her confirmed it beyond any doubt. And, if she were honest with herself, something else inside her wanted it to be true. She was not above pride, and a feeling arose within her that was similar to what winning races or getting top grades had done for her in school. She was special. But this feeling was immediately overshadowed by anxiety, by the shy part of her that hated attention and was overwhelmed at the thought that she had become the focal point for the forces of both good and evil across her entire country. Why did it have to be her? And furthermore, was it certain that it was her? Did that mean that people like Jalen, Torin, her classmates and her brothers, would not come to faith no matter what? It hardly seemed fair, for them or for her. But of course, God would know everything, and He would know what they would do under any circumstances ... she shook her head and decided to let those questions go. They were beyond her. It all was.

"I've finally silenced you." Justin's voice called her back to reality. She was on a train headed for California. She was the last believer in the country, being pursued by evil men who wanted to kill her, protected by angels, with a Bible and some money in her bag, and in three weeks everything and everyone she had known would be destroyed by warfare.

"Yeah," she replied quietly.

"How are you feeling?" the look in his eyes made her realize that he was probably wondering if he had done the right thing in sharing this news with her. But she was too consumed with her own situation to try to make him feel any better.

"I don't know … special? Scared?" She thought for a moment, and surprised herself with what came out next. "Loved?"

A look of pleasant surprise came over his face. "Tell me about that last one."

"Well, I don't know, just, really undeserving, you know?" Again, her own emotions caught her off guard. She was near tears. Where was this coming from?

Justin nodded approvingly. "I do know," he said.

Another thought occurred to Sarah, a relief because it took the conversation in a practical direction and allowed her some distance from her own feelings.

"But … really? I mean, I've actually wondered if that day was coming, you know, when we …" She stumbled over her words for a moment. *We?* It felt strange to use that word. Premature, somehow. But Justin had called her a believer, hadn't he? " …When, you know, we would just fade out, disappear. But there are still Bibles around, and you hear on the news about secret house churches, that kind of thing …"

"Well, yes, there are some who have already believed, and they have their own path to walk in the days to come. But there will be no one else, no new believers, not while this country exists in its current form."

"But, if they are around, and they get to stay, why can't I?"

"'Get to stay'? It's hardly a privilege, Sarah. Their future is a hard one, living in wartime in an unprotected land."

"Did you take their guardians away too?"

"He has not left them alone," he said, giving her a look that said *Sorry, none of your business.* "In any case, it will be a situation that your fragile faith is apparently not ready to handle. My orders are to get you out."

Sarah didn't argue with this. But she did have another question: "Why do they want to kill me?"

"Because you have a future they'd like to prevent."

"What kind of future?"

"I really don't know the specifics, Sarah. But if you believe, then I know it involves growing in faith, and at some point strengthening the faith of others. They hate the idea of both."

"If I believe? Didn't you just say I'm the last believer? I mean, I'm in this now, right? That train has left the station," Sarah laughed at her own joke, and turned to Thaddeus to see if he was laughing too, which he was. Neither of them saw that Justin's face remained serious.

"So then," Sarah said, turning back to him, "What's the plan? Where are we going? Mexico?"

Justin nodded. "Mexico."

Sarah let this new development sink in for a minute. Mexico. A whole different country. Somehow, this seemed to fit, and she found that she was more okay with this plan than she expected to be. "And what will happen when we get to Mexico?"

"I don't know. I've never been there," he said with a wry smile. "I only know that's your destination."

"Why not Canada?"

He shook his head. "No better than here."

"Oh." Sarah paused. It was a strange thing for her, a simple, uninformed girl who worked at a cafe, to have advance knowledge of the kind of events Justin was predicting. Her heart grieved for half a moment as another entire nation was added to the list of people whose imminent suffering she could not prevent. But she was unable to bear the weight of such thoughts for long, and she sensed that it was not her job to do so. If it was okay for Justin to focus all his attention on her situation, it must be okay for her to do the same. Another question occurred to her:

"How will we get across the border?"

The Mexican border was completely closed to civilians. Apart from a few tightly guarded roads that were reserved for cargo trucks, no one passed between the two countries. In most places, the border was a 40-foot steel wall protected by cameras and an alarm system that would report any activity or damage to the wall to nearby Army stations. If God was unwilling to miraculously provide her with money for her trip, she doubted He would magically transport her to the other side of the wall. So what was Justin's plan?

"I don't know how you'll get across," he said. "We don't need to worry about that yet."

Yet? They would be in San Diego by the end of the day. "You don't know? So, what, we'll just get off the train, walk up to the gate, and see what happens?

"Often, Sarah, I am called to obey one step at a time. Just like you."

She paused for a moment as something unexpected happened within her thoughts. She realized that what Justin had said was exactly the idea she had gotten from something she had read in her grandmother's Bible a few nights before. It was the first time, at least on a conscious level, that reading the book had informed her thoughts and caused her to see the world differently. It was like a new voice entering a choir and rising above all the others. She surprised herself by nodding in agreement with Justin's comment. "Like Phillip," she said.

"Phillip?"

"You know, Phillip. A guy in the Bible. An angel told him to start walking down a road, and didn't tell him why, and then it turned out that it wasn't really about the destination at all, but something cool happened on the way there."

Justin's smile was like a father's delight in his daughter's paintings brought home from kindergarten class. "I'm familiar with the story. I'm pleased that you are."

Sarah was still thinking. "Later in the story, he just disappears and magically appears in another place. So sometimes God does that too. Why can't He just do that with me?"

Justin shrugged. "I've seen it done both ways. There's always a reason."

Sarah nodded, then realized what he had said. "Wait, you've seen it both ways? Like, you've seen someone magically transported?"

"Well, I would prefer to say 'miraculously transported,' but yes."

"Can you tell me any stories?" Sarah asked eagerly.

"Sure. Once, there was this guy named Phillip ..." At this, Thaddeus chuckled loudly, and Justin broke into a playful smile.

"Shut up," said Sarah. "Wait. Really? Was that you?"

Justin's eyebrows raised mysteriously for a moment, but he didn't answer. "How's that form coming? We're almost there."

"You won't tell me?"

"Angels don't seek their own glory, Sarah. We just do what we are commanded to do."

"Fine. Okay, last question, and then I better fill out my form," she said, and turned to Thaddeus as she did so: "'Recreation?' So angels can just, like, lie when they need to?"

Thaddeus looked at Justin and they both chuckled, and Sarah felt that she was left out of an inside joke.

"What?"

"I cannot and would not lie, Sarah. Recreation," and he slowed the word down so she would get the joke, " ...re-creation ... is the perfect word to describe the purpose of your trip. You will never be the same after this."

Sarah rolled her eyes. "Angels are hysterical," she said sarcastically, and turned her attention to the paper on the small table in front of her. "Okay, fine. Recreation."

22
New territory

As Sarah filled out her paperwork, an unfamiliar landscape flew past the window at amazing speed. She was very aware of how small her world had been, of how small she herself was. She looked around at the passengers in the nearby seats, each of whom seemed to her to be an experienced, confident traveler. No one else seemed to be confused by the travel paperwork, or impressed by the speed of the train, or anxious about the coming security checkpoint. She glanced back and forth at the two angels on either side of her, and felt at the same time grateful and embarrassed. On the one hand, no one else on the train had an escort like hers. On the other hand, no one else seemed to need one. They were doing just fine on their own, at least for the moment.

She completed the form and tucked it into her pack, then stared out the window at the rolling hills that were rapidly turning into mountains as the train sped south. After a few minutes a pleasant female voice from speakers in the ceiling filled the cabin: "The train will be arriving in Medford in about 5 minutes. California-bound passengers, please have your travel forms ready. Upon exiting the train, proceed to the processing gate. Thank you." Sarah sat up straight and checked her backpack to make sure her money was in place and the Bible safely buried beneath her clothes. She fidgeted with one of the zippers until the train stopped, then stood quickly in an attempt to beat the crowd out the door. But she felt Justin's hand on her shoulder.

"Relax, Sarah," he said, "There's no point. We'll go last."

She soon saw that he was right. All the passengers rose and moved into the aisle at the same time, creating in an instant human traffic jam. There were doors in front of them and behind them, but at both ends people were fussing with jackets and luggage while other stood and glared at them impatiently. It would have been pointless to try to force her way through the crowd. The other passengers were eyeing the burnouts suspiciously and giving them extra space, but the men were behaving themselves for the moment, and there was no reason to panic or call attention to herself. Besides, the crush of people kept them from getting any closer to her at least until she was off the train.

When it was finally her turn to step out of the train and into the open air, her eyes followed the crowd as it made its way toward a massive wall made of iron bars, so that you could see the California side of the train station but not pass through. There was a gate, with a sign above it that said "Interstate Travel Processing." Many of the passengers from her train were forming a line there, and a few armed Soldiers stood nearby. The others, who had reached their destination, were dispersing quickly. But the men who had been shadowing her all day didn't join the line, nor did they disperse. Instead, a few took up positions standing next to the gate (off to the side, not too close to the Soldiers), and others simply loitered in the empty spaces between her and the line of people. They seemed to have no intention of attempting to cross into California. It was almost as if they were simply there to send her off.

Right now I'm the safest person in the country, Sarah told herself, and strode as confidently as she could toward the back of the line, through a gap between two clusters of the burnouts. As she did so, the spokesman who had eaten breakfast at the Cup and Saucer that morning stepped directly into her path. He glanced backward at the Soldiers, then briefly at her two escorts. Then he glared into her eyes and spoke softly and playfully:

"You're a long way from home, Sarah Martinez. Does your

family know where you are? Do you want me to give them a message for you?"

It took a moment for the threat to register in Sarah's mind. When it did she could not hide the fear in her eyes as she looked desperately to Justin. She was hoping for a word of reassurance. Surely he would tell her it was an empty threat, that Jalen and her father and brothers were protected, or that these men didn't even know who they were or where they lived. But he didn't. Instead, he looked at her almost without expression, and said simply, "You must entrust them to Him, Sarah."

As she struggled to process this, the burnout chuckled and shook his head. "That's a lot to ask," he said. Then his voice deepened. "My friends will be on their doorstep in ten minutes unless you dismiss these guys and come with me right now."

Sarah was surprised by her own response. She was deeply shaken and very much still processing the implications of this conversation. But she heard herself saying, "You're a liar," and she quickly brushed past the man and marched across the concrete to the back of the processing line. He did not follow her, but she heard him continue to chuckle as she walked away.

"Have it your way," he shouted after her. "But there's no escape, Sarah. Not for you or for them."

She reached the back of the line and was grateful that the delay had given all the other passengers a chance to line up first. With no one behind her, she could feel for the moment that she had a little privacy to collect herself. She was trembling badly, and reeling emotionally from the thought that right now, violent men could be entering her home and threatening Jalen and her father, all because of her. She fumbled in her pack for her paperwork, mostly to keep herself from crying.

"You okay?" Justin asked.

Sarah answered honestly, with an edge of frustration, "I don't know. It is a lot to ask."

"It's everything," Justin acknowledged. "He asks nothing less."

Sarah nodded and blinked away a tear. She was surprised to be slightly comforted by his words. She was also conscious that in the last few moments she had chosen and acted with a strength that was not her own. It felt good. She was growing. She could do this. Then she heard Thaddeus' voice at her side.

"Justin."

"I see it."

"See what?" Sarah asked.

"Well," said Justin with a strained smile, "it looks like the day's not over yet."

Sarah followed their eyes to the crowd on the other side of the bars, which was drawing nearer as the line continued to move forward. There were people hurrying to catch a train that was boarding, others standing around in clusters, talking casually, and others standing alone, engrossed in their phones. Then she saw him. A man all dressed in black leather, covered in tattoos, with bright green hair, leaning against the bars with his back to them. Then two more, standing together, chatting and watching the line of people coming into their side of the station. Bright green hair again. Further back by the trains, a group of four, all with green hair of various shades, all dressed in black. Her momentary courage was gone in a heartbeat. She had been so ready to let her guard down, to walk through the gate and feel at least some of the weight lifted from her shoulders. Now it appeared she would be hunted by a different breed of burnout all the way to Mexico. And would it even stop then?

"Justin, I can't do this."

"Yes you can."

"What do we do now?"

"Keep going," said Justin calmly. "We knew this was a possibility."

Sarah's fear expressed itself in anger. "We did?" she whispered hotly. "I guess I missed that part of the conversation. I do remember the part where you said we'd be safe!"

"What I said, Sarah, was that they wouldn't be able to cross the state lines. But there was always the possibility that they were coordinating with others. We've been seeing more and more of that lately."

The line moved again. Two more people and it would be her turn. Sarah felt panic rising within her. She turned to her protector again. "Justin, I can't! They'll be on the train, and everywhere we go. Can't you kill them or something?"

"No, not in public like this."

"But there will be more and more, I just know it! I can't take this anymore! Do something, please!" It had been a long day already, and Sarah was more tired than she realized. A part of her felt like she was being weak, like she probably should be able to go on, to stay calm and keep trusting. But the larger part felt that she was simply spent. Justin could see it, and he also knew that she was right: their stalkers' numbers were only likely to grow larger. At some point …

He nodded thoughtfully, then looked at Thaddeus. They looked at each other for a moment with such focus that Sarah felt she should not interrupt. Then the line moved again and the Soldier began his conversation with the woman directly in front of her.

"Justin?"

The two angels ignored her and continued their silent conversation. After a few more moments, as the woman in front of them proceeded to empty out the entire contents of her purse looking for her admission card, Justin finally turned his attention to her.

"Okay," he said, "new plan."

"'New plan'? Just like that? Are you sure?"

"Almost always, Sarah. New plan. No more trains."

Sarah considered the implications of this. "But everything else is so much slower."

"Time is not an issue. We need to get you completely away from these guys, off their radar. And that means getting away from main transportation routes."

"How will we do that?"

"As soon as you finish processing, head straight for that restroom over there," Justin gestured across the plaza on the California side of the station. "Go inside and lock yourself in a stall. These guys won't follow you in, because they don't want to get in trouble here. There is a woman in there who is dressed almost the same as you are who is getting on your next train. Thaddeus and I will surround her as soon as she leaves the restroom, and get onto the train with her. Your pursuers will follow us. They can see us, they'll assume we're with you, and we'll make sure they never get a look at her face. You take your jacket off and change into a different-colored shirt. Wait 15 minutes until the train has left, then hurry out those doors," he gestured again, "out of the station. Across the street and two blocks south is a bus station. Get a ticket for the bus going to Redding. It leaves in 25 minutes. Thaddeus and I will wait until the train is far away, then we'll exit and meet you when you get off the bus in Redding."

"Redding," Sarah repeated. "So you're leaving me? I don't know if I like this plan."

Justin smiled. "Only for a couple of hours, Sarah. And things will be much calmer after that. I promise. This will work."

"What about that other girl? Is this safe for her? Is she in any danger?"

"Not today," Justin said. "I'll make sure. Okay?"

"I think so," said Sarah.

"Next!" The Soldier seated in the processing booth beckoned for Sarah to move forward and present her paperwork.

Sarah stepped forward nervously, but the process was simple and routine. The Soldier examined her travel documents and the card she had been issued in Portland that served as her ticket onto the next train. She had a moment of worry that he would ask her destination, and that she would have to lie, now that she was no longer getting back on the train. But he didn't ask. He simply looked her up and down, eyed her backpack for a moment but didn't ask to see inside, and said, "Thank you. Next!"

When she stepped through the gate, the burnout who had been leaning against the gate straightened up and began to shadow her toward the restroom, but he didn't speak to her. She saw the others closing in as well. She sped up and moved as quickly as she could across the plaza. As the men moved closer, Justin and Thaddeus took up positions on either side of her. When she reached the restroom they turned and stood on both sides of the door, standing like sentries with their arms folded across their chests as she disappeared inside. The burnouts stopped and stood around in clusters near the door. A few chuckled and sneered, but they didn't speak, and neither did Justin or Thaddeus.

After a few minutes a young woman emerged wearing faded jeans and gray hooded sweatshirt, with long black hair spilling out from inside the hood and a backpack that looked like a school bookbag. Immediately the two angels moved to her side and escorted her across the plaza. She strode confidently toward the train that was boarding for southern California, and the groups of green-haired burnouts followed her. Once a pair of them came up right behind them, but Thaddeus turned and glared at them with such intensity that, while their pride would not allow them to show fear, they backed off and kept a respectful distance. The girl boarded the train, and so did the angels, and so did the burnouts, in groups of two or three interspersed among the other passengers, until the plaza was mostly empty again and the train began to move, slowly at first, but quickly gaining speed as it began its journey south.

Five minutes later Sarah Martinez emerged from the restroom and looked timidly around the plaza. It would be a while before another train came, so there were very few people around. None of them had brightly dyed hair. Sarah had changed into a light blue long-sleeved shirt and tied her sweatshirt around her waist. Having traveled so little in her life, she had a momentary feeling of freedom and excitement, despite the circumstances. She was on her own, away from family and routine, and her guardians had trusted her enough to make this part of the journey on her own.

The threat that had stalked her since the morning appeared to be gone, at least for now. The sun was hot overhead, and she realized she was hungry. She crossed the plaza and exited through a set of double doors that led her briefly into the inside portion of the station, where people purchased tickets and waited for their trains when the weather was bad. Another set of doors, and she was out on the sidewalk of an unfamiliar street.

Across the street and two blocks south. Redding. 25 minutes. That leaves me a little over 10 minutes. She scanned up and down the street for something to eat. Nothing in sight, and no time. Maybe there would be something at the station. She hurried across the street, worried at first because she saw no sign of a bus station. But then she saw it and hurried inside and looked quickly for the ticket counter. As she approached she pulled her wallet out of her backpack and said, "One ticket for the bus to Redding, please. And can you tell me where I can find some food?"

"Redding? Honey, that bus is boarding now. You won't have time for food. It's eighty-five dollars if you want to try to make it. Loading dock number 14." The middle-aged woman behind the counter pointed through a set of sliding glass doors across the room. Take a left after you pass through security. And you better hurry!"

Sarah was grateful to have cash in the right amount. She slid it across the counter and the woman pulled a paper ticket from a small printing machine. Sarah grabbed it and ran. Once through the glass doors, she found she was third in line at the security checkpoint, which required her to hand over her backpack to a Soldier. He reached in and felt around, but then handed the bag back to her and waved her on. She found the bus with the engine already running. She climbed the steps inside, ran her ticket through a machine next to the driver, and then made her way down the narrow aisle looking for a seat. Most were taken. Then she spotted an opening next to a young man who appeared to be about her age. They exchanged smiles and she sat gratefully, stuffing her backpack under her feet. She settled herself in her seat and let out a deep breath.

"You made it, huh?" he said pleasantly.

"Yeah." Sarah said. "Barely."

"Is Redding home?"

"Um, no." How could she avoid talking to him? Sarah didn't want to be rude. She also didn't want to appear unusual or even memorable. If only she had some headphones or something. She decided to shift the topic away from herself as quickly as possible. "Home is Portland, I'm just ... visiting. What about you?"

"Portland! I've heard it's beautiful. Me, I'm—well, home is sort of a fluid concept for me right now." He said this with such a winning smile that it was clear he was not looking for pity. He was free and he was enjoying his freedom. "I'm from here in NorCal, but you might say I'm in the midst of a transition."

It felt rude not to follow up on a statement like this. Sarah knew she needed to keep to herself and share as little as possible about her plans, but the opportunity for connection with another person (and a young, attractive, intriguing person at that) was appealing. Her life had become increasingly lonely lately, and she had faced tremendous challenges without anyone to share them with. What harm could come from a little normal conversation?

"Transition? Like, a new job or something?" Even as she asked this, Sarah knew she was off track. Something about his looks (his hair was a little out of control in a boyish, playful way), his clothes, and his attitude didn't fit with the working world.

"No, nothing like that. I'm getting ready to move."

"Oh, yeah, where to?"

"Colorado."

"Wow! What's in Colorado?"

"What's in Colorado? What's not in Colorado? Snow-capped mountains, natural beauty, awesome culture, great people, and, you know," he glanced around them and lowered his voice slightly, as if he felt a little silly making his next comment, "it's a nice safe place."

The statement was confusing. He seemed like a risk-taker, like someone who would be more inclined to pursue adventure than safety. The events of the last few weeks had made her paranoid, and Sarah began to wonder if this was someone who was somehow connected to everything else that was happening to her. "What do you mean?" she asked.

"Well, since you asked," he lowered his voice a little further "I—truth is, I'm kind of embarrassed. You don't know me, and this is going to sound dumb. But … well, have you ever heard of the Fortress Movement?"

Sarah stared at him blankly. "Sorry, no."

"Oh, good. That's what they're calling us on the internet, but it's not my favorite term. Anyway, some of us, more and more actually, are becoming convinced that things are not going in a good direction, you know, in our country." He looked at her as if he expected her to roll her eyes, but Sarah just listened. "Anyway, so, a lot of people, well, not a lot, but some of us, are starting to see that this country is weak, and we have enemies, and it just seems like it would be smart, you know, not to live too close to the edges."

"The edges?"

"Yeah, like the borders. Like, okay, this is where I start to sound crazy. I can't believe you're still listening. Everyone else writes me off as a wacko at about this point. But our country has all these enemies, and we keep making more people mad, all over the world, and we're not as strong as we think we are, and it just makes sense that if things are going to go bad, well, then the middle is probably where you want to be. I know, I know, I'm a paranoid, unpatriotic traitor. I can't even believe I told you all that. It's totally okay if you don't want to talk about it anymore, or, you know, at all."

"Actually," Sarah said, "I think it makes a lot of sense."

"Really? Are you making fun of me?"

"No, I can see it. I mean, you watch the news and things seem pretty bad." Something within her wanted to encourage him, and only partly because he was cute. Sarah could relate with the isolation that comes from having unpopular beliefs, and, while his beliefs were not the same as hers, they had enough in common that she instinctively wanted to reassure him, to help him feel a little more normal. It was what she wished someone would do for her.

"Exactly!" He was obviously excited to be understood. "I mean, with the recent economic sanctions, and the growing dissatisfaction with our foreign policy, anyone who's paying attention can see that it's really only a matter of time."

Now he had completely lost her. She had no idea what any of those things meant. It made her feel small, young, and naïve, but she didn't want him to know any of that. So she nodded and said, "Totally. So you're moving to Colorado. Like, right away? Is that where you're headed now?"

"No, still getting some things together. Me and a few friends from all over NorCal—Northern California. Leaving fairly soon, just getting our paperwork done and putting some money together. You really don't think I'm crazy?"

"I've heard crazier." Sarah said. Then her stomach growled noticeably, and she rubbed it in embarrassment. "Sorry," she said.

"Oh, are you hungry? I have a ton of food."

"No, don't worry about it. I'll be fine till we get there. Save your food."

"No, I insist. It's a two-hour bus ride, and I have more than I need. Here, what do you like?" He pulled out bags of nuts, dried fruit, and crackers from his well-worn backpack. "I'm Kyler, by the way." He offered his hand for her to shake.

"I'm Sarah. Nice to meet you, Kyler." She shook his hand shyly.

"Nice to meet you, Sarah. Have some crackers." His smile as he extended the bag to her was so warm, so genuine, and such a welcome contrast to the stresses she had endured so far that day, that any thoughts she had about keeping to herself for the rest of the ride were forgotten. She gratefully took the crackers.

After a moment of chewing and looking awkwardly out the window, she turned back to him to comment on the landscape, just to make conversation. But her mouth was still too full of crackers, some of which came out in a puff of crumbs as she said "Iff pretty here." Her face flushed red and she immediately started laughing at herself, and he joined in. Now the walls were completely down. He pointed out the view of Mt. Shasta through the windows on the other side of the bus, which required her to lean across him a bit to see properly. Then he asked her about life in Oregon, and told her about his adventures with friends in various parts of northern California. The conversation continued for the entire bus ride. He was so easy to talk to that Sarah felt none of her usual shyness with new people. They talked about favorite foods (as they ate all the nuts and the dried fruit), about books, about their dysfunctional families. It was the quickest and most enjoyable two hours that Sarah had spent in a long time. As the bus pulled into the station in Redding, she found herself disappointed that the trip was over.

"Wow, we're here already? That went fast." She said. She was not sure how to leave things. She was being pulled back to reality, and the reality was that she was on a journey, with a destination. She had plans, and there was no room in those plans for cute boys. She felt resentful of this fact, but didn't know what to do about it. What would Kyler's fate be in 21 days? Was he doomed to destruction as well? It didn't seem fair.

"Yeah, it did," he agreed, obviously sharing her disappointment. "Hey, uh, we should keep in touch." They were stopped now, and the other passengers were collecting their belongings, standing, and making their way toward the exit. He reached in his pocket. "Do you have a phone?"

A wave of guilt washed over Sarah's face, but he was already looking down at the screen in his hand and didn't see it. Sarah looked around the bus, but there were no angels to be seen. "Yeah," she said, reaching down into the bottom of her bag, "right here."

New Plans

Justin had told her not to bring her phone. She remembered it clearly.

Sarah was the kind of person who was always very aware of the rules, and she was incapable of doing the wrong thing without feeling guilty. But this did not mean she always did the right thing. Like anyone else, from time to time she allowed herself to be ruled by the simple fact that she wanted something, and she could find ways to justify her actions, sometimes beforehand, sometimes after the fact. The difference between her and most other people was that she was never very convinced by her own excuses. They were weak and she knew it.

She had told herself that she would just bring her phone to work that morning, because it was supposed to look like a normal day, and if she had left it home Jalen might have tried to bring it to her or something like that. She had planned to get rid of it at the train station, but then Thaddeus was there, and she was too embarrassed to reveal that she had disobeyed Justin. Then she had known, in the bathroom in Medford, that this was her chance, but she had told herself that if she threw it away or left it somewhere and someone found it, it would reveal that she had been there (although the train company's records would also do that), and that at this point it was better to keep it with her, just to be safe.

The truth was that she simply didn't want to let it go yet. To do so would be to let go of the last lifeline that kept her connected to her former life, to entrust herself entirely to Justin—really, to the One she did not yet fully trust. On a practical level, she was a simple girl traveling in the great big world, and it seemed foolish not to have this highly useful tool with her. Justin's instructions seemed over-the-top, unnecessary. Now, she told herself, she was glad she had the phone. She would have been embarrassed to explain to Kyler that she didn't have one, and she was glad to have a way to stay in contact with him. Logic said that there was absolutely no future to their relationship, but the connection she had formed in the last couple of hours was not one she was ready to relinquish yet. She gave him her number and took his eagerly, then looked back up at him.

"It was really good to meet you," she said shyly.

"Yeah, it was. I mean, good to meet you, too, Sarah," he said with the same charming smile as when he had offered her the crackers. "I hope we meet again."

This comment brought her back to reality a bit. "Well, who knows?" she said, but her smile was forced. She had to step off this bus, find Justin and Thaddeus, and find out what was the next step in their new plan. She was supposed to be in San Diego by this time, but now she was 600 miles short of that, and it was nearly time for dinner. What came next? She followed Kyler out of the bus, wondering about the stories behind all the interesting scratches and stains on his backpack. Both of them, she thought, were on adventures, stepping out into the unknown, but somehow his adventure was far more appealing. He was off with his carefree friends on a road trip to start a new life in an exciting place. She was alone, being chased by evil men and led by a guide who could not, or would not, tell her much about her final destination. It didn't seem fair. She forced herself to remember all that had led her to this point: her great-grandmothers' book, and the events of the last two weeks. She wasn't crazy. It was real; this was right. It was amazing how much all of that had faded into the background in the last two hours.

As she was thinking of this, she stepped off the bus and into the heat of the late afternoon in another new town. She realized that she literally did not know what her next step should be. Kyler turned around and said, "Goodbye, Sarah Martinez." Just when she was wondering what the appropriate gesture was for this moment—shake his hand? Hug him?—he smiled and turned away, and walked confidently toward the exit doors of the terminal.

"Goodbye," she said, taking a deep breath and sighing a little bit as she watched him walk away. Then she began to scan the terminal for Justin and Thaddeus. As she did so, she heard a noise that startled her: her phone was ringing. Quickly, she found where she had stuffed it in her bag and silenced it, then looked at who was calling. It was her father. She was embarrassed to realize that she had hoped, for half a second, that it was Kyler. That would have been exciting and fun; this was just the opposite. Her father never called her just to talk, or for any positive reason at all. If he called her, she was in trouble. She saw that she had already missed one call from him. It had been about six hours now since her shift ended at work. Probably, Jalen was worried, and had asked him to check up on her.

Of course, she wasn't going to answer. But now she had a real problem. She had to get rid of the phone, before Justin and Thaddeus showed up. But what if Kyler did try to call? Could she silence the phone, and ignore the calls from her family? No, that was silly. Sooner or later they would ask the police to use it to track her down. Even now, she had made it easier than she should have for them to trace her steps. And the truth was that there was no real point in maintaining contact with the stranger she had just met. Why hadn't she listened to Justin?

Then the phone made another noise. Not a call this time; a message. It was from Kyler! She opened it excitedly, but with growing anxiety as her guardians were bound to show up at any moment. It was a picture of a rack full of trail mix from the gift shop just outside the terminal, with a caption that read "In case you need to stock up." It made her smile, and at the same time made it entirely clear to her what she had to do. These messages would keep coming, and she would not be able to hide them from Justin. She quickly turned the phone's power off, looked around the terminal once more, then stuffed it back down into the bottom of her pack. She started walking toward the exit doors, somewhat aimlessly, unsure of how to proceed until her protectors showed up.

Suddenly she stopped. As she approached the doors, she was passing near to the line of people waiting to pass through the security checkpoint to enter the terminal. Midway back in the line was a man all in black, with an incredible amount of tattoos and piercings covering his face and neck, with bright green hair.

What should she do? There was still no sign of Justin or Thaddeus. He did not appear to have seen her, and she feared that if she changed course or pulled her hood on she would only cause herself to stand out. So she pretended that she had stopped walking to find something in her bag, then continued on with her face turned away from the burnout as much as possible without being obvious. For his part, the man showed no interest in her. He didn't even seem to be looking for anybody. He was more interested in the obvious discomfort his presence in the line created. When she was safely past him and through the exit doors, Sarah increased her pace and made her way out of the building, down a few steps and onto the sidewalk. She looked back. No one was following.

"Good job, Sarah. You handled that well." Justin was at her side. Thaddeus stood behind him.

Sarah was only slightly startled. His sudden appearances were less and less of a shock to her.

"Thank you. Where were you guys?" She was angry that she had been left alone to handle anything, but she realized that this was inconsistent with her desire, only a few minutes before, that her protectors would stay away long enough for her to keep a secret from them.

"We've been close. But we would not have been any help to you in getting past that guy. You did just fine without us."

"What do you mean?"

"Well, he wasn't looking for you. Many of them here in California haven't been mobilized to hunt for you yet. Because they are aware of our presence, we would have only attracted unnecessary attention."

Sarah felt her stomach turn a little when Justin used the word "hunt." It painted too graphic a picture of her situation. "So what now?" she asked without enthusiasm.

"Well, Sarah, now we need to find a place to sit and talk. Are you hungry?"

"I could eat." She did not feel like sharing with them that she had snacked extensively on the bus ride. It was time for dinner, and she would be glad to sit still for a bit.

"Okay, how about that little diner right there?" There was a small restaurant connected to the bus terminal. It looked cheap and was not at all crowded.

"Sure," Sarah shrugged. They made their way inside and immediately she was glad they did. The smell of hot food made her aware that the snacks had not really satisfied her. They found a table, and she was soon engrossed in the menu. It took her a moment to realize that Justin and Thaddeus, of course, were not looking at menus. They were looking at her. Justin noticed her awkwardness and dismissed it with a wave of his hand.

"You're just going to have to get used to it, Sarah. It doesn't bother us."

She looked back and forth at the two of them for a moment, sitting upright with their hands folded in their laps. "Okay," she said with a smile. "If you insist." She returned to the menu. A waitress appeared and put one place setting on the table. Sarah ordered a burger and fries, and waited to address her companions until the woman was out of earshot.

"So," she said, "what do we need to talk about?"

Justin shared a look with Thaddeus and then began: "Well, Sarah, things have obviously changed. Our plan to get you into Mexico by the end of the day didn't work out, and now we're faced with the reality that it will take multiple days to get you where you're going, and you will need to sleep …"

Sarah nodded.

"…and your pursuers will not." Justin paused to let this sink in.

"Oh. Right." Suddenly Sarah felt like she was back in her living room, facing ridicule from her father for being different from everyone else. "Sorry," she said in an embarrassed, frustrated tone.

"There is no need to apologize, Sarah. Your need for sleep is normal. It is the way you were made."

"But you said yourself, most people aren't like me. Everyone else gets by on sleep-replacers. And now I'm slowing us down and putting us in danger."

Justin smiled. "First of all, Sarah, let's be clear. We," he gestured to himself and Thaddeus, "are not in any danger."

Both angels smiled, but Sarah was not in the mood for joking. "Thanks, that makes me feel a lot better."

Justin continued, still smiling, but more serious. "And Sarah, sleep-replacers, like all drugs, have consequences, more than most people know. Sleep is a gift from your heavenly Father, Sarah, and the fact that He made you uniquely dependent in this way is not something to be ashamed of."

Sarah heard everything he said, but the word *Father* gave her a slight internal shock. It was a contradiction on so many levels. Her whole life she had only known one father, who ignored her, belittled her, and caused her to dislike and doubt herself. To think that she had another Father, who had her best interests in mind? Who had made her uniquely and loved her with all her flaws? But who considered a frustrating limitation a gift? And who was the mastermind behind war and bloodshed? She had too many questions, but she was not ready to ask them. So she simply said, "Okay, but the reality is I can't keep going, and they can. So what do we do?"

"Well, we'll need to get away from cities altogether. As I said, they're not all mobilized yet, but that will change. We need to completely disappear, in the hopes that they'll give up. By now they're aware you're headed south, for the border, so we'll need to find a place to cross that's less populated. We'll get to the edge of town, spend the night in a hotel, and in the morning we'll take back roads, hitchhike, and probably even do a little walking."

"Walking? But we have 600 miles to go!"

"More than that, actually. But we have three weeks, Sarah, and I think it's reasonable to say we can expect some things to go our way." He glanced upward as he said this last part, with a hint of sarcasm in his voice.

Sarah sighed loudly. "Isn't hitchhiking dangerous?" she asked.

"For single young girls who aren't accompanied by angels, yes."

She rolled her eyes at him and did not answer. Her food arrived and she began to devour it. After several bites, she held a french fry and offered it to Thaddeus. He smiled and shook his head.

"You sure? Man, you guys are missing out," she said through a mouthful of food. When she finished, she paid her check and they stepped out onto the sidewalk to find the sky much darker than when they had entered the diner.

"Follow me," Justin said. They walked for several blocks without speaking. Sarah found both the walk and the silence to be refreshing. It was a warm evening, and it felt good to stretch her legs after filling her belly full of greasy diner food. And the day had been so full that she was simply out of things to say, overwhelmed and suddenly exhausted. Just when she was beginning to grow tired of walking, she saw that they were approaching a small, clean, motel on a quiet street. Justin instructed her to go inside and get a second-floor room for one, which she did. After paying and receiving a key, she headed up a set of outdoor stairs to find her room. Justin and Thaddeus were behind her. Suddenly a thought occurred to her.

"Um, I don't know how I feel about sleeping with you guys in the room."

"Don't worry, Sarah, we'll be outside. We fully understand that it will be important for you to have some time to yourself, for reasons of privacy, and also just for your own growth."

Growth? What did he mean? Was this some kind of reference to Kyler, or her phone? What did he know?

"I don't understand," she said.

"Well, growth happens with a combination of experiences and reflection upon those experiences. It's hard for you to process what's happening in your life with an audience. It will be good for you to have some time to yourself in the evenings, and to do some reading, too."

"Got it. So, 'evenings,' plural, huh? How many 'evenings' do you think we're talking about?"

"I don't know, Sarah. Don't worry."

"Sure." She was opening the door to her room now. "Well, good night." She entered the room, shut the door, and surveyed the simple furnishings. She set her pack on a chair, and was headed for the bathroom when she turned, went back to the door, and opened it to find Justin and Thaddeus standing silently on either side of the doorway.

"You guys won't be cold out here all night? Or, do you need chairs or something?" She asked.

They laughed. "No, Sarah. Thanks for asking."

"Right. Of course. Well, good night." Once inside, she showered, and then put she same clothes back on—Justin had not instructed her to bring pajamas. She settled into a chair and pulled the Bible out of her backpack.

As much as she enjoyed reading, she often found it hard to begin. It felt like the moment she opened a book, a thousand distractions flooded her mind and prevented her from giving herself to the simple task of reading. But then there were times, like tonight, when her introverted personality found reading to be a wonderful escape. She could read as an alternative to thinking, to dealing with her life, and let the book do the thinking for her. It was refreshing not to have any decisions to make, no enemies to flee from. All she had to do was let her eyes scan the page. From the moment she opened the cover she felt her whole body relax. She had given a lot today, and now it was time to receive.

She read for half an hour or more before she began to feel sleepy. She was just trying to decide what to wear to bed when there was a knock on her door. Her heart froze for a moment, but quickly a voice came: "Sarah, it's Justin."

She opened the door, and rubbed her eyes, a little more than she needed to, to let him know she would rather be in bed.

"Sorry to bother you, Sarah. I realized that you should probably be a part of this. It's not something people normally get to witness, but in your case I think it's appropriate. Will you follow me?"

His words were mysterious enough to make her forget that she was tired and follow him without question. As she crossed the threshold she noticed that Thaddeus was not there. She followed Justin down the stairs and around the back of the building to a small backyard area with a modest lawn, a single picnic table, and a broken-down wooden fence, beyond which was an overgrown field of weeds, bushes, and small trees. Thaddeus was standing by himself in the middle of the grass. It was strangely silent.

"What's going on?" she asked.

Justin looked at Thaddeus, then back at her. "Thaddeus is being dismissed," he said.

"What? Why? He's been so great!" She turned and looked at her guardian angel, the strong, quiet protector who had watched over her since birth, of whom she had only recently become aware, and for whom she now realized she had developed a deep gratitude. "You've been so great!" she said, and turned back to Justin:

"I don't understand. Has he done something wrong?"

"Quite the opposite. Thaddeus has served well. His task was an important one, and it is now complete. You are safely in my hands. He will receive reward and a period of rest before his next assignment."

"But, we need him! There are so many of them! Don't you still need his help?"

"No, actually, having both of us here, as I said earlier, calls more attention to you from those who have the right kind of sensitivity. Our plan is to move undetected now. We only need one."

"So why not him? He's my guardian."

"Yes, Sarah, but you now represent something larger than yourself. You are the last believer under my protection as Supervising Angel of the United States of America. This task is mine."

Sarah was about to mount another argument, but instead she simply started crying. The fatigue of the day had caught up with her, and she was broken. She stumbled toward Thaddeus and put her arms around him, which he received awkwardly. She cried harder as he put an arm around her shoulders. "Thank you so much," she blubbered. "Thank you. I don't know … I don't know how …"

"It's all right, Sarah. You don't have to. My reward awaits me. It has been an honor and a privilege." He put his hands on her shoulders, as a way of looking her in the eyes and also bringing her hug to an end. "You will be fine. If I could choose a protector for you, I would choose Justin." She looked over her shoulder doubtfully. He turned her head back toward him and lowered his voice. "Do something for me, Sarah." She nodded. "Be brave. Don't ever give up. Keep learning and growing, and don't forget what you already know. Okay?"

Sarah nodded again through tears. She backed away and Justin approached Thaddeus. He raised his voice slightly and declared, "Thaddeus, faithful guardian, you have served well and are hereby released from duty until called upon. Your reward awaits you." Then he approached his friend and embraced him warmly. He stepped back and Thaddeus bowed slightly toward both of them. He looked upward, and for a moment appeared to raise just slightly off the ground. Then there was a flash of light, bright enough that Sarah covered her eyes. When she looked again, Thaddeus the angel was gone.

Her tears returned with full force. She turned without speaking to Justin and walked, stumbling, back around the building, up the stairs, and into her room, where she collapsed on her bed and was soon asleep.

24 On the road

The next morning Sarah awoke to the sound of Justin again knocking on her door.

"Sarah," his muffled voice said, "time to get moving. This place has a free breakfast downstairs you should take advantage of. It's only there for another half an hour."

Sarah opened her eyes and stared at the ceiling of the little hotel room. *20 days*. She had slept a long time. Yesterday had been exhausting. She reviewed it in her mind: sneaking out of the house, Thaddeus waiting on the sidewalk, burnouts on the MAX and at work, saying goodbye to Torin, the march to the bank, the constant presence of her pursuers, the train station, the ride south, the change of plans, the bus ride—meeting Kyler. Saying goodbye to Thaddeus. Had it really all been one day? Was she really doing this? Running away from home, believing in things she had no proof of, putting her life into the hands of an angel? An angel? And one who, more often than not, she found herself more frustrated with than grateful for? *Before it is all over, you are going to have to do a lot of trusting*. That's what he had said, that day at Java Stop. Looking back over the last 10 days—is that all it had been?—she felt like she had done a lot of trusting already. And it clearly wasn't "all over" yet.

"Coming," she said sleepily. "Give me a few minutes."

She readied herself, packed her things, and went downstairs.

After a quick breakfast, she checked out at the front desk and stepped out into the warmth of the morning. It was just after 9:00am, and already she didn't need her sweatshirt. It felt so different from Portland that she couldn't help but feel just a little bit like she was on a vacation. The blue sky and sunshine made the day seem promising. At breakfast she had been mulling over the events of the previous evening and relishing a bad attitude toward Justin, but at the moment it was hard to be anything but cheerful. Once they had taken a few steps down the sidewalk, and no one else was around, she asked him, "Well, what now, travel guide? What's the plan? Should I look for some cardboard and a big black marker? 'Mexico or Bust'?

He smiled. "Maybe later. First we need to go shopping."

"Shopping? I like the sound of that! I'm on a budget, you know. But I could use some shorts and stuff if it's going to be like this."

"No shorts. We're going to a sporting goods store."

Sarah didn't attempt to hide her disappointment. "Oh. What for?"

"A real backpack. And a sleeping bag."

"A sleeping bag? Like, for outside?"

"Yes, like for outside. We're not going to be able to do hotels every night. You're on a budget, you know," he smiled. She did not. "And there may be times when a hotel is not the safest option."

"'Times'? Won't I be in Mexico in just a couple of days?"

"I hope so. And do you know what your sleeping arrangements will be like after that?"

She stared blankly at him. Until that moment, getting across the border had been as far as her thoughts had gone. It was the goal. What would happen after that? What was the plan? Was there a plan? Just when her mind was beginning to spin with a hundred new doubts and fears, Justin interrupted her thoughts.

"Me neither. So you should probably have a sleeping bag. There's a store just a few blocks away."

They walked in silence for a minute while she debated which

question, out of the many she had to choose from, to ask Justin first. But when she opened her mouth, what came out wasn't a question at all.

"I'm still mad at you, you know."

"I know."

"I mean, for one thing, it just didn't seem like enough, you know? He protects me my whole life, and then there's just this pathetic send-off. 'See you later, Thaddeus, thanks for being there for me every second for the past 19 years.' His boss shakes his hand in some dumpy old field, and that's it? I mean, hasn't he earned more than that?"

"Absolutely he has. And he will receive it. Sarah, you're missing the fact that Thaddeus didn't expect, and couldn't really have enjoyed, any sort of reward while he was here. This is not the place for celebration, Sarah. This is the battlefield. His reward awaits him."

"Oh. Well, I guess I didn't think of it that way. Still, I wish I could have done more for him."

"Well, that's very kind, Sarah, and please don't be offended by this, but the thanks that matter most to us don't come from you. Most guardians never even get what you gave Thaddeus, and we're fine with that. Thaddeus is now in the presence of the One whose very words bring refreshment, joy, and pleasure." A slightly wistful look crossed Justin's face.

"And you're jealous," Sarah said. "You wish you were there."

"Not jealous. That's a human thing. I'm happy for Thaddeus. And yes, I look forward to my own day of refreshment. My reward awaits me. But not before the task is done. We're here." They had entered the parking lot of a large outdoor store. "I'll stay outside. Get a full-sized backpacking pack, and make sure it fits you. Get the warmest sleeping bag they have." He saw her open her mouth to object, and held up his hand to silence her. "The warmest they have. Again, make sure it's in your size. Look for items on clearance. Also, see if they have any freeze-dried foods that sound good to you.

When you get to the counter, the sales clerk will ask what you're preparing for. Tell him you're going to hike some of the Pacific Crest Trail—which is true, I believe we'll spend at least one day there. The man behind you in line will mention that he's headed east if you need a ride. Tell him you'd love one. I'll be waiting over there in his truck."

"What? How do you know that?"

"I know. Go."

Sarah felt like a soldier taking orders from a superior officer. She didn't like it. She entered the store and was overwhelmed by the sheer amount of clothing and gear, all of which came from a world she had no experience with. Did she need a warmer jacket? Some of those socks? What about a water bottle? Or a water filter? Justin hadn't given her enough instruction. She found the clearance section in the back of the store, and a backpack that seemed to fit pretty well. It had so much more room than her small pack that she couldn't imagine needing it. Still, she didn't want to have to explain to Justin why she hadn't listened to him. She found a sleeping bag, also on sale, that was rated to zero degrees. Zero degrees? Who sleeps outside when it's zero degrees? There was another that was for down to negative 15 degrees, but it was an ugly black whereas the first one was a pretty purple color. She took the purple one, along with the backpack, over to the food section. Everything was expensive, and unappealing. She grabbed some trail mix, and a couple of freeze-dried macaroni and cheese meals. Ugh. On her way to the counter she picked out a warm pair of socks and a water bottle that caught her eye because it had a cute little mountain goat on it.

When the man behind the register rang up her purchases, he said, "Nine hundred seventy-three dollars. You got some good deals."

"Yeah," said Sarah, disturbed that she was spending such a large chunk of her budget on items she couldn't imagine getting much use out of. She didn't have enough money in her pocket and had to dig down to the bottom of her pack to find more. She finally presented it to him and he began putting the smaller items in a bag.

"Gearing up for a big trip?" he asked with a friendly smile.

"Yeah, I'm going to be hiking some of the, um, Pacific Crest Trail?" Sarah hoped she was saying it right.

"Need a ride?" The voice came from behind her. She turned to see a tall, sloppy-looking man who was dressed like a rock-climber, or at least like he wanted people to think he was a rock climber. His broad smile was partially hidden by his shaggy blonde hair and unshaven face. "I'm headed over to the east side today."

"Actually, yes, that would be great," Sarah said, thinking to herself that she would never have accepted his offer if Justin had not prepared her to. "Are you leaving soon?"

"Right now. My truck's outside," he said. "Just let me pay for my stuff here." He was carrying a small stove and an armload of fuel canisters. Sarah nodded and lingered by the door, then followed him outside. As they approached his truck, she expected to see Justin standing nearby, or sitting in the bed, but he wasn't. Then she saw him: sitting in the small area behind the driver's seat. When she and the driver had both taken their seats inside, he winked at her and motioned for her to put her purchases back where he could take a look at them. She did so, and as the truck pulled out of the parking lot and made its way down the street he examined everything. Finally he nodded his approval and gave her a thumbs-up sign, which gave her an unexpected feeling of accomplishment.

"So, I'm Matthias," said her driver. His voice had a bit of a surfer quality to it that was entertaining to a girl from Portland. "Hiking the PCT, huh? That's awesome. You going solo?"

"Um, no, I'll be ..." she looked at Justin, who mouthed the word *supported*. " ...supported. And I'm not doing the whole thing or anything. Just a little bit. I'm Sarah, by the way."

"Sarah. Good. Supported is the way to go. I mean, no offense, but you look a little new to this."

"Yeah, I am," she said, and then, proud of herself for thinking of this, she said, "but you seem like a local. Maybe you can give me some advice." This received another thumbs-up from Justin.

"Sure, anything."

Justin interrupted and spoke aloud, and Sarah forced herself not to look in his direction. "Ask him where he can drop you off that's close to a trailhead, and how far it is from there until the trail crosses another highway."

"Yeah, um, I want to get started on a short section first, so will we be near any trailheads where you're going, and how far from there to the next road going south?"

"Actually, I can drop you off right at the trail here in a couple of hours, and from there it's only about thirty-five or forty miles to the next place your friends can meet you."

Sarah tried to remain calm. "Oh. Okay. Thanks," was all she said, but then she turned and mouthed *forty miles?* to Justin. He smiled and mouthed *that's perfect*. She shook her head but then stopped when Matthias turned and looked at her.

"Everything okay?"

"Yeah, fine. Perfect. Thanks so much for doing this." She said with a pretend smile, then turned and glared at Justin again. What was he thinking?

The ride passed pleasantly enough. The scenery was beautiful, and Matthias made conversation about hiking and mountain climbing and backpacking, most of which Sarah only half-listened to. It was still amazing to her that he didn't have more questions about her. From her perspective, someone who was shopping for a backpack that morning with no plan for how she was going to get to a trail 60 miles away that afternoon was suspicious, or crazy. But in his world this kind of thing was not at all surprising. It crossed her mind that he was just the kind of person they needed today. *Well done, Justin,* she thought to herself.

After about an hour and a half, they pulled over at a simple turnout in the middle of the woods, with a brown sign that said "Pacific Crest Trail."

"Here you go," Matthias said as he opened his door.

This is it? This is the middle of nowhere! Sarah thought. But she said "Oh, um, you don't have to get out. I've got it." She wrestled her two backpacks and shopping bag out of the car, realizing that an experienced hiker would probably have used the drive to pack everything neatly in the newer, larger one. "Thanks again."

Matthias was digging around in the back of his truck. He emerged and approached her with an armload of supplies. "Here," he said. "I don't need any of this." He set a small stove on the ground next to her pack. "I just replaced this today, but it still works okay. Enough to boil water." There were also two of the fuel canisters he had bought that morning. "And, I don't really like this kind, but it looks like you do." He handed her two more of the Macaroni and Cheese meals.

"Oh, wow, thank you," said Sarah, caught off guard by his generosity. "Thanks so much. You don't have to do this."

"No, it's fine," he said. "And here's some waterproof matches, just in case. I always carry a bunch of them. And a fork! Do you have a fork?" Sarah shook her head. "Always need a fork. Here you go. Be safe out there, okay?" He surveyed her pile of supplies, then looked her up and down, and then eyed the trailhead for a moment. "You sure you'll be all right?"

"Yeah, I'm fine. Just need to, um, take some time to put my stuff together, and then, you know, hit the trail!" She mustered as much enthusiasm as she could in an effort to convince him that she was doing this voluntarily.

"Well, okay then. Good to meet you, Sarah. Good luck." He opened the door of his truck. "You sure?"

"I'm sure. Good to meet you, Matthias. Thanks again."

The truck pulled away and she was standing alone amid the pile of her belongings that lay strewn in the dirt of the turnout. She turned on Justin and said in an aggravated tone, "Forty miles?"

Justin smiled, "Sarah, this is perfect. We've just accomplished our goal of getting east, away from the population center, and we did it using private, untraceable transportation from a guy who probably won't remember your name two days from now. We disappear into the woods for a couple of days and come out on the other side, where no one is looking for us, and we can hitchhike our way south from there. I know it's not what you were expecting, but I really do believe this is the best way to go."

The look on her face showed that she did not share his confidence, but she knelt and began to organize her belongings. She took everything out of the bookbag, stuffed the new sleeping bag into the lower compartment of the new backpack, and put her clothes, food, and everything else in the larger, upper compartment, with her money in a separate zippered pocket. At a moment when Justin appeared to be admiring the scenery, she slipped the phone, still turned off, into the compartment with the sleeping bag. Finally she put her Bible on top and zipped it shut. She stood and hoisted the pack onto her shoulders. It felt surprisingly good. She was glad she had chosen to wear sturdy running shoes for this trip. She felt strong and capable, ready for an adventure. She wished Kyler could see her like this.

Justin pointed to the small empty backpack at her feet and said, "Better hide that."

She bent down to pick it up and almost fell over. It was a reality check. Wearing the pack was one thing. Walking forty miles in it would be another. Maybe it would turn out to be closer to thirty-five. But she downplayed the strain it took to stand upright again, and carried the bag over to the edge of the trees.

"Think I might need it again?" she asked.

Justin shook his head. She shoved it behind a big tree and kicked some leaves and sticks over the top of it. "Okay," she said. "Let's go."

"Let's go," agreed Justin. He gestured for her to lead the way, and she took her first steps down the trail. The weight of the pack required a period of adjustment, and she spent the first several moments in a silent battle with herself, wondering if she was going to be able to do this, kicking herself for being such a weakling, and fuming at Justin for the continuing deterioration of their travel plans. Yesterday she had been on a train. A nice, comfortable train. Sitting in a chair as the miles flew by. Then a bus, where she had met Kyler. Now she was alone in the woods. It was hot, and she had no idea where she was, and this was her lot for the next several days. This sparked another thought.

"Justin, how long does it take to hike forty miles?"

"Well, today is half over. Probably the rest of today, and then, depending on how much climbing we do, and how fast you are, another three days?"

"Three days. Wow." She decided she was not going to talk to Justin anymore for a while. Her body was adjusting to carrying the pack and she was less overwhelmed and anxious than she had been for the first half a mile, but she was still not ready to forgive him. He had said that angels didn't always need to talk. Fine. If she had to walk in the woods, she would do so in silence for the rest of the day.

On the trail

The unexpected result of walking through the woods in silence for an entire afternoon was a level of internal peace that Sarah had never known in her nineteen years of city life. At first, of course, she was grumpy, then hungry, then, after she had stopped to eat some trail mix, grumpy again for another couple of miles. But then she began to notice the birdsong. It came and went, at times just a twitter or two here and there, and at times a chorus that echoed through the woods like joy put to music. It seemed, to her, like the sound of reassurance. Surely nothing bad could happen in a place like this, not while that kind of sound was filling the air. Once, she paused at a bend in the trail to discover a surprising view of a little valley and a creek running through it. She had crossed that creek only fifteen minutes ago; she had gained significant altitude but hadn't even really noticed the extra effort because she was so distracted by the birds. Occasionally she saw one and watched it flit through the trees for a minute or two. She also caught glimpses of cute little gray squirrels; they made her smile every time they scampered up a tree trunk at her approach.

They were not in an especially scenic part of the trail. Sarah's mental image of hiking had involved huge mountains and grand vistas. Instead, they were simply walking along a trail through the trees, occasionally crossing a creek or a small field of grasses and flowers. There were slight changes in elevation, but nothing serious. This was fine with her. She was in no mood to climb mountains, both because of the physical effort and the feeling of exposure she imagined that would involve. The woods seemed smaller, safer. She was able to go for long stretches of time without thinking about anything at all. Occasionally a twinge of guilt about those she had left behind, or of anxiety about what lay ahead, would cross her mind, but those issues seemed distant and unreal at the moment. Even more so, the green trees, blue sky, and slow pace seemed to be washing away the intensity of the past couple of days with every step. To her complete surprise, she found herself grateful for the present moment, even thinking that there was nowhere else she would rather be. This meant, of course, that Justin had been right. He had graciously been following her without speaking for a couple of hours now. There had been moments when she forgot he was there. She felt guilty for her earlier grouchiness. She would have to apologize at some point.

Twice they crossed paths with hikers headed the other direction. In both cases, the people were friendly, but didn't seem interested in stopping to chat. Sarah was grateful and realized this was because they were trying to make it to the road, probably to be met by someone who was picking them up, before the sun set. She started to think about her own evening plans. She couldn't go on enjoying the present moment all day. Sooner or later it would get cold and dark, and she had never spent the night in the woods before. What now?

"Justin?" She stopped and turned to face him.

"Yes Sarah?"

"Um, so, first of all … this is really beautiful. I'm glad we're here. I'm sorry I doubted you before."

"Easily forgiven, Sarah. I've been thinking about what it would be like to be in your position, and I'm sure the past two days have been even more stressful than, well, than any other time since you met me. I understand that you weren't expecting to disappear into the wilderness."

"No, for sure, but it's nice. So, that's what you've been thinking about all this time, walking along?"

"Not the whole time. But it has been nice to slow down and have the time to think. It's been a long time since things were as simple for me as a walk in the woods."

"Me too." Sarah smiled. "But I am starting to wonder about tonight. I'm getting tired. And hungry too."

Justin nodded and looked around. "Right. We should start looking for a place to camp. Let's keep going for another little bit and see if we can find some water and some flat ground, maybe a bit off the trail where you won't be seen."

Sarah looked over her shoulder, suddenly nervous. "You think they followed us out here?"

"No, no. But you're a single girl out here, and we're trying to avoid any kind of memorable contact. Even someone who was just trying to be helpful could slow us down."

"Okay." She shifted the pack on her hips and winced. She was going to be sore tonight. "But just a little further, okay?"

"Sure."

It was another twenty minutes before they found a spot that seemed right. Sarah filled her water bottle at a stream after Justin assured her that it was safe to do so. Then she walked up over a small hill and down the other side to a small clearing with a view of some bigger mountains, out of sight of the trail. Justin showed her how to operate the stove Matthias had given her so she could eat one of the freeze-dried meals. She boiled some water, added it to the pouch, and stirred until the steam stopped rising. When she tasted it she couldn't help making a dissatisfied frown.

"Not that great, huh?"

"No. Wish I had some salt."

"Hmm. Sorry."

"No, it's okay." She surveyed their surroundings as she ate. There was a grove of aspen trees across the clearing that were rustling with the evening wind. A few of the larger mountains they could see had snow on top. She had never been anywhere like this. Her head continued to swivel slowly back and forth as she took it all in, stopping every few moments to scoop more macaroni and cheese out of the pouch with her fork.

"I feel bad," she said after a while.

"Why?"

"Well, I mean, obviously, I'm the one slowing us down. You could go forever, and there's even a little daylight left. Maybe there's another spot a little further on ..." She stood slowly and could not hide how stiff she was.

Justin shook his head. "Sit," he said. "Let me explain something to you, Sarah."

He did not immediately continue, but looked upward for a moment as if searching for the right words. Sarah sat back down on the rock that had been her chair and waited while the angel collected his thoughts. Then he spoke:

"The people of this world, Sarah, they walk out their doors each morning and they are on a journey of their own making. They make their own choices, and they are often neither guided in those choices nor protected as they carry them out. They tell each other that 'everything happens for a reason,' but they are wrong, very wrong, about the reason for life itself. They have cut themselves off from the Reason. So when they find themselves in a situation where they're worried that things aren't going to 'work out,' they have every reason to be worried. There are no guarantees for them, because God has not promised to help them achieve their self-made goals.

"But you, Sarah, if you're a true believer, then it's different for you. You're not writing your own story anymore. You can trust that if you are faithful, things will, in fact, work out. You don't have to live in anxiety about every little detail, because you are being guided. You are being protected. And your Guide, your Protector, is not only the Reason, He is also reasonable. You can eat when you're hungry. You can sleep at night. You will get where you need to go. Does that make sense?"

"Yes, it does. Except ..."

"Except what?"

"Except that's the second time you've said 'if' I'm a believer. Other times you've definitely told me I am. So which is it?"

Again Justin delayed a while before answering. Finally he said,

"Two things. First, doesn't it seem a little backward that you're asking me that? If someone truly believes something, does someone else have to tell them?"

There was truth to this, and Sarah knew it. She thought for a moment. "I don't know, I mean, most of the time I believe. More and more every day, actually. But it's hard to hold onto. I mean, I don't want to complain, but how many people have to go through what I'm going through? Giving up my family and my job, believing crazy stories, chased by murderers, leaving home with ... you guys. It's a lot to ask," she ended weakly.

Justin shrugged. "I don't know about that. Someday you may see that this journey has been a great gift. You may even come to understand that everyone who believes walks a similar path. Some have had an easier time than you; some, actually, have had it much harder." He ignored the doubtful look on her face and continued, "In any case, here is the second part of my answer: I think, Sarah, that you believe as much as you know, but there are a great many things that you don't know yet. When the time comes and you are confronted with those things, your faith will again be called into question."

"And you don't know how I will answer that question?"

"All I know is that I have been told to ensure your safety on the journey. I cannot see into your heart, Sarah." He paused and looked around at the dimming sky. "I also know, as I was saying earlier, that there is always time for those things that are most important. There is still some light in the sky. I will leave you alone for a while, to read and have some time to yourself." He stood and pointed to the ground under a nearby tree. "I'd sleep there. Put everything back in your pack and keep it close. I'll keep the animals away. Goodnight, Sarah." He turned and walked back over the hill toward the trail.

Sarah felt a sudden chill, which distracted her from having any profound (or aggravated) thoughts in response to what Justin had said. It was going to get cold. She took out her Bible and a sweatshirt, put everything else in her pack, and then took the sleeping bag out of the lower compartment. When she did so, her phone fell out and onto the ground, but she quickly put it back in the bag and pulled the zipper shut. She rolled out the bag on some pine needles where Justin had pointed, and lay down to read. Then she realized she had no pillow. After a moment of squirming, she had the idea to take all the clothes she wasn't wearing and put them in the stuff-sack the sleeping bag had come in. She was pleased with herself when she put it under her head and it formed a perfect headrest.

She settled in and began to read in the dimming light. After a while it was too dark to continue, so she lay and looked up at the stars as they began to come out. They were like nothing she had seen in Portland, where, between city lights and clouds, the night sky was usually rather unimpressive. Here it was majestic. She had the thought, as the day's adventures began to catch up to her and her arms and legs felt suddenly very heavy, that the stargazing was a natural follow-up to her reading, that somehow the two activities were related. As she was pondering this, she began to notice hoots, chirps, and the occasional snap of a twig: the night-noises of the forest. But she was not afraid. *It's nice to have an angel around*, she admitted to herself as she drifted peacefully to sleep.

26 Further down the path

Sarah woke early. The combination of the light in the sky and the fact that she was freezing made it impossible to sleep any longer. She rolled onto her side and let out an involuntary groan. Her hips were sore. All night long she had rolled back and forth between her right and left sides, trying to stay warm and find relief for whichever part of her body hurt most at the moment. Now there were simply no comfortable positions left. She gave up and flopped down onto her back for a moment. *19 days*. Somehow the fact that it was less than twenty made it seem like time was about to start moving more quickly, like they were at the top of a hill and would pick up speed on the way down. She contemplated her situation. They had probably covered about 6 miles in their half-day of walking yesterday. Too far to go back. She was so sore that she didn't want to lie here anymore, and so cold that she didn't want to get out of her sleeping bag. She had to go to the bathroom, but had never done so in the outdoors before. She knew breakfast would be a lot like lunch yesterday: trail mix and dried fruit. The thought of three more days of this put her in the sort of bad mood that she had a tendency to cling to, because the bad mood was the only thing that was enjoyable at the moment. If someone tried to take it away she would fight to defend it, because to give it up felt, somehow, like losing a small part of herself.

"Good morning, Sarah! How did you sleep?" Justin came strolling over the hill looking exactly the same as he always did: clear-eyed, clean shaven, obnoxiously bright and cheerful.

"Terribly. I'm cold and sore and hungry and I have to go to the bathroom. People do this for fun?"

"It is the price that must be paid in order to see some of the most beautiful places in the world. And it gets easier and more enjoyable with time, or so they say."

Sarah lifted herself up enough to look around at the surrounding trees and mountains, which only the night before had seemed so beautiful and brought her such a sense of peace. After a moment she said "Not worth it," and flopped back down on the ground. Then a new thought occurred to her and she sat up quickly.

"Hey, I did my homework last night."

"Good for you. You read anything interesting?"

"Yes I did." She was already flipping pages in her Bible, then found what she was looking and read loudly, "'Are not all angels ministering spirits sent to serve those who will inherit salvation?'" She closed the book with a satisfied smile.

"I see," said Justin with a look of disappointment. "So you spent your time learning about what I'm supposed to do, not what you're supposed to do."

"Not entirely. I just think it's interesting that you were sent to serve me. So I was thinking: maybe today you should carry the backpack. Don't know why we didn't think of that before, actually." She was playful, but also partly serious.

"I'm sorry, Sarah, but it doesn't work that way. What do you imagine that would look like to other hikers we might pass? A backpack floating in mid-air?"

"Oh." She hadn't thought of that. "Okay, then, what does it mean for you to serve me, then?"

"I'm not sure you have the right understanding of service. Good parents serve their children, Sarah, but not on their children's terms." He paused thoughtfully, then continued, "Jesus served you, and continues to do so, but not always in the ways you would wish for. This is because He knows best."

"I see. And you know best, too? Or at least, better than me? Which means you don't have to carry my backpack? I think it get it." Her sarcasm had a lightness to it. The conversation was drawing her out of her foul mood without her realizing it.

Justin shook his head and did not answer. Sarah forced herself out of the sleeping bag and shivered as she put her shoes on. "Well, here goes something new," she said as she strolled off across the clearing toward the grove of aspen trees. She returned after a few minutes, and had clearly been thinking about something.

"You've never used that name before," she said.

"What name?"

Sarah paused and looked around, knowing it was ridiculous, that no one was around for miles. Still, she had been trained well by the world in which she lived, and she could not shake the feeling that she was about to do something slightly wrong. Finally her mouth formed the word: "Jesus."

Justin nodded. "It is not a name I use lightly. Truthfully, that is one of the few times I have used it outside the context of worship. Where I come from, we say that name often, but almost always in songs of praise. I guess it's a little hard for me to say it and not be worshiping. It seems wrong, somehow."

"Well, people don't say it at all, not where I come from. I mean, you hear things in school, and of course I've been reading," she gestured to the Bible that lay open on top of her sleeping bag, "but that's the first time I've ever said it."

"How did it feel?"

Sarah thought about it, putting her hand to her lips as if the feeling might still be there. "Good," she said.

"Good. Okay, Sarah, we have to get moving. You should drink a bunch of water, fill your bottle, have some food, and hit the trail."

"Ugh. Water? But I'm already cold."

"Trust me. You need to jump-start your metabolism for the

day, and start flushing all the lactic acid out of your legs. And you have a lot of work ahead of you. We need to cover about 13 miles today, if we can. It will get pretty steep toward the end, but there's another great place to camp near a water source if we can make it."

"How do you know?"

"I went and scouted it out while you were sleeping."

"You left me?"

"Not for long. I'm pretty fast when a certain someone isn't slowing me down."

"Ha ha ha." They were at the stream now. Sarah drank as much cold water as she could handle and then stooped to fill her bottle. "Ugh. You sure that's necessary, mister 'I'm-not-even-really-physical'?"

"Yes. You don't have to be a car to know how they work, Sarah. There are books on such subjects."

"I'll remember that," she said as she opened a bag of dried apples and chewed unenthusiastically. "All right, let's go. I can eat while I walk."

"Good girl. After you." Justin gestured toward the trail.

It was a hard day of hiking, but it went quickly. Sarah was surprised when Justin suggested they stop for lunch. They had already had a couple of snack-and-water breaks, and she did not expect to see that this time the sun was straight overhead. She had been enjoying the scenery, which was becoming more and more impressive as they gained elevation. But there was nothing especially scenic in this particular location as she sat on a log and rested her legs, and she was anxious to keep moving. She had found her rhythm and wanted to make as much progress as possible. It did feel good to take the pack off, but the food (dried fruit and trail mix) was hardly a reason to linger. Then she had a thought.

"Does being higher up mean that it will be even colder tonight?"

"Yes, I'm afraid so."

"I don't want to think about it. Let's keep going." She shouldered her pack and started off down the trail.

They reached the place that Justin had scouted out just as Sarah was starting to feel really hungry. Again, the meal was bland, but her hunger made it tolerable. And again, the setting was beautiful, and her time of reading and watching the stars was an experience of peace, joy, and wonder. And again, the night was miserable. She awoke (*18 days,* her brain reminded her) colder and stiffer and grumpier than she had the morning before. Justin sensed it and did not force conversation. It was only after they had been walking for half an hour that the silence was broken, and Sarah was the one to break it.

"I did my homework again."

"Yes? And what did you learn about angels this time?" Justin joked.

"Funny you should ask. Something about the 'sons of God and the daughters of men'?"

There was no answer. Sarah stopped and turned to face Justin, who looked displeased.

"What?" For some reason she enjoyed upsetting him. "I mean, it's in there! Isn't everything in there supposed to be true? I mean, if it was off limits, couldn't He have erased it or something?"

"That's very true. But it's hardly the point of the story, even of that story. I wish you would focus more on the things that apply to you, Sarah."

"Don't worry, I'm reading the other stuff too. But are you going to explain it, or not? Come on, what does it mean? What happened?"

"I was not involved in that." He sounded like the military, coffee-shop Justin from two weeks ago. Giving just enough of an answer to raise more questions. She refused to let him get away with it.

"Okay, but that's not an answer. Are we talking about angels here? Is that what it means? Did you guys—some of you—marry humans or something? I mean, that's crazy! You can't blame me for being curious."

"First of all, Sarah, can we keep walking?" She rolled her eyes, but turned and headed up the trail. Once they were underway, he continued. "Second of all, you need to understand that that book you have is like no other book. It is perfect. It contains exactly the information it is supposed to contain."

"Right, that's what I'm saying! So the angels-marrying-humans thing, if that's what it is, is in there, so it's supposed to be in there! So let's talk about it!"

Justin continued. "And what I'm saying, Sarah, is that when something in there is unclear, it is still exactly as clear as it's supposed to be. You have all the information you need, and you're not going to get any more. I can't fill in the blanks for you, because they're intentionally blank. I can't supply you with that kind of information. It isn't my place to do so, and it isn't your place to ask."

"Oh." This was hard to take. He had a way of reminding her of her 'place' just as she was beginning to enjoy a conversation that felt like normal friendship. She was silent for a while, long enough for it to be clear that her feelings had been hurt. Then Justin made an attempt to break the silence:

"But anyway, like I said, I can tell you that I was not involved in that. And ... in case you were wondering, neither was Thaddeus."

"Okay, new subject. Those trees are huge, aren't they?" Sarah gestured ahead of them to a grove of pines, grateful that Justin could not see that her face had flushed red. But she smiled, and he chuckled, and the rest of the afternoon passed with no tension between them. It was only toward the end of the day, as dinnertime approached, that Sarah began to feel uneasy. Things had been quiet for some time, and suddenly she spoke:

"Justin, I don't want to do this again. I'm tired. The nights are so hard. It's so cold and the ground is so hard. I can't keep doing it." She didn't propose a solution, and she wasn't trying to accuse or attack him. She was just being honest.

Justin nodded and thought for a moment. "Well, we've hardly seen anyone today. Maybe we could build a fire tonight. And look for some mosses or something to make the ground a little softer for you. I'm sorry I haven't been more sensitive to that. Thanks for telling me."

A fire sounded wonderful. Once they had found their campsite, Sarah found the matches Matthias had given her, and Justin talked her through the process of digging a small pit, gathering kindling, and stacking the wood into a small tepee. Soon the fire was crackling and Sarah was sighing gratefully as she warmed her hands. Even the macaroni and cheese tasted better. As she ate, Justin spoke:

"Sarah, I have a concern."

"What's that?" She was expecting something about the campsite or travel plans, and was caught off guard by what he said next.

"Well, it's a pretty unique thing, this … arrangement." He gestured back and forth between the two of them. "Most people don't get to see angels, Sarah. I'm afraid it's having some unintended effects."

"Oh. But, that was the plan, right? I mean, you showing up and warning me and everything, you were … under orders, right?" She looked skyward as she asked this.

"Of course. And it is still the plan. But you seeing us, getting so used to us, is—well, it's just not normal."

"Okay, but why is that bad?"

"Because you're not really supposed to have a relationship with us."

"Look, I know. I've let that go. I wasn't serious about that. I mean, he is cute, but he knew me when I was a baby, and that's just weird." Sarah smiled, but Justin was still serious.

"No, Sarah, you misunderstand. I'm not talking about a romantic relationship. I'm talking about any relationship. It's unusual for a person, like you, to form a bond with one of us. It might get in the way."

"Get in the way of what? Justin, do you understand that I don't have anybody else? I mean, who else would I talk to? Who else knows what I'm going through? I'm really grateful you're here. I like that part of the plan." Sarah was surprised to realize how true these words were, even as she was saying them.

"Sarah, I'm honored. Thank you for saying that. But let me

explain. The most important relationship in your life is with God, Sarah. With the Father, and the Son, and the Spirit. And while my presence in your life has done a lot to increase your faith in things you can't see, there's also the danger that you'll ... stop there. That you'll get so comfortable in dealing with me that you won't see the need to go beyond our relationship and start talking directly with Him. He also knows what you're going through, Sarah. You can talk to Him. And I won't always be around to talk to. You should think of me like training wheels, or crutches. Sooner or later you have to learn to walk, to trust, without my help."

His words made sense, and Sarah nodded as she considered them. But she was also still thinking about her own words from the moment before. She felt suddenly guilty about the fact that she had made it so plain she would rather travel with Thaddeus.

"That night, when Thaddeus left—when you dismissed him—I was rude to you. I'm sorry."

"Apology accepted, Sarah, and easily forgiven. I understand."

"You do?"

"Maybe better than you do. You have father issues, Sarah, and you react to men in authority in a certain way. You struggle to relate to me because your father didn't have your best interests in mind and wasn't worthy of your respect. And you're at the age where, appropriately so, you're breaking out from under his authority and becoming your own person. There are some things about me you like, but you don't like being told what to do, even by someone who is right. Thaddeus never told you what to do, so he was much easier to like. He was everything your older brothers should have been. That, and he looks younger." Justin said all this as matter-of-factly as if he had been giving the weather report.

"Wow. I was just saying sorry. I didn't expect to be psychoanalyzed by an angel."

"Well, I'm sorry. And I do accept your apology. But I don't want to get sidetracked from my original point. I am not your father, Sarah, but there is One who wants to be, if you will let him. I'm happy to be your guardian on this journey, but that's all I am. I just want you to make sure the relationships in your life are receiving the proper amount of attention."

"You mean all two of them? Noted."

"It won't always be this lonely, I promise. This is a season that serves a purpose. Hang in there."

"Okay." She sounded unconvinced. Then, after a moment, Sarah added: "I do talk to Him, you know."

"Good," Justin said with a smile. "Keep it up. And speaking of that, I think I'll give you some time to yourself now. You can tear up some of those big leaves down by the creek and put them under your sleeping bag. It might make things a little softer tonight, and warmer too. Goodnight, Sarah." He stood and walked out of the circle of light created by the dying campfire, leaving Sarah alone with her thoughts.

Breaking away

The cold and stiffness were easier to take when Sarah woke up the next morning, partly because she knew to expect them by now, and partly because she knew this was her last day on the trail. "One more time," she said aloud as she lay looking up at the pale blue sky. After a few more moments of trying to summon up the willpower to move, she realized that she had woken without her usual mental countdown. How many days was it now? Sixteen days? Seventeen? *17 days. I think that's right.* After three days on the trail she had begun to lose touch with the outside world. She imagined the busyness of Portland, Sacramento (the nearest city she could think of), or any other major city on this very same morning. Noise, traffic, stress—it was so entirely different from her current surroundings that it was hard to comprehend that that was the world most people were waking up in. She wondered if, when the attack came, the noise would be heard in places like this. *I could just stay here,* she thought. *If I had a warm little cabin. And a soft bed. And a servant to make me a hot breakfast.* This line of thinking was not helping her with the challenge of making herself get up. She sighed heavily and rose to the familiar routine of emerging into the cold air and then digging through her makeshift pillowcase to find as many layers as possible to put on while she packed her sleeping bag away. She would shed them gradually as the morning went on, but at the moment they were a necessity.

"Good morning! Ready to go?" Justin was sitting on the ground a little ways off, leaning against a fallen log.

Sarah glared at him for a moment. "It must be nice," she said as she forced herself to sit up.

"What's that?"

"Look at you. You never have to change your clothes, or shave, or sleep, or eat. You never get tired, or sore. You just sort of float along through all this. I don't know, it just seems pretty easy to me."

Justin laughed. "'Float along,' huh?" He looked around. "No offense, Sarah, but compared to where I'm from, this isn't that nice. And true, I don't have the same physical challenges you do, but believe me, what I do—what we do—isn't easy."

Sarah thought about this for a moment. "And you haven't been back there in 400 years? Is that hard?"

"Well, first of all, time is different for me. And no, I'm not going to explain that. Second of all, it's worship, Sarah. It's a voluntary sacrifice. I serve as a way of expressing love. If it wasn't hard, it wouldn't be much of an offering. He is worthy of nothing less."

Sarah nodded as she considered his words. "You've used that word before, too. 'Worship.' I thought that was like singing and stuff."

"It is anything we offer as a tribute to His greatness. Singing is one way to do that—frankly, one of the easiest and most enjoyable ways. Where I come from there is a lot of singing, and it is as much His gift to us as ours to Him. But worship takes other forms. When you look up at the stars at night and your heart is filled with gratitude and amazement, that is worship. When you left Portland, that was an act of worship, much like my service here."

After a moment of thinking about this, Sarah nodded again. "Okay. So I'm a worshiper now. I like that. All right, let's get this over with." She rose, completed her morning routine as quickly as she could, and soon was ready to set off down the trail, the last of the dried apples in her hand.

They walked without speaking for much of the morning. Justin had scouted out their route overnight and informed Sarah that they had about 9 miles to go. They were losing altitude now, making their way toward a saddle in the landscape where the next highway passed through. The trail was dry and dusty, and the additional weight on her back made the long downhill sections more punishing than Sarah would have expected. She was tired, dirty, and highly motivated by the goal of finding the road and bringing this part of the journey to an end. At lunchtime, as she forced herself to eat one more meal of trail mix, Justin broke the silence:

"You haven't given me any updates on your 'homework' today."

"Nope."

"Did you not read?'

"No, I read. Just … I don't know. Lots of death. Lots of blood. I just … I don't know. I don't feel like talking about it right now."

"That's fine."

But Sarah continued despite herself. "It's just … I mean, like earlier, when you were talking about worship, I totally get it, I'm totally convinced. It's all true and everything. But then, I think about what's coming …" she gestured in the direction she assumed was west, toward the coast and the population centers, "and it's pretty hard to understand."

"I can see how, from your perspective, it would be. I've been around people enough to know that some things take years for you to understand, and we have put you in a bit of a time crunch. Can I try to explain it to you?"

"No, I don't think so, not right now. I'm kind of too tired, you know? Maybe tomorrow or something. Is that okay?"

"Of course. That's fine. Let's keep going."

Midway through the afternoon things changed. The trail began to rise again, climbing steadily for about a mile before it began the final descent toward the highway. The cumulative effect of the previous three days began to take its toll on Sarah's legs. Shortly after the climb began, she started to sweat far more than she had at any previous point on the journey. She had been drinking plenty of water, but still felt too hot and tired to go on. Her legs ached and trembled. Halfway up, they took a break in the shade while she rested, and after a moment Justin spoke.

"Sarah, I'm afraid it's going to be uphill like this for another half a mile or so. I'm sorry I didn't tell you this morning; I didn't realize it would slow us down as much as it has. After that it's two more miles of slight downhill to the highway."

"It's fine," Sarah panted between sips of water. "I can do it."

"Well, that's the thing. I'm not sure we should. At this pace we won't get to the road until dinnertime or later. Then it's ten miles to the nearest town, and we'd be hitchhiking in the dark. We don't know where we're staying, or have any kind of a clear plan beyond this point, and I'd rather face those challenges in the morning, when you're fresh. I think we should get to the top of this rise and then find some shelter after we drop down a bit on the other side. Then we spend the night and have a short hike in the morning to the road, and we have all the rest of the day to find a ride, find a hotel, and rest up before the next leg. Sound good?"

"Not at all. You're talking about another dinner of macaroni and cheese, another night on the ground, in the cold. I can't do that, Justin. Look, I can make it. Just let me rest for a minute, and we can go. I need to get to that road tonight. Okay?"

"Sarah, I'm sure you could do it. It's not about that. I really don't think it's the best plan. I'm sorry it means another uncomfortable night for you, but we'll do what we can to make it tolerable. Besides, I don't think it's an accident that you have one more package of macaroni." He said this last part with a smile, in an effort to keep things light, but Sarah was in no mood for the joke.

"'Uncomfortable?' Look, don't talk to me like you know what it means to be uncomfortable, okay Justin? I'm miserable! I'm done! I've put up with a lot in the last few days, and you told me we would be done hiking today, and I am done, do you understand?"

Justin stared at her in surprised silence. Sarah waited for the rebuke, but nothing came. After a moment of watching his face, Sarah realized something that felt, at the moment, like a small victory. *He doesn't know what to do.* Her outburst, her irrationality and emotion, had given her the upper hand. On an unconscious level, she realized that she could win arguments with Justin more easily than she ever could with her father, because the angel would not be manipulative or make the argument personal. He didn't want to win, he only wanted to do what was right, and this gave her the advantage. Her fatigue and anger made it easy to ignore the part of her conscience that knew it was wrong to use this advantage. She continued:

"I'm not talking about this anymore. I'm ready. Let's go." She stood quickly to hide her stiffness, threw her pack on in a show of strength, and continued the march up the trail.

Her anger—against Justin's insensitivity, against the pain in her legs and the seeming endlessness of the trail—propelled her up the rest of the incline. She reached the top sweating but proud of herself, and only paused long enough to breathe in and out once or twice before beginning the descent. As before, going downhill was painful in its own way, and before long the incessant pounding began to take its toll on her knees and upper legs. But she was on a mission. She was going to reach that road, and she was never going to go backpacking again. Surely, when she reached the bottom, there would be a passing car that would give a young girl a ride into town. It crossed her mind to pray for this, but somehow that seemed inappropriate given that she was ignoring the counsel of one of God's messengers. She didn't care. She was too tired. Things would work out. Suddenly Justin spoke from behind her.

"We should stop here."

Sarah looked around. "Why? We're so close! Justin, I'm not sleeping on the ground again. I need a bed and a cheeseburger. Come on, don't do this to me!"

"Sarah, I'm sorry. I know it's not your first choice. But it will be getting dark sooner than you think. There's a creek here, we have enough food, and I really think it's a bad idea to rush this. I think we should stay."

Sarah paused. She knew she was being carried by the momentum of her own emotions, and of the journey downhill toward her goal. But she felt right. She felt justified. She felt strong and she wanted to be taken seriously. When she opened her mouth, the words came out: "Then maybe you should."

"What?"

"Maybe you should stay here. You said yourself I needed to learn to get by without you. Well, give me a chance then. Let me do this. I'll be fine."

Justin was a bit stunned. After a moment he said, "Sarah, I don't understand where this is coming from. Just yesterday you were talking about how you were glad I was around."

"Right, and you told me not to get too comfortable with it."

"Sarah, I know what I said, but you're not ready. Do you really think you can get yourself all the way to Mexico?"

"No, I'm not talking about that. I'm talking about taking a break for a day or two. Sort of a trial run. Come on, I know I drive you crazy. Wouldn't it be nice to have a couple of days off?"

"Sarah, I think that is a very nice way of saying exactly the opposite of what you mean. No, I don't want time off. I can see that you do, but you're not thinking clearly. And I'm afraid you're confusing comfort with need. This is not the plan, Sarah. You need to trust me."

Sarah bristled at his use of the word *trust*. He was always throwing that in her face. She also resented the implication that she wasn't tough enough to do what was right. She was tough enough. Tough enough to find a ride and a hotel room all on her own, darkness or no darkness.

"Justin," she said in an even voice, "I am not sleeping on the ground tonight." Then she turned on her heel and walked down the trail.

28
A different path

Sarah marched along in silence. She was used to this, but now it felt different somehow. It was the silence of being alone. Twice she turned and looked back to see if Justin was following her. He wasn't. Good. Fine. She didn't need a babysitter.

It was only when she caught her first glimpse of the highway that she began to doubt her plan. Of course, she was relieved and a bit proud of herself, but it was also a reality check. Now she needed a ride. She was at the mercy of whoever happened to drive by. What if no one did? Or someone who would do her harm? She pushed these thoughts from her mind as best she could. She would be fine. *If I can handle Portland, I can handle this,* she told herself. She reached the end of the trail, where she found a simple dirt turnout much like the one where she had packed her backpack 4 days ago. Across the road, she could see where the trail continued south, back into the wilderness. *Never again,* she thought gratefully. She removed her pack with a sigh of relief and sat down in the dirt next to the road. She took her shoes off, which elicited another sigh. Her socks were filthy, her feet were sore (*No blisters. That's kind of amazing,* she thought to herself), and her shoes would never be the same. But she had done it. It was over.

Sitting felt good for about 10 minutes or so. Then stiffness set in, and surprisingly, cold. Her back was soaked with sweat, and without the pack on to hold in her body heat she began to get a little chilled. There was a breeze, and the sky was beginning to dim. It was definitely evening. Not nighttime yet, but evening. She stood and put on her sweatshirt. Walking slowly back and forth without the pack on felt good, and kept her warm. But now she was starting to get hungry. She opened her pack and took stock of her food supplies. No more dried fruit. A handful of trail mix. And the last macaroni and cheese. She stuffed the dried meal back under some clothes and took out the trail mix. *Not enough for breakfast anyway.* She ate it all, but it did little to curb her hunger. She thought again about the macaroni. *No way. I'm having a cheeseburger tonight.* She drank the last of the water in her water bottle and waited.

Then there was the sound of a car. It grew and grew but after a moment it became clear that it was coming from the west, headed the wrong direction, further up into the mountains. Soon it sped past her in the far lane, its headlights on, winding away into the dusk. It was darker and darker in that direction. She looked west again, where the sun was setting. Ten miles down that road, there was a town, with lights and sidewalks and fast food and a cheap hotel. Would she have to walk? Ten more minutes went by. Nothing.

It crossed her mind that perhaps there would be no cars, that she would be punished for her disobedience. It was a frightening thought, but it did not lead her to repentance. Instead, an angry cry—she would have hesitated to call it a prayer—arose from within her. *Don't do this to me,* she thought. *I've done so much for you. Given up so much. A soft bed is not too much to ask. I didn't sign up to walk to Mexico.* Now the hunger and the chills were working together to make her miserable. Justin had explained at one point that a full belly keeps you warm at night, because your body has calories to burn, sort of like fuel for a stove. *Justin, the angel who knows everything,* she thought. Again she contemplated the macaroni and cheese. No. That would be like giving in. She would wait. She picked up her pack and carried it to the eastern end of the turnout, positioning herself there so a passing car would have time and space to pull over after they saw her. Then she sat as close to the road as she dared and waited.

In five more minutes a car came speeding past, going west. She rose and waved her hands, but it didn't slow down. She sat down again, dejected, as its noise quickly disappeared into the night. Yes, she would have to admit, it was almost night now. There was still light in the western sky, but there were stars in the east. What if no one came? Could she walk ten miles? She didn't think so. Should she at least start walking? That seemed unwise on this narrow mountain road. What if there were no more turnouts?

Then she heard another car. *Please,* she thought. She stood and waved, and the car slowed, then pulled over at the far end of the turnout. She picked up her pack and ran over to it. The back door opened, and she saw that there was only one seat available. The other three were filled with smiling young people. The trunk popped open and one said "You'll have to put your pack back there." She did so, and had to shove aside a case of beer to make room for it. Once she was inside, the driver said "Where to?"

"Just the next town. Thanks so much for stopping."

"For sure. Are you okay? This is kind of the middle of nowhere."

"Oh yeah. My, um, friends were supposed to pick me up but got stuck in traffic. I can just wait at a restaurant or something." This was a lie, plain and simple. But she needed to seem normal, and she would never see these people again. Did it matter?

"No problem. I'm Jaxon." Jaxon introduced the other two passengers, his girlfriend in the front seat, and the guy sitting next to Sarah, whose names she promptly forgot. Sarah gave her name and then answered some questions about her trip, making up a story about wanting to see if she could do an overnight backpack trip by herself. They congratulated her on her bravery and toughness, and talked about some friends they had who had undertaken similar adventures. Soon Sarah saw the lights of a small town ahead.

"Any restaurant in particular?" Jaxon asked.

"Just a place I can sit down and get a burger," Sarah said. "Thanks again."

When they dropped her off and she had retrieved her pack, Sarah congratulated herself on having been right about finding a ride. There were plenty of nice people around. The world wasn't such a big scary place after all. Her good mood and confidence increased with the first bite of a greasy diner cheeseburger. Yes, this was definitely the right call. She had cola and fries, and a huge chocolate milkshake for dessert. It seemed that her body could not get enough food. But she knew that it also needed sleep, and she didn't let herself sit for too long after finishing the meal. She paid her bill and asked the waitress about local hotels. Fortunately, there was one only a couple of blocks away. It was hard to get moving again. Already she felt like she couldn't have hiked another mile, and it was hard to imagine that she had walked as much as she had in the past four days. She found the hotel and got a room on the ground floor. *No stairs for me*, she thought. She was soon in her room, and forced herself to shower before getting in bed. She was asleep almost instantly.

When she awoke, it was clear from the light coming through the window-shades that the morning was well underway. She rose stiffly and smiled, because the stiffness reminded her that she was not hiking today. She had slept without dreams for nearly eleven hours. After a moment she realized how thirsty she was, and drank a big glass of water, which almost immediately made her feel more fully awake. She used the bathroom and showered again, just because she could. In the middle of the shower, she started to feel hungry. Wasn't there a free breakfast at this hotel? She hurried and got herself ready, then went out to the lobby without packing her things. They were just putting the breakfast items away, but she was able to get a muffin, a banana, and an apple. Back in her room, she ate them as she packed her belongings, most of which were filthy. This gave her an idea. Heading back to the lobby, she checked herself out and asked the desk clerk if there was a laundromat in town. Yes, but it was several blocks away. That was okay. She could handle a few blocks.

Outside the sun was shining high overhead, and she was able to get a better idea of where she was. The mountain town was even smaller than she had realized, with the east-west highway that passed through serving as the one main street. This meant she was unlikely to see any burnouts, but also that to continue her journey south she would first have to make her way west, back toward more populated areas, or east, toward Nevada. She didn't know if there were any other major roads before the state line, and she wasn't sure if it was a good idea to cross the border. She tried to mentally avoid the reality that she didn't know what to do next. Her plan had only gone as far as food and a bed. Now that those were behind her, she was directionless. But she liked the idea of washing her clothes. That, at least, allowed her to put off any major decisions for another hour or so.

She found the laundromat and washed all her clothes in one load. As they were washing, she sat and read a magazine someone had left, then found another one to read as they dried. Less than an hour had passed and she was already starting to get hungry again. But she forced herself to wait. She slipped into the restroom and changed into clean clothes, then washed another load of the clothes she had been wearing. While they were drying, she waited until there was no one else in the room, then took the opportunity to count all her money. She had around five thousand dollars left. It was going fast. She realized that eating at restaurants was a luxury she probably shouldn't indulge in too often. Through the window of the laundromat she saw a grocery store across the street. Perfect. She could stock up on breakfast and lunch supplies and eat cheap fast-food dinners. Once her clothes were dry and she had re-packed her entire backpack, she made her way there and left the pack with a clerk at one of the checkout lines. She strolled through the store, picking out enough fruit, crackers, cheese-sticks, salami, and granola bars to last for two or three days.

Sarah's self-satisfaction had continued to increase throughout the morning. It felt good to take care of these details, to plan ahead and get ready for whatever was coming next, all on her own. She was proud of herself for being so responsible. But as she stood in the check-out line, she was again faced with the reality that she didn't know what was coming next. Once she had eaten her simple lunch and packed away her purchases, what then? She found herself wondering if Justin would appear soon. Did she want that? What would he say? Should she apologize? She paid for her food and lugged her pack clumsily out the door, and found an out-of-the-way place on the sidewalk outside the store to sit in the sunshine.

She watched the people going in and out of the store as she chewed happily on a plum. It was nice to be eating fruit that wasn't dried. The sun warmed her face as she surveyed the half-empty parking lot. An older, beat-up van pulled up next to the sidewalk and several younger people spilled out, laughing and flirting with each other. Their cheerfulness made her smile, but it also made her a little envious, and raised the issues of loneliness and not fitting in that were always somewhere in the back of her mind. They were so happy. Would she ever be a part of a community like that?

Then the driver of the van, who was the last to get out and who had been hidden on the far side of the vehicle until now, came into view. Sarah's heart skipped a beat. Long, dark, floppy hair. Casual clothes, and a charming smile. Was it really him? She had a frantic desire to somehow make herself look more presentable, and could find nothing to do but reach for the scattered pieces of her lunch and gather them together before he recognized her and stopped where he stood on the sidewalk.

"Sarah?"

She acted like she had not seen him until this moment. She raised her head, tossing her hair as she did so, and said "Kyler?"

"Sarah, I don't believe this! So good to see you! What are you doing here?" He hurried over to her and opened his arms to offer a hug, leaving her no choice but to stand and receive it. He stood back and looked her up and down. "Look at you! Doing some traveling, huh? I can't believe this? What are the chances?"

Sarah could not find words. "Yeah," she said, smiling.

Her speechlessness was not an issue, because Kyler had enough energy for the both of them. He turned to his friends. "Everyone, this is Sarah! We met on the bus to Redding a few days ago." He introduced her to the whole group, two other guys and two girls, who all looked to be in their twenties and as free-spirited as their leader. "Guys," he continued, "can you just get me a sandwich or something? I'm going to stay out here and chat with Sarah."

As his friends went inside, he sat himself down on the sidewalk next to her backpack. "Is this okay?"

"Sure. I mean, of course." Sarah was still in shock from the surprise of seeing him. She sat down on the other side of the pack.

"You sure? I sent you a few messages, and you didn't respond to any of them, so I thought maybe you were trying to cut me off for some reason."

"Oh, no! I just turned my phone off right after we met, and then I went and did some backpacking for a few days."

"Backpacking? Wow, good for you! By yourself?"

Sarah only hesitated for a moment. "Yeah."

"Sarah, I'm impressed. But was that a part of your original plan? I thought you were down here to visit friends or something."

"Yeah, my plans kind of … changed." Sarah realized that this was the kind of incomplete answer that frustrated her when it came from Justin, but obviously she could not tell Kyler the whole story.

Kyler was used to people having parts of their lives that they didn't share with others, and he respected her privacy. "Okay," he nodded. "So what now? You don't look like you're headed back to Portland."

"No, I'm going … south."

"South?" He made quotes with his fingers as he repeated this. "Well, aren't you mysterious, Sarah Martinez? Any particular destination 'south'?"

His use of her full name had the effect of making her feel

known. In fact, everything about their interaction had a welcome familiarity to it. He acted as if they been longtime friends. It felt good, and made it easy for her to let her guard down.

She sighed and then said quickly, "Okay, the truth is, I'm going to Mexico." She said this while looking straight ahead, but then peeked out of the corner of her eye to see his reaction. His eyes widened a bit, but he didn't seem terribly shocked.

"Mexico? What's in Mexico? You know somebody there?"

"No, not exactly."

"Uh-huh. Interesting. You have a plan to get across the border?"

"No, not exactly."

"I see. So why are you going?"

How should she answer this? Was she even clear on the answer herself? "Well, actually, for some of the same reasons you're going to Colorado." She gestured toward the van, rightly assuming that he and his friends were on the road for the journey he had described to her on the bus.

Kyler threw back his head and laughed. "Ha! I knew it! I knew it! And that wasn't just because of talking to me, right? You were thinking along those lines even before we met?"

Sarah nodded.

"I knew it! Oh, this is great! Sarah, listen: you have to come with us. Mexico is a bad plan. Come to Colorado! It will be great! Oh, this is too cool."

Sarah knew that something within her had not been right ever since her argument with Justin, but this invitation was too bold-faced, too drastic of a change in direction, to accept. Even in her current state, her heart would not allow it.

"Kyler, I don't … think so. Thank you, but I just don't …"

"What? Sarah, listen to me, I admire your bravery, but let's start with the obvious: you're a young girl traveling alone, and it's not safe." As he made this first point he made a fist and then stuck out his thumb, then continued counting off his other reasons on his fingers. "They won't let you cross an international border without a visa, which I doubt you have. If you were to get across somehow, you're just as likely to end up in an unsafe situation down there as you are here. You won't be able to get a job, you won't have any friends …" at this point he gestured to his van, as if to say that she was instantly welcome in his circle of companions. "Sarah, you have to come with us. It's fate! I mean, what are the chances of running into each other like this?"

She did have to admit that it was kind of amazing they had ended up in the same town, at the same grocery store, on the same day at the same time, she after completing a four-day backpack trip and he on his way to leave the state forever. Was this somehow part of the plan?

Kyler saw her hesitation, and jumped in with a new proposal: "Sarah, I'll tell you what. It's about an hour or so to the Nevada border. And by the way, I have a fake ID that would totally work for you, so border crossings would be no problem. Anyway, just before we get there we'll cross a highway headed south. Let us give you a ride there—you're hitchhiking, right?" She nodded. "Perfect. We'll give you a ride, and I get the next hour to try to talk you into coming with us." Here he unleashed his most charming smile, and Sarah could not help but smile too. "If you still don't want to come when we get there, we'll just drop you off, and you'll be that much further along. Sound good?"

It did sound good. He had taken away most of her reasons to decline his offer. The one reason that remained was just a feeling, the feeling that somehow this was a compromise, that it's not what Justin would want. But hadn't she been right about coming into town last night? Like Kyler said, this would get her closer to her goal, and besides, Justin was nowhere to be seen. She had to do something, and this was the opportunity that had presented itself. She found herself nodding.

"Yeah, that sounds pretty good. Thanks, Kyler."

Just then Kyler's friends re-emerged from the store with their groceries. "Guys, Sarah's coming with us!" Kyler told them.

Sarah protested, "Well, not ..."

"...For a little while, anyway." Kyler winked at her.

This was a group that was used to last-minute changes in plan, and also clearly used to Kyler calling the shots. They were quick to embrace the new addition to their number. One of the guys—she had already forgotten his name—picked up Sarah's backpack and loaded it in the back of the van, and the other was happy to give up his seat next to the driver at Kyler's request, so Sarah could sit by him. It all happened a little too fast for Sarah. Before she knew it she was buckled into the front seat and the van was pulling out of its parking space.

She was instantly uncomfortable. Something didn't feel right. As they turned onto the highway, she involuntarily gripped the armrest and sat stiffly in the seat. She looked back at the grocery store, feeling vaguely that she may have forgotten something in the rush of the last few moments.

"Everything okay?" Kyler's friendly voice was reassuring, but she was too conflicted to trust it entirely.

"I think so. I just ..."

"Sarah, look, I know I put some pressure on you back there. I'll back off. I really am kind of worried about you. You seem nice, and I just hope you've thought things through."

This approach helped. Sarah calmed down a bit. "Well, thank you. The truth is, I don't know exactly what I'm doing. But so far I've been ... protected, and ... guided, if that makes any sense."

Kyler raised his eyebrows a little. "A little. I'm not sure I know exactly what you mean, but that's okay. You are an interesting girl, Sarah Martinez. So, you've been lucky so far. What if that doesn't last? What if you run up against a wall? Or," he continued with a smile, "what if you were 'guided' to meet up with us? I mean, like I said, what are the chances, right?"

"Don't listen to him, Sarah," said one of the girls from the back seat, "Kyler can talk anyone into anything."

"No, he's right," said the guy who had given up his seat, "you belong with us. You even out the ratio! We have totally been needing another girl!"

Sarah had noticed that they were sitting in three rows, with a guy and a girl in each row. Kyler turned his head briefly to glare at his friend, then looked apologetically at Sarah. "It's not about that," he said loudly so the whole van could hear. "I'm just really glad to meet someone who shares our beliefs, and I think it would be a shame for you to go off on your own when you might find that this" he made circles with his hand to indicate the whole group of them, "is where you fit."

Sarah did not know what to say. The other guy—was his name Axel?—joined in the conversation:

"It's going to be awesome, Sarah. My parents have this huge cabin up in the mountains. It's so beautiful, and we're all going to live there together. We'll stock up on food and chop our own firewood—we won't even need the rest of the world. Oh, I can't wait!"

Kyler looked at her and shrugged. "It is going to be pretty awesome. And besides, let's say we're right, and a war comes." The van got quiet. Kyler's friend were less interested in the political side of this adventure than he was. "Let's say there's some kind of an attack. It's going to happen at the borders, and who's to say you'll be any safer just because you're on the other side of the border? War is messy, Sarah. In that scenario, if Mexico isn't under attack, then they're potentially allied with our enemies! You think that's going to be a safe place? Actually, I sent you an article about attack scenarios a few days ago, just on the off chance you didn't think I was totally crazy. It's probably still on my phone. Guys, where is my phone?"

"Your phone is dead, remember man? You need to charge it," said the guy in the far back.

"Oh, yeah. Well, it would be on your phone," Kyler said to Sarah. "Do you have it?"

"It's, um, in my pack," said Sarah. She began to say something else, but Kyler didn't notice. He was yelling at his friend.

"Hey, get Sarah's phone from her pack, would you?"

"Where is it?"

"Um, in the bottom compartment," Sarah said.

The phone was found and passed forward. Reluctantly, Sarah turned it on. As she expected, it came alive with a variety of noises because of all the missed calls and messages from the past several days, mostly from her dad and Jalen. She ignored those and found the messages from Kyler, of which there were several. She blushed a little to realize that he had been thinking of her since they met. He helped her find the one with the article he had mentioned.

"Go ahead and read it," he said, "and tell me what you think."

Sarah's eyes skimmed the article, but her mind was a blur. It was a description of possible ways the United States could be attacked by enemy forces, along with some speculation about the safest places to be in each scenario, complete with a map. In every scenario, southern California and the surrounding area was completely shaded in red, which meant 'highly unsafe'. Her mind, though, was on the more immediate questions of how she had ended up in this van, how she felt about it, and what she would do next. She was unsure of the answer to any of these questions. Clearly Kyler's plan made sense on a rational, human level. There was no way she could explain to him that she had information, and protection, from another Source that was outside his experience and his plans. The right thing to do was to reject his offer and strike out alone, but what reasons could she give that would make any sense to him? And of course it was tempting to go along with him. To do so would mean friendship, and maybe romance, with one of the few people who had ever shown interest in really getting to know her, and loving her for who she was. It meant adventure, a place to belong, and the possibility of a reasonably comfortable life even after an attack came.

But none of these things were the reasons she had left Portland. She had to remind herself of that. Staying in this van would mean living with the guilt of knowing she had betrayed all that had been revealed to her in the past few weeks. Could she do that?

Probably not. Her conscience was too strong. A part of her heart raged against this. Why couldn't she be normal, like Kyler and his friends? Why couldn't she just enjoy life? Why did she have to be different? Why had she been chosen to know everything she knew?

So what would she say? She knew the right thing to do, but the situation presented a challenge on another level. Unless she was angry, Sarah had never been very brave when it came to saying things others wouldn't want to hear. It was one thing to make the right choice in her mind, and another to put it into words, to look Kyler in the eye and tell him no, when a good part of her heart didn't even want to. The few times in her life when she had really messed up, really broken the rules and gotten in trouble for it, had not been because of her own rebelliousness, but because of her inability to speak up for herself in the face of friends whose personalities were stronger. She didn't initiate trouble, but sometimes in her weakness she went along with it. She knew there was a very real danger this would happen in her current situation, that she would be unable to find the courage to say the hard thing and make Kyler stop the van, just as she had been unable to resist coming along in the first place.

"Finished? What do you think?" He interrupted her thoughts.

"Oh, um, yeah, it makes some good points. Listen, it's just a lot to take in, to change my plans so fast and everything. I need a little time to think."

"Sure. That's understandable. I'll stop pressuring you. We're coming up on your highway south in about half an hour. We can talk about something else for a while if you want." He reached down and turned on the radio, and soon he and his friends were engaged in a conversation about their favorite musicians.

Sarah was paralyzed. She did not want to stay in the van, and she did not have the courage to say so. Somehow she knew that she would have found it easier to be strong if she had not been in such a place of stubborn willfulness for the past twenty-four hours. She would have been more in touch with the Source of strength that she had disconnected herself from for the sake of a soft bed and a warm meal. Of course, then she would not have been in this position at all. Was that the right way to view this situation, after all? That if she had listened to Justin, she would not have bumped into Kyler at all, and that would have been better? Of course. Of course it was. But it was a hard reality to accept. It meant that she had been wrong all along, and would have to admit it, and it meant that she was being asked to trust the One who would deny her everything that Kyler represented.

Her thoughts were interrupted by Kyler slamming his fist on the dashboard. "No, man! No! I wasn't doing anything wrong!"

"What's up?" asked his friend from behind him.

"Army." Kyler pointed at the rear-view mirror. Then he cursed loudly, which was followed by an uncomfortable silence in the van.

Sarah turned and looked back through the dirty rear windows of the van. Two large military-looking vehicles were speeding up behind them, lights flashing. Kyler pulled the van to the side of the road, turned to his friends and said, "Okay, everybody, be cool. We don't know why they're pulling us over. Don't mention anything about crossing state lines. Tell them we're headed south, to do some backpacking with friends in Yosemite."

He was impressively quick with the lie, which did not make him more attractive to Sarah. Her heart was racing, but she told herself that someone like Kyler would probably be driving without the proper registration, or something like that. Still, it was strange that there were two vehicles, and that they had come out of nowhere, so quickly. Kyler rolled his window down and Sarah saw him put on his charming smile like someone had flipped on a light switch. But this was clearly not a routine traffic stop. Four armed Soldiers, two on each side, exited their vehicles even before they had come to a full stop and ran up alongside the van. The two in front pointed their rifles at Sarah and Kyler.

"Whoa, gentlemen, what's going on?" Kyler raised his hands in the air and looked as innocent and respectful as he possibly could.

The Soldier who spoke had no interest in conversation. "We're looking for a Sarah Martinez," he said. "Is she in this vehicle?"

Arrested

Kyler involuntarily spun toward Sarah. He had clearly been expecting this encounter to be connected to his own previous dealings with the Army, and probably with good reason. He looked at her questioningly.

The Soldier addressed her directly now. "Sarah Martinez? Step out of the vehicle please."

Trembling, Sarah opened her door and stepped down out of the van, tripping as she did so, but catching herself. Rather than offering assistance, the Soldier nearest to her took a step backward and kept his gun pointed at her.

"We will require all of Ms. Martinez's personal belongings," the Soldier on Kyler's side said with raised voice so as to be heard in the interior of the van. He seemed to be the commanding officer. Kyler's friends quickly passed her backpack forward. They slid the van door open and delivered it to the Soldiers without making eye contact with them. Kyler took her phone from where it rested on the dashboard and passed it out of his window.

"Is that it? Nothing else?"

"No sir, that's it."

"And what is your connection to Ms. Martinez?"

Kyler looked at her briefly with something like an apology in his eyes.

"Um, she was hitchhiking and we picked her up."

"That's it? You don't know her?"

"No, sir. She said she was from Portland."

"Did she try to give you anything?"

Now Kyler looked genuinely confused. "No, sir. Nothing. Have we done something wrong, sir?"

"Not that I'm aware of, son. Although I wouldn't recommend picking up hitchhikers in the future."

"Yes, sir. Thank you. Sorry, sir."

"Now, if I have my men search your vehicle, are they going to find anything else belonging to Miss Martinez?"

"No, sir."

"Would they find anything else that shouldn't be in there? Weapons?"

"Oh, no, sir, not us. Just food and stuff. You know, camping supplies. So sorry about this," he nodded in Sarah's direction. "We had no idea."

"Okay." The commander looked at his men as he said this. "Let's load her up." Then he said to Kyler, who had ceased to be useful to him, "You may go."

"Yes, sir. Thank you, sir," Kyler said politely. He put the van into gear and pulled slowly onto the highway, leaving Sarah standing in the middle of the circle created by the four armed soldiers. She had been in a state of shock since Kyler had denied he knew her. At that moment, the pain of his betrayal was as bad as the fear of what the soldiers would do with her. A part of her knew that this was not entirely fair. The truth was, Kyler didn't really know her. He had no reason to stick up for her, and much to risk if he did so. Still, the things she had seen in him in the past few minutes—his anger, his ability to lie and manipulate, and his quickness to protect himself at the expense of others—made her angry with him and with herself. She had let herself believe that he was something better than what he was, and it hurt to discover that he was so flawed, and that she meant so little to him.

And now he was gone. Fear welled up within her as she watched the van shrink rapidly away, leaving them alone on the side of the small mountain road. There were no other cars in sight, and the air was still. The commanding officer stepped closer to address her. A small tag pinned to his chest pocket said Sgt. Parsons. He was older than the other three, with some colored patches on his uniform indicating his superior rank. He also had a way of speaking that sounded somehow more intelligent than she had always assumed Soldiers would be. He was clearly used to being in charge, and his voice was at the same time powerful and effortless. He held up her phone and said, "A lot of people have been looking for you, Miss Martinez."

Her heart sank as she realized that they had found her because she had turned her phone on. Justin had been right. Again. Internally, she kicked herself and at the same time allowed herself a little anger toward Justin. A part of her knew that being wrong about something was not a good reason to be angry with the person (or angel) who was right, but it was an automatic reaction. Besides, where was he now? Wouldn't this be a good time for him to show up and rescue her? Would he kill these Soldiers? Were they evil, or just doing their job? Or (and this thought filled her with fear all over again), maybe he would never come. Maybe this was her punishment for going her own way, not trusting him. She had known it was wrong to go with Kyler. She had created this situation, and probably she would have no help getting out of it. She was on her own now.

Then she realized what the Sergeant had actually said. Why would anyone, besides her parents, be looking for her? She spoke timidly, "Who is looking for me? What did I do wrong?"

He looked at her piercingly and, without answering at first, took two purposeful strides over to the soldier who was holding her backpack. Then he spoke with his back to her as he searched through her belongings.

"Your parents called you in as missing several days ago. Normally we don't spend a lot of energy on missing persons, but they mentioned you had been acting strangely, and that you had taken this," he removed the Bible from her pack and waved it in front of her, "with you."

Sarah winced as he flipped through the pages. His strong, careless hands could easily destroy this thing that had become so precious to her.

"Is this your writing?" he asked.

"No, sir. It's my great-grandma's."

"Uh-huh." Then he noticed her squirming and realized what her fear was. "Oh, don't worry, I'm not going to hurt it. This is evidence. This is coming with us, along with you. Let's go." He motioned for his men to usher her into the first of the vehicles, then turned his back and began walking toward the second one.

"Wait! This isn't fair! I haven't done anything wrong!" Sarah surprised herself; she had not meant to yell, but fear made it hard to control her voice. The lead soldier spun on his heel and walked back toward her, not stopping until his face was just inches from hers. He spoke quietly and clearly:

"Oh, I think you have, Miss Martinez. I think there are a lot more of these." He held up the Bible again. "I think you are guilty of distributing them, and of transporting them across state lines. Furthermore, I think you have done so in cooperation with some of our nation's enemies. These are serious crimes, Miss Martinez. Now, I know that you are young, and it may be that you have been deceived into doing the things you've done. But you will be detained in my custody until such time as I can determine exactly what you've been doing, who you have been talking to, and what their plans are. Is that clear?"

"No! I mean, yes, sir, but I didn't do those things. I mean, yes, I brought that one into California, but that's it. Nothing else. There aren't any more and I don't know what you're talking about with all that other stuff. Please, I'm sorry. You have to let me go! I have to ..." she stopped herself before revealing her travel plans or the reason for them, but it was too late. She had aroused his curiosity.

"Have to what, Miss Martinez?"

"Nothing. Never mind."

"No, I'm interested. Where exactly are you going, Miss Martinez?"

Now she was stuck. "Nowhere," she said lamely.

"Right. Let me tell you something, young lady: you are going to tell me where you are going and what you are doing. But there will be time for that once we get indoors. Let's go." He started to turn away again.

"Wait! Don't I have rights? Don't I get a phone call and a lawyer and all that?"

The man sneered. "Miss Martinez, I have sworn an oath to protect my country against all threats, large and small. There are people out there, many of them believers in this book," he again shook the Bible in the air, "who seek to undermine the values of my country. They are unpatriotic traitors. They are full of hatred. They maintain illegal relationships with my country's enemies. I suspect that you may be one of them. And until I can determine exactly what kind of threat you represent, you have no rights."

"This is crazy! No!" Sarah involuntarily jerked away as one of the Soldiers placed his hand on her shoulder. This resulted in four strong hands taking her by the arms, lifting her slightly up off of the ground, and carrying her to the truck, where the other Soldier had opened the back door. Inside there was a simple plastic bench and bare metal walls. Her arms were suddenly wrenched behind her and she felt handcuffs snap roughly onto her wrists.

"No! You can't do this!" Sarah continued to struggle uselessly as the third Soldier now lifted her up by her ankles and the three of them set her quickly in the truck, then shut the door with a clang. Sarah found herself in complete darkness. Then the vehicle started to move. Two big bumps as it pulled onto the road convinced her that it would be worth trying to get seated on the bench. She was curled up on the floor with her hands cuffed behind her. To get up meant pushing off the ground with her knees and the side of her face, and as she did so the truck hit another bump. It hurt, and knocked her down, but she was determined, and on the next attempt she found herself upright on her knees. From there she was able to stand briefly on her feet, turn quickly, find the bench with the back of her legs, and sit.

Once she was seated, the tears came almost instantly. She was so afraid. And she was so alone. Kyler had betrayed her. But so had her parents. And Justin had abandoned her. Even God … no, she didn't allow herself to entertain that thought for more than a moment. But it was there. And if He had, could she blame Him? She had failed utterly. All she had needed to do was listen to His messenger, and to the voice within herself that she knew was from Him, the one that she had ignored when Kyler flashed his charming smile. Now she was in darkness, in every way. Whatever lay at the end of this drive, it wasn't Mexico. It wasn't the freedom and peace she had experienced as she lay under the stars. She was at the mercy of other powers now, and before her lay a future of punishment, of compromise, of something less than what could have been. She wept and wept until she had no more tears as the truck bumped along toward an unknown destination.

Transported

The ride was much longer than Sarah had expected. Eventually she stopped crying and simply sat in the darkness, too emotionally exhausted to think much about anything. Her lower back was still stiff from the backpacking she had done, and sitting on the bench with her hands behind her back became increasingly painful, but there was no way to find relief. The wall behind her was angled inward, making it impossible to lean back. The bench was too narrow to lie down on. It seemed that the whole compartment had been designed to keep its occupants uncomfortable.

After what seemed like several hours, the truck stopped, and then a moment later the door squeaked open and Sergeant Parson's face appeared.

"Halfway there. This is a bathroom break."

Sarah squirmed her way to the end of the bench closest to the door. She did have to go to the bathroom.

"Just halfway? Where are you taking me?"

"You will be detained at a federal correctional institution while I conduct my investigation. Now, if I take these handcuffs off, are you going to give my men any trouble?"

"No, sir." Sarah decided not to pursue her question any further. Based on how long they had been driving, she figured that they were probably headed back to Portland. The thought pushed her further into the discouragement that had settled on her during the long drive, a feeling of hopelessness so deep that its effect was to make her numb. She stumbled out of the truck and was momentarily disoriented by the light in the sky. It was evening, but it was still much brighter than the total darkness of the past few hours. She looked around and saw that they were at a highway rest stop, which at the moment was occupied by only one other car, far at the other end of the parking lot, where an older man was walking a small dog. As the Soldiers escorted her to the restroom her thoughts were filled with all the progress, physically and spiritually, she had made on the journey south over the past week. Now it seemed it was all being taken away, mile by mile, as the truck carried her back to where she had started.

When she returned to the truck, Sergeant Parsons was standing by the door with two plain-looking granola bars in his hand. "Eat these," he said. "We have a long way to go."

Sarah took them without speaking, grateful to be climbing into the back of the truck without handcuffs on. The door clanged shut and she sat down on the bench, tore open the wrappers, and began to chew the food mindlessly. It was bland but surprisingly filling. When she was done, she noticed that the road they were traveling seemed to be relatively smooth. Maybe she would try sleeping. She lay down on the bare metal floor. No position was comfortable, but after a while she discovered that if she lay on her side with her arm under her head, she could relax. She was tired, and the loud hum of the truck, combined with her desire to hide away from what was happening to her, soon put her to sleep.

She woke to the sound of the truck's metal door. Light filled the compartment along with the sound of chuckles from the Soldiers who had opened the door. Instantly, shame washed over Sarah's face. It was a feeling she had not had to deal with in Justin's company, but now she was back in the world of real people, most of whom considered sleeping a weakness.

"Did we disturb you, princess?" The men laughed as she rubbed her eyes and rose to a stooping position. She had decided to adopt a policy of not speaking unless it was absolutely necessary, so she ignored them and climbed down to discover that they were inside a large concrete room, a sort of parking garage with other Army vehicles, equipment, and loading docks. Sergeant Parsons was nowhere in sight. Two Soldiers took their places at her side as another led them up a ramp to an unmarked door, while another followed behind. Each of them carried a rifle as well as having a pistol in a holster on his belt. *Really? For me?* Sarah thought. It seemed ridiculous that a shy little girl who was barely out of school should warrant this much attention from the Army. *Me and my little book*. She smiled at the thought of what her great-grandmother Sarah might think of all this. Then that thought was replaced as she remembered that she had failed her great-grandmother, failed the book and all that it stood for when she failed to trust. Her smile disappeared. She was led down a gray corridor, past several more unmarked doors, around a corner, and finally into a plain room with a bed, a sink, a toilet, and a large mirror on one wall which she assumed allowed people on the other side to watch her every move. One of the Soldiers gestured toward the bed and she sat obediently.

"What now?" she asked, but the man simply shut the door without a word. She looked around the room and sighed. She was still tired, and it was bedtime, but just as she was beginning to look for a light switch the door opened suddenly and Sergeant Parsons entered.

"Well, Miss Martinez. How was the ride?"

Sarah didn't want to answer, but was afraid that things would be worse if she were rude. "Dark," she said.

He chuckled. "My men tell me you were sleeping. Can I get you some Ampheine?"

"It won't help. I'm a Sleeper."

"Really? Interesting. Well, then I'll let you sleep in a moment. First, I'd like to share with you something I learned on our drive today. I've been taking a look at your phone." He pulled it from a chest pocket in his uniform and showed it to her. "Can you guess what I found?"

Sarah shrugged, prepared for some sort of false accusation she would have no way of disproving.

"Attack scenarios. Battle plans, Miss Martinez! Casualty estimates, safety routes … not the kind of thing most girls your age are reading. Can you explain that to me?"

Sarah's face turned red. The message! She was at once internally furious with Kyler, and at the same time had an urge to protect him. Whatever he had done to her, the situation was mostly her fault, and he didn't deserve to be handed over to this man. She struggled for words, then gave up and simply said,

"It's not what you think. You wouldn't believe me if I told you."

"Of course. Who is Kyler Anderson?" He was looking at the phone again. "Is he a friend of yours? A fellow dissenter? Was that the young man driving the van?"

Sarah said nothing.

"Well, in any case, we'll find him, and anyone else you are in communication with. Things just got a lot worse for you, Miss Martinez." He turned and moved toward the door, slapping his hand on the wall as he went out. "Better get used to this room."

The door slammed and immediately Sarah remembered that she had meant to ask something. She ran to the door and banged on it with her fist, shouting as loudly as she could, "Wait! Can I have some food?" There was no response, and she had no way of knowing if she had even been heard. She resigned herself to the fact that she was going to go to bed hungry, and resumed her earlier search for the light switch. But there was none. It took her a few minutes to realize that this was intentional. She was in a prison cell, and it was designed to be as tamper-proof as possible. The walls were bare, the bed was bolted down, the mattress was thin and covered in thick plastic. There was no bedding. There was nothing to break, nothing to throw, nowhere to hide anything. And no light switch. She sighed and lay down on the mattress facing the wall, telling herself that it was slightly darker this way than if she were looking out on the center of the room.

Sarah's thoughts were angry as she waited for sleep to come. She was tired of beating herself up for her own part in what had happened. Now she began to list for herself the things Sergeant Parsons had said that were simply not true: she was not a Bible smuggler. She was not a part of some massive conspiracy. She was not a traitor, not in league with the enemies of her country. And there was no evidence that she was, other than his own speculation that might have come from conversations with her parents, and maybe Torin. There was that one article on her phone, but she couldn't be blamed for what someone else had sent to her. It wasn't fair.

She stared at the wall, thinking along these lines for a while, when something caused her to begin thinking about the difference between this night and those she had experienced on the trail. She thought of the beauty of the stars compared with the harsh fluorescent lights of this room. She remembered reading her Bible in the fading evening light. Now it had been taken from her forever. She remembered Justin saying she had more to learn, and thought about how much she had not yet read. Had she read enough? She tried to remember some of the things she had read most recently. As she mentally reviewed the stories she had been reading near the end of the book of John, the thought came suddenly: *You were falsely accused.*

It was immensely comforting. She let the thought wash over her, holding onto it as long as she could. *You were falsely accused. You know how it feels. It looked like you were at their mercy, but you weren't.* It was the brightest spot in her day, better than the false freedom of eating a plum in the sunshine of her rebellion. But inevitably it led to another thought, one which she tried to hold off, but it came anyway: *I haven't been praying.*

It was an important moment, but Sarah didn't know how to handle it. It was an invitation to repentance, though she would not have known to use that word. But she wasn't ready. She was unsure of what lay on the other side of such an act, and did not know what to do with her own guilt. She held onto it, though a bit more loosely than before, and allowed herself at the same time to cling to the partial comfort she had found a moment before. *I am not alone*, she thought, and it was enough to allow her to drift off to sleep in relative peace.

Detained

15 *days.*

Sarah woke suddenly, and for no apparent reason. She was alone in the room of bare walls and bright ugly light. It was a strange relief that her internal countdown had resumed. 15 days. It gave her a strange sort of hope that, no matter how long the Army intended to keep her here, one way or another things would be changing dramatically in a couple of weeks. Would she still be in this room? Would the building itself be attacked? If it was a federal building, this was likely. Would she die in the initial missile strike? If not, what would happen to prisoners when the enemy took over? What sort of means would the Army use between now and then to try to get information from her that she truly didn't have?

She considered these questions calmly. At least for now, she was able to rise above them. She knew in this moment that the Army was not really in charge of her life. Her internal state did not depend upon her external circumstances. But she was impatient. She did not look forward to spending endless hours in this cell, waiting for ... what? She wanted something to happen, and at the same time didn't expect that anything good was coming.

There was a clicking sound from over by the door. Sarah stood and found a tray of food on the floor that had been passed through a slot which was now closed. It was an unappetizing breakfast of toast and flavorless eggs, but she was hungry, so she ate it. Then she lay back on the bed. At home she had enjoyed opportunities just to lie on her bed, stare at the ceiling, and think, but the brightness of the lights in the ceiling of this room made that difficult. She shifted onto her side, but that felt too much like going to sleep, and she didn't need any more sleep at the moment.

She rose and explored the room, looking for anything of interest that she hadn't noticed before, but there was nothing. She stood in front of the big mirror and studied herself, then began to wonder if someone was on the other side of the glass, watching her. She waved into it and said, "Hello?" but then felt silly for doing so and wandered to the other side of the room. Above the sink she saw that there were some scratch marks on the wall. She looked more closely and discovered that they were actually letters; someone had scratched the word "liars" into the paint. She wondered about the story behind the word. It was the only unusual thing in the room, and it intrigued her. Someone else had been in this room, someone else who felt falsely accused. Maybe they had been. Maybe this was where the Army brought people they intended to treat unfairly. The thought made her shiver, but she took a deep breath and pushed it from her mind.

Hours went by. Eventually the food slot clicked again and a glass of milk, a peanut-butter-and-jelly-sandwich, and an apple appeared on a gray plastic tray. The apple was mushy, but the rest wasn't bad, and she was hungry. After eating she took the lunch tray, sat on the floor against the wall, and begin to spin the tray on the floor on one of its corners, perfecting her technique over the next few minutes until she could get it to remain spinning for several seconds. Then she took the tray that had brought her breakfast and began to work on spinning one with each hand at the same time. No matter what she did, the one in her right hand always spun longer. Just as she was becoming absorbed in her game, a woman's voice came over a hidden speaker from somewhere in the ceiling and said "Please return your meal trays through the meal slot. Thank you." Sarah sighed, stood, and slid the trays through the slot, not wanting to show any signs of rebellion to her captors. But then she looked up and addressed the ceiling:

"Hey, what am I supposed to do? What happens next?"

There was no response. She was afraid to invite the Army to pay more attention to her, but her boredom was becoming larger than her fear. She walked over to the mirror and knocked on it.

"Hello? Anybody in there? I want to talk to someone. You can't just keep me here like this. I want to talk to my parents."

Still nothing. She sighed and sat down on the bed again. She found herself longing for her meal trays, then laughed at herself for thinking this. *If you're going to wish for something, wish for more than plastic trays,* she told herself. Then she flopped down on her back and shut her eyes. Maybe she would take an afternoon nap. But no, the lights were just too bright. They seemed even brighter than they had been before. Were they really, or was she just getting more tired of them?

The afternoon passed like the morning. She alternated between lying on her bed and wandering around the small room, from the bed to the door to the mirror to the sink and back again. Her thoughts wandered too, from Kyler to her parents to Justin and Thaddeus to the beauty of the stars. Finally there was another click at the meal slot, and this time Sarah went running over and put her head down near the floor. "Hey!" she said, "you can't just keep me in here!" But there was no response.

She ate her dinner and spun the tray a few times before voluntarily sliding it back through the slot as a gesture of good faith. She told herself that someone like Kyler would probably hold onto the tray just to stir up trouble in any small way he could, and she wanted it to be clear that she wasn't that kind of person. Time continued to pass. After a couple more hours of pacing, she guessed that it was nearing bedtime. It was strange not to have clothes to change or sheets to pull back. She simply lay down and rolled over to face the wall. It took a long time to fall asleep—her day hadn't exactly been very tiring, and she could not help but wonder when her door would open and things would go from boring to ... something else. But eventually she slept.

14 days. Sarah woke to the sound of her breakfast being delivered. When she stood, she knew that she had slept long and hard, and that she was now nearly fully recovered from the soreness and fatigue of backpacking. She told herself that all she needed was a shower and she would actually feel somewhat refreshed, despite her circumstances. She put her mouth to the meal slot and shouted into the hallway, "Hey, do I get to shower?" knowing that even if she were heard she would probably be ignored. She ate the breakfast of oatmeal and yogurt and waited.

She waited all morning, and nothing happened. Lunch came, then dinner. All day she lay down, stood up, paced, spun her meal trays and then returned them. She asked questions of the mirror, of the ceiling, and was met with silence. She stared at the word "liars" and made up stories about the person who had scratched it on the wall.

After she had returned her dinner tray, she got a drink of water in her hands from the sink and lay back on her bed. It was too early to sleep yet; she just wanted to digest her meal a little. But suddenly she felt cold. And the light from the ceiling seemed brighter than ever. She rolled over on her side and hugged herself to warm up, but still couldn't get comfortable and stood back up, hoping to warm up by pacing the room for a bit. As she approached the door, suddenly it opened and in stepped Sergeant Parsons, the first person she had seen in a day and a half. She was so startled that a small scream came out before she could stop it. He seemed amused by this and said,

"Good evening, Miss Martinez. How is your stay so far?"

As far as she knew, this was her one opportunity to talk, and Sarah was not going to waste it. "It's too bright in here, I need a shower, and I'm getting cold. You can't keep me here like this. I haven't done anything wrong. I want to talk to my parents."

Sergeant Parsons simply smiled. "Step over against the wall, Miss Martinez." He pointed toward the mirrored window. As he did, a younger Soldier entered the room behind him carrying a rifle, which he aimed directly at Sarah. All her anger gave way to dread, and she cowered as she obeyed his order. As soon as she did so, two other Soldiers, carrying what appeared to be power tools, hurried in and knelt down at two corners of her bed. There was a loud noise that echoed in the small room as they removed the bolts that kept her bed fixed to the ground. Then they moved to the other two corners and did the same thing. Then, carrying their tools in one hand, they picked the bed up with the other, tilting it on its side, and quickly carried it out of the room.

Sarah did not know exactly what she had been expecting, but it wasn't this. Still deeply afraid, she asked with a trembling voice, "What are you doing? Where are they taking my bed?"

Sergeant Parsons addressed the Soldier with the rifle first, but without taking his eyes off Sarah. "You may go," he said in a commanding voice, taking a handgun from his belt at the same time. The Soldier immediately obeyed, shutting the door behind him. The Sergeant pointed his gun at Sarah and kept it aimed at her as he spoke:

"You won't be needing a bed for a while. And it's going to keep getting brighter in here, Sarah, and it's going to keep getting colder." This was the first time he had used her first name, and it had the effect of making her feel like his hatred of her was more personal, not merely a matter of doing his job but of some kind of wrong she had done to him. He looked around the room and gestured at the walls as he continued:

"Did you know that this room has speakers built into the walls, and that it's also entirely soundproofed? No one outside can hear what goes on in here. So I've arranged to have an alarm go off—a fairly loud one—every ten minutes in this cold, bright room. You see, you, Sarah Martinez the Sleeper, are not going to sleep until you tell me everything you know about your friends, the enemies of my country. You're going to tell me anything you know about upcoming terrorist attacks, and about Bible distribution, and anything else you're involved in. Now, you can just tell me those things now, and I'll have the boys bring that bed right back in. I'll even turn the lights off for you. But if you choose not to do that, I think you'll find that a couple of days from now you'll be more than ready to talk. Now, have I been clear?"

Sarah nodded. Curled up against the wall, trying not to look at the barrel of his gun, she was near tears, but spoke as normally as she could, "Yes, but I don't know anything! I'm not hiding anything, I promise! There's nothing I can tell you! Really! Please, you can't do this. I want to talk to my parents."

As she made this last request, she saw the flash of a smirk cross his face. A new fear entered her mind, and she found the courage to look him in the eye as she gave voice to it.

"Do they even know I'm here? My parents, did you tell them you found me?"

Instead of the shame she had been hoping for, he met her gaze with a sort of satisfaction, and said, "No one knows you're here, Sarah Martinez. You are all alone. Now, do you have anything you want to tell me before your night begins?"

She looked away, shook her head and spoke quietly. "There's nothing to tell. Please don't do this. I'm innocent." A tear slid down her cheek.

"No, Miss Martinez, what you are is a really good liar. But that will change. Have a good night."

Sergeant Parsons turned, knocked on the door, and it opened. He stepped through and slammed it behind him. A moment later, the lights increased in brightness to the point that she couldn't look directly at them. Shortly after that it became noticeably colder in the room. Sarah sat on the floor and hugged her knees for warmth, wondering how this would end. How would she endure this? What would he do when she couldn't give him any answers? Would the torture become more extreme? She was not yet panicked, but there was a rising feeling of urgency within her. Surely this could not go on.

Then the alarm went off. It was like the sound of the fire alarm in her high school: a jarring, grating, incredibly loud noise, actually two noises at once, one a sort of siren-like beep and the other like the squawking of a giant mechanical bird, each happening at the same time so the sounds overlapped one another in a chaos that made you want to cover your ears and leave the room as soon as possible. It continued for about thirty seconds. Sarah had been wondering if possibly at some point she would become so tired that she might sleep through the alarm, but now that seemed highly unlikely.

Six or seven cycles of the alarm passed before she began to feel truly tired. Up to that point, she had been trying to distract herself with her usual activities in the room, even doing jumping jacks a couple of different times to warm up. Each time the alarm went off it was startling, but she simply plugged her ears and paced around the room until it was over. But now she really wanted to go to sleep. Tired of walking around, she curled up in a corner that she guessed was possibly the farthest away from the hidden speaker. She took off her outer shirt and draped it over her head and arms, as if she were hiding under a very small blanket. Then the alarm sounded again. She plugged her ears and waited until it was over, then lay her head against the wall.

When the alarm went off again she had already fallen asleep. It woke her so suddenly that it sent a shot of adrenaline running through her system, like when her brothers used to scare her by jumping out from behind a door. What followed was a feeling of despair. This was going to happen every ten minutes? She simply couldn't take it. What would she do?

And then she knew what to do. *God, help me,* she prayed. *I don't know what to do. I need your help.* At once, she had the sense that her prayer was heard, was welcomed, but also that she could not pray this prayer without also addressing some other unfinished business.

This time her walls were down, and she was ready. *I'm so sorry. Please ... forgive me.* She hesitated at the word *forgive.* It was a word she rarely used. Certainly no one else in her family used it, and she realized in this moment that she probably couldn't have given a clear explanation of exactly what the word meant. Had she ever seen real forgiveness? Was this even the right thing to say? But she was beyond defending herself, beyond bargaining. She had nothing to prove and nothing to offer. She just needed help.

As soon as she prayed these words, Sarah's heart was flooded, not at first with the feeling of being forgiven, but of being truly sorry. Up to this point she had pretended that she was not wrong, blamed Justin, made excuses. Now she felt the weight of her own disobedience and it nearly crushed her. She cried, then sobbed, but as she did it was like the feeling of setting down a heavy backpack at the end of the day. They were tears she had carried for too long, and it was right and good to be rid of them.

Then the alarm sounded again. Her fingers went into her ears and her tears dried as she waited out the awful noise. When it was over, she was calm. She wiped her face, and sat reflectively for another ten minutes, not praying or thinking anything in particular, but simply allowing what she had just experienced to soak into her heart. Then another alarm, which she barely noticed. She plugged her ears, but otherwise her mood of reflection was uninterrupted. Somehow, the sound seemed further away this time.

When it was over, she uncurled from her position and stretched herself out full length on the floor against the wall, with her head in the corner and her face toward the wall. She arranged her shirt over her head again, covering as much of her back and shoulders as she could. In this way she passed the night. She was still cold, but it was manageable, and she was able to doze off for a few minutes at a time, plugging her ears each time the alarm woke her.

Interrogated

Without windows, Sarah had been able to tell night from day only by the arrival of her meals. After countless cycles of the alarm, she started to feel hungry, and rolled over from her position each time the sound stopped to see if her breakfast had been delivered. It didn't come. She began to wonder if starvation was to be another form of her torture. But after nine more alarms, suddenly it was there, and she realized that this was probably the normal mealtime and that she had just underestimated how long the night was.

She ate the breakfast and returned the tray immediately. She had no desire to play games now, and needed both hands to plug her ears. She assumed her position in the corner and waited. But no alarm came. Surely it had been ten minutes by now. She waited a bit more: nothing. Gratefully, she pulled her shirt back over her head and almost immediately started to drift off.

Suddenly the cell door opened and a loud voice broke the silence: "Good morning, Miss Martinez!" Sarah woke with a start and could instantly feel the effects of her miserable night. Her body had been so hungry for real sleep that to be pulled back out just as she was starting to sink into it was truly a miserable feeling. Everything in her was begging to cling to the sweet rest she had just tasted. To be denied this made her feel groggy, weak and irritable. At the same time, she was aware of a calmness, a confidence that while she may be uncomfortable at the moment, things were going to work out all right. Somehow this was connected to the knowledge of being forgiven, though she couldn't put her finger on exactly why one was related to the other. She rolled over to see Sergeant Parsons quite near her, taking a seat on a folding chair he had carried in. He sat backwards in the chair, with his arms folded on the backrest. Behind him were two Soldiers armed with rifles.

"So, are you ready to have a conversation?"

Sarah sat up and faced him. She even looked him in the eye. She felt herself filled with an unexpected inner strength, which did not counteract the physical weakness she was feeling, but caused her to believe that it didn't matter. Her weakness was no obstacle to things unfolding as they should.

"Yes I am," she said.

He looked pleasantly surprised. "Good. Smart girl. Things were not going to get any better from here. So you're ready to tell me the truth?"

Sarah nodded. "I will tell you everything I know."

Now he looked pleased but skeptical. "Okay then. Let's see about that. First: are you a Bible smuggler?"

"No. I mean, I carried my Bible into California, but that was for personal use. I never intended to show it to anybody else. I don't have any others."

"Why did you travel to California?"

"Recreation."

"Come on now, Miss Martinez. An evasive answer like that only arouses my curiosity. What's in California?"

"Nothing in particular. I was just passing through. I went on a little backpacking trip, and then I was moving on."

"Moving on? So where were you headed next?"

Sarah was not ready to give the full answer to this question, but still tried to answer truthfully. "Honestly, I'm not exactly sure."

"So you're just some sort of innocent young girl out to see the world? I see. An innocent young girl who runs away from home, carries a Bible in her backpack and has battle plans on her phone?"

"Those aren't battle plans! It's just some conspiracy theory website a friend sent me!"

"I know very well what it was meant to look like. And I know the kind of people who produced it. Are you a part of the Fortress Movement?"

"No."

"Are you a part of a terrorist organization?"

"No."

"Are you in the employ of any nation seeking to do harm to the United States of America?"

"No."

"Are you aware of an imminent attack on the United States of America?"

"Yes."

The reply came from Sarah's lips before she had time to think, but she had no regrets about saying it. She had made up her mind not to lie. She had nothing to lose. She was amused to see that Sergeant Parsons, for a moment, was speechless. He remained composed, but it was obviously an effort to control his voice when he finally asked his next question:

"When?"

"Thirteen days."

Now he inhaled and sat up straight in his chair. He glanced at one of the two Soldiers behind him, then proceeded.

"That's some pretty specific information for someone who is neither a spy nor a terrorist, Sarah Martinez from Portland. Do you want to change any of your earlier statements?"

"No sir."

"Well then, how does a sweet little girl like you know that an attack is coming in thirteen days?"

Now Sarah was the one to pause and take a deep breath. This

was it. It was not that she had, or should care about having, this man's respect. But now was the moment when telling the truth would make her look like a fool, and it took a moment for her to become comfortable with this fact. She collected herself and continued:

"An angel told me."

Sergeant Parsons laughed out loud before he could stop himself, as did the two Soldiers. "An angel? You expect me to believe that?"

"No. But it's true."

"Okay, I'll play along. Where did you meet this angel?"

"At a dance club."

It was clear that he could not tell if Sarah was being sarcastic as a way of withholding information, or if she was crazy. If she was stalling and wasting his time, his usual tactic would have been to raise his voice, make bigger threats, and employ more aggressive forms of torture. But something about the simplicity of the girl before him aroused his curiosity enough that he decided to let the conversation play out.

"At a dance club?" he said with amusement. "You met an angel at a dance club and he told you that there was an attack coming in thirteen days?"

"Well, no, he told me later, at a coffee shop. And at the time it was thirty days. I know it sounds crazy, but it's true, and no matter how much you torture me, this is all I can tell you."

"I see." He nodded. He was beginning to lean toward the opinion that he was dealing with an issue of mental illness, but he hadn't entirely given up on gaining some useful information. Perhaps this girl had spoken to a real live person, a spy of some kind, who had shared something with her. "So how did you know it was an angel?"

"I'd rather not say. He proved it to me. Let's just leave it at that."

"Fair enough. Did this 'angel' tell you who the attackers would be? Or give you any other details about what was going to happen?"

"No. I guess it was none of my business. He just said that it was coming, and I needed to leave town with him."

Parsons couldn't contain a chuckle at this. A picture was

forming in his mind of a confused, mentally ill young girl who had been taken advantage of by someone very creative. "He wanted you to leave town with him? And you did? Oh, my. So where is your angel now?"

Sarah rested her chin on her knees. She knew how all of this sounded, and she didn't care, but she did hate to be reminded of why she was in this situation. She sighed. "I don't know."

His responded with mock sympathy: "Your angel left you? I'm so sorry to hear that."

"No, it's my fault. I sort of … went off course."

"I see. But you were going to carry on, without your angel, weren't you? That's why you were 'passing through,' isn't it? You're not just a free spirit out exploring the world. You really believe something is happening thirteen days from now."

"Yes sir, I do."

"So where are you really headed, Miss Martinez?"

"Mexico. I was headed to Mexico."

"Of course. And how did you plan to cross the border?"

Sarah shrugged. "I don't know. That was His job."

"The angel?"

Sarah paused. "Not exactly."

Sergeant Parsons studied her face for a minute, nodding gently the entire time as he processed everything he had heard. "You are headed to Mexico because you believe an angel told you to flee the country because of an imminent attack, and you believe that *God*," he put special emphasis on the word, "was going to magically open the gates for you and let you escape."

"Yes sir."

"And what about the rest of us? That doesn't seem very fair of God, to give you a warning and take you to safety while the rest of us burn, does it?"

This was the very question that Sarah had been asking herself, but now that she was on the other side of it, she saw it differently. "Do you believe in Him?"

It was the first time she had asked a question. Normally he would not have responded, but Sergeant Parsons was becoming increasingly convinced that he was not dealing with someone who posed any sort of real threat. He looked her in the eye and said, "No I do not."

Sarah met his gaze. "Well then maybe that's your answer."

The Sergeant frowned and stood. This conversation had ceased to be a good use of his valuable time. He folded his chair and took a step toward the door. Sarah, emboldened by the realization that he had no more interest in her, called after him:

"You think I'm crazy, don't you?"

Experience had taught him that it would be a mistake to insult her at this point. He had no desire to escalate an argument with a mentally ill prisoner. "I think you and I disagree about some things, Miss Martinez." He continued to move toward the door.

She called after him. "But you don't believe I saw an angel, do you?"

"No, Miss Martinez, I do not," he said over his shoulder.

"Then can I ask you a question?"

He sighed, and resigned himself to the fact that the conversation was not quite over. He turned and faced her again.

"Sure."

"Why did you leave me here for a day before you came and talked to me?"

The question caught him off guard. It seemed irrelevant. He was growing impatient. "Because, Miss Martinez, believe it or not, there are other things going on in this world that that have nothing to do with you."

Sarah smiled. "That's what I thought. Things kinda falling apart out there?"

This got his attention. He stepped closer. "Why? What else do you know?"

"I know people need angels a lot more than they think they do."

He rolled his eyes, turned, and strode out of the room.

Forgotten

Hours passed. The alarm did not sound again. Eventually lunch came, after which Sarah fell asleep until the click of the meal slot awoke her at dinnertime. This meant that after eating she was not tired, and returned to her earlier routine of pacing the room and lying down to stare at the ceiling, although this time without a bed to lie on. After a few minutes of this she realized that the lights were back to their usual brightness. The temperature had returned to normal as well. She began to hope that this meant her bed would be returned, and perhaps even that the lights would go out at some point. Sergeant Parsons had mentioned that. But he had apparently forgotten his promise. Hour after hour, she was alone with the silence of her thoughts. The peace from the previous evening remained, but at the edges of her mind a question was seeking to force its way in, to create a foothold for fear within her: What now?

Sarah woke on the floor with her head in the corner of the room, in the position she had adopted the night before. She did not remember lying down or putting her shirt over her head, but she did have a sense that she had slept a long time, and that it was a new morning.

12 days. This was a frightening thought. While the number was still in the teens, the destruction Justin had foretold seemed a long way off, especially back when it seemed safe to assume she would be long gone before the deadline came. Twelve seemed like a very small number. She sat upright and took a deep breath, consciously fighting the anxiety that sought to consume her. She forced herself to think back to when she had first met Justin, and to mentally review once again all the events that had happened since then, this time keeping mental notes on which events had happened on which days, just to make sure her countdown was accurate. Thinking through everything in this way made her realize just how quickly everything had happened. Had it really been less than three weeks ago that she was living her simple life, arguing with her parents, working at the Cup and Saucer each day, neither hunted by evil men nor accompanied (to her knowledge) by angels? She smiled at the thought of the small, selfish dreams and everyday problems that had occupied her thoughts in those simpler days. Again she was aware that her heart and mind had changed as much as her circumstances since then. Thaddeus had been right. Whatever happened, she would never be the same.

Then discouragement came. She looked around at the walls of her cell and felt a deep sense of waste. It was true that she had seen amazing things and grown in unexpected ways, but what was the point if all of that had only led her to ... here? It was such a pathetic ending to what could have been a great story. *What was meant to be a great story*, she told herself, *until I blew it*. Thoughts like this made her wish her room were equipped with a Wall. It would be nice to be distracted, not to have to think at all, for a while.

The meal slot clicked, signaling breakfast. She ate and then decided to see how long she could play her game with the meal tray before the robotic woman's voice came over the speaker. But it never came. She spun the tray until she got bored, and then it became a new part of her routine: pace, stare at the ceiling, spin the tray, repeat. After lunch she was able to continue to develop her skill with two trays. Still no voice, no reprimand. Dinner came. She spun trays until her back became tired of sitting on the floor, then, on an impulse, took one of them and hurled it at the mirror. It bounced off harmlessly. She waited for a response, but none came. She sighed and continued spinning, pacing, staring, spinning, pacing, staring, until she could sleep again.

11 days. Sarah was angry almost as soon as she woke. Her anger was partly at the Army, for trapping her in this situation and then, apparently, forgetting her. It was partly at God, for the same reasons. And it was partly at herself. After breakfast she angrily shoved the meal tray back through the slot, along with one of the extra ones from yesterday. She pictured Sergeant Parsons at a desk somewhere, eating a donut and dealing with important matters, completely unconcerned about the fact that she was still sitting in this room, going crazy.

After a couple of hours, though, she found that she could not live with herself in a state of anger. As she stood staring at the word "liars" scratched into the cell wall, she realized that the blame that filled her heart was no longer satisfying. It would only hurt her, not Sergeant Parsons at his desk, certainly not God. She decided instead to sit down on her bed and make a mental catalog of all the things she remembered from her Bible reading. For some reason, though, at the moment she could think of very little. It was frustrating. She knew she had read a great deal, and she knew that some of it had sunk deep into her heart, that she had been forever changed by it in a way that was not dependent on her memory. But still, it would be nice to remember something. Apparently, though, this was not a good time for mental challenges. Again she wished for a Wall to stare at. Still, at the very least she had been able to fight off, for now, the toxic attitude that had greeted her at the start of the morning.

The rest of the day passed like the one before. No one came, nothing changed. Sarah had a hard time getting to sleep that night. She was more aware than ever of the hardness of the floor, and her body was simply not tired. Eventually, long after she had taken her position in the corner, she slept once again.

10 days. This time Sarah woke to a feeling of numbness. She expected that the day would be exactly like the one before, and it was too exhausting to be angry, or hopeful, to wrestle with regret or with big questions. What was the point? She passed the day without smiling and without tears, but she sighed a lot. She paced, stared, spun her trays, and ate her meals. When she lay down to sleep in her corner, though, something snapped. It was too much to ask her to go back into that corner again. What was the point of all this? What was it for? It felt like she deserved something: information, or at least hope, and she was beyond the point of manufacturing hope from within herself. It had to come from the outside. She sat upright and prayed angrily, and aloud:

"Hello? Are you there? What is going on? What is the point of this? I said I was sorry, right? So what happens now? I can't ..." her voice broke unexpectedly. "I can't do this. What are you doing?"

There was no answer, of course. Not that she had expected one. But talking to the walls and getting no response felt like it proved her point. And now that she was allowing herself to say what she felt, it was hard to hold back:

"It's all your fault!" She was yelling through tears now. "None of this was my idea! You're the one who dragged me out of my life into this ... crazy nightmare! I didn't ask to be special! I didn't ask to believe! You did this! You said you wanted me, and now you've left me here because I made one little mistake! I'm sorry, all right? What can I do? What am I supposed to do?"

Again, there was silence. But then, suddenly, a thought, a memory—an answer?—came into her mind. *You do not have because you do not ask.*

She remembered reading that. It was about prayer. What did that have to do with anything? *What haven't I asked for?* She thought for a moment, and when the answer came, it made her blush with embarrassment, and smile at herself a little bit through her tears: *I haven't asked to get out of this cell.* Was it that simple? Would that really work? It seemed impossible. And if it was possible, did that mean she had only had to endure the past several days because of a technicality? Because she hadn't said the right words? That didn't seem right. Still, it was hard to believe that it was as simple as asking. But what did she have to lose?

"Fine," she said aloud, "I'll ask: Please get me out of this place."

Would it happen immediately? She stared at the door for a moment. Nothing. Should she ask again? Then another memory came, something about a woman who wanted justice. *Then Jesus told his disciples a parable to show them that they should always pray and not give up.* And there was also something in there about praying without ceasing. Okay. So she would keep praying. And she would try not to give up hope. She asked one more time before lying down to sleep:

"Please help me. I'm so sorry. Please get me out of here."

Then she committed herself to asking again the next day, all day long, for as long as it took. She lay down in her corner and was soon asleep.

Nine days. Sarah remembered her commitment as soon as she opened her eyes, and made it the newest part of her routine: pray, pace, spin, stare, repeat. Pray, pace, spin, stare, eat. *God, please get me out of here.* She was proud of herself as she lay down in her corner that night. In a strange way, it had been a good day.

Eight days. God, please get me out of here. It almost felt as if she was praying before she was fully awake. *Please do something amazing. I know I don't deserve it. But please. It doesn't make sense for you do to everything you did for me and then leave me here. Please get me out. I will go wherever you want and do whatever you say. Please, I need your help. Get me out.*

The morning passed quickly, much like the day before. Pray, pace, spin, stare, eat. After lunch, though, she felt her willpower waning. What was the point of saying something she had already said dozens of times? Either He had heard her, or He hadn't, right?

She prayed once or twice in the afternoon, and again before going to sleep, although a bit of her enthusiasm was gone and it felt at times like she was just saying empty words. Still, she had made a commitment. She would not allow discouragement to defeat her this easily. *Please, get me out. I'm trying to have hope. Please.* And then she slept.

On the run

That night Sarah had a dream in which she felt a tap on her shoulder and opened her eyes to see Justin standing over her. She was not surprised to see him. He put his finger to his lips to indicate that she should be quiet. She rose and followed him to the door of her cell, which he opened as if it had never been locked at all. He led her down the corridor, but instead of retracing her steps to the garage where she had entered the building, they took a turn that led them to another door, which he also opened. They were now in a hallway of offices. After passing several doors, he stopped in front of one and pointed through a window. There, leaning against a desk, was Sarah's backpack. She opened the door—it wasn't locked either—and discovered that sitting on the desk was her Bible. As she took it to put into her pack, she saw a framed picture of Sergeant Parsons standing with another important-looking Army official. She smiled and shouldered the pack, then Justin beckoned her to follow him down the hallway again. The building was entirely quiet. In another minute they stepped into a large entryway, with shiny granite floors, elevators, and a large desk, behind which slept two armed Soldiers. Justin again motioned for her to be quiet, and they walked silently across the floor to the large glass entry doors that led out to the street.

When they emerged, the first thing Sarah noticed was the

warmth. It seemed to be very early in the morning; light was growing on the horizon in one direction, but for the most part the sky was dark, although she didn't see many stars. But the air was as warm as she would have expected for the middle of the day. There was also a sweet, unfamiliar smell, and the noise of a surprising number of cars on the road for this early in the morning. Something didn't feel right; everything had the sort of surreal quality that she was used to noticing just at the point of realizing she was dreaming, shortly before waking up.

"Justin, what's going on? Where are we?" she asked.

The angel smiled his characteristic patient smile and said, "It's good to see you too, Sarah. And you're welcome. We're outside the Federal Army Building in East Los Angeles, California. It's five o'clock in the morning and you are no longer a prisoner. We need to hurry and get out of the area before your absence is discovered. I'd suggest catching a taxi."

"Los Angeles. Wouldn't that be nice?" Any moment now Sarah expected to open her eyes and be greeted by the dull white paint of her sleeping corner.

"What do you mean?"

"What do you mean, what do I mean? I mean, isn't this …?" Sarah's voice faded and she began to look around carefully. She stared at the sidewalk, the glass doors of the building she had just left. She stepped back and read the sign over the doors: Federal Army Building, East Los Angeles. She listened to the traffic, and sniffed the air. She stared for a moment at her own hand, then placed it against her face, then gently slapped herself. "Wait. What? What! This is real?" She looked around herself again and then back at Justin. "Justin, is this real? Are you real? This isn't a dream?"

"Not a dream." Justin raised his eyebrows playfully. "But we do need to hurry. I can explain later."

"Justin! You did it! I'm out! Thank you!" Sarah impulsively threw her arms around him and squeezed him as tight as she could, releasing him again before there was time to feel awkward. There was no one on the sidewalk, and she was too excited and relieved to be concerned with being seen or heard. "Do you know what this means? It worked! Justin, you would be so proud: I prayed and it worked! I asked to get out, which seemed impossible, but here you are, and now I'm out! And we're in Los Angeles? Is that a miracle? Did He change it from Portland somehow, because I prayed, or was I always here?"

Justin was laughing before she finished gushing. Now that she had paused to take a breath, he stopped chuckling and said, "You were always here, Sarah. As it turns out, our backpacking trip put you just far enough south to be under the jurisdiction of the Southern California Field Commander, which meant, because of some Army regulations, that you had to be transported here. But we really should go. I can explain more once we're out of the city. Now, will you please come with me?" He turned and began to walk down the sidewalk.

Sarah's head was spinning, but she hurried to catch up. Then, after a few steps, Justin stopped suddenly and looked intently at her backpack.

"What is it?" she asked.

"Let's leave your phone behind this time."

Sarah's face flushed red and she lowered her eyes. Sheepishly, she slid the pack off, opened the lower compartment, and reached inside. The phone wasn't there. Then she remembered that Sergeant Parsons had been looking at it at one point. When she opened the main compartment, it was sitting right on top, under her Bible. She took it out and turned it over in her hand, deeply aware in that moment of all that it represented. "Justin, I'm so sorry," she said.

"All is forgiven, Sarah. Your only penance is that you have to run over to that trash can," he pointed to a receptacle about fifty yards past the entry doors in the other direction," and put it in there to throw them off."

Sarah smiled and quickly did as he said, and felt a sense of lightness when the phone slipped from her hand and thunked into the empty can. She returned to him. "Okay. Ready."

"All right. Let's go." Justin began walking and talking at the same time. "So this is the plan: The Army now knows you're headed to Mexico, and they'll be looking for you along the main roads and at the main points of entry, so we need to head east and get away from people again ..."

Sarah interrupted: "But why would they care where I go? Don't they just think I'm some crazy girl now?"

"Well, yes, the sergeant had pretty much dismissed you as a dead end, which is why he left you alone for the last few days. But now you're an escapee, so you just became a priority again."

"I guess so. And hey, how do you know they know I'm going to Mexico? I thought you left. Where have you been this whole time?"

He gave her a mysterious smile. "Not far. Now, as I was saying, we need to get a taxi, head east out into the suburbs, and from there the desert, and then we'll look for a place to cross over that's a little more obscure. You're not going to like hearing this, but I think it would be wise to stock up on some food and supplies, because this could still take a few days. And I think we'll want to invest in some untraceable transportation. How much money do you have left?"

"Um, I don't know, five thousand and some dollars. If I still have my wallet."

Justin eyed her backpack again. "You do. And that should be enough. So let's see ..." He looked around at the traffic that was beginning to fill up the street they were walking down. "That should do." He pointed across the street to where a taxi was parked. As they were waiting for a stoplight to change and let them cross, he continued to give her instructions: "Tell the driver you need to get to the nearest grocery store. Once we're underway, mention that you have farther to go and that you'd like to buy a car, but that you're in a rush and don't have much money. Then just see what happens."

"We're going to buy a car? Justin, I've only driven a few times in my life, and I'm terrible in city traffic."

"It'll be fine. We're not going far, a hundred miles or so, mostly in wide open spaces."

They arrived at the taxi as Sarah was processing this. She opened the back door and sat down, trying to act like someone who rode in taxis all the time.

"Where to, honey?" asked the driver. He was a middle-aged man, unshaven and with greasy hair, who gave the immediate impression that he had been driving a taxi for many years.

"Um, the nearest grocery store, please?"

"Any one in particular? I can think of a few, but none of them are all that close."

"Well, I'm headed east, so, is there one that direction?"

"Sure." He pulled out into traffic without saying any more. They drove for about ten minutes as Sarah did her best to pretend that Justin wasn't sitting right next to her. New questions came into her head the longer the drive went on, but she knew now wasn't the time to ask them. Then the driver spoke again:

"Headed east, huh? You buying a lot of groceries? You gonna need a ride when you're done?"

"Um, no, not many groceries, and a ride would be great. Can you wait?"

"Depends on how far you're going. I don't like to get too far from downtown."

"Well, the truth is, I'm going a long way. I actually need to buy a car, but I can't afford much and I'm kind of in a rush."

This caused the driver to sit up in his seat and take a closer look at Sarah in his rear-view mirror. "I see." He paused for a moment, then went on: "I have a friend who might have a car to sell you. Cash only." He glanced at her again in his mirror.

Sarah looked at Justin, who gave her a thumbs-up. "Perfect."

At the grocery store, Sarah bought fresh fruit, muffins, bagels, two deli sandwiches, salami, jerky, cheese, crackers, candy, and trail mix. This last item was Justin's recommendation—Sarah told herself she would buy it just to satisfy him, but she wouldn't eat it. When it was all piled on the checkout counter, it seemed like a lot of food. It filled two grocery bags, and she guessed that it would last her several days. She prayed that she would be over the border much sooner than that, but then remembered that she still had no idea what awaited her once that happened. She wanted to ask Justin about it, but there were too many people around.

Back in the car, the driver said, "I called my friend and he says he only has one vehicle available right now, an older truck. You still interested?"

"Sure," said Sarah, "sounds great."

They rode along on freeways and busy streets for another fifteen minutes or so, and Sarah was glad to see that they were still headed east. They turned off into a residential neighborhood that was nestled up against some dusty brown foothills, and followed side streets to the very edge of the houses, where the subdivision met the desert. There, at the end of a long dirt driveway, was a mobile home with a barking dog on the end of a chain and a few vehicles, or at least parts of vehicles, scattered around the property. Sarah glanced at Justin questioningly as she opened the car door, but he nodded as if to say "Yes, this is the plan."

A man in a dirty white tank top who looked a lot like the taxi driver came out from behind the house, wiping his hands on a rag that he then tossed onto the porch. He extended a hand to Sarah and said, "Raphael tells me you're interested in my truck."

Again, Sarah did her best to act like she was comfortable in the situation. "Yeah, I mean, I'd like to see it."

He pointed her to a dirty white single-cab pickup. "That's it. Runs great. Here, let me start it up." He walked over to the truck, took a set of keys from the visor, and started the engine. Sarah knew nothing about cars, but it sounded right to her. She trusted Justin, but she also wanted to get out of this place as soon as she could.

"Okay, then. How much do you want?"

"Six thousand." He stopped the engine and stepped to the ground.

"I only have four thousand."

The man looked at the taxi driver and frowned. "No way. I can't let it go for that."

Sarah involuntarily looked at Justin, then tried to pretend she was just thinking. Now what should she do? She didn't have enough, and she felt too weak and vulnerable to bargain with this man. She had nothing to offer, and he had no reason to do her any favors. Then Justin turned and spoke to her.

"Sarah, look him in the eye. Ask him if he has insurance on the car."

She wanted to question him, but couldn't.

"Is it insured?"

"What?"

"The truck, do you have insurance on it?"

"As a matter of fact, I do. So what?"

Justin spoke again. "As him if he has the title."

"Do you have the title?"

"Yes, young lady, I do. But what do you care? You don't have the money anyway."

"Tell him the truck isn't worth six thousand. Tell him you'll give him four thousand, he can keep the title, and in a week he can report it stolen."

It was all Sarah could do to keep from looking at Justin at this point. She felt like a character in one of the movies her dad watched. But she put on her best tough-girl face and said, "Look, we both know the truck isn't worth six thousand. What if I gave you four thousand dollars and let you keep the title, and you wait a week before you report it stolen?"

The man looked at his friend again, who shrugged. He smiled and nodded and said, "Well, you're a surprise, aren't you? Okay, young lady, that's good enough for me. You have cash?"

Sarah produced the money, then pulled it back just before giving it to him. She had thought of something.

"How much gas is in it?"

"Half a tank or so."

"How far will that take me?"

"I don't know. Hundred miles, maybe a hundred and fifty."

"Okay." Sarah was proud of herself for thinking of this. Fewer and fewer vehicles even used gas, and finding a gas station was not always easy.

She handed him the money. The man counted it, nodded again, and passed a few bills over to the taxi driver. Then he said, "All right, you know where the keys are. This conversation never happened." He turned abruptly and walked back behind his house. The driver got in his car and sped off, and Sarah and Justin were left standing in the dust next to the truck. Sarah turned and asked,

"Was that dishonest?"

"Not at all. You didn't cheat him. He was trying to cheat you. You just had to speak his language a little bit. He got a fair price for his truck. You don't need the title. And in a matter of days, if he survives, he won't be able to find gas for it anyway."

"So I wasn't being deceitful?"

"No, Sarah, you were being shrewd. But I'm glad you're concerned about it. Now, come on, let's go."

Sarah had already put her groceries in her backpack on the cab ride. She took out a muffin and a banana, then put the pack in the back of the truck, opened the driver's door, and nervously climbed inside. The truck started smoothly once again, and she was relieved to see that it was an automatic. She put it into gear and slowly crept down the driveway, becoming accustomed to the feeling of being in control of a vehicle. Aside from mandatory driver's training classes in school, she had only driven a few times, in her brother Alyx's car. He had always sat in the passenger seat, giving instructions, teasing her, and worrying about his paint job. It felt good to know that the paint job on this truck was nothing to worry about. She gained confidence as they made their way back along the slow residential streets, then a larger street with stoplights and multiple lanes. Justin guided her to the freeway onramp, and she let out a whimper as she sped up and entered the flow of traffic. But it wasn't long before there were fewer and fewer exits, and then the buildings started to give way to sagebrush. They were in the desert. She let out a sigh of relief and resettled herself in the seat, and allowed herself to relax enough to start talking.

Into the wilderness

"I'm almost out of money, you know."

"I wouldn't worry about it, Sarah. That money wasn't going to be worth anything in another week."

"Huh. I guess so." *7 days. Is that right? Is it that soon?* For a moment she was struck by how surreal her situation was. "Justin, is it true? I mean, the whole attack thing? Is it really happening, a week from today?"

"Yes, Sarah, it really is. And I'm really glad you're getting out."

"But you don't know how we're—how I'm going to get across the border?"

"No, I don't."

"Or what happens when I get to Mexico?"

"I honestly don't know, Sarah."

"It kills me that you're okay with that. I mean, what if I get there and it's just as dangerous, except you're gone? I don't even know where I should go, or what to do! What if nobody helps me, and I can't find a place to stay or a way to get food and stuff?

"Does that seem likely to you?"

Sarah took a breath and thought for a moment. She knew what Justin meant. She had been taken care of up until now. There was no reason to think that wouldn't continue. "I guess not. Still, it's hard not to know anything about what's coming."

Justin smiled but didn't answer. After a minute Sarah spoke again: "It's pretty crazy that the Army drove me five hundred miles closer to my goal without knowing it."

"And gave you food and a free place to stay for the past nine days."

"Yeah." Sarah hadn't thought of that. She pondered it for a moment. "Especially since it all happened because I left you and went off with Kyler. I mean, it's almost like ..."

"Almost like what?"

"Almost like it was supposed to happen that way. I mean, does it mean that what I did was good, since it worked out for the best?"

"Not at all, Sarah. There is a world of difference between those two things."

"Which two things?"

"Between 'good,' and 'worked out for the best.' First of all, we will never know if it was best. All we can say is that it worked out. Second, your life is in the hands of the One who can bring great good out of real evil. In no way does that mean that evil is good. It just means He is that amazing."

"That doesn't make sense."

Justin sighed patiently. "Then let me give you an example. The Son was betrayed. He was abandoned, He was falsely accused, He was mistreated and killed. None of that was 'good.' Those who were guilty of those acts were wrong, and they are responsible. But it 'worked out.' It was part of the Plan—in that case it *was* for the best. It was for you, among others."

Sarah stared at the road. "Yeah ... I guess I've never really understood that part."

"Which part?"

"You know, the Jesus part."

To Sarah's surprise, Justin laughed out loud, so abruptly and loudly that it startled her. It was more than a chuckle; it took him a moment to compose himself, long enough for Sarah to become slightly embarrassed and offended.

"What's so funny?"

"'The Jesus part'? Sarah, are you serious?"

"Yes, I'm serious, and stop laughing at me! There's a lot in there," she referred to the Bible in her backpack by nodding her head in its direction, "and some of it's pretty confusing! I'm learning a lot, but I guess I've never really gotten why he had to die like that. I mean, I read Hebrews, and that helped a lot at the time, but now it's kind of fuzzy in my head again."

Justin calmed himself. "Okay, I'm sorry. I just didn't realize that this is … where things were. But it's fine. Actually, it is my great honor to explain."

"Well, please do," said Sarah, still hurt.

"Okay, Sarah. Let me start by saying that there is a sense in which everything you have read, and everything you have learned about God, is 'the Jesus part'. He is everything. By the Father's design, the Son is the rightful recipient of all glory and honor. He deserves to be praised, worshiped, trusted, obeyed, and loved above all else."

Even as He said these words, Justin was visibly caught up in worship. It was as if saying them was a great relief, as if this was what he wished to be doing all the time, and other duties, while necessary, were less of a joy, and less important, than giving praise to the Son he so clearly loved. For a moment he was completely distracted, and when he looked at Sarah again he was surprised to see a tear making its way down her cheek.

"I know," she said quietly.

"Sarah, what's wrong?"

"I know," she said again, "You're right. That is what He deserves. And I didn't give it to Him."

Justin smiled slightly. "And there is your answer, Sarah."

"What?" She brushed the tear away.

"'Why He had to die like that.' It was because people eat the fruit that poisons them. It was because they don't trust Him, and they won't let go of their phones, their back-up plans. Because they run away with strangers who do not love them rather than trusting in His faithful love …"

"Stop!" said Sarah, and burst into tears. "I said I was sorry, okay? I can't do anything about it now!"

"And that's exactly my point, Sarah. How do you feel about those things you did? How do you feel about the nights you went to The Grind when something in your heart told you not to? How do you feel about the way you treated your father, and Jalen?"

"Stop it! What are you doing? I feel terrible, okay? I feel guilty!"

"And there's nothing you can do about it?"

"No, of course not!" Sarah was furiously wiping away tears so she could keep driving. This was the insensitive part of Justin that had made her want to be free of him back on the trail. She wished she was not trapped in the cab of the truck with him so she could just run away.

"But He has."

"What?"

"He has done something. About your guilt. That's why it had to happen, Sarah. Because you couldn't do anything, but something had to be done, so you could be free of it."

Sarah calmed down slightly. "What do you mean? Just a second ago you were just calling me a terrible person, beating me up about what I did. Now you're saying I don't have to worry about it?"

"No, Sarah, you are the only one beating yourself up. I am trying to answer your question, to explain 'the Jesus part.' I'm trying to tell you that you are forgiven, you are loved, because of Him. Do you remember when you asked me if I thought you were a real believer?"

"Yes."

"And I said that you believed as much as you knew, but more tests would come, and they would reveal the true nature of your faith?"

"Yeah, I remember. And then I failed the test," Sarah said glumly.

"No, Sarah, you misunderstand. This is the test. Right now."

"What do you mean?"

"I mean, a test of faith is different from a test of character. You happen to be undergoing both. But the most important question is not 'Will Sarah always do the right thing?' it's 'Does Sarah trust? Will she embrace what is offered to her?'"

"So if I let Jesus take my guilt, while I go free, then I'm a true believer? That hardly seems fair."

"It's not fair. You might as well get used to that. In this relationship, Sarah, there will always be a great imbalance. You will almost always be on the receiving end. You will get better than you deserve. You will lose your temper with an angel, and in return get free transportation, room and board. That's just the way it works."

Sarah smiled, and rolled her eyes at the same time. After a moment of thought she said, "So what's to keep me from taking advantage of that?"

"I think you know," said Justin.

Sarah nodded. She drove in silence for quite a while, deep in thought. Miles of brown desert, broken only by pale, spring-green clusters of sagebrush, passed before she spoke again. Then she said,

"So, just believing in God doesn't make someone a … believer, I guess?"

"No, Sarah. You're not a believer until you cry out for mercy. Think of it this way: your friends in black believe most of the same things you do about God, and they know as much as you do about Jesus. Would you call them believers?"

"No."

"Would you call yourself one?"

Sarah was quiet. "I think so. I mean, not that I want to be like them. I just—need a little time, you know? It's all new."

Justin nodded. "You're getting pretty low." He pointed toward the gas gauge. It read less than a quarter of a tank.

"So what do we do?"

"Well, we can't cross the Arizona border, which is coming up in a bit. We should look for a place to turn south."

They drove on. A string of low mountains appeared on the horizon, stretching away to the right, toward Mexico. They grew larger and larger until Sarah could see green patches in the small valleys created by little folds in the earth.

"Mountains mean water," said Justin. Sarah nodded. She was just beginning to allow herself to think about backpacking again. She did not look forward to it, but she felt stronger than last time, even a little ashamed of the complainer she had been less than two weeks earlier. She resolved not to let the experience crush her this time.

A sign indicated that they would reach the Arizona border crossing in twenty miles. A minute later, an exit off the freeway appeared. There were no services, in fact no buildings at all. The exit seemed to be there only for the sake of access to a ranch that lay on the north side of the road.

"Here," said Justin.

Sarah exited and, without speaking, took the small, unnamed road that wound its way south toward the foothills of the mountains. They drove on, seeing no other signs of life, for another twenty minutes or so, moving more and more slowly as the road became narrower and less maintained. Then it abruptly turned to dirt. Sarah stopped for a moment.

"Keep going?" she asked.

"Keep going. As far as you can."

They bumped along on an increasingly rutted and uncomfortable road through the sagebrush, toward the mountains, for another half an hour. Then the truck sputtered to a stop. Sarah looked at the gas gauge. Empty.

"I guess that's it," she said.

"I guess so," said Justin. He nodded toward the brown hills in front of them. "I don't think you had much more road anyway."

"So what now?"

"Well, it's mid-afternoon, and you've had a tiring week. It looks like some clouds are coming in, which is a great gift. It means shade, and possibly water in the mountains. I'd recommend spending the evening right here. Sleep as much as you can, and enjoy having some cushioning." He patted the truck's seat. "I'll do some scouting and try to find a good route to the border."

Sarah looked around them, not thrilled at the idea of being left alone here in the desert. Logic told her that no one on the entire planet knew where they were right now, but she had already gotten used to the comfort of Justin's protective presence.

"You sure it's safe?"

Justin also looked around. "Yes. Don't worry, Sarah. There is no one around for miles. And I won't be gone long."

"Okay." Sarah made the decision to cut worry off, to trust Justin and simply not think about it anymore. She got out of the truck and rummaged in her pack for some fresh clothes. When she looked up, Justin was gone, so she changed, relishing the feeling of the clean material against her skin. She tried not to think about how long it had been since she had showered. A cool breeze caused her to look up and see that Justin was right: gray clouds were threatening to hide the sun at any moment. Maybe it would rain. At the very least it wouldn't be too hot to spend the rest of the day in the cab of the truck. She grabbed her sweatshirt and a deli sandwich, along with her water bottle (she had remembered to fill it at the grocery store), and went around to the passenger seat of the truck. She ate the sandwich, drank a little water, and lay down to try to sleep. But she found that she was more excited by the events of the day than she was tired from the past week. After a few minutes of tossing back and forth she gave up, got back out of the truck, and retrieved her Bible from her pack. She sat down on a nearby rock to read, but the wind kept turning the pages, so she went back to the truck, locked the door, and turned with her back to it, using her sweatshirt as a pillow behind her lower back and extending her legs across the bench seat.

Having the book back in her hands was like being reunited with a friend. It was the same feeling as being reconciled with Justin: the past was forgiven, and she was able to pick up where she left off. At first, she read simply for the pleasure of doing so. After over a week in her cell with nothing to do, thinking she would never see her great-grandmother's handwriting again, it was a joy to turn the pages with her fingers, to find comfort in the words of the book as she had in her bedroom back home. But after a while she found herself seeking out places that struck a deeper chord in her heart, that helped her understand all that she had been through, that answered her questions. From there she went deeper still, losing track of time and reading words that felt as if they were being spoken out loud, for the very first time, by a living Voice directed at her very soul. She found herself reading over and over again a passage that she didn't even remember turning to. Every few words would lead her into a prayer that would last so long that by the time she returned to the passage she would have to start over, and the process would repeat.

"Good book?" Justin interrupted her thoughts by appearing at the opposite window, which she had opened at some point when the air in the cab got stuffy.

Sarah raised her head and tears were running down her face, though she was barely aware of them. She looked back at the page in front of her and read aloud with a broken voice: "From this time many of his disciples turned back and no longer followed him. 'You do not want to leave too, do you?' Jesus asked the Twelve. Simon Peter answered him, 'Lord, to whom shall we go? You have the words of eternal life. We believe and know that you are the Holy One of God.'" Her tears increased as she finished, but she was smiling as she wiped them away.

Justin nodded approvingly. "I'll give you some more time," he said.

After a while Sarah emerged from the truck, pulling her sweatshirt on, and found Justin seated on the rock where she had attempted to do her reading.

"Sorry about that," he said.

"About what?"

"Interrupting you. I should know better than that."

Sarah waved her hand and dismissed his apology. She found a seat on another rock. "No big deal. Don't worry about it, Justin. I've had plenty of time to myself lately." She grinned. It was nice to be joking with him again. "So, what did you learn?"

"Well, it's a little over sixty miles to the border. If we stay along the foothills here, there are a couple of places to get water in the first half of that, but the last part is pretty dry. No towns or roads between here and there; just one abandoned highway when you're almost there. I'm sorry, Sarah."

"Why?"

"Because it's hotter and dryer and farther than our last trip. There aren't any really steep parts, which is good, but you'll have to average over ten miles a day, with no trail. It's going to be hard."

"Well, were we supposed to go a different way?"

Justin looked a little surprised. Sarah didn't seem to be upset with him. She looked determined, strong. "No, I don't believe so. This is the plan," he said.

"Then it's okay." She stood and walked over to the truck, digging into her backpack for the other deli sandwich and an apple. When she returned, she sat and ate in silence for a time, looking thoughtfully up at the mountains. Then she spoke without looking at Justin, still partially lost in thought. "They walked a lot, didn't they?"

"Who walked a lot?"

"Jesus and those guys. I mean, they went all over the place, and they didn't have cars or anything, so they walked, right?"

Justin smiled. "Yes they did."

"So they slept on the ground. He slept on the ground. Right?"

"Right. Quite a bit, actually."

Sarah nodded, still staring at the mountains. She took a few more bites of her apple. "Okay," she said after a minute, then rose, threw her apple core into the sagebrush, crumpled the wrapper of her sandwich, and said "I'm going to try to get to sleep early. Goodnight, Justin." She walked to the truck, then turned and looked back at him.

"Hey, Justin?"

"Yes?"

"Thanks for coming back. Thanks for getting me out. Sorry I didn't say it earlier."

Justin smiled. "You're welcome, Sarah. Don't worry about it."

Sarah got her sleeping bag out of her backpack, then looked upward. The clouds still looked like rain was a possibility. She put the backpack on the ground and slid it under the truck, wincing at the cloud of dust that enveloped it, but telling herself this was better than finding it wet in the morning. She climbed into the cab, unpacked the sleeping bag, and put her sweatshirt and some other clothes in its sack to create her makeshift pillow. Once she was settled, she stared at the ceiling for a while and wondered if she had made the right choice. Maybe it was too early to try going to bed. Had she been rude to leave Justin all alone out there this early in the evening? Then raindrops started to patter on the roof of the truck. A few at first, then more and more until it was a steady rain that washed down the windshield in a steady sheet. The sound was relaxing, and rather than keeping her awake it made the prospect of falling asleep seem much more likely. She smiled at the thought of Justin sitting out there in the rain, somehow untouched by it, or at least unbothered. She rolled over on her side and closed her eyes, and all at once her early-morning escape, the fear and frustration and near-torture of the past week, and the emotional and spiritual roller-coaster of the day caught up to her and overwhelmed her body and spirit, and she was asleep within seconds.

Company

6 *days.*

Sarah's eyes opened to what seemed like full daylight in the cab of the pickup. The sun was still low in the sky, but there were no clouds in sight and it was already heating up. She was instantly too warm in her sleeping bag, so she wriggled out of it and sat upright. She sat for a moment rubbing her eyes and yawning, but it was still too stuffy and uncomfortable in the small space where she had slept for, she guessed, the past twelve hours. She opened the door and discovered with relief that the morning desert air was still fresh and spring-like. The ground was slightly damp from last night's rain, and the smell of the sagebrush, so different from anything she had known back home, caused her to breathe in deeply through her nose and let out a grateful sigh. She knew what was coming: at some point very soon, she would put the backpack on and take those first heavy steps. But she was still able to enjoy this moment. Birds sang, and small desert flowers added color to the scene. It was a beautiful day.

She looked around for Justin, but didn't see him, so she took the opportunity to sneak off behind one of the larger bushes and use the bathroom in what felt like relative privacy. When she returned, Justin was sitting on the rock once again.

"Well, I didn't miss that," she said with mock grumpiness.

Justin chose to ignore this comment. "You slept well," he said.

"Yes I did. That is the most comfortable truck seat I've ever slept on." She was in a good mood. She dug her pack out from under the truck, proud of herself for thinking ahead and keeping it dry. She dusted it off and lugged it over to the rock next to Justin. She opened a bag of dried fruit, but Justin shook his head.

"I'd eat the heavy stuff now, so you don't have to carry it."

Seeing the wisdom in this, Sarah dug deeper and found an orange and a bagel. She ate them both, but then was so thirsty she drank about a third of her water bottle. Justin saw her eyeing what remained and said "Don't worry about it. There's a place to refill in a few miles." Grateful, she drank all she wanted and then stowed it in her pack.

"You should unload anything you don't need," he said. "Like that stove, for starters."

Sarah looked around, then stood and emptied the contents of the backpack on the rock where she'd been sitting. She realized it had felt light a few minutes earlier because her sleeping bag was still in the truck. She retrieved it, repacked it, and began sorting through everything else. When she was done, she took an armload back to the truck that included the stove and fuel, a pair of pants, a shirt, and two pairs of socks she had brought from Portland. All that was left was her sleeping bag, her Bible, water bottle, and food, her sweatshirt and the long-sleeved shirt that had been with her in her cell, and one extra pair of socks. She stood taking stock of it before packing it away.

"Your shoes seem to be in good shape," commented Justin.

Sarah looked down at the beat-up running shoes. They were dirty, but intact. "Yeah, I hadn't really thought about it. Good thing, huh? I guess we'll see how they handle this next part."

"I have a feeling they'll be fine," he said.

Sarah was lost in contemplating the best way to pack her things, and didn't respond. When everything was stowed, she lifted the pack and hefted it up and down a couple of times, appreciating how much lighter it was.

"Wow, that stove was heavy. This is going to be so much better," she said.

"I'll remind you of that at dinner time," Justin replied.

"Don't worry, I have plenty of trail mix," Sarah said sarcastically. "All right, let's go. Do we need to do anything with the truck?"

"No, I don't think so. No one is looking for you out here."

"Okay, then let's go!" Sarah started down the dirt road. The combination of a good night's sleep, the freshness of the morning, and the lightness of her pack and of her heart gave her an energy that carried her easily through the first few miles. The road only lasted for the first twenty minutes or so, but it wasn't difficult to choose a relatively straight path through the sparse sagebrush. With the mountains on their left, they went gently up and down along the foothills, high enough to have a view of the flat desert to the west. As the sun rose higher, this view became less and less beautiful as the starkness of the desert at mid-day revealed itself. Sarah started to sweat, but her spirits were still high.

As Justin had said, they found a small stream trickling out of the mountains at the low point of a small fold in the earth. Sarah started to fill her water bottle, but Justin stopped her.

"Drink the rest of what you have first," he said. "Fill your belly AND your bottle."

"I'm really not that thirsty," Sarah protested.

"Sarah, things are going to get hot. We need to be smart about this. You should drink every chance you get."

Sarah complied without further argument. And the water did taste good.

"You know, it's a good thing it's spring and that it rained last night. This stream won't be here in another couple of weeks," Justin said.

"What luck." Sarah smiled and glanced upward. "Okay, on we go."

The land rose ahead of them. They had begun to climb one of the larger foothills. All they could see behind it were even taller mountains, and it became clear that to maintain their current elevation they would need to break right, back toward the west. After a few minutes Sarah stopped to catch her breath.

"Which way?" she asked. "Should we head over there?" She pointed ahead and to the right, to what seemed to be a clear path around the steep hill in front of them.

"No, I don't think so. It will take us too far off course, and leave us out in the middle of the desert. There's more water and shelter this way."

"Justin, it's getting steep. I'm tired."

"I know. But remember I scouted this yesterday. If you can just push on over this rise, it drops back down into the foothills again. You just can't see it from here. There's actually a nice little valley on the other side, with some trees and a little bit of a meadow."

"A meadow?" Sarah looked doubtful.

"Well, not exactly, but it looks like it used to be cultivated, kind of an abandoned field. It's a pretty little spot. The closest thing you're going to get to an oasis on this trip. I actually wish it were a little further along so we could spend the night there. But anyway, it's the right way to go. Trust me."

Sarah took a deep breath. "Okay," she said, and pressed on.

In fifteen minutes they crested the hill and Sarah was drenched in sweat. But Justin had been right. Below them a grove of juniper trees was spread out all along the hillside, and beyond that a flat area with knee-high grasses growing in it, still showing a hint of spring green. On the far side of this the land dropped again toward the level of the foothills and began to look like much of what they had already crossed. Sarah could see more trees on the far side of the meadow, and a glint of running water among them. She could also see that in the distance, beyond the foothills, the small mountain range dwindled and then disappeared altogether, leaving the land flat all the way to the horizon.

Then she saw movement. At the far edge of the meadow, emerging from the trees, were small dark figures, first two, then three, then several more.

"Justin!" She gripped his arm and pointed. "What is that?"

Justin looked and stiffened. "Get down," he said, and took her hand. She stooped low and he led her down to the nearest tree she could hide behind.

"What is that? Are those people?"

"We need to get further into the trees," he said. They rushed forward again, downward, until Sarah felt the relief of shade and of knowing she was no longer exposed.

"Justin, what's going on?" Sarah panted. "Who is it?"

"Take a look," he said.

Sarah leaned out from behind a tree and peeked through an open spot in the branches. They were closer now, and some of the figures had begun to cross the field. There were many more of them now. They were definitely people. They were all in black, but among them were a few dots of bright, unnatural color. Blue, and green, but also red and yellow. After a moment, Sarah saw clearly that it was their hair. She also saw the glint of sunlight reflecting off of shining metal. She gasped and covered her mouth, and pulled back behind the tree. She could not speak.

Justin was scanning the field. "There are over forty of them," he said without looking at her.

Sarah whimpered. "How did they find me? I thought we were safe!"

"Sarah, don't be afraid," said Justin. But she was unable to obey him.

"What do we do?" Her eyes were wide and panicked. "Can you fight them? Can you beat that many?"

"No," he said matter-of-factly. "Not that many. And they've gotten stronger."

"What? I thought you couldn't be killed!" Sarah's voice was a harsh, desperate whisper.

"I can't. But I can be overpowered temporarily. I can be slowed down. Remember, they don't care about me. They just want to kill you. And I can't protect you from this many."

"But they're just people, just a bunch of burnouts, and you're ... you!"

"No, they are more than that. Their power is not their own; it comes from another source."

"Well then what's the plan? Can we call for ... backup or something?" She looked heavenward. "Maybe Thaddeus or someone could come help?"

"I'm afraid not. Doubtless they have prepared for that." He looked upward too. "They have been setting up this moment, and their agents will be in place to slow down any aid we would send for."

"So what, we just lose?" Anger was the only thing keeping Sarah from despair.

Justin spoke calmly. "No, Sarah. You're missing the point. We don't need any help."

"What?"

"If we needed help, we would have it. The fact that we don't have it tells us that we already have what we need. Like the money. There was enough, right?"

Sarah didn't like this, but she knew it was true. "Fine. So what's the plan?"

"Well, first of all, as I said, you don't have to be afraid," said Justin, and then quickly explained his plan of attack.

Showdown

There were no witnesses to the battle that took place that day. Elsewhere, life went on as usual, and the world took no notice as Justin the angel strode out onto the field to face his enemy under the bright blue sky. Only heaven watched.

The men in black had been waiting for the last of their number to drink from the stream that emptied out of the meadow. When they saw Justin emerge from the line of trees and begin to cross toward them, there were shouts and battle cries, and they quickly organized themselves and marched forward to meet him. When they were close enough, one spoke:

"Where is she, angel of light?"

"You will never reach her." Justin revealed his shining blade and stood ready.

"Oh, I think we will." The speaker was tall, with bright yellow hair and a savage look. His black leather shirt had no sleeves, and his arms were long and thick. He spoke with a strange sort of wildness and detachment, as if the man standing there in the sunlight were not the one speaking at all. "We are many, and we are strong, and we have come on a mission from our great master. We will not fail!"

"You have come only to your death," said Justin.

"Now!" said the yellow-haired leader. At once the crowd of men charged at Justin with their blades swinging. But not all of them.

They were spread out in a line about fifteen men wide and three deep, and while those in the middle attacked Justin, several at either end ignored the fight and began sprinting toward the far end of the field. They were hunting for Sarah.

"No!" yelled Justin. He swung his blade and killed three of the men who were already upon him, including the leader. Then he turned and ran after those who had broken free. With blazing speed, he caught two and struck them down in mid-stride. But then a blade pierced his back.

The effect was momentary paralysis. He froze for a moment, cried out in frustration, then turned and killed his attacker. Several more leapt at him and he fended off their blows, his arms moving too quickly to see. He slew them and turned and ran again, catching two more who were more than halfway toward the trees. Then a crowd overwhelmed him. As he fought off the strokes of eight different attackers, he saw several more reach the treeline. He killed several, but when he turned to break free again he felt a sword slice into his side. His cry was like a man straining to lift an object of incredible weight. He fell, and immediately two more blades pinned his legs to the earth. From where he lay he swung his sword parallel to the ground and brought several more men down in a heap. Then a short, thick, red-haired opponent jumped directly on top of him with a short blade, and plunged it into Justin's chest, then lay with his full weight on top of the hilt. Others piled on. Between their legs, Justin could see that at least ten had reached the trees. They were yelling and using their blades as machetes, hacking branches off the small trees and kicking up dust as they made their way up the hillside. "There's nowhere to hide, little girl!" they yelled. "It's over!"

But Sarah wasn't there.

Sarah was running.

Downhill run

"You don't have to be afraid," Justin had said, "but you do have to run."

"What? I'm exhausted. They'll catch me."

"No they won't. Take off your pack. Hide it up in that tree. And then run that way." He had pointed west, along the edge of the trees, to where the hill that formed the edge of the meadow fell away toward the desert. "Run around all of this, on the other side of that hill, down where they can't see you. Go all the way down there," now he pointed south, past the trees below the meadow, "And then make your way back up until you find water. Find a place to hide, maybe in those lower trees, and then wait for me. I'll make sure they chase us back in the direction we came from. That should buy me enough time."

"Enough time for what?"

"Don't worry about it. I'll meet you at the bottom of those trees. Can you do it?"

Sarah had followed the route with her eyes. "Around all of that? How far do you think that is?

Justin surveyed it quickly. "About a mile and a half."

"Ugh. I'm more of a sprinter," Sarah said with a wry smile. A determined look had replaced the fear in her eyes. She took another look at the meadow. "So much for my oasis."

"Yeah, sorry about that." Justin said with a slight grin. "Now go. Run, Sarah."

So she did. At first, along the upper edge of the trees, she had to pick her way carefully, ducking her head and often glancing to the left, afraid that she would reveal herself. Though she was far away, she winced every time a twig snapped. Then she came out of the trees and was exposed for a few seconds before dropping down over the rim of the hill and losing sight of the trees and the meadow altogether. She covered this bare ground with all the speed she could, and then had to slow when she encountered some steep downhill. Once she was confident she could not be seen, she turned to the south again and began to run at a pace that felt as fast as she could manage for a mile and a half.

The terrain did not make it easy. The ground rose to her left so that she was annoyingly off-kilter the entire time. She had to dodge sagebrush and the occasional juniper tree. But her course was slightly downhill, and she was propelled by fear. And it felt good to run. Whereas backpacking required mental effort, forcing her body to do something it didn't want to do, running was to her like breathing. She could just let her body take over and do what it loved to do. She could feel the stiffness in her legs from the last couple of weeks of backpacking and sleeping on the ground, but the more she ran the more all of that seemed to be flushed out of her system. Soon she was flying, feeling as uncatchable as she had in her track days back in school. She jumped over a small bush, because going around it felt too slow, then lifted up her eyes to scan the terrain ahead, looking for a clear path that would allow her to go even faster.

Then a thought entered her mind: *This is better.* In that moment running was actually preferable to simply sitting back while angels swooped in and solved her problems. It gave her something constructive to do, made her a partner. She could not swing a sword, but she could run. And it gave her an outlet for the rush of adrenaline that had flooded her system when she saw that she had been followed, tracked all this way out into the desert, by her enemy. It was perfect. A good plan. She shook her head at herself and wondered how long it would be until she learned to trust. Then she charged on.

After about ten minutes the land dropped away ahead of her and she realized it was probably time to veer left before she got too low and had to climb up a long way to find shelter in the trees and wait for Justin. She was well below the rim of the hill that formed the base of the meadow, and seemed to be nearing its southern end. And she was getting tired. Sweat drenched her forehead and her upper legs began to feel weak. Her throat was coated with dust. With each passing moment, running was less and less enjoyable, and she found that she was no longer thinking about running away from anything; she was thinking about running toward water. She had exhausted herself, and anxiety began to creep into her mind. Compared to backpacking ten miles, running for ten or fifteen minutes *was* a sprint. She wouldn't be able to go on without water. What if she couldn't find it? Had Justin been successful? How long would she have to wait?

To her left the hill was getting steeper, and she saw that if she went any further it would become a wall that might prove difficult to climb. She chose her spot, stopped running and allowed herself to catch her breath as she approached it. Then the sweat began to pour. She was instantly hot, and it created a desperation within her. She climbed up the hill and was relieved to see that she was well below the level of the meadow. Below her, scattered trees filled the space between her hill and the next one, and she heard the trickle of water among them. She half-ran down the hill, trying to be as quiet as she could and glancing up to make sure the enemy had left no stragglers down here below the field. She reached the stream and plunged her hands in, lifting up cups of water and washing her face, then drinking deeply, then soaking her hair, then drinking some more. She sat panting for just a moment, then forced herself back up and found a seat with her back against a tree facing downhill, where she would be hidden from view if anyone was looking from above. She closed her eyes and waited for her breathing to slow. *Thank you*, she prayed. *Thank you.*

Up on the field, Justin rose from a pile of slaughtered opponents. The rest were now spread out on the hillside that he and Sarah had descended, making their way higher up and farther away from him. Such was their pride that they believed their comrades had been able to destroy him. He looked back toward the lower end of the meadow and smiled. It had been a good plan. Sarah was safe down there, and his enemy was now scattered, headed in the wrong direction, and less than half its former number. Then his head turned back toward the hillside and his face turned grim. He did not relish what he must do now, but he wasted no time. With purposeful strides, he pursued the remainder of the enemy into the trees.

When he rejoined Sarah, she was dozing, with arms folded on her knees and her head resting on them.

"Wow," he said, "you're faster than I thought."

"Hmm?" She opened her eyes and stretched. "Sorry. What do you mean?"

"Well, I figured you'd beat me here, but I didn't think you'd have time to take a nap." He sat slowly against a nearby tree. "How long have you been here?"

"I don't know, maybe twenty minutes?"

"Wow," he said again, then with a distracted look he turned and looked back up toward the field. "It took a while."

"Are they all … gone?"

He nodded but didn't answer, still gazing back up the hill. Sarah thought she saw sadness in his eyes.

"I'm sorry, Justin. Sorry you had to do that. But thank you. Thank you so much. I mean … you know … your reward awaits you."

This made him smile. "Thank you, Sarah. Hey, do you want to eat some lunch? This is a good spot, and I'd like to sit here for a few minutes if you don't mind. You should also drink as much as you can and then fill up your water bottle."

"Well, I'd love to, but I have a hike ahead of me first. I have to go get my pack, remember?"

"No you don't; it's right there." Justin pointed to where Sarah's backpack was leaning against a tree behind her.

"You brought my pack! Didn't you say that was against the rules?"

"No, what I said was that it would look strange for your pack to be floating along all by itself. But there's no one out here to see, and I just felt like doing something nice. I knew you'd be tired after your run."

"Well, thank you. It's a great surprise." Sarah found cheese, crackers, and salami, and begin making herself a lunch. "By the way, did I hear you say that you wanted to sit still for a minute? Are you tired or something? I thought nothing affected you."

"Everything affects me, Sarah, just not in ways you can always understand. I'm not tired in the way you're used to thinking about it, but encounters with evil like that leave me ... drained, I guess you could say."

"So did they hurt you?"

He shook his head. "Again, not in a way I can explain. It's a spiritual, or maybe an emotional, kind of pain. It pains me to be hindered from my task, and to see evil gaining ground. I'm fine now."

"Just tired," Sarah clarified, with a twinkle in her eye.

Justin chuckled. "Sure. Just tired. How's your lunch?"

"Delicious," Sarah said through a mouthful. "I'm telling you, you're missing out. So, yellow and red—is that Nevada and Arizona?"

"Yes."

"How did they find me?"

"Well, like you, Sarah, they are in touch with very real spiritual powers. They have inside information. They were probably mobilized when you escaped, and once they saw where you were headed they came together ahead of you to cut you off. It's a good thing we encountered them here, where there are places to hide. Out there," he pointed south toward the flat horizon, "it would have been much harder."

Sarah nodded, acknowledging that once again Justin had been right. "But how can they all work together like that? What about the borders?"

"The Army has much bigger problems at the moment. Things arc falling apart all over the place, and there are plenty of places to cross state lines other than the highways. And they are growing more powerful. The time is near and they are becoming bolder, taking bigger risks."

"So will more come after me?"

"No. We sent a clear message today. And it's pretty remote out here. They face the same challenges you do: water, food, heat. To be honest, I was really surprised to see them this far out of the city. But they'll leave you to the desert now."

Sarah was looking at him doubtfully. "That's what you said yesterday. You said we were alone out here."

"I know. And we were. I knew this group was coming; I saw them on my scouting mission. But they were too far away to reach us last night, and I wanted you to get a good night's sleep."

"What?" Sarah sat up straight. "So why didn't you just kill them then? Why put me through all this?"

Justin shrugged. "Orders. It wasn't the right time or place."

Sarah surprised herself by not getting angry at this news. She shook her head and repeated, "Orders. Huh." She took a long drink from her water bottle, then filled it at the stream. She put on her pack and said, "Okay, lunch is over. Ready?"

Still seated, Justin shook his head. "I'm impressed, Sarah. I half expected you to want to spend the night here. That was quite a run, and here you are ready for more."

Sarah shrugged. "I was afraid. And kind of mad. Makes me faster."

Justin slowly rose to his feet. "Well, those aren't the best reasons to run, but they worked well enough for today. Okay, I'm ready. Let's go."

"Wait, what do you mean? I'm being chased by crazy evil men through the wilderness; don't I have the right to be a little angry and afraid?"

"Certainly, Sarah, and that's not what I meant. For today, those were completely appropriate things to be feeling. I just meant that fear and anger can only keep you going for so long. They aren't the best motivation in the long run—pardon the pun."

"Okay, so what is the best reason to run?"

"I'll tell you some other time."

Sarah groaned and started down the hill. She knew it was pointless to pursue the conversation further. "So, what's the plan for the rest of the day?"

"The plan for the rest of the trip is to head south. As far as we can today, and then one more day will probably take us to the end of these hills. That will be our last water. Then it's thirty miles of desert to the border."

It was a hard reality, and Sarah was grateful that she didn't have to face it today. "All right," she said. "Off we go."

A good conversation

"Okay, Justin, I'm ready."

They had been trudging along, up and down little hills, for a couple of hours. On the uphill portions Sarah could feel the effects of her run. She was slower than she wanted to be, and started sweating as soon as she had to put forth any real effort. But the downhill portions weren't bad. They had just enjoyed a brief snack-and-water break, and they were picking their way down an especially bushy hillside. Sarah's comment broke what had been a long, peaceful silence.

"Ready for what?"

"Ready for you to explain all the death."

"Oh. Okay. And by that do you mean all the death in the Bible, all the death today, or the attack that's coming?"

"All of the above, I guess. It's just still hard for me to wrap my mind around. I mean, I believe more and more, and I know He's good. Most of the time. I mean, not that He's good most of the time, just that most of the time I know it. But there's still this big question, and I keep picturing what you talked about at Java Stop that day, people scared and dying and bleeding and everything, and I think, 'How can He do that?' And it's the same when I read the Bible. I just don't know how to feel about all of it. I mean, when you saved me from those guys in the subway, I was glad, but then they were dead, and it just seemed so ... harsh. So final. And I feel bad questioning Him. I don't want to be ungrateful or, like, say anything I shouldn't, but it's hard to know what to do with it ... you know?"

Justin took a deep breath. "Well, actually, Sarah, I don't know, but I'll take your word for it. And that's probably a good place to start. If we're going to have this conversation, then you have to understand that there are a couple of areas where I have a much different perspective than you. I don't approach this issue from a human point of view. My experience differs greatly from yours."

"Well, that's why I'm asking. I want your perspective. So what do you see that I don't see?" This was a genuine question, but they had also begun to climb again, and Sarah hoped to make Justin do as much of the talking as possible for the next few minutes.

"Two things. First of all, it's interesting to me that so many in your culture are so offended by death, by bloodshed, and yet they have seen very little of it. They are bothered by the very idea of those things, and they act as if the only way anyone can believe in a good God is to hide away from the reality of the pain in this world. But my experience is exactly the opposite. What are unpleasant ideas to most people are realities to me. What you read in history books, I have witnessed firsthand. I have seen so much war, Sarah, so much murder, so many car accidents. I have been there for genocide and for plagues. I'm not the one hiding my head in the sand; I have seen more death than you can imagine. And it has never, not once, caused me to doubt the goodness of my God."

"So what's your point? That angels have stronger stomachs than people? I think I already knew that."

"No, the point is that so many treat death as the final proof that there is no God, or that He is not good. And they're wrong. They say, 'Look at all these terrible things. How can anyone say there is a good God?' Well, I have looked at those terrible things. More closely than they have. And I still say it."

"But it's different for you, right? I mean, you are an angel, Justin."

"That's true. I have an advantage even over people like you, who do have faith. What you are still hoping for, I have seen. The goodness of God is not a question for me. I have stood in the presence of the Answer. And I know it seems like that puts me at an unfair advantage, but that's what I'm telling you. I see it differently. Bloodshed raises a major question for you, but not for me. Not at all. So I can try to help you as you wrestle with this issue, but I can't relate to it."

"Hmm. Okay. But I've seen how sad it makes you. I mean, you're not some cold-hearted killer. It does bother you, right?"

"Absolutely. And I think, or at least I hope, that is because in some small way my reaction to it is the same as His. He is not some cold-hearted killer either, Sarah. That's what I'm telling you."

"But He is a ..." Sarah stopped herself short of saying what she wanted to say. It felt like crossing a line. "I mean, He does kill."

"Yes He does. So let's talk about that now. It brings us to the other major difference between me and people."

"Oh, I already know this one: you never have to eat or sleep or go to the bathroom, you never get cold or hot, your clothes never get dirty ..."

"Very funny. No, the other difference I was thinking of is that people have completely lost sight of their position as creatures, and I have not."

"What do you mean?"

"Well, Sarah, to put it bluntly, one of the most amazing things that I am witness to on a regular basis is when people, who are made out of dirt, feel completely free to throw questions in the face of the One who made them out of dirt. They challenge Him as if they had a right to do so, and He puts up with it! You are a mild example, but even you have spoken to God in ways I would never dream of. It is a reminder to me of how much more loving He is, how much more patient, than I am."

These words stung, but Sarah failed to see how they related to the question at hand. "Ouch. Okay, so the answer is that I have no right to ask and I should just shut my mouth?"

"No, sorry, that wasn't meant to be a rebuke. I'm just making the point that people are often very confused, very misguided, when they speak about their 'rights.' The truth is that you have no rights. And neither do I. We are creatures, and every good thing we enjoy is a gift. So when someone asks, 'How can God take away someone's life?' I want to ask, 'Did they have a right to that life?' Or, to put it differently, did He not have the right to take it? Ask yourself this, Sarah: Do you believe that people have a right to live a long and happy life? Is that guaranteed somewhere? Or even more specifically, because this is really what most people are saying when they argue this issue: Do people have a right to live a long and happy life with their backs turned to God?"

This was new territory for Sarah. "I suppose not," she said slowly.

Justin continued: "Have you read in the Bible where it says "The wages of sin is death"?

"Yeah, I think so."

"Well what you have to understand, Sarah, is that that is not some kind of arbitrary punishment. It's not as if God just got mad and decided he would kill everyone who sinned. It is a statement about His very nature, the very nature of reality. God is the source of life, the only one. To turn away from God is to turn away from life. People cannot, and should not, live forever without God. It is a great mercy that they live any amount of time at all. For those who reject their Creator, death is *right*. It is what should happen. And He always knows exactly when it should happen. It is never a mistake, and never more or less than what is deserved."

"What about the people who do trust Him?"

"That's even easier. I can promise you that no one who has crossed over to life with God has ever harbored any ill will about being taken too soon."

Sarah pondered this for a couple of minutes. Then, as their path turned downhill again, she said, "Okay, so I can see the logic of what you're saying. God gives life and has the right to take it. Sin deserves death. But it still feels like those are just ideas. I keep thinking about what it's really going to be like when the missiles and the soldiers come. All that panic, all the hurt people and dead bodies? I mean, you can justify it all you want, but it's still pretty awful."

"Agreed. But again, probably not as awful for me as for you. People die every day, all the time, Sarah, and every single time someone dies it is because their Creator has decreed that it is their time, and He absolutely has the right to do so. The fact that He decrees that a large number of them die at the same time doesn't change much for me. It bothers the people of your world because they think those people had a right to a long and happy life on their own terms, and that if there is any sort of God, then His job was to help them toward that goal. That, and it confronts them with the inevitability of death on a scale so large they can't ignore it, which makes them uncomfortable. But the reality is that those people were made to know and love God, and if they weren't interested in that then death was their destiny at some point anyway. From a heavenly perspective, the fact that He brought it a little sooner is somewhat of a minor issue."

"Wow." Sarah thought for a while. Her heart was far more prepared to accept these things than it had been a few weeks earlier, but it was still a lot to take in. She hiked on for a while before speaking again.

"Okay, but why?" she finally said. "Why does this have to be the way it is? If He is the Creator, why make things this way? Why not make them different?"

"Aha. Now we are getting somewhere. You are taking us into deep mysteries, Sarah. Good for you. This is a question I can only partially answer. Frankly, it can't be answered as well in a single conversation as it can over a lifetime of growing in faith and reading your Bible. But for now, I'll give you a short answer, so you'll be sure to remember it: It's worth it."

"What? What's worth what?"

"All the pain, all the death, is worth what's coming. As you read your Bible, you will see that God created a wonderful life for people, but people didn't trust God. They sinned, rejected Him, and introduced thousands of years of awful pain onto the earth. In the midst of all that, the Son came, receiving death into Himself on behalf of those who will trust Him, defeating it, and offering life in its place. And that life surpasses what was here before. One day all the death and pain will be no more, and the life of the Son will remain. And we will see that what people have with God at the end is better than what was at the beginning. And you will say to God: 'Now we see. You were right. It was a good plan. It was worth it.'"

Sarah tried to imagine all the pain and death in the world, from the beginning of history, wrapped up in a giant ball. She thought about the lifeless, depressing atmosphere of her own home. She thought about Torin's secret heartache as she gave herself to man after man who did not love her. She thought about prisons and playground bullies, about torture and abuse, about children's hospitals, and about war after war after war, down through the ages. She saw the earth as that giant ball of sin and pain, a dull gray color, desperately lacking in hope. And she saw that hope was being offered; it looked like a glimmer of golden light, brilliant in intensity, but for the moment seemingly much smaller than the enormity of the earth's misery.

"It's a lot to believe," she said. "I mean, it's a lot of awfulness to make up for."

Justin acknowledged this. "I know it seems that way. But take it from a witness, Sarah. I have seen the one thing that makes up for all the death, all the bloodshed. And I can tell you that it is greater."

"Wait, you've seen the future? I thought you said it took faith."

"I'm not talking about the future."

"Then I'm confused. What are you talking about?"

Justin paused a moment. He was walking behind Sarah and she could not see his face, but there was a noticeable change in his tone, a deepness and a reverence: "I'm talking about *the* death. *The* bloodshed. I'm talking about the Victory."

It felt wrong to keep walking. She turned to face him. "You saw it?"

He nodded, and there were tears in the angel's eyes. "We all did."

"What was it like?"

He shook his head. "Again, Sarah, where I come from we don't speak of these things. We sing. But it was … beautiful."

Sarah didn't press for more details. She felt she understood. Then she realized that she was wiping tears from her own eyes, and she turned to hide them. After a few steps she said, "So, from that point on you didn't have many more questions, I guess?"

"Well, I never did. Questions are more of a human thing. There are things I wonder about, but I trust. I will say that since then I have served with an even greater joy. The plan is good, Sarah."

Sarah took a deep breath and sighed. She looked out at the landscape in front of her. It was nearly dinnertime. She could see the end of the mountains, and their life-giving water, clearly now. *One more day, and then the desert,* she thought. But she clung to faith. "The plan is good," she repeated.

After another hour they arrived at a small stream and found a flat area next to it that would be suitable for sleeping. The water was warmer this time, and not as clean, a reminder that they were dropping in elevation. Sarah ate her dinner of cheese, crackers, and dried fruit, with a few pieces of candy for dessert. After sitting around for another hour waiting for darkness she was hungry again, so she ate one of her breakfast muffins. Then she sat in the dirt and stretched her legs, groaning occasionally.

"Sore?" asked Justin.

"Yes. What a day."

"It was quite a day, wasn't it? You ready for more tomorrow?"

"Not right now. But I will be by then. Hopefully tomorrow will involve less running."

Justin laughed. "I can guarantee it."

"Will you go scouting tonight?"

"I will if you want. But there's really nothing out there now."

"No, it's fine. I trust you."

"Well, it's nice to be trusted."

"You've earned it. You were great today. I was thinking, I haven't said thank you enough. Thanks for protecting me, and keeping me company. And for talking with me. That was a good conversation today. I appreciated it. I want you to know that I'm really grateful for you."

Sarah did not realize it, but these were things she would not have said if she did not truly believe she were forgiven for going her own way the previous week. She spoke genuinely, out of a certainty that their relationship was intact, without the burden of false guilt. Justin smiled at her freedom, and at her kind words.

"Well, you're welcome, Sarah. I feel the same way. Now try to get as much sleep as you can. Big day tomorrow. Probably the last one where you'll want to hike in the daytime."

"What do you mean?"

"Well, when you get down there," he pointed to where the hills met the flat desert, barely visible in the fading light, "walking in the sun will take too much out of you. You should make as much progress as you can at night, and try to find some shade and rest during the day."

"Wow, now that you say that it's so obvious, but I wouldn't have thought of it. Okay. One more day hike. And it's downhill. I can handle that."

"Yes you can. Goodnight, Sarah."

"Goodnight, Justin."

A new chapter

"Sarah."

Sarah opened her eyes see to Justin standing over her, quietly speaking her name.

"Sarah. Wake up."

She had been sleeping hard. Her body was sore, and she squinted at the brightness behind him. It seemed the sun was already rising.

"What is it?" she asked hoarsely.

"It's love, Sarah."

"What?" The strangeness of his words brought her more fully awake. She sat up, rubbed her eyes, and looked at him. "What's love?"

"The best reason to run. It's not fear, and it's not anger. It's love. Love is the best reason. I wanted to tell you."

"Okay." Sarah didn't know what to do with this. "Thank you for waking me up to tell me that," she said sarcastically. She flopped back down in her bag and rolled over onto her side. "Now if there's nothing else urgent, can I have a few more minutes?"

Then she woke up. The sky was still dark, with a hint of lighter blue in the mountains to the east, where she was facing. She looked to the west and could still see a number of stars. Birds were beginning to sing faint songs from their hidden perches in the sagebrush. Her head felt foggy. It had seemed like full daylight when Justin spoke to her a moment ago. Had it only been a dream?

She sat up. "Man, that was weird," she said. "You were in my dream. And not like I dreamed about you, but like you really came into my dream, interrupted it sort of. It was intense. I think it woke me up."

There was no answer.

"Justin?" she asked. "Are you around?"

Nothing.

"Justin?" She raised her voice. "Hey, did you go scouting?" She wriggled out of her sleeping bag, stood and turned a complete circle, scanning the bushes and rocks in the dim light for his silhouette. "Where are you?" All was silent. Her yelling had momentarily scared the birds. She listened and looked.

And then she knew.

When you get down there, walking in the sun will take too much out of you. You should make as much progress as you can at night. Not we. *You.*

But she wasn't ready to accept it yet. She turned another circle and yelled louder. "Justin! Justin!"

She walked up a few paces from the streambed where she had slept for a clearer view to the south, as if she might see him returning from surveying their route. But even as she did so, she knew he would not be there.

"No, no, no," she said to herself, then screamed again, "Justin, you can't leave yet! Don't leave! I have so far to go!"

But Justin the angel was gone. She knew he would not return.

Sarah crumbled and wept. She sobbed. Her tears created a small dusty puddle between her legs on the ground. But they were tears of sadness, not anger. She knew that to become angry would be like a step backwards, like forgetting all that she had learned from him. She grieved the loss, but accepted it. "I'll miss you," she said to the southern horizon, imagining that he had gone before her, clearing the path to her destination.

A few minutes later, as her tears dried, she wiped her face and took stock of her situation. She looked at her pack, and at the route ahead of her, and said aloud, "Okay, Sarah, what would Justin say about this?"

It took her a moment to think through what Justin would, in fact, say. Then she answered herself: "He would say that if he's not here, then I don't need him. He would say that the plan is good."

She wiped her face again, then rose and wiped her hands on her jeans. She drank some water, then filled up her water bottle. She used the bathroom and ate her breakfast of a bagel, dried fruit and a piece of jerky listening to the birds, whose songs became louder and louder as the sun began to rise. After another sip of water, she topped off her bottle, and put everything in her pack. She hoisted it onto her shoulders, adjusted the straps and shifted the weight on her hips until it felt just right. Then she took a deep breath as she stood looking down at the day's journey as it lay spread out before her. The angle of the light at this moment made everything seem close, as if she would be able to reach the desert in far less than a day, but she knew that would change as the sun rose higher.

"Okay," she said aloud, and lifted her eyes to heaven. "You and me."

The desert

5 days.

Sarah made good time all morning. The route was still more downhill than up, and her legs felt good. For a while there were even a few clouds that provided intermittent shade. She didn't drink much water. When she guessed it was lunch time, she stopped and ate the last of her cheese, some nuts, crackers, dried fruit, and a piece of candy. It was enough, but she did notice that her food supplies were starting to look a bit low. She held the bag of trail mix in her hands for a moment, then stuffed it back down below all the other food.

About two hours later the land dipped down into a small wrinkle, and at the bottom ran a small trickle of water. Sarah looked west and saw that further down the slope it disappeared entirely. She looked south and saw that she was now only a mile or two from the flatland. "This could be it," she said aloud to herself. She wasn't terribly thirsty, but she forced herself to drink the entire contents of her water bottle. Then she filled it from the trickle of water at her feet, which required her to dig out a low spot in the dirt and press the lip of the bottle down as close as she could to the ground. When it was full, she lifted it and eyed with disgust the grit and sand that swirled in the bottom. But she knew she needed it. She also knew that there was no way that this amount of water would be enough to get her through the next thirty miles. But she was choosing not to think about that, partly out of denial and partly out of faith. Things would work out. They had to.

The foothills gave way to flatland a bit before dinnertime. Sarah was not mentally ready to begin making her way across the desert yet, so she stopped at the base of the hills and found a place that felt slightly sheltered to eat her meal. She missed having cheese, but did the best she could with the jerky, nuts, crackers, and another bagel. She sat and enjoyed being off of her feet and watching the sun sink lower behind the sagebrush. Then, before darkness came, she remembered her Bible and opened it. The page fell to Psalm 121, which she read out loud without really making a conscious decision to do so:

"I lift up my eyes to the hills—where does my help come from?

My help comes from the Lord, the Maker of heaven and earth.

He will not let your foot slip—he who watches over you will not slumber;

indeed, he who watches over Israel will neither slumber nor sleep.

The Lord watches over you—the Lord is your shade at your right hand;

the sun will not harm you by day, nor the moon by night.

The Lord will keep you from all harm—he will watch over your life;

the Lord will watch over your coming and going

both now and forevermore."

The smile on her face grew with each line that she read, and at the end she shook her head in amazement. She read it through again and mentally replaced the word "Israel" with "Sarah." It was as if these words had been written just that day, just for her, at this time in this place. She shook her head again as she thought about Torin and her father and all the terrible things people believed about this book. She lifted her head up and said "Thank you," then turned to look back and the path she had walked so far. "So, my help is not in the hills. Okay." She began re-reading the words of the Psalm, and after a moment stopped short as a new realization came to her.

"I feel good," she said, stretching out her legs and wiggling her feet in the air. She thought for a moment more, then nodded, having made up her mind. She reached into the pack and found her small bag of candy. There was a bit more left than she would usually eat in one night, but not enough to be at all satisfying tomorrow. She ate it all, then stood and shouldered her pack. She looked back again at the hills and the place on the horizon the sun was setting, to get her bearings. The moon was beginning to rise in the east. *Perfect*, she thought, then took her first steps away from the hills and into the desert.

As Sarah walked, she calculated how much ground she might gain by a few hours of extra walking tonight. Three hours at two to three miles an hour would be another six to nine miles! She was proud of herself, and thought that Justin would be proud too. Her pack seemed light and it was an adventure to be walking out in the desert alone as the sun set and the stars began to appear. *It really is beautiful, in its own way*, she thought. The blue and purple shades in the eastern sky slowly chased the oranges and reds over her head and then out of sight, below the horizon in the west. The stars multiplied everywhere except where the half-moon overpowered them. There was enough light to make out the silhouettes of the sagebrush and tumbleweed, and Sarah was able to keep a fairly straight path. From time to time she would stop and simply gaze upward, turning and looking in all directions to take it all in. Once she did this for so long that she became completely turned around and had to bend down to find her own footprints to be sure of her direction. Three hours passed in worshipful silence.

Then she came upon a small cluster of rocks, a few of which were as big as she was. Their presence here seemed significant, though she did not know why. She was so encouraged by her own progress, the beauty of the night, and how good she was feeling, that she had been telling herself she would press on all night, and sleep as much as she could the next day. But she could not ignore the feeling that she should stay here, by the rocks. She stood there for several minutes. She felt silly, but it became a genuine struggle to make the decision. The idea of pressing on made her feel strong, brave, and independent. Stopping now felt premature and unnecessary. But when she took a few steps past the rocks, she immediately had the sense that she was ignoring a voice that it was unwise to ignore. So she stopped, sighed, and turned back. She opened her sleeping bag, found the biggest rock, and snuggled up next to it, much as she had the wall of her cell back in Los Angeles. As soon as she was lying down, fatigue overtook her, and she slept.

She was awakened by a noise a few hours later. It sounded like the skittering of a small animal across the rocks, but when she sat up she couldn't see anything, and she was too tired to get up and do any serious looking. She was confident that there was nothing out here large enough to harm her, and her food was stored as well as it could be. She shifted to a new position and began to lay back down, putting her hand on the rock to lower herself. Unexpectedly, the rock was cold. In fact, it was wet.

Startled, Sarah put her hand to her mouth. Yes, it was wet. Her body, thirstier than she had realized, demanded more. She sat up again and looked closely at the rocks. The moon had set, but peering in the starlight she could see that all of the rocks were covered in dew. The sand around them was dry. The rocks, because their lower halves were buried in the earth, hidden from the sun, had cooled overnight and collected what little moisture was in the air. Suddenly the situation felt urgent. She must collect this water. She glanced eastward and saw that the horizon was just beginning to turn light blue. She realized that in a couple of hours these same rocks would be dry and hot. She smiled at the fact that, for once, she had listened to the right voice within her when she decided to stay here. But how would she collect the water?

Then she noticed that her sleeve was slightly damp. She turned to her pack and dug for the long-sleeved tee-shirt buried at the bottom. She lay it out on one of the larger rocks and let it soak up as much moisture as it could. Then she tried to wring it out, but it wasn't wet enough. But there were several more rocks to go. She found her water bottle, and drank about half of its contents, then went from rock to rock, soaking up water with the shirt. Finally it was wet enough to wring out into the bottle. When the bottle was full and she had one more rock to go, she took another drink and then filled it again. Again she lifted her eyes and said, "Thank you."

Afterward the shirt was still wet, so she balled it up and dug in her pack for the plastic bag that held her breakfast muffins. There was one left. She ate it and then stuffed the shirt inside, sealed it, and put it back in the pack. She was about to get back in her sleeping bag when she stopped herself. The air was cool. Now was the time to walk. She would rest in the middle of the day, when the sun was hot. She hadn't had much sleep, but this was the smart thing to do. She put on her shoes, packed up her sleeping bag, and set out toward the southern horizon as the stars began to fade and the morning light grew in the east.

Thirsty

4 days.

Sarah was grateful for the countdown in her head. It was a more reliable measure of progress than her estimates of how far she had walked. She knew she would deceive herself into thinking she had gone farther than she actually had. Who knew how fast or slow she was actually walking at this point? The desert provided no milestones. But she did know that whatever else happened, four days from today things in the world would change dramatically, and that at that point she would be glad to be here, on this journey, rather than in the world she knew back home.

She made slow but steady progress all morning. When the sun grew hot, she took out the wet tee-shirt and tied its sleeves around her forehead, draping the rest of the shirt down the back of her neck and leaving one sleeve long enough to reach her mouth so she could suck the moisture from it. She also unashamedly turned the plastic bag inside out and licked it, laughing at herself as she made a mess on her cheeks, but thoroughly enjoying the wet muffin crumbs and drops of water. The cool material on her neck felt wonderful, and she felt good enough to keep walking until nearly noon. By then the shirt had dried and begun to moisten again, this time with sweat. But it still felt good to have her neck shaded, so she kept it on.

She was hot, but didn't feel terrible, and was tempted to keep going. Sitting still felt like a waste. But she remembered Justin's words: *Walking in the sun will take too much out of you.* She told herself that she didn't want to sweat out all the water she had gotten from the rocks the previous night, so she found the largest sagebrush she could and sat down next to it. The shade it provided was far from adequate, but by draping her sleeping bag over its top she could create just enough of a space to lay down out of the sun. But of course the shade kept moving. She ate a small lunch of jerky, the last of her nuts, and the last of her dried fruit. Somehow the nuts and dried fruit were better than trail mix, because she had chosen them, and could eat them separately. Trail mix, with its salt-covered raisins and unappetizing mixture of things she would never buy individually, felt like true survival food. And she had had more than enough of it on her last backpacking journey. But she was down to one more bagel, a few more pieces of jerky, and some crackers. Soon she would have no choice. She packed the food away and lay down in the dirt about a foot ahead of the sleeping bag's shadow, using her sweatshirt for a pillow, hoping to sleep.

But it was just too hot. All afternoon she lay there restlessly, chasing the shade and dozing occasionally, but never really getting good rest. Finally she slept for perhaps an hour before dinner, waking up as the sun heated the denim of her jeans to the point of discomfort. She took a swallow of water to make eating possible, then had some more jerky and crackers. She wanted the bagel too but knew it was better to wait. With a sigh she opened the bag of trail mix, picking out a few raisins just for the taste of something sweet. She put the food away and assessed the position of the sun. It was still too high, and she knew she would sweat too much if she started walking now. So she waited another hour, then shouldered her pack as the shadows of the bushes grew longer.

This evening's beauty was the same as the last. The colors of the sky, the brilliance of the stars, and the comfort of the moon were again sources of amazement and peace. But Sarah was not exactly the same. Last night's energy and optimism had faded. She was tired. Although she had slept on the ground many nights, this afternoon's nap on the bare ground, without the protection of her sleeping bag, had made her feel dirtier than ever before. Her clothes were dusty, and her throat felt the same. She stopped for a drink of water after the sun went down, but tried to restrain herself from drinking too much. "Now all I have to do," she said, attempting a little humor to boost her own spirits, "is find a rock in the desert in the middle of the night." She smiled grimly and trudged on.

A long time passed, and she saw no rocks. She was becoming discouraged. She had been hoping that this night's pattern would be the same as the last, that she would find a stopping place that would allow her to get some real sleep in the darkness. But she found nothing. The hours blurred together as she stumbled between sagebrush under the stars, most of the time not even seriously looking for rocks, but simply hoping—perhaps believing—that at some point she would come across some. It crossed her mind once or twice just to stop and lie down, but she knew that if she did she would wake in the hot desert with a little over half a water bottle, and any rocks she did come across would then be dry. She walked on. She was too tired even to pray in anger, to vent her frustration at the situation. She just walked. The Milky Way swept over her and gave her more of a sense of the spinning of the earth than she had ever had before. She felt small and weak, and began to think that if God did let her die in the desert, then He certainly had the right to do that, and even if she never knew the reason for any of this, perhaps it wasn't her place to know.

Then she tripped on a rock. It scraped her shin slightly as she fell onto it, which woke her out of her walking dream. Her hands and pant leg were immediately wet with dew. She scrambled quickly to her feet to avoid soaking up any more of it. She looked eastward and saw that the sky was again beginning to brighten. She had walked all night. The rock at her feet was a bit smaller than her kitchen table back home, and it was the only one in sight. It was roughly rectangular and rose only about a foot off of the desert sand at its highest point. She knew this would not be enough water to wring out of her shirt and fill her bottle. And she knew that water in her body was more important than water on the back of her neck. So she took off her pack, knelt down, and began to lick the rock.

She started at the bottom, down at the edges near the dusty soil. She licked upward and tried to keep her hands off the rock as much as possible so as not to waste any water. The rock was fairly clean, although she wondered after a few minutes how dirty it would have looked in the daylight. In any case, the taste in her mouth was more than tolerable. And it was water. She completed one side and lay on her back on the half of the rock she had already licked, resting her tongue and cheeks. Then, staring up at the stars, she began to laugh. She pictured how she would look to someone else, a young girl out in the middle of the desert in the wee hours of the morning, licking a rock. She imagined Kyler walking through the desert with his friends and coming upon her, and his amazement that she would choose this path over the life he had described to her in Colorado. But there was no bitterness in her laughter. She did not wish for Colorado, not even now. She was grateful for a rock to lick. The plan was still good.

And then Sarah was given a great gift. All at once she pictured herself, not just at this moment in the desert, but all along her journey, as the rest of the world would have seen her. She saw herself walking the streets of Portland to the bank and the train station, flanked by burnouts. She saw herself riding the train alone, changing plans and catching a bus, sleeping in cheap hotels, shopping, backpacking, hitchhiking. She saw herself in her cell, on the streets of Los Angeles, buying a truck from men of questionable character. She saw that at every stage of her journey, she had appeared to be completely alone, and never had been. And she saw that it was the same now. Unless it was God's plan, she was in no more danger of dying of thirst than she would be if Justin and Thaddeus had been there at her side, carrying backpacks full of water. She laughed again and rolled back over to finish licking her rock. When she was done, her upper body was trembling from holding herself in an awkward position for that long, her tongue was raw, and her cheeks were sore. But she felt as if she had just drunk a full water bottle, and her heart was light. She curled up on the sand next to the rock on the western side, where she would be in the shade the longest, and put the sleeping bag over herself like a blanket rather than crawling inside. She covered her face and head with her extra shirt and closed her eyes in peace.

The heat woke her in the late morning. *Three days.* She was still partially in shade, but the dark color of her sleeping bag had begun to absorb the sun's rays and it was quickly becoming stifling underneath it. She pulled it off and sat up, looking around sleepily for a moment as she considered her situation. She had a little more than half a bottle of water. Her path to the south was unbroken desert. It would be foolish to walk in the heat of the day. Staying here was the best option. But as the sun approached its peak, there was no shade anywhere. What could she do?

Sarah rose and took her pack in one hand and her sleeping bag in the other and moved herself to the other side of the rock. This side was slightly higher, and at some point it would begin to provide some shade. In the meantime she leaned up against it and arranged her shirt on her head once more. The sun was hot on her jeans, but nothing was exposed to the sun except her hands. She pulled out all of her food and set it on the ground in front of her. Bagel, jerky, crackers. Trail mix. And this would be the last of the jerky. She ate it with a few crackers and allowed herself a small drink to wash it down. Just half a bottle of water now. Then she realized that she was nearly halfway through another day. *Three days. Maybe ten, fifteen more miles? Can I make it?* And then another thought: *Make it to what? A magical tunnel under the wall and a secret oasis on the other side? With a cheeseburger stand?* She smiled and intentionally cut herself off from any more thoughts in that direction. Neither fantasy nor despair were helpful now. She just had to keep walking.

But not yet. Somehow she had to pass the afternoon without

getting too hot. She took out her Bible and let it fall open to the Psalms again. This time her eyes fell on Psalm 63:

> Oh God, you are my God, earnestly I seek you;
> my soul thirsts for you, my body longs for you,
> in a dry and weary land where there is no water.
> I have seen you in the sanctuary
> and beheld your power and your glory.
> Because your love is better than life, my lips will glorify you.

Her great-grandmother had underlined the words "Your love is better than life." Sarah sat looking at them for a long time, admitting to herself that their message was beautiful, but still somewhat foreign to her. She imagined what a great woman her Great-Grandma Sarah must have been, and wondered what it had been like to live in her time, when those who had faith in God gathered openly, and Bibles were not considered dangerous. She kept reading. Again it was as if the words were written for her. They expressed a faith and love for God that, while beyond what she had at the moment, were a picture of who she believed she was becoming. Later in the Psalm there were words of promise that, despite appearances, the powers that stood against God would ultimately lose. She found herself sighing deeply, as if she had just had a satisfying meal. Or a drink of water.

She intended to keep reading, but discovered that she was uncomfortable. A small rock was poking out of the ground under her leg. She took hold of it and it came up easily in her hand. It was about the size of a tennis ball, and left a small indentation in the dirt. She sat looking at this hole in the ground for a moment and then had an idea. Using the rock as a scraping tool, she dug away at the dirt, starting with the small hole she had already created. Soon the indentation was the size of a loaf of bread. And the ground underneath the surface was darker, and cooler, than the dirt on top. Excitedly, she began scraping nearer to the big rock.

After a few minutes she had created a small trench of cool earth next to the rock that was half as wide and half as long as her own body. Already it was big enough for a child to hide away from the sun. She began to sweat, and slowed her pace. In twenty minutes she had scraped away a small hollow in which she could lie down and be completely shaded. When she settled into it, she signed with relief. It was much cooler than sitting against the rock with the sun on her legs and head. And she was lying down. If she was going to walk all night again, and if there was any chance she could sleep now, then she needed to try. She put her extra shirt under her face so it wouldn't be resting directly on the dirt, then forced herself to sit up again and gather her food, Bible and sleeping bag and put them away in the backpack. Then she lay back down. It took a few minutes for her breathing to slow from the work of digging out the hole. When she had calmed down, she shut her eyes and was soon asleep.

Journey's end

This time it was hunger that woke her. Sarah opened her eyes to the beauty of twilight in the desert, and realized that her body was telling her it was time for dinner. She had very little to offer it. She sat up and rummaged in her pack for the last remaining bagel. In some ways, this was the beginning of her day, so it seemed appropriate to eat something resembling breakfast. After the bagel and some trail mix, she had a sip of water, then put everything in the pack. Then she stood, found her bearings, and began walking south.

The walk this evening was pleasant, not as enjoyable as the first time, but better than the all-out exhaustion of last night. She was grateful to have gotten so much sleep. Soon, however, she found herself distracted from the beauty of the night sky by thoughts of food. And water. She had been walking for days, and her body simply needed more fuel. She snacked on a few crackers, then told herself she would go at least two hours before thinking about food again. But it was impossible to measure time with any accuracy, and soon she was allowing herself more. After another forced break, she gave up. Sometime around midnight, she stopped and took the crackers out of her pack, then put the pack back on and kept walking, carrying the bag of crackers in her left hand and eating them with her right. Soon they were gone. Her hunger was somewhat satisfied, but now her mouth was salty. She told herself she would take a thousand steps before allowing herself to have a sip of water.

This goal, at least, Sarah was able to stick to. Counting her steps gave her something to do to pass the time, and it felt like she was making progress. When she did stop to drink, she took just the tiniest sip, and swished the remaining water in the bottle to get a sense of its weight. It felt light. She held it up to the starlight and could see that she had about one-third of the bottle left. *That's it,* she thought. *No more tonight.* She walked on through the night, her thoughts mostly blank. She had enough energy to keep up a modest pace, but she was too tired, hungry, and thirsty to pray or wrestle with deeper questions. The prayer of her heart was a wordless, fragile hope. Occasionally, when she did try to put words to it, the only word that came was a simple *Please.* At the moment, this was all she could manage, and it felt like enough.

Soon the sky grew lighter in the east. Sarah had seen no rocks or any change in the landscape the entire night, and did not hope to. Her mind was only half-awake and she had no clear plan. She told herself she would just keep walking on into the daytime until it was too hot to do so, and then ... what? She didn't know. When the sun rose, she stopped to watch it for a moment, and it felt good to stand still. *Two days.* One way or another, the journey was nearly over. This was comforting. She lowered her head again and marched on, picking her way around sagebrush and tumbleweed as she had for days. She tried not to think about the fact that she was already getting warmer.

Then suddenly the sagebrush stopped and she was walking on gravel. The ground swelled upward slightly and she raised her head to see the reason. There in front of her was a cracked, broken band of concrete, stretching from east to west as far as she could see in either direction. The paint had long ago faded, but it appeared to have been a major road at one time, abandoned when the Army had mandated the Buffer Zone: no civilian residences or activity within ten miles of the Border. What was it Justin had said? *No towns or roads between here and there; just one abandoned highway when you're almost there.* She put up her hand to shade her eyes from the sun and looked south again. Then she saw it. Perhaps half a mile away, tall enough that only a few mountains could be seen beyond it, was a huge wall. It appeared to be the same color as the concrete of the highway, and it too stretched as far as she could see in either direction. If not for the brightness of the sunrise and the fact that she had been staring at her feet, Sarah would probably have noticed it sooner.

I made it! For the moment Sarah was untroubled by the question of what came next. The fact that she had covered more miles than she had realized, and that her walking was nearly at an end, was enough for now. She stood looking at the wall for several minutes, allowing herself to rest, and then began to scan the landscape between herself and her goal, looking for the easiest path through the low bushes. Looking west, everything looked exactly the same. In the other direction, the sunrise made it hard to see, and again she shielded her face. After a moment her eyes adjusted, and she realized that she was looking at a building. A building! Or at least, it appeared to be a structure of some sort. It was down the highway about as far away to the east as the wall was to the south. She looked back and forth between the two, then decided it would be better to explore the building first. She had no plan for what to do when she got to the wall, and she had been walking all night long. And it was getting hot. The building, whatever it was, would at least provide some shade, and a place to get off her feet.

Energized by her new discoveries, Sarah walked quickly. The hard, unforgiving surface of the road was already getting hot, and it made her grateful for the sandy ground she had been walking on. But it was nice to walk in a straight line, without any bushes in the way. Soon she neared the building, which sat about fifty feet to the north of the highway at the edge of a wide turnout. It was a dilapidated wooden structure with bits of peeling white paint left in a few places, a little wider than her house, but with only one story. A broken sign dangling from the roof said "Ice Cream and Smoothies." A large front window had been broken out and replaced with plywood, and across the wood were spray-painted the words "Se Vende." *For Sale. Now that's funny*, thought Sarah. She pushed on the door, which creaked open. She had a brief fantasy that somehow she would find a stash of unspoiled ice cream inside, but the coolness of the shade was almost as good. She sighed in relief. It appeared that the place had been pretty well cleaned out before it was abandoned. A large main room was completely empty, as was the space behind the counter. A small back room contained a sink, some shelves, and what appeared to be a walk-in freezer. She tried the sink, but of course there was no water. But the freezer was a pleasant surprise. Purely by virtue of its insulation, it was even cooler than the rest of the building.

Off to one side of the main room was another door. Sarah opened it to discover a small bathroom. She chuckled to herself. It was a luxury that would have made her quite happy under other circumstances, but she had been taking in so little food and water it was doubtful she would even need it. She poked around for a few minutes more until she was sure that this was all there was to the building. She mentally took stock of what her little discovery had gained her: no food, no water, but shelter from the sun and the heat. She reflected on the fact that her journey south for the last two days had been all guesswork, based on the path of the sun. She could just as easily have come to the wall at a place miles to the east or west, and missed this building entirely. Chances of finding it were no better than they had been with the rocks. She lifted her head and whispered with a dry, cracked voice, "Thank you."

But what now? She set down her pack and stepped outside to gaze at the wall from the shade of an awning that hung over the door. Based on the walk she had just taken, she guessed it would take her ten to fifteen minutes to walk all the way to the base of the wall. How tall was it? What would she do when she got there?

If she couldn't find a way through, it meant a total of half an hour of walking in the hottest part of the day to get back to shelter. Her water was nearly gone. No, it was wiser to wait at least until the cool of the evening to go have a look. She stepped back inside and drug her backpack to the walk-in freezer. She lay down and discovered that getting comfortable on the hard floor was actually more difficult than it had been in the desert sand. But after her long night's walk, she knew she was tired enough to sleep under almost any circumstances. Lying on top of her sleeping bag and using her sweatshirt as a pillow, she stared up at the wooden ceiling and expected to drift off immediately.

Instead, she felt her stomach growl. She growled back at it and rolled over on her side, trying to ignore the demands of her body. But they only increased. Food. Water. Her stomach began to ache slightly. She sat up and took out the bag of trail mix, which was still about two-thirds full. She took a generous handful and chewed it slowly. The dryness of her throat made it even less appealing, and hard to get down. She swallowed it in gulps, like a child taking her medicine. Then she took another, smaller handful, and did the same. Now the bag was half empty. She found her water bottle and took a small drink, larger than a sip but still far less than she wanted. She guessed there were about two more drinks like that left in the bottle, and the last one would carry with it a fair amount of sand. She set it aside and lay down again. Mercifully, she had satisfied her stomach enough that it allowed sleep to overcome her eyes.

But hunger woke her again in the middle of the afternoon. Her stomach was aching as before, and this time she knew she couldn't afford to do anything about it. She lay on the floor of the bare room, stretching lazily and weighing the discomfort of lying on a hard surface against the effort it would take to stand up. Eventually she did stand and made her way back to the front door. The view was unchanged, apart from the fact that the sun was in a different part of the sky. She had perhaps two hours to wait until the air began to cool, so she went back inside and strolled lazily around the main room. Remembering the game she had played with the trays in her cell, she looked for something she could use to distract herself. But there was nothing. She retrieved her Bible, but then sat staring blankly at it. She was not in the mood to read. She went back in and got her sleeping bag, then spread it out on the floor of the main room where she could stare at the ceiling and also keep tabs on the progress of the sun.

Her stomach continued to ache. The time passed slowly. Eventually, though, the light coming in through the broken windows began to change. She packed everything away, telling herself that this was what a person with faith would do. *Like I'm never coming back*, she thought. She stepped outside and felt that it was still fairly hot, thought it was now late in the afternoon. She was anxious to do something, but knew the danger in overheating. *Okay, half an hour more. At least twenty minutes.* She sat in the doorway and watched insects flit back and forth in the sagebrush at the edge of the turnout. A lizard made its way across the concrete in front of her. Prior to this week, she had never seen a real lizard, and this was the biggest yet. She watched it with fascination until it scrambled out of sight, grateful to be distracted by something genuinely interesting. When it was gone, she waited another minute and then could stand the boredom no longer. "Okay," she said as she stood to her feet, "here we go."

She had gone no farther than the other side of the road before she stopped to wrap the shirt around her head. It was hot, but tolerable. She knew her back would be sweaty under the backpack, but trusted that she was close enough to the end now that losing a little moisture would not matter. Walking quickly, she weaved past the bushes that covered the small plain between the road and the wall.

It grew larger as she approached. Soon she could see that it was at least forty feet tall at this point. She looked for any kind of marking or deviation, but found none. She half expected to find some kind of maintenance door or an obvious tunnel that had been dug underneath, but there was only dirt and concrete and sky no matter where she looked. Drawing even nearer, she saw that it was topped with razor wire, and even appeared to be slightly angled outward toward the top, creating an overhang that made her dizzy when she stood at the base and looked up. Sarah wondered if even a lizard could climb it. She reached out and touched its surface. The concrete was a pale color and not as hot as she had expected. But its hardness was discouraging. She smacked it, and the force of her blow was completely absorbed by the stony material. Her hand stung; the wall was unaffected. She could hit it a hundred times as hard and it would make no difference. As she stood there, looking back and forth, east and west, the wall seemed to her to have a personality, insensitive and cold. It reminded her of Sergeant Parsons back in her cell. It didn't care about her problem, the uniqueness of her situation. She could throw herself against it and cry, lie at its base and die of thirst, and it would not care.

So now what? Sarah felt silly and small. What had she expected? Why was she even here? She sat down against the wall and looked back toward her building, a dot in the desert. Should she go back? Had she missed something? Was this the plan, or not?

She sat for perhaps an hour. There was enough faith in her to wait this long, to believe that now that she had arrived, done her part, something would happen. The sun sank low, and the noise of insects increased. Her stomach began to hurt. She had eaten no lunch, and now it was dinnertime. She had half a bag of trail mix, and she was at a dead end: a forty-foot wall in the desert that gave no indication it was going to miraculously open for her anytime soon.

She stood again. "I'm here!" she shouted to the air. "I came! Now what?"

The insects buzzed in the still desert air. The western sky was orange. Her stomach growled.

"Aaaah! What am I supposed to do?" Sarah remembered Justin's comment about creatures speaking to their Creator with respect, but at the moment she told herself that perhaps a little disrespect would at least get a response. "Is this it? What do I do now?" Then she realized that this was the wrong question; it no longer applied. She rephrased it, and her voice dropped from a yell to a simple, sincere plea as she did so. "What are you going to do?"

There was no answer. No change. After another half an hour of watching the sun set, Sarah decided that it was better to spend the night indoors. She began the march back toward her building. She stopped and looked back several times in the first few minutes, still clinging to a shred of expectation. But it continued to stand silently, mocking her hope, and soon she stopped looking back. She trudged the rest of the way back to the building slowly, conserving her energy. Nevertheless, when she arrived, she was as hungry as she had ever been, and her dusty throat was begging for a long, cool drink of water. She picked up a rock and threw it angrily at the "Ice Cream and Smoothies" sign, but missed.

Once inside, she unpacked in the freezer once again, and sat for a moment staring at the bag of trail mix. She opened it slowly and ate half its contents, grateful for each bite but far from satisfied when she was done. She took a drink of water and let it sit in her mouth for a while before swallowing. Then she lay down. Now that she had arrived at the border and had found shelter, she saw no reason to stay awake through the night. She wasn't going anywhere. And she was tired. She lay down and stared at the ceiling for a moment. "Did I do something wrong?" she asked the wooden boards above her. No answer. She wondered how things would be different if she had obeyed Justin on the trail that day. Would she be safe in a bed somewhere, with a full belly? Had she ruined everything? Was she being punished after all? Then she stopped herself. There was no point in these questions. She was here now. Either the situation could be redeemed, or it couldn't. There was nothing else to be done. She turned over on her side and slept, curled up in a ball with her hands on her aching stomach.

Waiting

One day.

Sarah woke from a dream of war. Many times her imagination had painted a picture of what Justin had described for her that day at Java Stop, and sometimes those pictures found their way into her dreams. She always pictured Torin and herself at the Cup and Saucer, hearing the noises and seeing people running down the street screaming. This time she had somehow known that Jalen was at the mall and had been trying to call her on her phone, but the phones weren't working.

It's tomorrow, she thought. *And I won't be there. I'm in an ice cream shop in the desert, trying to climb a forty-foot wall.* She sat up and looked at the bag of trail mix and the water bottle. *But there is a plan,* she told herself. *Surely, something will happen today.*

She determined to put off eating for as long as she could. She went out and took her seat in the doorway to look at the wall, standing indifferently in the distance. Instantly she began to doubt herself. What exactly was she waiting for? For someone to show up? For Justin to arrive, scoop her up in his arms, and fly her to the other side? Or Thaddeus? Would the wall simply fall down, or be swallowed up by the earth? And what then? How long would she last on the other side? What about food and water?

She rose, frustrated, and walked aimlessly around the main

room. She sat on the counter restlessly for a moment, then had an idea. She got down, went outside, and collected a handful of pebbles. Then she went back inside, grabbed her trail mix, and sat down on the floor against the counter. She began tossing the pebbles, one at a time toward the far wall, trying to see how close she could make them land to the baseboard. It took several minutes, but when one came to a stop just resting against the wood, she cheered and rewarded herself with a single raisin from the bag. The next time, a minute later, she had a peanut. Soon she was out of pebbles and had to get up to collect them before starting over.

As she improved, the trail mix began to disappear faster and faster, but the game still stretched for probably over an hour. Then she was down to the final three items: two peanuts and a piece of some unidentifiable dried fruit. Sarah studied them in her hand for a moment, then impulsively ate all three. She tossed the pebbles that were left in her hand in the general direction of the door, then sat for a while staring at them. Finally she rose and went into the freezer, and came back out with her water bottle, which now contained a single drink. She took her seat once again and stared at the water for a long time. Should she save it? Was that wise? Or was drinking it now proof of just how real her faith was? How much good would one little drink do her anyway?

She opened the bottle and closed it again. She got up and went to the doorway and looked out at the wall. *Please*, she prayed. Then she lifted the bottle to her lips and drained it dry, doing her best to savor the drops that rolled down her throat, and at the same time partially gagging on the sand and grit that found its way to the back of her tongue. She spit it out and dropped the bottle on the ground, then thought better of this and went and put it in her pack, in case a source of water presented itself later. While there she retrieved her Bible, but again found that she couldn't concentrate when she tried to read it. Or perhaps it was that reading it felt like doing something for God, and she didn't feel like doing anything for Him until He did something for her. She was ashamed when she realized that this was the state of her heart. But she was too tired, too hungry and thirsty, too frustrated, to do anything about it.

She sat in the doorway again and looked for lizards for most of the afternoon, glancing up from time to time to look at the wall. *Still there*, she joked to herself. When she started to feel too hot and noticed herself starting to sweat, she retreated to the freezer. She returned to the doorway as sunset approached, and watched the changing colors of the sky yet again. They were still pretty, but sadder somehow with the run-down building and roadway as part of the picture. Sarah watched the first few stars come out, but then started to actually feel chilly for the first time in days. Without calories to consume, her body was shutting down, and in the absence of sunlight had a harder time heating itself. *Like a lizard*, she told herself with a chuckle, then went inside to get her sweatshirt. She watched the moon rise and the stars fill the sky, waiting to feel tired enough to sleep.

Eventually her eyes began to droop, and she went in to snuggle up in her sleeping bag. But standing in the freezer looking at her few belongings strewn on the floor, she changed her mind and dragged them all out into the main room. She spread the sleeping bag out on the floor where she could see a piece of the sky through one of the broken windows, and then crawled inside. Somehow, it felt good simply to have survived the day. Nothing had happened, but that was okay. She was still here. As she drifted off to sleep, Sarah had the strange thought that in a way it was a gift to be starving and thirsty. If she had more mental energy, she might be highly anxious about what the next day would bring. As it was, she couldn't worry about such things. A sort of resigned peace had come over her. Perhaps she would die. Perhaps enemy soldiers would find her and take her prisoner. She was powerless in any case. There was nothing she could do but wait.

Breakthrough

That night as Sarah slept, a coordinated attack against the United States of America began. For the first phase of this attack, hundreds of undetected submarines approaching the Pacific, Atlantic, and Gulf coasts drew near enough to launch low-flying, short range missiles at over thirty major cities. These huge submarines also contained thousands of ground troops, who would be deployed shortly afterward in the chaos that followed the missile strike. The missiles were all launched at precisely the same moment, which was about an hour after sunrise on the Pacific coast.

One of these missiles, launched from the waters near San Diego, contained a slight manufacturing defect. A small warp in the metal casing near its nose prevented it from being completely airtight, and when it was released from its tube at great speed from fifty feet under the ocean's surface, a tiny amount of seawater leaked in. The water caused an electrical short in the missile's guidance system, and shortly after being launched it went spinning wildly out of control. The other missiles from its submarine streaked together in a tight cluster toward the population center, but this one broke away and rose high above the rest in a great spiraling arc across the sky, over the city to the east. When its small fuel supply was expended, it began dropping rapidly, falling directly on the line between Mexico and the United States. Against all odds, it finally struck the ground five feet to the north of the border wall out in the middle of the uninhabited desert, directly south of an old abandoned ice-cream shop. The explosion decimated the wall, sending huge chunks of concrete flying hundreds of yards through the air on the Mexico side.

The impact shook the ground, and even half a mile away the noise was like being inside a cloud during a thunderstorm. Glass broke in the ice-cream shop, and Sarah woke with a start. Despite thirty days of anticipating exactly this moment, she was momentarily confused and wondered if there might be an earthquake. She sat up and steadied herself with her hands on the ground, preparing for the next tremor. When it didn't come, she pulled her sleeping bag off and crawled toward the door, preparing for disappointment. The wall would still be there, or perhaps it would be destroyed and soldiers would be marching through it.

What she saw instead was a huge cloud of dust obscuring the portion of the wall she had visited two nights ago. It was clear that something had happened—but what? She waited, but the dust was slow to settle. Finally, unbelievably, she saw a gap in the wall: clear sky where gray concrete had been. She stumbled to her feet and stepped outside, and began to frantically search the sky. What did this mean? Were there planes? Were more explosions coming? She looked back at the wall. Were there troops? No. It didn't make any sense for an enemy to destroy the wall at this point, or send soldiers into the middle of nowhere. She stood staring for a long time. Could it be that this was for her? Should she go?

Then she heard the helicopters. Despite its plain appearance, the wall was equipped with sensors, and cameras at regular intervals, to detect any breach of the border. The explosion had sounded the alarm in a small Army base in the desert twenty miles northwest of Sarah. As part of the enemy's strategy, all US satellites had been taken off-line at the same time as the missile strike. This meant there was no way for the Army to know if this breach in the wall, unlikely as it may seem, was another point of entry for the enemy. A small company of attack helicopters had been sent to investigate.

At first, the faint chop of the helicopter blades, coming from her side of the border, filled Sarah with panic. It meant that she could not sneak quietly through the hole in the wall. She would be seen, and she would be captured. Her presence out here in the middle of nowhere, right next to a hole in the nation's defenses on the day of a major attack, would certainly cause them to bring her in for questioning. She was already suspected of being an enemy spy. She pictured her cell from the previous week. Where would they put her this time?

She considered hiding, but shook the idea off quickly. She had no food or water. The Army would probably station Soldiers at the gap. Now was the time. She stepped further away from the building to get a view of the helicopters. They were still a long way off. Then, for some reason, she imagined that Justin were with her. If he were, what would he say? *He would probably say*, she thought, *that I should be more impressed at the fact that there is a hole in the wall than that there are helicopters coming.* She looked back at the wall. It really was a miracle. She had prayed for the impossible, and it had happened. Her weak faith had wavered, but she had still been heard.

Her panic turned to resolve. She looked back at the helicopters, then back at the hole in the wall, half a mile away. She spoke aloud: "I believe." Her toes flexed and pushed off the ground, and in a few steps she was across the road.

Then she skidded to a stop. "Wait!" she cried into the air, whether addressing God or the helicopters she did not know. She turned and sprinted back across the pavement and into the building, where she shoved her hand into her backpack and came out with her great-grandmother Sarah's Bible. Then she flew out the door and began to run.

For three hundred yards Sarah ran faster than she ever had. Carried by a burst of energy that came from the feeling of once again being hunted, she gave her body free reign to do what it loved.

Then her legs began to tire. The reality was that she had eaten and drunk almost nothing in the past few days. Her muscles began to tighten, her strides became shorter, and it seemed there was nothing she could do but slow almost to a walk. The noise of the helicopters seemed louder. She looked behind her and they were much larger than they had been. Probably they had seen her by now.

"No!" she cried out, and to her surprise the word came as a sob. "Please! I believe!" She forced a few more steps, then came to a stop. She bent double, crying and catching her breath at the same time.

A ray of sunlight glinted off the gold edging of the Bible in her hand, catching Sarah's eye. She stood upright and looked down at the book in her hand. Then she remembered: *It's love, Sarah. Not fear, not anger. The best reason to run is love.*

She raised her head and caught sight of a small gap on the far side of the missile's impact crater, a place where she could see past the rubble to a patch of sunlight on the level of the ground. The noise of the helicopters faded from her consciousness. *I'm coming, Jesus,* she prayed. *I'm coming.*

Three more steps and she was running again. Slowly at first, then faster. *I'm coming. I'm so sorry. Sorry for everything. I'm coming. I love you.*

She could no longer feel her legs. There was no sound, only the growing light of the gap in the wall. *I love you, Jesus. Almost there.* She reached the crater and slowed only slightly to pick her way through the chunks of concrete and razor wire. Her lungs filled with smoke and dust, but she stumbled through the gap in the wall and kept going. The wall was no longer the finish line. She ran on, coughing and stumbling over sagebrush, until it was well behind her. Her pace slowed, but she didn't stop until she had put another quarter of a mile between herself and the border. Then, finally daring to look back, she saw that the helicopters were just landing and Soldiers were beginning to explore the crater. As far as she could tell, none were looking in her direction.

Had they not seen her? Or had they just decided to let the desert kill her? That seemed like a real possibility at this point. Now that she had stopped running, thirst overwhelmed her. She looked to the south and saw nothing but more of the same, flat desert she had seen for the past several days. Then something caught her eye. Something was shining on the horizon, perhaps a mile away. Was it water? A stream? Could she make it that far?

She began to walk. Everything in her body cried out for relief, but there was none to be had. The sun was growing hot. There was no water, no shade—feeling as she did at the moment, it seemed likely that she might die before evening even if she simply sat still. She might as well walk. She took another look back to reassure herself that the Soldiers had no interest in her. No one was following. She set her eyes on the shining ribbon and forced step after painful step.

For a while it seemed that she was making no progress at all. Her throat stung with thirst, and it occurred to her that it was odd she was no longer sweating. She stumbled more and more often. At times the stream, or whatever it was, seemed to disappear and she wondered if she had been hallucinating. But finally it began to grow larger. Another few minutes and she would be there. She tripped and fell to her knees, and it was several moments before she gathered the strength to stand again. She told herself she would not stop again until she reached it.

As she got closer, the moment came when Sarah realized that it could not be a stream. Instead of being lower than the surrounding terrain, it seemed to be elevated a few feet above the desert. A few more steps and she was sure: it was a road. Part of her realized that she had never really had much hope that it was water. That would be too easy. But she was too drained of emotion to be angry. She kept walking until she reached her goal. At the end, she fell to her knees and crawled up the gravel onto the road's shoulder, then lay face-down, using her arm to protect her face from the heat of the pavement.

46 Salvador

Sarah lay that way for several minutes. She had not yet lost consciousness, although she expected that she soon would. For the moment she was enjoying the feeling of lying down, and wishing she still had an extra shirt to cover her head and face. Then there was a loud sound, the roar of an engine followed by the crunch of gravel, and she opened her eyes to see the four tires of a truck parked on the road not far from her. Then she saw boots and a pair of jeans, and heard a man's voice say, in English but with a thick Mexican accent, "Hey, are you okay?"

She didn't move or speak. She tried, but during the time she had been lying still everything inside her seemed to have stiffened. She groaned and tried to lift her arm, but barely managed to stir.

"Oh, man, you're in bad shape. Where did you come from?" The boots and jeans turned and went back to the truck, then returned and knelt by her side and she felt the incredible sensation of water on her cheek and lips. It brought her to life and she involuntarily strained toward it, taking awkward sideways gulps that caused her to sputter and choke.

"Easy, easy," said the man. "It's going to be okay. You been out here long?"

Sarah managed a raspy reply. "No, just this morning." He

looked at her questioningly, so she added "Well, longer than that, but I had some shelter along the way."

"Where you headed?"

"I don't know. I'm ... I don't know. It's a long story." She took another drink, and sighed with gratitude so deep she felt like smiling and crying at the same time.

"I see." He looked at the state of her clothes, then lifted his head and looked north toward the border. After a moment he seemed to make the decision not to ask any more questions. "Well, you're lucky I came by. This road doesn't get used much anymore. I live out in the desert on my little ranch," he gestured to the east, "but I come into town on Sunday mornings to go to church. Any other day of the week, and you might have been lying there a long time." Then he spotted her Bible lying on the ground. "Looks like maybe you were headed to church too." He grinned.

Sarah smiled back. "I guess you could say that."

"Well, can I give you a ride?"

"That would be great."

The man helped Sarah to her feet and led her to the passenger side of his truck. When they were both seated and pulling onto the road, she was overwhelmed by the smell of warm food coming from a covered pot on the floor next to her feet.

He noticed her eyeing the pot. "Help yourself. Once a month we have a meal together after church, and I always bring my famous tamales. When's the last time you had any food?"

"Well, I had a little bit of trail mix yesterday. And the day before that. But nothing warm in about a week. It smells delicious. Are you sure?"

"Si, absolutely. There will be a lot of other food when we get there. Listen, I have a daughter who is about your size. I'm going to call her and have her meet us there with some clean clothes, okay?"

Sarah's mouth was already full of tamale. She nodded gratefully and he dug a phone out from the pocket of his jeans. A conversation followed, but it was in Spanish spoken too fast for Sarah to keep up. After a few minutes the man hung up and said, "Okay. She'll bring you something. So, will you need a place to stay?"

Sarah's head was spinning. Water, food, clothes, and now shelter?

"Well, yes, but you don't have to ..."

He cut her off. "No, it's fine. My daughter has a room. My grandkids are loud, but they're sweet kids. We'll get you rested up and then you can figure out where you're going, okay? Besides church, I mean." He grinned again.

Sarah had finished her tamale. "Thank you so much. This is all so nice. I mean, you don't even know me."

"I know you were all alone by the side of the road in the desert. If that were me, I would hope someone else would do the same."

"Well, thank you. Thank you very much." Sarah took another long drink and lay her head back on the seat of the truck, pacing herself before eating another tamale. The past ten minutes had been overwhelming, but she gave herself permission to receive the gifts that were being offered to her.

Then her driver spoke again. "By the way, my name is Salvador. Salvador Martinez." He extended his hand for her to shake.

"Really! I'm a Martinez too! Sarah," she said, and took his hand.

He smiled warmly. "Well then, you're family. Nice to meet you, Sarah Martinez."

They drove in silence for a few more minutes while she ate another tamale. Then they entered a small town and wound through narrow streets until they arrived a small, simple-looking chapel with a white cross mounted on the roof. People of all ages, clean and dressed nicely, were making their way into the building or standing around in groups talking excitedly. *Probably about the war,* Sarah realized. She and Salvador found a place to park, and he came around to help her out of the truck and to carry his pot of tamales. As they walked to the entrance, he greeted friends and introduced them to Sarah. They were so kind to her that she barely remembered to be self-conscious about her appearance. From within, there came a sound Sarah had never heard before: the sound of voices joining together in worship. It sounded like joy, like freedom. Years later, out of all the things that happened that day, it was the memory of that singing Sarah would treasure most. It was, she thought, the most beautiful sound she had ever heard.

Epilogue

In another realm, a place indescribable in terms of physical location or distance, the angel Justin strode majestically down a corridor of light toward a great throne.

His appearance was greatly altered from what Sarah had known on earth, although she would have recognized him by his face. He wore no black jacket, but a robe of white. He was huge, and power and dignity graced his movements. His face shone as if joy and beauty filled his entire being. Anyone from earth, seeing him like this, would have been tempted to worship. But as he approached the throne, Justin bowed low.

"Rise, faithful servant," said the Voice from the throne.

"My task is complete, Lord," said Justin as he stood upright. "My humble efforts are an offering of love."

"You have served well," said the Voice. "Your reward awaits you."

Justin did not answer, but nodded humbly.

"Are you saddened?"

Justin nodded again. "A bit. This part of the Story is sad, Lord."

"Yes, it is. But it is only a part. Glory is coming, Justin."

"I know." Justin's smile at this was deep and genuine.

"And this is in no way a failure on your part. It is the Plan."

"I know," the angel said again.

"Then rest, Justin, and receive your reward."

"Thank you, Lord." Justin turned to go, but after a step he turned back and said, "Lord?"

"Yes?"

Justin hesitated a moment. "The girl? The one at the end?"

"Sarah?" The Voice spoke her name with tenderness and warmth.

"Yes, Lord."

"She is saved."

And if you had been standing there, you might have thought that something like a tear formed in the eye of the mighty angel, although it is said that such a thing does not happen in that place. He nodded gratefully and said again, his voice trembling slightly, "Thank you, Lord." Then he turned and made his way down the corridor of light to receive his reward.

And so Jesus also suffered outside the city gate to make the people holy through his own blood. Let us, then, go to him outside the camp, bearing the disgrace he bore. For here we do not have an enduring city, but we are looking for the city that is to come.

—Hebrews 13:12-14

Printed in the United States
By Bookmasters